I0846659

THE BRIGHT SPOT

THE BRIGHT SPOT

Book One of The Bright Spot

SHAWN RABEN

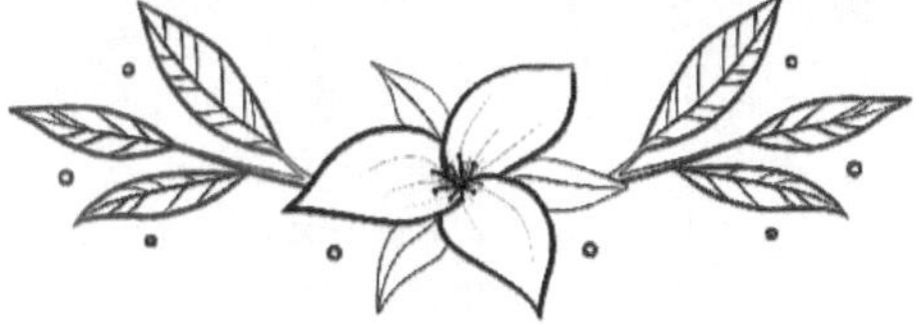

Redmatter Creations LLC

THE BRIGHT SPOT

Published by Redmatter Creations LLC
www.redmattercreations.com
www.shawnraben.com

Developmental editing by Maryssa Gordon
Copyediting and proofreading by Emma Moylan
Map design by Shawn Raben (partially created using Inkarnate)
Additional artwork by Sarah Keller

Cover design by Shawn Raben
Interior formatting by Shawn Raben

ISBN: 979-8-9913889-0-0
First Edition
Written, edited, and published by humans

NIVALIS

Map enhanced by Azura Seren

Mino Section, 28th Orbit

For my grandfather, Larry Castro,
Who makes the best breakfast sandwiches.

Contents

Content Warning

While this book is quite tame compared to other books without a content warning, I want my readers to feel comfortable, knowing what they are getting into. The Bright Spot contains depictions of:

- Violence, death, and gore
- Attempted suicide and suicidal thoughts
- Allusions to, but not expressly written sexual assault
- Cannibalism
- Drug abuse
- Mild language

Acknowledgments

This novel has been a true labor of love. It's hard to believe we are finally here. Finally published. This novel has been in the making for over two years now. Hundreds of hours have been spent on writing and editing. Countless nights have been sacrificed to create my greatest personal achievement to date. Of course, there are people who helped push me across the finish line. Without them, this book would not exist.

First and foremost. Thank you to my editors. Thank you, Maryssa Gordon, my developmental editor for going through my AWFUL second draft and making sense of it. I promise the next book won't be so bad. Without you, my book would've fallen apart.

Thank you to Emma Moylan, my copy editor, who painstakingly combed through the text, and polished the heck out of it. Work provided by copy editors and proofreaders is invisible and typically goes unnoticed by the reader, which is why I want to extend the largest thanks in your direction.

Ultra thanks to my ALPHA reader and biggest BackerKit supporter, Dan King, who has a character named after him.

Super thanks to my beta readers, Tobi Raben, William Parker, Alan Ouderkirk, Brenna Dia, and, of course, Jared Burch.

Extending another thank you to Tobi Raben for going above and beyond during her beta reading. This book wouldn't be where it is without her.

Mega Thanks to my BackerKit Cross-Collab partner, Belinda Crawford! Check out her book *Gamer.*

Let's not forget some other BackerKit friends who have been a HUGE help with my book. JC Spark and Aimee Cozza. Please support them and buy their books, *Dire Contact* and *The Warm Machine.*

Special thank you to all of my backers on BackerKit. Forty-two of you believed in me and my project, collectively raising $1,633 to make it happen. Thank you so, so much. I hope it's worth the wait.

Some backers went the extra mile and donated a considerable amount more to my project. These amazing people are Sarah and Ken Keller, Gina and Russ Campbell, Billy Tidyman, and Dan King. Thank you, guys, very much!

Thanks to my dad, Jordan, who introduced me to the worlds between pages.

Thanks to my mom, Sarah, who always pushes me to greater heights. I hope I push you that way, too.

Thanks to my fiancé, Caroline, of course. Sorry you have to listen to me ramble about my books all the time. Hopefully you'll soon see why I'm so excited to share this with you.

Thanks to Brandon Sanderson for his writing lectures, Pierce Brown for inspiring my prose, and Matt Dinniman for bringing comfort during dark times. None of you will likely read this book, but you guys mean a lot to me.

If you enjoyed reading this novel (heck, even if you didn't), consider rating it on Amazon or Goodreads. Maybe even give this copy to someone else.

Thanks to you for taking the time to read my book. I hope you enjoy *The Bright Spot.*

Preface

It's important to understand that this story does not take place on Earth, but rather a separate planet. This planet developed similarly to our own before the dissolution of its society. You may recognize familiar vocabulary like "ottoman" or "Épée," but of course, neither the Ottoman Empire nor France ever existed here. Because of this change, on Nivalis—the planet where this story takes place—people here have a slightly different vocabulary from our own. The residents here don't use the word "years," but rather measure time in passings—each passing being 340 days long. Twenty passings make one orbit, as it takes that long for the planet to make one orbit around the sun. It can be hard to follow along at times since the sun never sets, seasons don't pass, and everyone alive is within "walking distance" of each other.

There is a glossary at the end of this novel. If you forget a term, you can refer to that.

Follow the Light. Ride with the sun.

Part 1

Light

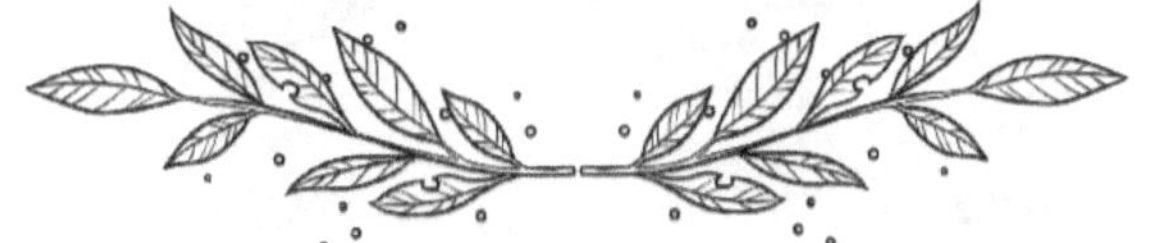

1

The Hunt

It's the planet that intrigues me. Not the star.
From the Journal of Azura Seren. Turseno section, 28th
orbit

The beast's eyes meet my own. Its endless black voids draw me in as I stare at it through the sights of my crossbow. I keep my grip firm, despite the need to wipe my sweaty palms.

His horns rise like a crown of living wood, catching the pale light above. The size of the beast could feed our group for days.

I hold my breath, remaining still. With a twitch of a finger, the latch falls, launching the bolt through the air. It whistles before finding a home in the dirt.

The buck leaps away in the opposite direction, invisible in the mess of trees.

A voice behind me: "Only you could miss a buck that big." Startled, I reflexively pull my knife from my belt, before processing who it is.

"Whoa, buddy. It's just me." Oberon, my hunting partner, holds up his hands. "Do you even know how to use that knife?"

"Light, Oberon." I swear, attempting to suppress my adrenaline rush. I take a deep breath. My hands shake and my heart pounds in my chest. "I think my sights are off," I say in between breaths.

The bald man gives me a stupid grin accentuated by his cleanly cut beard. A few white strands poke through his facial hair, despite not being much older than myself.

I take another breath. "Come on. Keep your mouth shut."

We both scout through the forest together, following the tracks the buck left behind. "I thought I was supposed to take the northern side of the forest?" he whispers.

"I didn't realize I was in your territory," I lie, keeping my voice lower than his.

A rogue twig snaps underneath my weight. Birds in the trees above us rush away. "Nice going," he says, giving my shoulder a gentle push.

I remind him what a middle finger looks like.

We keep walking, avoiding any more misplaced paraphernalia. I didn't realize my eyes were stuck to the ground rather than ahead until Oberon holds his arm out to stop me.

Our buck stands alone not fifty feet in front of us. His neck is craned toward the ground, eating a purple flower—SpringStep.

While rare, SpringStep grows wildly in the forests of Nivalis. When consumed, it nullifies pain and enhances cognitive ability. I stay away from the three-petaled flower because of its addiction rate and mind-altering effects. That doesn't deter us from using it as bait though. Deer and rabbits can't get enough of it.

"Let's see if your sights are actually off," Oberon whispers, taking my crossbow from me. His own weapon hangs from his belt, resting partially on the ground.

Oberon aims. I hold my breath, waiting for him to shoot. Minutes pass. I almost say something but the crossbow jerks in his hands. I don't see the bolt in the air. Only in the screaming buck's eye. It falls to the ground with a *thud*.

"That's how you do it." He hands me back my crossbow. "Sights are good," he says, forcing himself up. The dying creature is still alive, breathing shakily. The bolt must not have sunk deep enough to kill it. We stumble over to the deer. He wheezes and grunts, trying to move. I see fear in his eyes when I unsheathe my knife. Hopefully I can spare this creature from suffering much more.

"In the name of the Light, I thank you for your sacrifice. For your body and your blood." The knife glides across its neck and a dark red fluid pours out of the opening. The forest turf underneath turns black. In seconds, the tense animal goes limp.

"That still weirds me out," Oberon says, pulling the bolt from the dead creature's eye.

"What? Offering my thanks after they offered their body?" Standing up, I wipe the blood from my blade with a cloth.

"Yeah."

"The Light placed this animal here so we can eat. It's the least we could do."

Oberon doesn't reply. He's focused on something on the ground. I know he thinks it's dumb, but to me, it's about respect. He bends down and picks up a rock next to the animal's head. "Oh, Brena's going to love this." He holds it up for me to see. The light reflects a myriad of different colors. I can't help but admire it.

Oberon places the stone in his pocket and lifts the body onto his shoulder. An hour-long walk back to camp is nothing to us, even with a 150-pound carcass. We've been walking our entire lives and will continue until our last step.

Smoke from our caravan's fire billows into the bright sky. The moon hangs low, while the sun perpetually stays in place above our heads.

I place the carcass on the butcher's prop-up table. Mattias, the local butcher for the Brightest, scrunches his small nose in displeasure, distorting his ratlike facial features.

"You are late." He snorts. "We didn't think we'd get to eat tonight. Everyone is starving." His high-pitched, nasally voice makes me want to sew his mouth shut. If he weren't a mouth breather, someone would have done it by now.

I ignore his passing remark, but Oberon can't ever do the same. "At least we're out there sweating our asses off while you sit around and do absolutely nothing for two days." His outburst is unnecessary, but tension has always been high between them.

Mattias smirks. "Sounds like an excuse for you two to sneak away and be scandalous. What about your wife and daughter, Obie?" he snarls.

Oberon's cheeks redden. I can feel the heat emanating from him. "I'll snap you in half, little man," he shouts, stepping forward. My arm extends in front of him, hopefully preventing him from fulfilling his promise.

Mattias gives us a sly look before equipping his cleaving knives to dig into the carcass. I lead Oberon to the campfire where everyone gathers for dinner. "I want to kick his teeth in," Oberon grumbles.

"I know. Me too."

A breath passes before a child's voice sounds behind us. "Dad!" It's Brena.

Oberon's shoulders visibly relax, and his normal color returns to his face. "Hey, pumpkin! What you up to?" She holds her arms behind her back and smiles. "What you got there?"

Excitedly, she reveals a red tulip. "Wow!" Oberon exclaims, taking the flower and putting the bud up to his nose. "Mmm, very pretty. I'll trade you." Oberon lifts his shirt pocket and pulls out the same rock he showed me earlier. The light catches its flat side, reflecting blues and greens. Brena gasps, eyes going wide. She observes it closely before grasping it out of her father's palm. "Don't lose it!"

"I won't," Brena beams before running off to show her mother the rock.

Oberon swings the tulip toward me. "Would you look at that?" He twists the stem in his fingers and the petals twirl in the air. "When was the last time you saw one of these?" He hands me the flower. The stem is cool to the touch but I can hardly feel the softness of the petals with my calloused fingers. I lift it up to my nose and inhale. The fruity aroma floods my lungs, reminding me of a time, many passings ago in Elyndra, when we traveled through an entire field of these flowers. That was the last time I saw one.

The moment is interrupted by a hand landing on my shoulder. To my right, between Oberon and me, is

Hadrian, the leader of the Brightest. His thinning hair is stark white, the sign of an aging man. His other arm rests on Oberon's shoulder. The rapier attached to his hip presses against my side.

"Good to see you two are back safe," Hadrian says. His warm and inviting voice lessens the tension in my shoulders. "That's a pretty big buck you brought back, huh?"

"Not the biggest, but it should keep us fed for a couple of days," I say, trying to engage in his small talk. I expect him to continue talking about the deer or our hunt, but he changes the subject.

"I'm not sure if you two are aware, but I've been wanting to surprise the Brightest." He removes his hands from our shoulders and positions himself in front of us. His clean white robe trimmed with gold sweeps through the grass at his feet. "Tomorrow we will be approaching the city of Solace. We won't be entering the city, but we will be staying in its neighboring suburb for the time being. You may have been too young to remember, but that's where I met you and your parents, Caelius."

He is right. I didn't realize we were so close. Had it really been twenty passings? If we're that close to Solace, that means we are dangerously close to the Octoro Bridge—the last place I ever saw my mother and father.

When I don't respond, Hadrian continues, "If you guys could scout ahead and make sure that the suburb, Hollyard, is safe for us to stay, that would be great. Don't want to run into any raiders. If you see anyone there, turn right back around and report to me." His eyes light up, remembering something. "Oh, and one more thing," he starts, "please avoid the church in the town. It's a church of the Light but teaches the wrong scripture. I'll give the same speech to the other members while you two are gone."

"You can count on us, Father," Oberon says. Hadrian gives us a pat on the back before walking away, his white and gold-trimmed robe following behind him. How did he keep it so clean? Oberon turns to me excitedly and says, "Dude, I can't believe Hadrian finally wants to stay somewhere. We can just relax for a while."

It is uncharacteristic for Hadrian to want to halt our travels. He's always trying to ensure we are constantly on the move. "Don't you think that's a little odd?" I ask. "What do you think changed his mind?"

"Who cares? He's an old fart. He probably needs some rest too. Who knows how long he has left before someone needs to take over his position?" Oberon says. "Just take this moment and enjoy it. We'll get to be the first ones to check it out!"

The idea made me feel slightly uneasy. Even if there are no raiders in the town, they tend to follow closely behind. How long can we stay before they will need to be addressed?

How long could we afford to be behind?

I am the first to wake up. I remove my blindfold and the harsh light of the sun blinds me as my eyes try to adjust. It's impossible for me to sleep without a blindfold, though a few other members are able to do it. Some wagons offer a cloth shade from the sun, but those are reserved for mothers and their children, pregnant women, and Hadrian. Married women would try to get pregnant just so they can stay in a wagon instead of walking. It is even encouraged by Hadrian to increase the population on Nivalis.

Dolora and Brena sleep in one, but Oberon isn't permitted to join them. I wonder if that puts a strain on their relationship.

Bodies of men, their spouses, and teenagers sleep on the soft grass, all wearing blindfolds. I step carefully over the bodies, being careful not to wake anyone up. I find Oberon near the edge of the group. Drool leaks from the corner of his mouth and pools up near his ear. I kick him slightly in the ribs. He groans, barely reacting.

I crouch down and lift his eye mask. He squints from the light. "Wakey, wakey," I tease, letting go of the mask. It snaps back against his face.

"Ow," he groans, feeling at his mask.

"Come on, sleepyhead," I whisper, grabbing his arms, pulling him up. He struggles to stand, mumbling something incomprehensible. "Don't forget your crossbow." I grab it from the ground and place it against his chest. He holds on to it with one arm. "Come on! I thought you were excited to scout the town."

We walk ahead for a couple of hours, following the same road that most take while they travel around the world. The main road cuts right through Solace, but this one takes a detour around the city and through a small suburb known as Hollyard.

The grandness of the buildings of Solace in the distance staggers me. It seems impossible anyone could make something so tall. The warm-colored brick skyscrapers are accented with vines, creeping and clustering vertically. Chunks and corners of some buildings are broken off. I try to imagine what it looked like without the vines and deterioration.

We've traveled through other cities like Westco and Lunace, but they don't compare to Solace.

"That sure is something, isn't it?" Oberon says in awe, a bit more lucidity in his voice. He is staring at the city as well. It's like seeing the mountains for the first time, yet it invokes a different feeling. It's hard for me to believe that men built this at one point.

I almost completely miss the little town in its shadow. In the center of the residence is a massive willow tree. Twice as tall as the tallest house—tiny in comparison to the city.

"Caelius, look!" Oberon interrupts my gawking. He points at a figure about half a mile away. They're trekking into Hollyard.

The figure disappears in the mess of houses. "What are they doing?" I ask. "Is it a raider?"

"I dunno." Oberon shrugs. "Should we find out?"

"No. We should go back and tell Hadrian to steer clear." Other caravans don't typically travel this close to the edge of the Bright Spot, but it's not unheard of.

"Ah come on!" Oberon presses. "Maybe it's a girl and you can get yourself a girlfriend, finally."

At my ripe age of twenty-six passings, I'm expected to have a wife and at least three children by now. I roll my eyes. "And if we get ambushed?" I ask, ignoring his comment.

"Do you see anyone else? Where would they even be hiding?"

"The houses, Oberon. Especially if they know we are coming."

"You're so lame, you know? I'm going in anyway," Oberon says, taking the initiative and walking toward the town. I keep my crossbow ready and apprehensively follow him.

2

The Willow

While it was previously speculated, I was able to
confirm that a passing takes three hundred and
forty days.
From the Journal of Azura Seren. Turseno section, 28th
orbit

Oberon and I can see Hollyard in the distance. As we near the city, my eyes scan the landscape, searching for anything, or anyone, that may bring us harm. The grass on the side of the road stands to our waists. My hand subconsciously hovers over my crossbow as anyone could be hiding in there.

"Don't you ever get tired of all this?" Oberon asks. His voice pulls me from my thoughts. His tone is in stark contrast to his whimsical stride.

"What do you mean, specifically?"

"Like the Path," he says. "You know—walkin' round this planet over and over until we die? Why did they get to live in paradise?" He gestures toward the city miles away. "They could just live in one place their entire lives and build these massive buildings. And we are merely stuck with their scraps." I can tell he's been thinking about this for a while now. "I just want to be able to raise Brena normally. The last thing I want is for Hadrian to change his mind on staying here."

I understand what he means. It's hard to imagine what a stable life would look like. We've been traveling since birth. My parents had a house here when I was only six, though they stayed for less than a passing.

Hollyard's massive willow tree is the first thing we visit. From a vantage point, it seems to be planted right in the center of town, inside the looped road of a cul-de-sac. The grandiose nature of the tree strikes me with an awe like Solace as we draw closer. The diameter of its trunk had to be about ten feet across and stood over thirty feet tall.

Oberon gawks as well. The leaves dome over us, softly touching the ground, providing shade from the sun. It is a beautiful experience. We stand there together, taking it all in.

I almost forgot about the mystery person we saw— almost.

We survey the town after we finish admiring the tree. Wooden poles stand tall, erected from the grass. Each pole is connected by thick metal cables. A few lay sideways on the ground, blocking the roads. Relics from the past.

I want to find the house I used to live in, but my memory of this place is blank. Other extravagant houses sit on the perimeter of the cul-de-sac, but none are familiar. "I'm gonna be the first to call dibs on the house I want!" Oberon shouts. Before I can respond, he points at a tall brick house painted black. "Like that one!"

Most of the houses have completely deteriorated over the last six hundred passings; the roofs have caved in, or the wood structures failed to hold them up. The few that are still intact have been built with brick and mortar.

I follow Oberon up the steps of the house's large porch. The design on the outside is elaborate. Faded gold trim lines the windows weaving an intricate floral pattern. He turns the handle and pushes the door inward. It squeals loudly as it swings away from us.

The interior is just as intricate as the exterior. A staircase leads to the second floor. To the right is an opening to a living room, and opposite that is the kitchen and bathroom.

"Oh yeah, Dolora is going to *love* this," he says, peeking around the corners before running up the stairs. He disappears into a room on the left. I also peer around his house. *Could this be the same one I grew up in?* I can't be sure.

Before I can survey the rooms on the first floor, I hear Oberon's muffled voice through the walls. "Caelius! Come here, quick!"

My mind races at every possibility. Did Brena follow us without us knowing? What if it was that mystery person? I stumble up the stairs, and what I see is the last thing I expected.

Oberon is holding a large orange cat in his arms. "Caelius. Kitty!" His stupid smile splits his face, and I can't help but grin.

"Look, he likes me." He pulls out a piece of venison jerky, and the cat accepts the offering. It makes smacking noises with its mouth as it attempts to chew the tough meat.

"I think he just likes your food," I say.

"I'm gonna call you 'Beef Iron Mutilator,'" Oberon says, bopping the cat on the nose.

"Beef Iron Mutilator?" I ask, dumbfounded.

"Yeah! Beefy for short," he responds. "I wanted to name Brena that, but Dolora said, 'No can do.'"

"Good for her."

He glares at me. "Mah?" the cat says to Oberon.

"I know! Can you believe the nerve of this guy?" Oberon replies. "Some people, Beefy."

I roll my eyes. We need to get back to making sure this place is safe. Maybe I'll find my own home in the process. "I'm going to go look around," I say. "You guys are welcome to come with."

I don't think he heard me because he continues to feed the cat.

I leave Oberon's new home and begin searching for my own. It doesn't take me long. I don't know where I'm going, but my feet do. I count the intact houses on the way. We could house everyone in the Brightest, maybe more.

My breath catches in my throat when I see a brick house with a large, distinct window. Its green paint flakes away in patches, peeling like bark. My home.

The door creaks open and I peer in. It enters right into the living room. Nostalgia crashes over me—sudden and cold. The room is dim and the only light comes through the window. The ceiling used to be so high up, but now I can touch it with my hand.

An old brown couch lies against a wall. Springs and padding extrude from the cushions. The wooden floor underneath bears scratches from the furniture's legs. The end table with a pattern along its legs has fallen over onto its side. Someone created this table, painstakingly carving this design. They had to have measured each component precisely for everything to fit together.

These relics of the past give me whiplash. That person is dead now. There's no one to tell him his craftsmanship is exceptional—that his work is appreciated. I try to envision myself in this house over six hundred passings ago, before the Freezing of the World. I would sit next to the love of my life on this very couch, watching our children play together. It's so hard to imagine a world so different from this one—a world where you wouldn't freeze to death in the Darkness.

Other pieces of old tech intrigue me. A flat rectangular box rests face down on the floor. A wooden box with knobs sits on a side table. A clock hung on the wall, frozen in place. Its hands display a singular time. I don't know how to read it.

The kitchen is sectioned off from the living room. How many meals were prepared here? How long had this house been standing before the Freezing of the World? For being over six hundred passings old, this house is in great condition. I still see the remnants of white paint on the kitchen cupboards.

My room is exactly how I left it. The sheets are unmade and soggy, with a slight stench of mildew. I'll need to wash or replace these sheets somewhere—maybe I'll just burn them. Light peers through the window onto a sun-bleached section of the carpet. In the chest at the foot of the bed are clean, dry sheets.

When was the last time I slept in a bed? I can't remember. I've been sleeping on the ground my entire life.

The bathroom isn't very different from the other bathrooms I've seen during my travels. Though this one has a bathtub. Like the others, the toilet is completely dry. Rarely, they are filled with water. Messing with knobs and dials on the appliance provides no response. If we are planning on staying, I'd like to get that working again. I leave it for later, heading to explore the next room.

Something catches my attention in the mirror above the sink. It is only a light reflected from the window. Blue eyes meet mine in the reflection. Eyes of someone very familiar. Staring back at me is a man—not a child. I'd somehow let my dark hair grow past my ears. More hair thinly paints my cheeks, chin, and lip. I'm the same age as my parents when they lived here.

My parents' room is the last unexplored space. It's laid out identically to mine but mirrored. The bed is the same size as my own, the dresser stands at the edge, and a nightstand is placed in the corner. I lightly brush my hand against the sheets, focusing on their soft texture. They slept here together. Somehow, they both fit. Seeing their room again nearly brings me to tears. I can't cry though. I've cried enough over them. I pull the comforter up to my face and breathe in, hoping to capture any last bit of their scent.

Instead, I'm greeted with the mustiness of mildew. Sighing, I set the comforter back. These should get thrown out too, but could I bring myself to do that?

I make one last pass, scanning the room, collecting my crossbow and head out to find Oberon. I make a mental note of the house's location—only a couple of blocks south of the cul-de-sac.

The location of the moon in the sky tells me it is midday. Have we been here for that long? What about that individual we saw earlier. I feel foolish for forgetting about them. Where are they now? Are there others ready to ambush me? Could they be hiding in one of the houses? Or did they go to the city?

I warily make my way to Oberon's new residence, hand hovering over my crossbow, just in case. I've never killed anyone. I'm not sure if I could. But I want to be ready if I must.

I barge into Oberon's house to find him on the floor in the living room, playing with his cat. Were they playing this entire time?

"Caelius!" Oberon shouts. "Look at what Beefy can do." He pushes himself off the ground and the cat sits, staring up at him. Oberon reveals a piece of jerky from his pocket and the cat watches intensely. "Okay, Beefers, time to show Caelius what we have been working on. Speak!" he commands.

"Mah," the cat screams.

"Good boy!" Oberon puts the jerky in front of the cat's face, and it snatches the meat out of his fingers, making a smacking noise as he chews.

"That sure is … something," I say. Oberon's stupid grin is contagious. In any other case, it would be impressive. I can't help but wonder how much jerky he wasted. Oberon should have been doing something more important this entire time, instead of training a cat to speak. But to be fair, I didn't do much either.

"Come on, Hadrian and the others should be here soon," I say, waving my hand.

They follow me outside, where we see a woman swinging by her neck from the willow's branches.

3

The Woman

The interval between when the sun begins to illuminate a specific point and when it moves beyond is referred to as a passing.
From the Journal of Azura Seren. Corono section, 28th orbit

O beron!" I sprint over to the hanging body, and he follows quickly behind. How did I not notice this a moment ago? I must not have seen her behind the curtain of leaves. I draw my knife and we move like clockwork. He offers his hands for me to step onto, as if reading my mind.

He pushes me upward, allowing me to grab the branch. With effort, I lock my arms over the branch, fumbling with my knife. "Hold her legs," I shout. Oberon quickly obliges, lessening the tension on her neck.

The serrated edge saws through the rope with ease. The rope falls loosely and I drop to the ground. Oberon lowers her gently onto the grass. I hastily remove the rope from her neck revealing a bloody gash from where the rope cut. Her neck's not broken, which is good, though she's going to have a scar there for the rest of her life.

She is a black-haired woman; her tear-stained face suggests she's in her thirties. Her gown is torn and bloody, suggesting signs of a recent struggle.

How long has she been here? This had to have happened while we were exploring our houses, right?

A ragged breath. She's still alive.

Did she do this herself? Or did someone else hang her? Her ragged appearance suggests the latter. I don't know what to do; Hadrian should be here any moment.

"Oberon, follow the path back and get Hadrian. Bring him here," I command. He hesitates, face blanching. "Now! I'll stay with her until you get back."

"What if it's a trap?" he asks, voicing my concerns.

There could be a group of people hiding, ready to ambush. If he leaves, I'll be alone—mostly. I grunt, "I'll be fine, just go!"

Oberon sprints in the direction we came from, and Beef Iron Mutilator stays with me, rubbing against my arm.

My hands move aimlessly, not knowing what to do. I've never had to tend anyone. Is she thirsty? Her lips are dry; maybe I should give her some water.

I retrieve my flask from my coat pocket and pour water into her open mouth. She coughs, spewing water in my face.

Her pained eyes connect with mine and I feel a hand tightly gripping my arm. I whip my head to the side, looking behind me, making sure I'm not about to be attacked.

"Tommy," she croaks.

"It's okay. You're okay," I assure. I can't heal her, or tend her wounds, so I do what I can to comfort her until Hadrian arrives. The cat tries stepping onto her chest, but I push him aside.

The tension squeezes my stomach as we sit quietly for minutes, maybe half an hour. She stares at the dangling rope above, breathing softly, fully lucid, but not present.

I hear footsteps and see Oberon and Hadrian running down the road toward us. "What happened?" Hadrian asks, breathing heavily.

"We just found her like this. We'd been exploring the town and found her hanging here," I say, my hands had stopped shaking but my voice exposes my fear.

"Step aside," Hadrian says. He pushes the cat aside with his foot and rests a hand on the woman's neck. "In the name of the Light, restore this woman."

Light reflects slightly where Hadrian touches her. She gasps, swinging a hand up to her throat. Hadrian takes a step back. She looks around, eyes full of fear. To her, we are three strangers staring back at her. Her breathing comes in waves, but she remains silent.

"Caelius, why don't you watch over her while she recovers?" Hadrian sighs. He turns from her and examines us both. "Oberon, thank you for swiftly retrieving me. The rest of the Brightest should be here soon. We will convene under this tree." He walks back in the direction he came.

"Can you walk?" I ask her. She sits up, bringing her knees close—silent. Her distrusting eyes give me pause.

"It's okay," I say, trying to comfort her. "We'll take care of you." She makes eye contact with me, but she does not respond. "I'm Caelius, and my friend is Oberon. We are just people trying to survive before we found you. The one who healed you is Hadrian. He is the leader of our small group." I'm not sure what else I could say other than a single burning question. "Are you with anyone else?"

The woman's face turns and she whimpers. She pouts softly as she falls sideways onto the ground. Tears flow from her eyes and land in the grass underneath.

I look at Oberon, hoping he will know what to do. His face is covered with bewilderment. He shrugs, helplessly. I want to help her. I don't want to presume what's best for her, but she shouldn't be left alone.

There's a chance that whoever hung her on the willow, could still be around, if she didn't do it herself. What if it's a group of people? We would have seen another by now, right?

"Is there something I could do to help?" I ask softly. "If you need a group to stay with, Hadrian is welcoming to all newcomers. It's dangerous to be walking the Path alone."

She isn't my responsibility. If she wants to run away, I won't stop her. It is, however, my responsibility to make sure she gets the help and resources she needs if she decides to stay.

Chattering fills my ears and down the road I see a group of people with wagons walking toward us. The Brightest have arrived.

Our group's doctor, Stella, is running our direction. Her casual clothes hardly suggest she's our doctor. She's likely the smartest person in the Brightest. Why didn't she come back with Hadrian and Oberon earlier?

She gets down on her knees and examines the crying woman. "Is she hurt?" Doc Stella asks, prodding around, checking her pulse.

"I—I don't know," I stutter.

"Okay, help me carry her."

She moves and grabs the woman under her armpits and I grab her legs. We carry her into a nearby house where we lay her on a bed. "Is she going to be okay?" I ask Stella.

"She'll be fine. She just needs some rest. I'll monitor her for now," the doctor says. I don't know Stella personally, but I trust her.

I exit the house and watch as people disperse into buildings and structures on the street. Many others admire the massive willow tree in the center of the cul-de-sac. The rope remnant dangles from where I cut it. I should remove that.

"This willow was here last time I visited," Hadrian says next to me, interrupting my thoughts. He'd been waiting. "I forgot how large it was."

"I've never seen anything like it," I say in awe, thankful for the distraction. I lean against the railing on the porch, admiring the distinct flora with drooping leaves. I tremble thinking about the woman's fate, signified by the dangling rope.

"Crazy how our planet can come up with the most beautiful of things," he says. "Do you remember the Luminous Forest? I think you were about nine or ten passings old."

"How could I forget? That place is creepy as hell."

"Ah, you get used to it. At least I have," Hadrian says.

I hesitate, not sure how to express what I'm about to tell him. "Father Hadrian, Oberon and I saw that woman before coming into town." He perks up at that. "She was alone from what we saw, but I'm not sure. It's possible she lured us into a trap, whether she meant to or not."

Hadrian's brows could pierce steel. "What do you mean?"

"I think someone saw her walking alone and tried executing her by hanging. Maybe as a sign for us to leave?"

"And you didn't see anyone else?" he asks.

"No, I was looking for my old home," I say with shame.

Hadrian sighs. "Let's not rule out the possibility she tried killing herself. Thanks for bringing this to my attention. I don't think there's much to worry about," he says dismissively. "Why don't you show me the home you found."

If Hadrian isn't worried about others being here, then maybe I shouldn't be worried either. He's the one who receives divine guidance from the Light. If there's anything to worry about, he'll be the first to express it.

Hadrian follows me for the short walk, and we step inside. He examines the kitchen and living room. "Are you liking your new home so far?" he asks, taking a seat on the couch, evaluating its comfort. "Oh," he grunts.

"I think this place definitely needs a new coat of paint, but so far, I'm pretty happy with it," I say. Hadrian sticks his hands down into some of the holes in the couch, feeling around. Is he looking for something?

I give him a tour of the kitchen, bathroom, and the bedrooms. "You could use some curtains there," he says, pointing at the window in my room. "I'm sure Tremain or one of the seamstresses has some extra cloth you could lay over that window. That should make it easier to sleep."

"I'll keep that in mind." His small talk unnerves me. Usually, he talks like this before he unloads something important.

"You have a nice place here, Caelius. I'll admit, I'm jealous." Hadrian shoves his hands in the pockets of his clean gold-trimmed robe.

"Are you going to find a house for yourself?" I ask him. Hadrian isn't incompetent, but he is old. He's the one who decided to stop and rest so he should get first pickings on the house he wants.

"Ah, no, probably not. I like my wagon," he says. "You know. I'm just used to it." He smiles weakly, looking tired. Not the kind of tired you get from a sleepless night, but the kind that peers through the eyes of someone too long-lived. He has to be over sixty passings by now. At first it seemed uncharacteristic for him to want to rest in a quiet little suburb. But in this movement, I understand completely.

"Caelius," he starts, standing in my doorway "about your parents ..." He doesn't meet my eyes. Instead, he looks to the side at something. He has something to say. His mouth stutters and after a moment, he finally says, "They were good people. I'm sorry they aren't here with us now."

I nod slightly. I've gotten over their disappearance. I've accepted that they are likely dead somewhere. I just wish I had the chance to say goodbye. "It's okay, Father. It's not your fault."

"No, it is my fault," he admits. "They were under my protection, and I let them run off. For that, I apologize."

I want to give him a hug, but I can't bring myself to do it. He steps outside into the sunlight and meets up with other caravan members. I follow along, finding a place in the grass next to Oberon and Dolora.

Reyus and Efram chat excitedly about something they found while searching Hollyard. I attempt to eavesdrop on their conversation, but I'm interrupted by Oberon. "The girls love the house," he says. "Which is good because I don't think Beefy would like the idea of living in a different place."

I don't reply, trying to figure out what those two men were discussing, but they had already finished their conversation.

The cooks wasted no time getting dinner prepared. They started a campfire as soon as they arrived and have cooked up the meat for today. One by one, the children pass out the food to each of the adults. Brena brings food to her dad and mom first. Most children start with their parents. She brought my serving next.

"Thank you, Brena," I say. She runs off to pass food to more people. Oberon, Dolora, and I sit together on a curb in front of the willow tree. Once Brena is finished passing out food, she joins us with her own plate.

"Hey, did you ever get that girl's name?" Oberon whispers to me. Does he not want his wife to hear him talk about another woman? "You know, the one we found?"

"I barely talked to her," I reply in between bites of food. "Who knows if she even plans on sticking around?"

"Maybe you can get yourself a girlfriend, eh?" He nudges me in the side with his elbow. I do everything in my power to not blush. The woman is not my type and the last thing I want to do is take advantage of someone's vulnerability.

"Nah, I don't think so," I say.

"Dude, why not?" He sounds shocked. "You're gonna miss this opportunity to get laid?"

"What are you guys talking about?" Dolora asks from next to Oberon. He snaps upright, looking very guilty.

"Oh, ha ha, nothin'. Just hunting stuff," he lies. She shakes her head and turns her attention back toward her daughter. "Think about it, buddy," he whispers.

I don't want to think about it. I think I'd rather wait for the right person to come along. I definitely don't want to get stuck in a relationship that I am not happy in.

Even though Oberon and Dolora aren't perfect for each other, they make it work somehow. Oberon is crass and spontaneous, whereas Dolora is calm and reserved. I know he constantly annoys her, but she still loves him despite that. Would I be able to do the same with someone I love? With our living conditions, I can't be too picky about who I might decide to wed.

I can't deny I've been feeling the effects of loneliness lately. Having some companionship would be nice. Oberon is fine to have around, but, well, he's Oberon. I hope eventually I could find someone outside of the Brightest, but I have no intentions of leaving.

Could this newcomer be my future wife? I still don't even know her name. She hasn't said a single word to me and I'm already thinking of our future together. Damn it, Oberon, for putting these thoughts into my head.

I take another bite and hear an unfamiliar sound. "Mraw?" The suddenness startles me and I nearly choke on my food.

"Beefy!" Oberon screeches. "Come here, little meathead!" The cat, Beef Iron Mutilator, hops over to Oberon and jumps up onto his lap. "Aww, baby kitty!" Oberon pets him, followed by smelling his head, followed by kissing his head, which is then followed up by him trying to fit the poor animal's head in his mouth. The cat pushes back and Oberon squeezes him tightly against his face.

Dolora looks at him with an unreadable lingering expression. She sighs slightly and pushes herself off the curb, her plate empty. Oberon doesn't even notice her leaving while he continues to love on the animal. Despite all of Oberon's strangeness toward the cat, it does not leave. It seems to enjoy the attention. Or rather the little pieces of steak Oberon feeds him.

Dolora sits with a group of other women who accept her excitedly. I'm glad she has a group of other girls to confide in. Oberon can be hard to deal with at times.

Three men sit on the concrete in front of us. Beef Iron Mutilator is distracted by the newcomers. The cat approaches the leftmost individual—Efram, a skinny man who promptly scratches the tabby on the head. His thin mustache and goatee line his mouth as he speaks. "How are your guys' crossbows holding up?" he asks us.

Eyeing the two men sitting next to him, Reyus and Lew, I speak softly, unsure of their part in the conversation. "Fine." Efram would have come alone unless he had something larger to share. "I think my crossbow sights could be off," I add.

"They're not, I checked them," Oberon blurts. Still, Reyus, a clean-shaven Misuran man, extends an arm. I allow him to inspect my weapon. Beef Iron Mutilator bumps his head against the bottom of Reyus's hand holding my crossbow.

"I only ask, because we found something … pretty cool while exploring the town," Efram says. He leans in close to whisper, "We think it's an abandoned smithy."

A smithy? Isn't that how they used to make blades pre-Freezing?

Efram reads the puzzled expression on my face because he explains further. "If you need a new knife, sword, arrowheads—Light, even animal traps—we can finally make it."

"Ha"—Oberon smacks me on the shoulder with the back of his palm—"there you go, buddy. Maybe you'll find out that the crossbow really isn't your thing after all."

The joke isn't funny, but I smile anyway. "Nah," I say, "I don't need to learn another weapon. I'm good enough with a crossbow. When did you guys learn to forge metal anyway?"

This time Lew speaks up, his voice soft-spoken but assured. "I have a little bit of experience from my previous caravan. I'm going to show these two how it works later tonight. If you want a weapon like Hadrian's, we can make you one. We thought we'd come to you two first since you guys are the only other people here who help defend the Brightest." There's a pause before he adds, "Other than Hadrian of course."

I'd always thought of Hadrian's rapier as a holy weapon, not something that can be crafted. Which is a foolish assumption since it's just steel. "I'm good but thank you," I tell the three. A sword would only make me more like Hadrian, which is not something I'd ever want.

4

The Park

If there weren't an extra degree of rotation, we
could stand in one place for eternity without ever
leaving the sun's warmth.
From the Journal of Azura Seren. Corono section, 28th
orbit

Drool pools from my lips onto the carpet underneath me. How did I end up on the ground? I remember tossing and turning the previous night, but I don't remember choosing to sleep here. I reach to remove my blindfold and notice I hadn't put it on.

Bright light peers through the window, illuminating the sun-bleached spot on the carpet. Hadrian was right; I need to get some curtains. Maybe there's a sheet of fabric I could snag from one of the wagons. I push myself off the ground and leave my bedroom, peering into the bathroom.

Other places have functioning bathrooms. Is there a way to get mine working again?

Twisting the handles on the sink does not provide any results—neither does pressing the lever on the toilet. Finding more valves underneath both appliances, I give those a hard twist as well—nothing. Am I missing something?

I round my house and urinate outside. If we are going to be living in houses for the near future, I want to use everything my house has to offer.

I look inside through the back window, my room on the other side. A window next to this one reveals my parents' room. Something catches my eye. A red valve handle is attached to the foundation, almost completely obscured by grass. If it weren't red, I'd have missed it. "WATER LINE," the label reads.

When I'm finished, I give the handle a hard twist and it hisses loudly. I jump back, startled, checking my surroundings. It sounds violent, but if this allows me to use the sink, I'll leave it.

Making my way toward the cul-de-sac, where the Brightest set up camp, I see a large group of bodies lying on the ground near the tree. Maybe they share the same discomfort with their beds as well. It will be a while before we are accustomed to our new way of living.

Our storage wagon is planted a couple dozen feet away from our residential wagons. No one wants their sleep interrupted by someone who just needed a smoker. I move the curtains of the wagon over and climb in. It's dim, but the cloth allows just enough light to pass through. The seamstresses leave extra clothes in here in case they need them.

A large roll of white fabric rests against the wall of the wagon. This will be enough for my window, and there will still be plenty left when I'm done. I grab the roll and my mind drifts in the direction of that woman we found.

I pop open the lid of a chest containing clothes for women. I dig around searching for a fresh set of clothes and pull out a garment by the shoulders—a blouse with a floral design. I search more, finding leggings to go with it. Hopefully, these are the right size.

I shut the lid and exit the tented wagon, reflexively squinting from the sun's light and trek toward the woman's house.

"What're you doing up this early?" Oberon says, startling me. He is sitting on the same curb we sat at the previous night.

"I'm always up this early. I could ask the same thing about you," I reply, resting the clothes over my shoulder.

"Couldn't sleep," he says, cracking his fingers. "Playing dress-up?" he teases half-heartedly.

Something seems off about him. I don't know if he is tired or if something is bothering him. "The woman we found needs some new clothes, so I wanted to bring her some."

"That's nice of you," he says, smiling slightly. He stretches his next finger, and it cracks with a loud pop. "So many passings spent sleeping on the ground makes it impossible to sleep on anything else. Dolora and Brena love the beds, though. Dolora says it reminds her of the maternity wagons." As men, we would never know what it is like to sleep in a maternity wagon.

"I slept on the ground," I admit. "I must've rolled off." He chuckles at that.

"I'll probably do some 'splorin later if you'd like to come with," he says. "Gotta stretch my legs a little."

"Yeah, sure. Let me know when you're ready," I say, continuing my walk to the newcomer's house.

When I arrive, the woman's door is closed. I don't want to barge in, in case she is sleeping or not decent. "Hey, I have some clothes for you if you wanted something else to wear," I shout into the closed door. I wait a moment for a response—nothing. Is she even here? Maybe she's still asleep. Everyone else is. I almost set the clothes in front of the door before it clicks open.

She still wears her tattered clothing, and her pained eyes connect with mine. I pass the clothes over to her and she accepts, holding them tight, not breaking eye contact. Her timid gaze reminds me of a rabbit's. Any motion may send her running.

"Thank you," she mutters. Her other hand begins to close the door.

"Wait," I interject. "I never got your name."

There is another awkward delay before she says, "Lyria," and closes the door.

Oberon sits in the same place I left him, still popping his knuckles, but they refuse to crack. He stands up when he sees me approach. "You ready?" he asks impatiently. We both carry our crossbows, just in case we aren't alone in this town.

Raiders don't tend to travel this far ahead, but we still need to be careful. Running into another caravan could be just as dangerous. Oberon and I are efficient with a crossbow, but we've only ever killed deer. Hopefully we can keep it that way.

"Sneaking off together again without telling your wife, Obie?" a snotty voice says from behind. Mattias.

Oberon closes his eyes and takes a deep breath. He is about to say something, but I speak up first. "It really isn't your business. We are just scouting the town. That's all."

Mattias scoffs. "Right. You think the others haven't noticed you two sneaking off? People are starting to get suspicious. Some think you are being unfaithful to your poor wife." He crosses his arms smugly and there's a hint of a grin on his face.

Oberon's turns red hot. He speaks before I can stop him. "You better choose your next words very carefully." He steps forward, standing mere inches from Mattias, fists clenched.

Mattias is unfazed. "Or what? Do you not want people to think you two are secret lovers?"

"I'm not cheating on Dolora, and if I hear a peep about it from anyone—" He does not finish the sentence. He is probably twice Mattias's weight and could hurl him across the cul-de-sac.

"You'll what? Lay one on me? Which will it be, a fist or a kiss?" Mattias gives a slight smirk, tapping on his cheek. He spins on his heel to walk away.

It's all lies. Oberon and I have never shown romantic interest in each other. But is Mattias planting that seed in people's minds? I didn't have much to lose, but it could harm Oberon's relationship with his family.

Oberon remains silent. He holds his hands up in front of him, staring at bloody palms. He grabs Mattias by the arm. The little man turns back sharply, and I see a hint of fear in his eyes. Oberon releases him, leaving a bloody handprint around the butcher's arm.

"Come on, Obe. Let's go," I press.

"I want to kill him," Oberon murmurs when we are out of earshot. "What makes him think he can spread lies about me? Why is he so bent on trying to ruin my life? Why can't I figure out how to do the same to him?"

I choose a direction and start walking. He continues to complain about Mattias and I let him rant. He needs to get it out. I just wish they could keep their mouths shut.

The trees in the little town bloom as the air warms up. It's a miracle they can survive the harsh, nineteen-passing long winter. Many of the trees stand in front of decaying homes. They are tall, but none can match the figure of the central willow tree.

Compared to these other trees, the willow seems ominous. Being underneath its drooping leaves feels warm and welcoming, a type that you feel deep inside, yet unfamiliar and uneasy.

Our shoes tap lightly on the concrete as we explore more of Hollyard. Like most places we travel, it's barren and empty—devoid of life. Occasionally a bird would flee from our arrival, but there is little to suggest that other people live here. I lower my guard slightly. Each house has a unique form of age. Vines creep in and along some buildings. Green tendrils worm their way inside every crack and crevice. Other buildings are reduced to rubble. Few express little to no structural damage. We pass a park with an open field stretching hundreds of feet across. Its deteriorated playground looks more dangerous than fun.

Oberon is in a slightly better mood; his shoulders are much more relaxed, and his normal color has returned to his face. "Brena would like this," he says, examining the playground.

"I don't think you should bring her here," I say cautiously. My footsteps crunch on the woodchips as I approach one of the slides. I put a small amount of weight on it with my hand and the slide splits in half, crashing to the ground.

Oberon's eyes show defeat. "I dunno what his deal is." He's talking about Mattias again, I realize. "Why does he want to be an arse so bad?" I stay silent and let him vent again. "He only picks on us. I don't see him picking on anyone else. Is he trying to trick my wife into leaving me so he can have her for himself?"

Unexpectedly, Oberon puts his palms against his eyes and yells. We are far enough away from the camp that no one could hear him, though the volume catches me by surprise.

When he is done yelling, he looks up at me, face red.

"Better?" I ask.

He nods—before an arrow impales him in the back.

5

The Murderer

*The old scholars had the tools to deduce that it
takes almost exactly twenty passings for the sun
to make one full orbit around the planet.*
From the Journal of Azura Seren. Corono section, 28th
orbit

Oberon yells again, this time in shock, his back arching. The arrow sunk itself into his left shoulder. His thick coat should have stopped most of it. My crossbow unhooks easily from my belt and I raise it up to my face, looking around for the attacker. Oberon does the same, straining, not bothering to remove the arrow.

The thrumming in my chest accelerates. If there is just one attacker, we could probably handle it, but if there is a large group, we might be in a tough situation. We've never had to kill, nor defend ourselves from attackers, and we've been thrust into a situation we aren't prepared to handle. Could I truly take another man's life? An arrow to the heart—not much different from hunting.

I search frantically but don't see anything. A deeper fear sets in. The attacker could be anywhere, from any angle.

There's soft galloping behind me. I quickly turn to see a creature on all fours bounding toward us from behind a house. There's no time to react before it leaps onto Oberon, knocking him to the ground. The sound of snapping is accompanied by Oberon's screams. The creature's long fur dangles against the concrete below. I've never seen anything like it before.

A bolt looses from my crossbow and I miss. I always miss. The four-legged animal snaps its teeth mere inches from Oberon's face. I drop my crossbow to equip my knife and run toward them. With all the strength I can muster, my boot slams against the creature's ribs. Thrown to the ground, I stand over the animal, knife raised. But it's not an animal. It's a human.

I hesitate for too long. The human creature grabs my leg and pulls me down with a force I didn't think possible. I land hard on my back and my attacker climbs on top of me.

The human creature opens his mouth, exposing sharp teeth, and slams his head down. With speed, my knife moves in front of my face, pointing upward. The entirety of my blade punctures his eye socket, burying itself deep in his skull. Blood gushes out, covering my face.

The creature goes limp on top of me, I push it off gasping for air.

"Oberon," I say in between breaths. "You okay?" I ask, stumbling over to my friend to help him up. Next to him on the ground is the back half of the arrow. That's what had made that snapping sound.

"I'm fine," he says. "Just freaked." He takes a deep breath before nudging the body with his foot. "Looks like you *do* know how to use that thing," he says, pointing to my knife, wincing. I try to reply, but I have no words. The human's face is covered in blood. The intact eye stares blankly into the sky.

Its fur isn't actually fur, but some kind of suit to make him look like an animal. Oberon and I exchange glances.

Oberon tries to help me remove the bloody suit from the attacker, groaning in pain every time he moves his arm. I gesture for him to just allow me to remove it. Inside is a normal-looking man.

"Raiders? Already?" Oberon asks, flustered. "We just got here."

Could he be a raider? Or was he here before us? I stare into the lifeless man's eye and see the pain and anger. The knife—my knife—sticks out toward me, asking me to grab it.

I feel numb. This man lived a whole life, and I ended it in a split second. Did he feel pain when he died? Was killing him the only thing I could have done? Couldn't we have just taken him hostage and let Hadrian decide what to do?

What if that was me on the ground, staring into the sky? It could have happened as I was also a split second away from death. I imagine myself being stabbed by other people invading my home. My life fleeting away as my heartbeat slows to a halt. If I died now, I would have lived a life of no accomplishments. No one to love, no one to care for. No children or grandchildren of my own. Oberon's legacy is his daughter. If he died, he'd live on through her. Hadrian didn't have a wife or children of his own. Is this how Hadrian feels? Alone?

Hadrian has the Brightest. At least that's his accomplishment. They look up to him. They need him. But the last thing I want is to be like Hadrian. Running a group and making difficult decisions is not something I could do. I wouldn't be able to love, lest they get in the way of my leadership. A group wouldn't want to follow me, anyway. They require someone strong. How could I be strong if I can't even handle killing someone trying to hurt me and my loved ones?

"Come on, we should head back," Oberon says as if nothing happened. "Hadrian will wanna see this." I snap out of my trance, and Oberon tosses the stringy suit over my shoulder. He looks me in the eye. "I'd carry this, but you know," he says. He notices the look in my eyes. "You good, man?"

"I just—," I stammer. "I never—" The words have a hard time leaving my lips.

"Hey, it's alright. He tried to kill us," he reassures. "If you didn't do what you did. We'd be dead."

"Did I have to take a life to save a life?"

"Sometimes you do," he says. "We take the lives of deer to save our own. We squish poisonous bugs to protect our kids."

He means venomous, but I don't correct him. But he's right. How is this much different from killing an animal for food? It felt different, though. Like it *took* something from me.

It was easy—so incredibly easy to take a life. One moment, that man was perfectly healthy; the next, a knife lodged into his skull. The same could have happened to me, or Oberon.

A better-aimed arrow could have punctured an important organ. I could have had my face bitten off if I didn't have my knife. Regretfully, I retrieve the weapon from its holding place in the raider.

"Let's go." Oberon leads the way back to the camp. I follow closely behind, white knuckle gripping my crossbow. I'm still unable to shake the feeling of unease.

If there is one, there ought to be more.

When we return, we seek out Hadrian, even though I'd rather just lie in bed. When we approach his wagon, he sticks his head out of the curtains, as if he knew we were approaching.

"Oh, it's just you two," Hadrian says with a sigh of relief. "What happened to your face?" he asks in shock.

I sling the suit off my shoulder and onto the concrete ground underneath. I then use the front of my already bloody shirt to wipe more blood from my face.

"Looks like raiders are scouting the area," Oberon says.

"Really?" he asks incredulously. "We've only been here a day." Hadrian's expression drops in defeat. He steps out of his wagon tent to observe the mass of cloth.

"Yep, one leaped onto Oberon and was wearing this," I say, still tasting the attacker's blood in my mouth.

"Ah, a ghillie suit." Hadrian stares at the pile of strings on the ground. It looks like moss. "I've seen these a time or two, though they are quite rare." He doesn't speak for a couple of seconds and shrugs. "Seems like you guys handled it just fine."

Oberon and I look at eachother. We both suffered from this encounter, and it feels like Hadrian doesn't care.

"Well, Father. Actually—" Oberon speaks before someone behind us cuts him off.

"Oberon John Winters!" It's Dolora. "What in the name of the Light happened to you? And what is this?" The arrow tip is still lodged in his shoulder. He cries out in pain when she pokes it. Dolora's expression could kill. Her hands move to her hips when Oberon speaks.

"It's nothing," he blurts out. "Just a little injury."

"Just an injury? You two disappear without telling us and return with an arrow sticking out of your shoulder," she scolds. "What would have happened if you were killed? Don't you ever think about me and Brena? You're lucky Mattias told me you two were heading off somewhere. I don't even want to know what you were doing." Her words sound like Mattias's.

"Dolora, I—"

She turns on me and shoves her index finger into my chest. "And you! Aren't you supposed to be protecting him? You guys go out with crossbows all the time. Surely you know how to use them by now, right?"

I roll my eyes. She doesn't realize that I *did* protect him. I saved his life. If it weren't for me, Oberon *would* be dead. But I can't say that, because it would just escalate the issue.

I can't help but notice that something is different. She doesn't normally act like this. I do not want to get caught up in whatever Oberon and Dolora are going through. But why did she drag Mattias's name into this?

Hadrian watches these events unfold before him, but he does not intervene. I look around, and do not see Mattias anywhere. Where is that little rat-faced bastard? Likely snickering to himself in a bush while all this takes place. Light damn him.

Dolora flips around, nearly hitting me with her hair, and stomps off to her house. Oberon sighs deeply, putting his hands against his face. "Well, I should probably get this removed," he says finally. "Doc Stella will not be happy to see my face again after that incident with my ingrown toenail."

According to Oberon, he had an ingrown toenail so bad that when our caravan's doctor, Stella, tried to remove it, she vomited on his foot. Oberon exaggerates his stories, so I don't know how truthful that is. Although I do believe that even just looking at Oberon's feet could cause someone to retch. He leaves dejectedly toward Doc Stella's tent.

I stare at the broken arrow in his shoulder. The gears in my brain jam. Who shot Oberon?

"Thanks for bringing this to my attention," Hadrian says at last, bending down to pick up the ghillie suit.

"Father, I don't think that's the only raider living in our town at the moment," I say, frantic, meeting his wide eyes.

"Explain yourself," he demands.

"The raider who attacked us wasn't carrying any form of ranged weapon. No bow, crossbow, or arrows to go along with them," I explain, cringing at the memory of blood pooling out of the raider's eye socket onto my face. "There's a chance he dropped his ranged items, but I think someone else shot Oberon."

Hadrian's eyebrows sit flat with concern. "If what you're telling me is the truth, it could be very dangerous for the Brightest. I'll station Lew, Reyus, and Efram. They'll each do eight-hour shifts watching our community for attackers. You guys are good with crossbows, so I'll have you two as a second line of defense." His hand brushes up against the hilt of his rapier as if reminding himself that it is still there.

He then drops his guard and meets my eyes, showing a different type of concern. "So he was your first one?" he asks softly.

I nod, dropping my eyes to the ghillie suit in his arms.

"I remember my first kill," he said. "It wasn't a raider. It was a friend." He places a hand on my shoulder and I wince reflexively. "He'd betrayed us—sold us out. We all would have died if I hadn't made a decision. No one believed me when I told them the truth. I know what I did was for the good of the Brightest, even though I was branded as a killer from then on."

"But, Father, I—," I stammer, meeting his eyes, "I'm not—a killer."

"Yes, Caelius." He sighs. "You are."

6

The Snake

*They gave each passing its own name and named
each section of the planet after them.*
From the Journal of Azura Seren. Corono section, 28th
orbit

The three smiths, **Lew, Reyus**, and Efram, are assigned guard shifts, each lasting a third of each day. While one would be on watch, the others would rest. They'd trained with ancient blades, exhibiting skill only achieved by long, drawn-out hours of practice. In the very few instances our camp was attacked, the three would clear the threat before it became a problem.

They have killed people. How did they live with that? Perhaps they block it out? How could you suppress a feeling like this?

My eyes stay wide open. I dare not close them. For when I do, I see the raider in stunning detail. Underneath the tattered cloth suit, was a man. It was hard to see anything but a man. Not an animal or forsaken creature. But someone with parents, friends, hobbies, and ambitions. I remember the folds in his face, the lines supporting his eyes, the creases created by the mouth, the wrinkles painted on his forehead. I remember his dry, chapped lips and hairy nostrils. Perhaps my mind created something that didn't exist to humanize this creature who attempted to kill me.

But that's what he was, wasn't it? He was a human, so why do I want to refuse to see him as such? Maybe it's my mind trying to justify what I've done. As if lying to myself would allow me to pretend I'm not a murderer.

Hadrian chose to stay here, in Hollyard. He knows it's dangerous. He knows that we are going to get attacked again. He knows he's putting everyone in a difficult spot, but he doesn't seem to care enough to do anything about it. I'd expected him to tell everyone to start packing up to leave after I told him of my encounter.

Oberon chose to go scouting. If he didn't scream, maybe he wouldn't have drawn attention to us. Maybe the raiders had their attention on us before he screamed.

Mattias chose to antagonize him. If Mattias had kept his mouth shut ...

I want to blame Mattias for this, but I can't. He didn't have anything to do with the attack. Maybe Oberon wouldn't have wanted to go exploring, but maybe he'd decide to explore anyway. At least now we know what possible dangers await us in this town and no one needed to die.

I blame myself. I had the choice to not kill the attacker. Though had I not chosen to defend myself, I wouldn't be here. Instead, Oberon would have dealt with the consequences.

Less than a day ago, I'd been worrying about my romantic future—marriage and children. It's funny how quickly priorities change.

I can't help but think of that woman, Lyria. What horrors did she experience before joining the Brightest? Had she killed anyone? Maybe she chose not to kill, which almost cost her life. I don't know what she'd gone through, nor do I want to speculate, so I force her out of my mind.

Maybe that raider is the same one who hung her?

What takes her place in my mind is the weapon I used, my knife, sunken deep in the eye socket of the creature— the man. The memory plays over and over in my mind. Oberon gets shot and knocked to the ground. My crossbow bolt misses by mere inches. My boot knocks the attacker off my friend. The attacker pounces on me. My knife meets his eye as he comes down to bite my face.

It plays again. Oberon gets shot. Crossbow bolt misses. My boot knocks him off. He sinks his face into my knife.

Oberon. Bolt. Boot. Knife. Oberon. Bolt. Boot. Knife.

I grab my hair in an attempt to pull the memory from my skull and discard it. It's buried deeper than my fingers could penetrate.

What's the threshold for a broken mind? Mine should have broken by now, right? Is it this? Am I there?

My breathing slows along with my heartbeat. Worse things could have happened. Oberon could have died. I could have died. Maybe we both could have died, leaving the Brightest in danger.

In a moment of clarity, everything feels fine. I saved his life. Maybe I saved more lives within the Brightest.

It was so damn easy to kill. Could I do it again? Did I … enjoy it? Maybe the dread I felt is how I expected to feel after killing someone. Maybe I was playing a part.

Replaying the memory in my mind again, I instead find peace in the experience. The blood pours out of the man's skull, down my arm and onto my face. It gushes out in waves—the same way the buck's blood had after I slit its throat beneath the forest trees.

"In the name of the Light, I thank you for your sacrifice. For your body and your blood," I whisper, reciting the prayer I say when taking the life of a deer.

Finally relaxing, I drift off. The carpeted floor underneath me, as well as a thick blindfold, pulls me down into a deep slumber.

Water from the sink spills over the edge of my canteen and I take a sip. The water is so clean. Do I even need to boil it? As a child, I'd drink from the river. My mother's voice plays in my mind telling me to stop or I'll get sick. Sure enough, I contracted a terrible stomach bug, making me incapable of keeping anything down. I learned my lesson from that.

I leave my residence, holding a hand up to block the sun. Fewer people lay on the ground this time. I guess more people have acquainted themselves with their own homes.

I love being up before anyone else. I can be productive, getting things done without people noticing me. Often, I would go out hunting and return with food before the day even started. If Oberon could wake up as early as I do, I'd go every morning. Hunting alone is dangerous. If I get in trouble, it's nice to have someone there to help.

Having someone to banter with is also appreciated. Old legends have it that the silence of the forest has maddening effects.

An old children's story tells of a young boy who traveled through a nearby forest alone. He was there for only a week. When he returned, he saw things and spoke to people who weren't there. He murdered his family in his delusion and killed himself afterward.

It was likely a story written to discourage children from running away from their caravan, but stories didn't exist if there wasn't some truth behind them.

When we traveled through the Luminous Forest, Hadrian assigned everyone buddies who *anchored* each other. Something about the forest caused people to lose their sense of direction and disappear. They'd hallucinate, seeing things and hearing voices, not unlike the boy in the story. A blanket of fog carpets the floor of the Luminous Forest and unrecognizable creatures lurk in the bushes. Despite the sun being overhead, the coverage provided by the trees darkens the landscape. Walking around the forest instead of through it is rarely an option due to its sheer size. The Path goes right through the center of the forest and takes longer than a full passing.

The forests here aren't like that—at least not to that degree of intensity. We wouldn't need to worry about the Luminous Forest for another couple of passings. Hopefully, I'll be dead by then.

"We are low on food again," a nasally voice says. It had to be Mattias. Couldn't I enjoy one day without him bothering us? I stretch my neck back, looking toward the sky and take a deep breath. "If you guys don't go hunting, I won't have enough food for everyone," he says.

"Yes, Mattias. I know. Thank you," I respond, trying not to inspire him to speak more.

"If I don't have enough, you guys will not be getting a plate tonight."

It's too early for me to care. The moon hasn't even broken the horizon. I just walk away.

"Maybe I should come with you on your hunts," Mattias adds, catching my attention. "Make sure you aren't screwing around."

"You? Hunting with us?" I almost laugh. "Sure, buddy." I know Oberon would be pissed if I let him come with, but maybe this experience will get him off our backs. He'll see the amount of effort we put into feeding fifty people.

"What time are we going? Will I be getting a crossbow too? We better be back so I can have time to prepare the food."

"I will keep you updated," I say, shooing him away with my hands. Thankfully, he leaves. He's probably on his way to bother some other poor person who's awake at this hour.

Walking around the cul-de-sac, I find Lyria sitting cross-legged against the tree. The dome-like leaves droop down, providing a natural barrier from the sun, shading her from the heat. She wears the floral blouse I picked out. Her hands feel the grass underneath. Her dark hair flows effortlessly, resting on her shoulders. Her eyes are accented by her round and gentle face. Cautiously, I approach.

"Tommy would have loved this," she says, eyes still trained on the grass in front of her.

"Tommy?" I ask, sitting in the grass a few feet in front of her. It was the first word she said after I cut her from the tree.

"It's a shame he couldn't be here—to be in a community that cares for each other." A moment passes. "My son. He went missing." Her gaze breaks from the grass and meets mine. Her eyes hold pain, but not tears.

"I'm sorry," I say, almost a whisper.

"He and that girl, I think her name is Brena, would have been good friends. They're the same age." Her voice is solemn. "I try to convince myself he's still out there, but I don't know."

"What happened?" I ask, catching a glimpse of the dangling rope fragment above us.

She breathes heavily, hesitating. "I was in a camp. The Meridas. I was a pink. I got pregnant with Tommy and imagined him growing up in that environment. He'd grow up as a red and eventually become just as bad as Jack himself. So, I ran away. I thought nothing out there could be as terrible as living with the Meridas." She tosses a small stone beyond me.

Many questions flood my mind. What does it mean to be a pink? A red?

"Jack?" I ask.

Her lips tighten. I don't think she wants to discuss this topic, but she speaks anyway. "Jack Merida. He's the leader of the Meridas. I'm his—one of his wives."

"You two are married?"

"Not quite." Her knees come up to her chest and she holds them tight. "As a pink, I was more of"—she hesitates again, her breathing shaky—"a whore." Her eyes close when she says it and she hides her shame with her hands.

Waiting a moment, I change the subject. She doesn't want to relive this memory. If her son and Brena are the same age, and she left while pregnant, then she's been on her own with Tommy for nearly six passings. "So you left when you were pregnant? How have you guys survived this long? Have you been on your own this entire time?" I can't stop the questions as they pour out.

"We traveled with a few other moving caravans, but none lasted very long. I learned a lot on my own. I didn't have a choice," she said. "Either learn to live or learn to die." Those words resonate within me. "If I didn't have my son, I'd have given up. In a way, he'd saved my life."

Her eyes track the grass again, focused on something. Her hands move quickly, snatching an object. She lifts a garter snake by the neck, which wriggles and squirms.

I flinch when she snaps its neck. The tail drops, going limp, swaying back and forth. She didn't even hesitate. "When you're starving, snakes and bugs aren't such a bad meal."

The snake is dropped into the grass between us. Does she want me to take it? I don't think I can. Her survival instincts might be beneficial in the forest. I want her out there hunting with us, not Mattias.

"Do you know how to use a crossbow?" I ask, curiously.

"No, why?"

"Do you want to learn?" Her eyes meet mine, brows raised.

"I don't think anyone here would trust me with a weapon," she says quietly. "More for my own safety."

"I'd love to teach you sometime. Hunting is a very important skill." I pick up my crossbow, standing up.

"Hunting and using a crossbow are two different things," she says coyly. "I know how to hunt." The tone she used catches me off guard. I feel a grin tugging at the corner of my mouth.

Oberon is the better shot; he'd be better at teaching her crossbow. "Would you teach me something in return?" I can't help but ask.

She points at my waist. "Your knife. It's dull. Maybe I could show you how to sharpen it."

It's the same knife I used to kill the raider who attacked Oberon and me. The memory plays back in my head again—my knife sinking into the raider's eye socket as he lunges downward at me. Why did I still carry it? I should have thrown it away—or left it with the raider.

"No." I panic. "I can't. I'm sorry." Already standing, I speedwalk back to my house. I would not kill again.

7

The River

Janero, Febro, Marto, Abro, Mino, Janao,
Janio, Agero, Sebero, Octoro, Nevoro, Dektoro,
Plino, Vereno, Turseno, Corono, Cayano,
Hylano, Retuno, Fonalo.
From the Journal of Azura Seren. Corono section, 28th
orbit

Light flickers through the leaves as Oberon, Mattias, and I traverse the forest south of Hollyard. Mattias wears one of my spare hunting suits. It's a little large for his figure making him look ridiculous.

Even though the suit is made for reducing noise, Mattias knows little to nothing about hunting. Birds and smaller animals quickly flee due to his carelessness and heavy-footed approach.

"Why don't I get a crossbow?" Mattias complains.

"You're here to watch our process," I say quietly. A twig snaps underneath his foot scaring away a tree-dwelling squirrel. "Hey, watch where you step. You're being too loud."

"If I knew I wasn't going to have my own crossbow, I wouldn't have come. You promised we'd talk about getting me one," he whines.

"Shh." Oberon puts a finger against his own mouth and miraculously, Mattias shuts his.

We trek into the depths of the forest, keeping an eye out for natural landmarks to help us find our way back. Birds above us chirp and call out to each other. A woodpecker drills its beak against a tree. A group of bunnies bounds in the direction away from us. A low roar echoes through the trees as the wind conducts its natural orchestra. My shoulders lose their tension when I breathe in the scent of the humid air.

It's unfortunate the road after the Octoro Bridge doesn't contain many more forests. The rest of the Brightest should experience this at some point. Most refuse to explore this side of nature because of their experiences in the Luminous Forest.

How could I blame them? How could I convince anyone that these trees are not hostile?

Mattias spits and swats at his face. He'd walked right into a gnat cluster. I didn't even realize I'd ducked right under it. "Ew. They got in my mouth," he cries, spitting and rubbing at his tongue. Oberon and I can't help but snicker at his misfortune. He is way too loud, but seeing Mattias out of his usual element is such a treat.

"Welcome to the real world, buddy." Oberon chuckles. "Out here, you need eyes in every direction. Never know when something is gonna *jump* out at you." Oberon leaps slightly toward Mattias on the word "jump" and he flinches, putting his arms up.

"You guys sure you haven't seen any snakes out here?" Mattias asks, sounding worried. I regret not taking the snake Lyria killed to tease him. Mattias hasn't experienced a normal forest, and I take advantage of that.

"You know those hallucinations you experience in the Luminous Forest?" I ask. "They're real here." His eyes widen even more. I've never seen the little man so afraid in his life. "Remember seeing those ten-foot-tall snakes?" I tease, remembering how the Luminous Forest had played on his fears.

"But how is that possible? That was fake—a hallucination. Just like you said," he sputters.

I can't help but laugh. It sounds diabolical in my ears. "What do you think those hallucinations are based off of?"

"Fear, right? Those hallucinations stem from your greatest fear. That's what Hadrian said!" His voice sounds doubtful and he waits for me to say I'm just messing with him.

"You guys better make sure I make it back alive," Mattias says after I don't respond. "I've gotta date tonight."

Oberon and I perk up at that statement. Our eyes lock. A date? A woman wants to go on a date with Mattias? Surely, he is messing with us now.

"Alone time with a dead deer is not called a date," Oberon says. "It's called messed up." He giggles quietly, but Mattias does not find it funny.

"Ha, good one," he mumbles. "But really, I do have a date."

"You're joking," I smirk, crossing my arms, still not believing him. "Who?"

"You should know her. Lyria."

I freeze at the mention of her name. Lyria?

"Lyria?" Oberon asks. "Who's that?" I see his face as he puts the pieces together. "Oh yeah! That's the woman you like—the one we found at the tree, right?" Oberon asks. Mattias's cheeks flush.

"Yeah," I say after a moment. Mattias is the last person Lyria should interact with. She doesn't know him like I do. But that's not my call to make. I should be happy for them, if that's what she wants. I can't help but feel hollow at the thought of it.

"Oh, so," Mattias starts, "she's already taken then?"

Before I can speak, Oberon blurts out, "Hey, man, just 'cause there's a goalie, don't mean you can't score." He grins stupidly. I resist the urge to punch him in the gut.

It's quiet for a while as we continue our trek deeper into the forest. A loud rushing indicates a nearby river. Where there's water, there's a deer. The ocean east of us is thawing out, causing all the water to rush westward. The current roars, moving quickly. Anything caught in the water will be swept away.

The three of us sit in the bushes along the bank. The rushing water allows us to speak louder at a normal volume. "So, Lyria, huh?" I ask Mattias. "When did you get a chance to talk to her?"

"When you two snuck off yesterday, she introduced herself to everyone." Mattias snorts. "I asked if she wanted to spend time together and she said yes." He shrugs his shoulders. "Some women just want a direct man sometimes."

My stomach sinks and I know it's jealousy. Mattias is likely exaggerating the event, but who knows? Maybe she sees something in him.

I let it go. If it's what makes them both happy, then I will support it. Maybe she'll make him a better person.

"You know, it's really nice to have some guy time with you two," Mattias says. "It's good to get away from the group. I'm glad that I could experience this." Oberon and I stay silent as he continues. "I can't wait to see the look on everyone's faces when they see me carrying a deer on my shoulders. I'll be the hero of the Brightest."

He may be an asshole sometimes, but I admire his childlike enthusiasm. Oberon and I both know he wouldn't be considered the hero—just another spoke in the wheel.

Oberon smirks, "You want to know what it's like to carry a deer on your shoulders? Try picking me or Caelius up and walking five miles."

Mattias grins. "Obie, you're like the size of three deer. You're the main resident of Obie city."

Oberon lets out a short laugh. "Good one! Obesity. Hadn't heard that one before."

Are they bonding? This might be the first time where the two aren't at each other's throats. If they can keep this level of banter, it seems like things might be looking up for the two of them. If they became friends, or at least acquaintances, I wouldn't have to deal with them bickering anymore.

"Wait a minute," Oberon says, pausing. They both stand a couple of feet from each other. "I hate you." Oberon shoves Mattias back and he falls, again to the soft soil underneath.

They both laugh again, and Oberon offers a hand out to Mattias, which he takes.

Maybe we are too harsh on him. He doesn't seem to have many friends or be admired by anyone, despite having an important role in the group. Could I see myself actually being friends with him? Could I see Mattias and Lyria being happy together?

"I think it's time for a change," he says. "I want to come hunting with you guys more. Maybe we could go in shifts, since three hunters may be overkill. I could get my own crossbow and clothes. Maybe I could even teach you guys how to butcher!"

Oberon and I look at each other. I'm unable to find the right words to say. Mattias hunting with *us*? It seems unnatural. Could I really deal with him in the forest alone? Could Oberon? I think I could look past it if he doesn't antagonize us. I'm alright with some lighthearted joking, as long as I know it's just banter.

Mattias gasps, reaching for my crossbow. The weapon tugs on my belt loop. Panicking, I reflexively twist my hip. Mattias, still holding on to my crossbow, flings to the side before the belt loop rips, sending both him and my crossbow down the riverbank.

He rolls down the hill, screaming. My crossbow lands in the mud. Hooves pound against the ground on the other side of the stream. A good-sized deer scampers away. He had seen it before us and wanted to be the one to shoot it.

Mattias splashes into the rushing current. Wasting no time, Oberon shuffles down the hill toward the river. I follow him watching Mattias struggle to stay afloat.

"Help!" Mattias yells in between gasps, reaching out of the water. I quickly weigh the options and consequences in my head before leaping into the water after him.

The water is deadly cold. If I wasn't operating on adrenaline before, I am now. In an instant my arms and legs numb. What matters is that they still operate.

I should get out now and save myself, while I still can. It won't be long until my body locks itself up. But I've already committed to this. I need to follow through.

I don't panic. Instead, I keep an eye on Mattias's flailing body in front of me. The weight of my clothes nearly pulls me under as I swim forward. Faster than I'd anticipated, my arms struggle to move. If Mattias panics while I'm holding on to him, he could take us both under.

I snatch him by the shirt. Fear shines in his eyes and he pulls in closer, holding on tight. "Caelius," he says with purple lips. "Caelius."

"It's okay. I'm here," I reassure him. I can practically feel the pounding of his heart.

Oberon shoves a long branch into the water in front of us—he can pull us out. I let the current bring us closer and take a gamble, hoping I have enough strength to grab on to the branch.

With effort, I reach out and grab the slippery wood with my free hand. My hands are numb from the ice-cold water. "Hold on!" Oberon yells. He grounds himself against a tree, trying not to fall in with us, and pulls hard, fighting the strong current. His face strains, turning red. If I could just swim toward the shore …

Something hits Mattias, and he flies backward, his hug breaking. Now he floats behind me, our hands connecting like a splitting rope. I hold his hand with the little strength I can muster. I feel my grip on the branch slipping. If we stay in this water much longer, we are both going to die.

I take a look at Mattias behind me, freezing water splashing against my face. I see the man I am holding on to. I'm supposed to hate him, but in this moment, I only feel pity. This is the same man who helps feed the group. It's also the same man who's been making our lives harder.

I remember what Oberon said to me yesterday. Sometimes we must take a life to save a life. Right now, I need to save my own.

The fear in his eyes tells he knows I have decided his fate. "In the name of the Light," I say in a prayer, inaudible over the roar of the rushing river, "thank you for your sacrifice."

He has no time to respond.

I release my grip.

Instead of being taken by the river, he stays in place behind me. He must be holding on to the branch with his other hand. "Come on!" Oberon yells.

I lift both my feet and push off of Mattias. The action propels me up toward the shore and pushes his body deeper into the depths of the river, forcing him to let go. I hear him screaming as he is carried away by the relentless current. With numb fingers and a lot of effort, I pull myself out of the flowing water.

"I'm not a killer," I'd told Hadrian. Shivering, I pick up my crossbow from the ground.

Hadrian's voice answers in my head, "Yes, Caelius. You are."

Another voice, unfamiliar and wispy, layered upon itself, joins him. "I think I understand you now, Caelius."

At least I'm alive.

The End of Part 1

8

Interlude I: The Priest

Hadrian

Light peeks through the curtains of Hadrian's tented wagon, illuminating the scripture in front of him. He attempts to absorb the message on the page, but his attention drifts.

Grunting, he starts over, reading the beginning of the left page for the third time. His finger rests underneath the first word. Whispering the written words aloud, his voice sounds strange, unfamiliar. "I tell you this: Follow the Path and I will bring you light."

Hadrian reads these scriptures completely each passing. He interprets differing meanings from the text—almost like it changes its words every time he reads it. Who is Hadrian supposed to follow? Is he to worship the Light or the Path? Maybe follow the Path and worship the Light? Isn't that the same thing?

How long until he ends up like Rancis? Rancis was a strong leader. He was a leader Hadrian admired. When Hadrian was a kid, he wanted to be just like Rancis. He wanted to gain his favor and be viewed positively by him. Until finally, it worked. Rancis appointed Hadrian to be his right-hand man—his "Grafter." It was a nickname Rancis used for him, but he never learned what it meant.

They traveled together for many passings. While Rancis spent most of his time leading the Brightest, Hadrian focused on his swordplay. Rancis had a rapier made specially for Hadrian. It's the same rapier that lies next to him now. The same rapier that eventually ended Rancis's life.

He told Caelius his first kill was because a friend betrayed him. It wasn't a lie. Something needed to be done. Hadrian always felt like he was the one who betrayed Rancis. Learning who Rancis really was helped him justify his decision. He tried banishing the image of Rancis chewing on a detached human arm.

He still remembers the first words the Light had said to him. They replay in his mind with a bone-chilling voice.

The Light gave him directions and the plan to overthrow Rancis because he'd stopped following the Light's will. Hadrian knew it to be true, as the Light's words are truth.

Rancis's stomach popped like a fruit when Hadrian's sword penetrated it. In hindsight, it was the best thing he could have done. He didn't want to kill him, but Rancis was unfit. The Light deemed him unworthy of its power.

Hadrian ascended as the new leader of the Brightest. Chosen by the Light to lead and spread the scripture. The Light wouldn't turn on him, like it did his predecessor. He is everything the Light needs.

Hadrian forces himself to concentrate on scripture again. His book is the only one they have in the camp. The rest of the Brightest don't even know it exists. He plans to keep it that way. Hadrian's purpose is to take the words of scripture and interpret them for his followers. He purposely leaves out things in his teachings for various reasons. But it all points to one reason—how could he teach the scripture of the Path if he didn't fully understand it himself?

He sees himself like a muddied glass window. The Brightest would view the scripture through him. Some things are better left obscured for their own protection. If they knew the truth among these pages, they'd leave. The truth is almost too much for *him* to handle.

Would it be so terrible if some made their own decisions, unfettered by Hadrian's influence? People hardly questioned Hadrian's actions. They let him get away with anything. At times Hadrian needed someone to ask if he was making the right decision on an issue. These problems he's faced over the many passings wore him down. Most of his solutions were morally wrong. People blindly accepted each difficult choice he'd made without question.

Caelius almost convinced Hadrian that staying here was a bad idea, but he eventually relented. Maybe if Caelius had pushed a little further, Hadrian would have made everyone pack up.

Four passings ago, the Brightest stumbled upon a lonely man distraught with hunger—Jance was his name. Seeming to be mentally sound, Hadrian allowed him to join. As Jance slowly comforted himself within the group, he became unruly, hostile, and dangerous. It started with minor arguments with other members. Eventually it escalated into threats and violence.

After Jance lit an occupied maternity wagon on fire, Hadrian felt like he had no other choice but to put him down. No one stopped him. Not a single person questioned it. Afterward, they acted like he never existed. That bothered him.

The words blend together as he tries to read again. He shakes his head, knowing he'll have to continue tomorrow.

The book snaps shut in Hadrian's hands, revealing the title—*The Path*. Its origin is unknown. Was it written before the Freezing of the World, or after? The scripture reads as it was written after the Darkness froze—unless it was prophetic, predicting its future—Hadrian's present.

Amplified footsteps patter from outside his wagon. He pulls the curtain to the side, expecting someone to be standing there—no one. Sticking his head out, he sees the Brightest member who had just walked by his tent—Lew.

Maybe he really is becoming more paranoid.

Anything outside the range of his sound bubble is muted until someone walks close enough. Hadrian dismisses the bubble and the world around him increases in volume.

He breathes in through his nose, letting the familiar scent of morning air fill his lungs. A few members sit around the fire cooking breakfast. Hadrian hadn't eaten in many passings. The sun provided him the nutrients he needed. That didn't stop the food from looking delicious, though.

It was nice to finally be back in Hollyard, but he did not forget his reasoning for being here. There is a BlightStone in Hollyard, and he has been tasked with locating it. The only people who might know where it would be are Caelius's parents. Too bad they are dead. Hadrian figures the first place to look is also the most obvious one.

Caelius is out hunting with Oberon and Mattias, leaving his house unoccupied. The handle on the front door clicks and he pushes it open. It's dark inside. The only light comes through the massive window in the living room. Miraculously, the window is still intact after all these passings.

Hadrian had only seen a BlightStone once. He harvested it from Rancis after killing him, taking it for himself. He'd forgotten what it even looked like.

Hadrian searches Caelius's house, hoping his parents would have hidden it here somewhere. The search yields no results as he checks the kitchen cupboards, bathroom, bedrooms, and even in the cushions of the couch.

Where could it be? "Light. Now would be the time to speak," he says aloud.

The Light used to speak to him. Not anymore. Previously, it might have given him clues on where to look, but now it's silent. It hadn't spoken to him in many passings. Hopefully, he didn't do something to make it upset.

"Light, please," he moans, defeated. "I'm trying to follow your request, but I can't do it if you don't point me in the right direction."

Hadrian feels something touch his consciousness. Could that be it? The Holy Light? Or is that something his mind fabricated? Hadrian waits for it to speak to him.

Nothing comes.

How would he ascend if he couldn't find a single stone? What would happen when he does ascend? Who would lead the Brightest? Would his spirit still be present on Nivalis? What would they do if it wasn't? They already proved to him they require a strong leader to survive. None of them are equipped to make difficult decisions. Did Rancis know Hadrian would end up replacing him? Would someone need to replace Hadrian?

He walks a short distance before reaching the cul-de-sac. Members congregate around the willow tree landmark. A few seamstresses work on making more clothes. A handful of men work on building another wagon. Another three men are practicing their sparring under the shade of the willow.

"Lew," he calls. The skinny man stops in his tracks. He and Reyus lower their weapons and jog toward Hadrian.

"Yes, Father?" Lew asks, hardly meeting Hadrian's eyes.

Hadrian examines the man. His head bends low, and he stares downward. He is a good lad, though timid at times. Hadrian needs something from him and his friends.

Hadrian unsheathes his rapier, letting it rest on both his palms. Lew's eyes widen, connecting with Hadrian's. "Lew," Hadrian says, "take this sword and make an identical copy omitting the insignia."

Lew sighs with relief. Did he think Hadrian was about to kill him? What kind of man did they take him for? Lew sticks his hands out and Hadrian gently places the weapon in his palms.

9

Interlude II: The Father

Oberon

Caelius's body goes limp and falls to the soil underneath. "Caelius!" Oberon yells, sprinting over to him. He presses his fingers against his cold neck, checking his pulse. Thump—thump—thump. The rhythm is too slow.

Is this hypothermia? How does that work?

Caelius's lips are purple and his face is devoid of color. "Oh, Light," he whispers to himself, not knowing what to do. "Caelius, get up." He slaps his face lightly. There's no response. His mind races. Caelius needs medical attention. Oberon lifts Caelius up and slings him over his shoulders. His friend's body rubs against his still fresh arrow wound. He collects Caelius's crossbow and clips it to his belt loop.

It is like carrying a deer. Although Caelius's body is soaked and freezing. His clothes make him nearly twice as heavy. But that is no issue for Oberon. This is why they both hunt together. In case one of them can't make it back.

But what about Mattias? He is a valuable member of the Brightest. Who would butcher the meat? They were just starting to get along. Should he turn back and try to save him?

No. He needs to save who he can right now. Caelius needs Doc Stella immediately. Hopefully it isn't too late.

Oberon's legs struggle to run. His shoulder wound aches.

Caelius mumbles, "Oberon?"

"I gotcha, buddy, don't worry." Oberon fails to mask the worry in his own voice.

"I killed him, Oberon," he mumbles. "He could have lived, but I kicked him away."

"You did whatcha had to do. It's not your fault."

"I kicked him away," he repeats. Whether it's true or not, Caelius is clearly not thinking straight. Each step feels heavier than the last. If he is going to make it back alive, he needs to stop running.

He runs for miles. Each natural landmark helps him find his way back. Relief comes in small batches when he passes the oddly shaped boulder, and the unique mushroom patch.

How long had he been walking? Oberon lost track of time completely. He can see Hollyard in the distance; behind it, the city of Solace. He can do this. Just a few more steps. *Gotta make it to Doc Stella's.* He stumbles, feeling like he is walking through honey.

He is just within earshot of the camp. "Hey!" he yells as loud as he can. If one person could hear him, they'd alert the others. "Medic! Doctor! Help!"

The people in the distance scramble. Four of them sprint to Oberon. The others flee, likely to alert Doc Stella and Hadrian. The four men's faces become clear as the distance closes. Relief washes over Oberon when he sees the familiar faces of Reyus, Lew, Efram, and Donovan. Oberon slings Caelius off his shoulder into the men's arms. They carry him the rest of the way. Oberon takes a deep breath, savoring the loss of extra weight.

Caelius is in their hands now.

Oberon walks through his front door and is greeted by Brena. "Daddy!" she yells, throwing herself at him with a hug. He nearly topples over.

"Hey, bug," he says, placing a hand on her head. "How was your day?"

"My day was good. Mommy and I painted!"

"Oh yeah? Show me!" Brena sprints to the other room, her red hair bobbing as she runs off. She is so pure of heart. She doesn't deserve to live in a world this terrible. Mattias's body is likely still floating down the river. What would Oberon do if it were her instead?

After a moment, she returns, holding something clattering. She opens her hands and reveals a couple of very colorful rocks.

"Oh wow, these are so pretty." He grabs the top one, thoroughly inspecting it. It's a landscape of a field of trees with the sun high in the sky. The sun has a smiley face on it. To others, it's just another painted rock. To Oberon, it's everything.

He examines the next rock from her palm. This one is bare, save for some painted words. "I love Daddy," it reads. A little red heart is painted underneath. Oberon's eyes water up. What would he do if something happened to this tiny person? He couldn't imagine his life without Brena.

He will do what he can to protect her in this evil world with cannibals, raiders, and rapists. He signed up for that job when he became a father.

A voice interrupts his thoughts. "I'm sorry I got mad at you earlier," Dolora says softly next to him. She stands in a doorframe with her arms crossed.

"It's okay," Oberon says, a rogue tear escaping his eye. "It's just been hard lately. For Caelius and me."

"I know. It's been hard for me too." She sighs. "It just feels like I'm the only one raising our daughter, you know?"

This admission hurts worse than being shot with an arrow. She's right. Oberon hardly spent any time with them. But what was he supposed to do? He couldn't get anything done if he were at home all the time.

How long had she felt this way? What could he do to be better? It was unfair that she had to do this alone. It was unfair to Brena that she didn't get to see her father. But he had responsibilities.

"You don't mean that do you?" Oberon chokes. Doesn't she realize all that he does for them? For the Brightest?

"You're never here. You're always missing, out on some adventure with your pal. I just need you to be more present."

"I am present," he says, pain leaking into his voice. "I'm here right now."

"But you're not," she says. "You're here physically, but I can tell you're off in another place—a place in your head."

"In my head?"

"I just want to be a part of that place," she says. "I don't want you to forget that you have a wife and a daughter. If you get injured or die out there, I don't know what I'll do." Oberon has no words. Dolora continues, "You've been so distant these last few passings. I just need reassurance that you do love me—that you love Brena."

Oberon chokes, forcing himself to speak. "I provide." He stops. *Light, what can I say?* "I provide for this family. I provide for the Brightest. I can't just stop hunting. Everyone would starve!"

"I'm not asking you to stop hunting; your desire to provide and travel into the unknown is what I love about you," Dolora cries. "I'm asking you to show me that you love me."

Oberon does love her. He loves her more than anything. He just doesn't know how to show it, how to prove it. They've been together for so long. Not once did he think she felt this way.

Oberon doesn't show his love like everyone else. Others hold hands, kiss, say "I love you." Is Oberon broken inside? Is there something wrong with him? What could he do to fix himself?

She needs him to be more present. But what if he stayed home instead of hunting with Caelius and Mattias? "Caelius would have died if I wasn't out there with him," he says. "We go together so we can both return safely." Oberon's mouth tastes salty. A tear had snuck in between his lips.

Beef Iron Mutilator appears from behind the doorframe and rubs up against Dolora's legs. She doesn't acknowledge the animal.

"Oberon, please, I just need to know I'm not alone in this. Raising a child is hard! It's very hard." Dolora cries too. "If you don't love me enough to help me, then fine. But at least show that you love your own daughter."

His emotions go from sad to angry. "Don't you dare!" he shouts, putting a finger in her face. Beef Iron recoils at the sudden volume, his back arching.

Brena shrinks running off, scared. She hates it when her dad yells. Oberon dials it back slightly.

"I put my life on the line to make sure you two are safe. Mattias died and Caelius nearly joined him, and you're upset because I'm out of the house for a little bit too long? Do you understand how stupid and selfish that sounds? I can't believe you would insinuate that I do not love you two."

"I didn't say that!" Dolora shouts back. "You always take my words out of context and twist them to fit your own agenda!"

"Well, you—" Oberon is cut off by the sound of a horn. The vibrations shake the house, and they are both silent. *Raiders.* He meets her eyes. A million words are unsaid. What awful, yet perfect timing.

"Just go!" she yells.

Oberon grabs his crossbow and runs outside. There's static in the air, and people are fleeing back to their own homes, where they believe they're safe.

Are Dolora and Brena safe in their house? He shouldn't leave them alone. What if someone breaks in?

He shakes himself out of it. He can't think about that right now. There is a job that needs to be done, and that is to protect.

Hadrian, Lew, Reyus, and Efram congregate in front of the willow tree. Each one carries their own sword. Oberon and Caelius are the only ones in the group who use ranged weapons. And Caelius is in recovery right now.

Hadrian looks surprised at Oberon's arrival, like he didn't expect him to show up. He stops his speech to acknowledge him. "Ah, good to see you came to help. The more the better," their leader says. He returns to addressing the group. "Scouts say that a small group of raiders is funneling in from the northeast, north, and northwest." Hadrian swings his finger in those directions. He lowers his voice and meets Oberon's eyes. "Now, son, are you sure you can fight?" Oberon didn't know the answer to that question. He'd never used his crossbow defensively. Maybe Hadrian knows that. Oberon doesn't want to put his life on the line, but it gives him time to process Dolora's words.

"I'm sure," Oberon says with uncertainty. Dolora's words echo in his mind: "*I don't want you to forget that you have a wife and a daughter. If you get injured or die out there, I don't know what I'll do.*" It didn't matter if Oberon lived or died. He would go through any means necessary to keep those two alive.

"Good," Hadrian says. "Reyus, Lew. You guys station northwest." He points toward the city of Solace. "Oberon, Lew. You two—"

A creature appears from the side of a nearby house, charging at them on all fours. No, not a creature, a man wearing a ghillie suit—similar to the one he saw a few days ago. Oberon lifts his crossbow, aims, and pulls the trigger. It doesn't fire. There isn't even a bolt loaded into it. Oberon had been too panicked to even load his weapon. The creature stands, swiping a clawed fist at the nearest person. Efram dodges the attack and counters with his own, slicing the sword across its kidneys. The attacker recoils, stunned. Efram lifts his sword and buries the blade in the man's chest.

"That wasn't very smart of him," Oberon jokes. No one laughs. His cheeks flush and he feels shame for not having his crossbow loaded. His hands shake. Only a moment ago, he was ready to die for his family. That same belief isn't so strong now. If he'd been alone, what would have happened?

"It's a drone," Reyus replies. "They're seeing how we would react. They have eyes on us. Light knows how many."

Hadrian finishes his thought. "Efram, Oberon. You two station over there. Shoot any ranged raiders that you see." He points toward an intersection in the road. They should be able to defend from attackers from any angle. "Reyus, Lew—northwest. I will stay here near the tree defending the residences. If you hear me calling, return immediately."

The men split, running off in different directions. Oberon and Efram don't even make it to the intersection before being attacked by two more raiders. Oberon is ready this time and unleashes a bolt into a raider's bare chest.

The raider does not fall and instead barrels toward Oberon. *That should have dropped him. Why didn't it?* The raider leaps, wrapping his arms around Oberon, who is too big to fall. Efram quickly sticks his broadsword into the raider's side. The attacker howls and releases Oberon. He gets a better look at the naked chest of the raider. Except he isn't naked. He wears a type of leather armor made of human skin. The armor is slightly more tan than the raider himself and displays nipples and a belly button. Could it be the skin of a previous victim?

The second raider jams a bone knife into Efram's shoulder. He screams in pain. The raider shoves his knife downward, throwing Efram to the ground, instead of cutting. Oberon is fast with his hands, efficiently reloading his crossbow before launching his next bolt into the raider's head. He drops limply.

Scanning their surroundings, the realization that he had just killed his first human being strikes him. He remembers Caelius's first kill and how much it had affected him. Strangely, Oberon feels nothing but relief in this moment. Looking at the raider's lifeless eyes, he's reminded of what kind of world they are living in. It's a wonder he hasn't had to kill before.

Oberon offers his free hand and pulls Efram up. "Damn it," Efram swears before pulling the hollow bone knife from his shoulder. It clatters on the ground when he drops it. Blood stains Efram's shirt from where he'd been stabbed. "Keep your eye out," he warns. Efram presses a boot on the first raider's neck. Bones crunch under his weight, and the life drains from the raider's eyes.

Not a breath later, an arrow buries itself in the dirt next to him. This arrow is as thick as the one that shot him days ago. Oberon traces the arrow's direction, finding no one on the rooftops above.

He notices the archer too late. He's nearly invisible, hidden in a ghillie suit among the bushes between two houses.

Oberon raises his crossbow and releases a bolt toward the attacker. He doesn't miss. The bolt implants itself between the raider's eyes. The raider releases his grip on the bow, sending an arrow flying through the air, missing Oberon by mere inches.

He turns to check on Efram just to see the arrow sticking out of his chest. Efram looks up from the arrow, meeting Oberon's eyes. Fear.

"NO!" Oberon screams. The man falls back, blood gurgling from his mouth. "It's okay, buddy. I'll find help."

He whips his head around, searching for anyone who could help him. "Hadrian!" he shouts. "Hadrian!" There's no response. Hadrian can't hear him. "Medic! Somebody. Help!" He continues shouting. No one comes. Not even a single raider is drawn to his yelling.

Efram's eyes meet Oberon's before losing focus. Oberon grabs his hand, squeezing it tight. Efram's gurgling breathing has stopped, his chest failing to rise again. The arrow appears to have punctured one of his lungs.

Oberon won't accept this. "No, don't you go! Please, just stay alive a little longer," he cries out, squeezing Efram's hand harder.

His eyes stare into the distance, despite Oberon's pleading. Efram does not move. Bile rises in Oberon's throat.

What could he have done differently? If he'd spotted the archer sooner, maybe he could have saved his life. He wasn't good enough. How could he be expected, as a father, to protect his child, if he couldn't protect his friends?

He feels shame for even thinking that. He had to accept the truth—he did what he could, and it wasn't enough. It's never enough.

Part 2

Dimming

10

The Captive

*Looking for any indication or documents as to
what might have happened nearly twenty-nine
orbits ago is next to impossible.*
From the Journal of Azura Seren. Cayano section, 28th
orbit

My body aches as I gain consciousness. I groan in pain and light presses against my eyelids. A stack of blankets pins me to the bed. I struggle to breathe, daring to open my eyes. Is that my nightstand? I'm so groggy, I almost don't even recognize my own room. What happened?

"Caelius, I see you're finally awake," Hadrian says from my doorframe. He walks into the room and sits on the side of the bed near me.

"What …?" I struggle to say.

"Oberon told me you leaped into a river to save Mattias after he fell in. You're lucky Oberon was there to pull you out and bring you back. I know you and Mattias had your differences—but if you truly jumped in to save him, I commend you. It takes a very brave person to save someone, especially those they dislike."

Mattias. Light above, I *killed* him. I didn't jump in to save his life; I jumped in to make sure he didn't climb out. Hadrian calls me brave, but it's the wrong title. The fuzzy memory keeps me from making out what happened and what didn't. How much of it was a dream? I can't remember.

I shiver despite being under a stack of blankets. I'm cold, so very cold. My bones feel as if they are made of ice, freezing the flesh around them. It's agony.

"I understand this is hard for you," Hadrian says. "Thank you for doing what you could. It shows that you have real integrity. An integrity only found in the strongest leaders." Hadrian's expression drops, his eyes breaking from my own. "Though, your bravery didn't come without consequences."

"What?" I ask again. What did he mean? Is Oberon okay?

"The doctors tried everything to reattach them. Between the frostbite and the infection, there wasn't much they could do."

Reattach them? Something is off. What does he mean? He looks down at my arm and I follow his gaze. I stare at my left hand, resting on the bed. Two fingers are wrapped in bandages. The other three are—missing. My thumb, index, and middle finger are completely gone. Oh Light. My crossbow. How am I going to use my crossbow?

I check my right hand. Each finger is also individually wrapped. They are all present, although unresponsive.

"I'm sorry," Hadrian says. "They really did try. They told me movement in your other fingers should resume within the next few days. We are very lucky to have you still with us. I'm sorry Mattias couldn't be here, but your bravery did not go unnoticed."

Bravery. The word sickens me. It wasn't bravery. It was cowardice. I didn't save Mattias. I'd killed him.

I recall the events again. Mattias attempted to take my crossbow to shoot a deer. My belt loop ripped and he fell backward, tumbling into the river. I don't think we claimed that deer.

With great effort, I force the words out. "Did you— eat?"

"Don't worry about that. We made it by with some leftovers."

I feel guilty. We failed our job as providers. Even if we brought back food, who would butcher the meat? It's my fault Mattias died. It's my fault I lost my fingers. It's my fault the Brightest didn't get fresh dinner. I speak, straining: "Can't you—heal my—?"

Hadrian cuts me off. "I'm sorry, Caelius. It won't work."

"But—the Light—"

"The Light chooses who to heal and who not to heal. The Light uses me as a vessel to deliver its warmth."

I lay my head back on my pillow. If I can't hunt and provide, who am I? I'm worthless. There's nothing else I'm good at. I could try learning how to butcher meat, but there's no one to teach me. Oberon would need a new hunting companion while I stay behind as a cripple.

"How long?" I ask, my voice sounding clearer in my ears.

"Three days. You've been in recovery for three days."

The front door to my house creaks open. A fat, bearded, bald man walks into my room. Oberon. "Hey there, buddy, I was wondering when you'd wake up." His voice is solemn and quiet. I'd expected him to burst into the room full of energy. Did something happen while I was asleep for those three days?

"Heard you lost your fingers there." He smirks before saying, "Don't you worry, you still got your pecker. I checked." He chuckles, trying to lighten the mood. It's not convincing. I raise my hand to flip him off. I can't. My middle finger is gone, likely hiding in one of the nurse's ice boxes.

This reaction makes him chuckle, but his eyes show pain.

"What happened, Obe?" I struggle to ask.

"Hadrian hasn't told you?"

"He's had a lot on his plate. He just woke up," Hadrian says, grimacing.

"There was a raid."

"A raid?" I croak. If I were more lucid, I would have yelled it. There are many things I want to say, but can't. *There was a raid? Is everyone okay? What did I miss? When did it happen?*

"Yes, there was a raid," Hadrian says. "But why don't you get some more rest and we can talk about it later?" I need to know more, but I can't articulate my thoughts into words before they leave me alone in my room.

The weight of the situation hits me all at once. I'll never use my left hand normally again. Those fingers are gone forever. I can't hold my crossbow like this. I'll have to come up with a different solution. If I hadn't jumped in the river to save Mattias, I wouldn't be in recovery, missing three fingers. Light burn him in the afterlife. He died anyway, and I get punished.

I feel guilty for even thinking that way. I truly am a murderer. I've killed two people in two days. That would keep me up if I weren't still so exhausted.

My eyelids shut and I quickly drift to sleep.

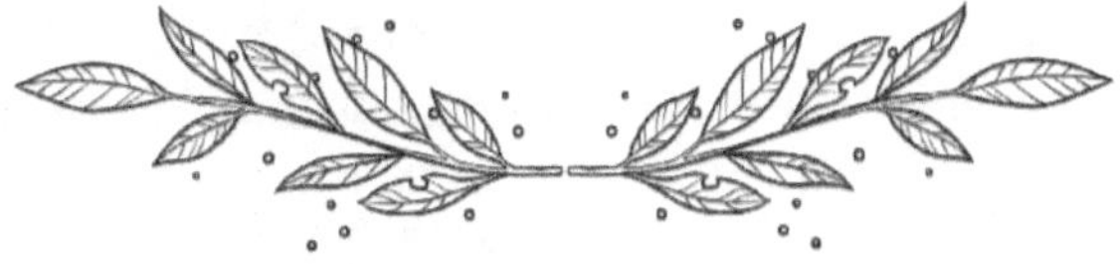

A dry throat revives me from my slumber. I cough hard, pain spreading through my chest. I attempt to grab the waterskin on my nightstand, but it slips through my hand. My fingers …

I'm reminded of that memory. I'll be reminded every time I look at my hand. The one where I doomed Mattias to death.

Mattias may have deserved a hard kick to the groin, but he didn't deserve to die. Would I have died too if I hadn't used him as a launch pad?

The waterskin fits better in my right hand. I pop open the lid and pull. The water painfully moistens my mouth and is gone in seconds.

It takes more strength than I expected to shove the blankets off me. I wobble, nearly falling over when I stand up. I guess that's what happens when I don't use my legs for three days.

The doorknob to my house's front door feels strange in my left hand. I reposition and use my right. I won't be getting used to this anytime soon.

"Good to see you moving around again," Hadrian greets. How long had he been sitting on my porch waiting for me? "Are you feeling any better?"

"Somewhat," I reply, wincing at the ache in my legs.

"Good man." He stands up and slaps his gloved palm against my chest. I stagger slightly and he hobbles off, away from the cul-de-sac. I look toward Oberon's house, seeing something in the distance. Someone I don't recognize is tied to the trunk of the massive willow tree. People typically congregate in that area. But this time, there's no one else.

I limp to the tree to get a better look at him. Rope binds his gangly figure to the trunk, pinning his arms. He's likely my age, but the grime on his face makes him look ten passings older. Faded tattoos crawl down the side of his neck. His beard is littered with bald patches and he has long dirty brown hair.

"Keep staring and you'll lose your other fingers," he hisses gruffly. He speaks with a lisp. Each *s* dragging like a knife over stone. I am taken aback by this comment. I shouldn't interact with him, but curiosity gets the best of me.

"Why are you tied up?" I ask stiffly.

"Why don't you ask your dad." Something about him unnerves me. The air feels colder around him. Are his teeth—sharpened? He looks like a shark, ready to tear flesh apart. Did he have each tooth ground down? I can't imagine the pain of that process.

"What's your name?" I ask, overstepping my boundaries. Hadrian isn't someone to capture and hold hostages, so why this man?

The man responds by spitting in my face. I scrunch as the wet spittle hits me. I wipe the spit off with my sleeve. I'd get more information by asking other members. Why did I think this captive would tell me anything?

I look back and Hadrian still hobbles down the street a couple of blocks away. He turns into a cube-shaped, concrete house on the right. Glass juts from the empty frames where small windows once sat, and a wide opening—about the width of three doors—gapes along one side. It's a garage. Other homes here have them attached. I follow Hadrian inside.

Hadrian, Lew, and Reyus chat in a circle. The concrete walls are lined with tools and weapons. In the center of the room is an anvil and next to that is a coal forge. Its embers glow a bright orange and a thin piece of metal glows devilishly above it. This must be the smithy Efram was talking about.

Where was Efram?

Reyus notices my entrance and waves his greeting. A solemn expression is plastered on his and Lew's faces. "Caelius," Reyus says, "Hadrian was just talking about you. I'm sorry to hear about your hand. He wanted us to make you something for your bravery."

There's that word again—bravery. My stomach twists at its mention.

Hadrian gives Reyus an "are you serious" look. Reyus must have spoiled a surprise. I pretend I didn't hear it.

"Efram told me about this place," I say, looking around. It is in rough shape, although with some work, they could make this place look great. I doubt they are going to spend the extra time on that, though. I let curiosity get the best of me. "Where is Efram anyway?"

The two young men's expressions drop. Hadrian answers for them. "This last raid made me realize how underprepared we are in the case of another attack. Reyus and Lew have proficiency in blade smithing. With this forge, anvil, and all these unused materials, everyone in the Brightest could have their own weapon."

He didn't answer my question, which tells me enough. "I'm sorry," I say. "Are you guys okay?"

Again, Hadrian answers for them. "They're fine."

I pick up the hint. It still doesn't stop me from being irritated with Hadrian. They're grieving and he's trying to push it under the rug. Changing the subject, I ask, "Are you guys able to make me a crossbow that I can use one-handed?"

Lew's lips tighten. "You'd still need your other hand to pull back the string. It may be possible to make a hand crank for one-handed cocking," he says. "As much as we would love to make you one, we're blacksmiths, not engineers."

He didn't mean to discourage me. Hunting is going to be impossible. On the other hand, without a crossbow, maybe I wouldn't be able to kill anyone else.

I'm still a killer. I don't need a crossbow to kill. Mattias proved that. Hell, even the first raider who attacked Oberon died from my knife.

I remember why I followed Hadrian here. "I wasn't there for the raid. Who's the man tied to the tree?"

Hadrian takes a deep breath, trying to choose his next words. I can tell he has been thinking about this all day. "Caelius," he finally says, "I need you to make a decision on my behalf."

"What?" I ask. "What do you mean?" Hadrian's the one who makes the decisions.

He pulls out a talisman from his unnaturally clean gold-trimmed robes. It's the insignia of the sun. He holds it up between us so I can see it clearly. "I'll need you to convert the raider to the Light. Or—" He unsheathes his rapier with his other hand. "If he is unredeemable, take his life." He places his rapier in my face-up palms. Upon closer inspection, it isn't his rapier. The familiar insignia of the sun isn't on the handguard. It's a different symbol.

My face numbs. I almost topple over. "You want me to what?"

"Redeem him or kill him," Hadrian repeats concisely.

"Why can't you do that?" I stammer. Panic sets in further. He's asking me to kill again.

"I can, if you want. But I asked you to do it."

Sweating, I look down at the rapier in my hand. The sharp tip looks like it could penetrate stone. The symbol embossed on the handguard is a circle with two smaller circular cutouts. The top left cutout symbolizing the sun, the bottom right cutout symbolizing the moon.

"I can't take this. The sword I mean …" I falter. "This is made for killing. I'm not a killer. Please take it back." My hands tremble as I try to shove it back toward Hadrian, pleading for him to retrieve it. He doesn't.

"When will you have the capacity to protect your people?" Hadrian asks flatly. The words hit me like a ton of bricks. He turns around and leaves through the open garage. I am still frozen there, holding the sword—*my sword*—in my hands. Reyus and Lew return to work.

11

The Redeemer

*Almost two hundred thousand days after the
event and still no one knows what really
happened.*
From the Journal of Azura Seren. Cayano section, 28th
orbit

I pace back and forth on my house's lawn. I glance at
the captive a couple of hundred feet away. He's still
tied to the tree. I do not want to talk to him. Darkness
freeze Hadrian for making me do this. Why couldn't he do
this himself? How am I supposed to convert him to the
Path if I'm not a priest? The Light hasn't blessed me with
the knowledge like it has Hadrian. Even if I could convert
the captive, how would I know he still wouldn't kill us all?

The rapier wobbles uncomfortably against my hip.
Reyus and Lew gave me a scabbard to keep it in, but I'd

almost rather hold it. The constant bouncing of the scabbard maddens me.

My other option is to kill him. It would be the easy way out. But I can't take another life. I don't even know how to use my sword. I take a deep breath and march to the raider against the tree. He doesn't look at me before he speaks.

"I was wondering when you'd come back." He speaks as a snake might, hissing each syllable. "You come to kill me? Well, do it swiftly." His neck tattoos stretch down under his shirt and his grimy hair leaves an imprint on the tree behind him.

"No, actually." I hesitate. "I'm here to save you." I take a seat in the grass in front of him, hoping the rope holding him is strong enough. His sharp teeth unnerve me as he speaks.

"You're gonna set me free?" he asks, raising his eyebrows. "Better do it now before the rest come."

What would happen if I freed this man? I assume he'd lunge at me and tear out my throat with his teeth. What does he mean by "the rest?" Other raiders? Do they know he is being held hostage?

"No, I'm here to show you the Light's warmth," I tell him.

"Oh, so you're one of those religious junkies, then?" The captive breaks his gaze to roll his eyes. "Come back when you're ready to kill me instead."

"If you give your life to the Light, Hadrian may free you."

He reacts slightly to that. It's subtle, but it's there. A twitch of the eyebrows. Hope? Or a spastic muscle? He makes a guttural sound in his throat, preparing to spit. I scrunch my face, leaning away. Luckily, instead of in my face, he spits a wad of mucus on the ground.

I don't even know where to begin. Why do I feel like the one with a disadvantage? He's the one tied to the tree. I take a breath, resetting my thoughts. "Let's start out easy. What is your name?" The raider just glares at me. "I'll start if it makes you feel more comfortable. I'm Caelius."

Still, the captive refuses to speak. Instead, he bears his teeth. If he intends to freak me out, it's working. But I won't let him know that. I stare him in the eyes. Fire blazes behind his pupils, burning devilishly.

I break, feeling uncomfortable. I hide the shame in my defeat, standing up and leaving without saying another word.

I grab a bowl of dinner instead of having it served to me. I sit next to Oberon who hasn't gotten a bowl yet. We sit on a curb like usual, but Dolora and Brena eat with Dolora's friends.

Oberon is unusually quiet. After a moment, I break the silence. "Did you go hunting alone this morning?" I ask.

"Yep," he says shortly. I knew something was bothering him earlier, though I didn't know what. He usually would go to great lengths discussing his hunting experience.

"What's wrong?" I ask.

He exhales. "I don't know," he says. "I thought life would finally be normal after coming to Hollyard. Apparently, that's not the case." I know what he means. Life has been much harder since we arrived. "I get shot, Mattias dies, we are attacked, we both kill for the first time, and to top it off, I'm *still* having issues with Dolora." I look at her, laughing with her friends.

"You killed someone?" I ask. The food doesn't seem appetizing anymore. "I'm sorry. I couldn't sleep after what I did to that first raider." Oberon and I share a burden now. We are both killers.

"It doesn't bother me like it bothers you, I think." He hesitates. "It feels good knowing that I can help create a safer place for the children in the Brightest, especially for my daughter." Oberon's expression is flat as he stares off into the distance. "I'd kill again if I have to. I'd kill a thousand raiders to keep Brena safe. Maybe I should kill the man tied to that tree there." He points at the captive.

I wouldn't stop him if he tried. At least it wouldn't be my problem anymore. I don't think Hadrian would be upset if something *happened* to the captive. After all, Hadrian has killed many raiders in the past himself.

A man walks past us giving me a mean scowl. He's a Brightest member, but I don't know his name.

Oberon notices it too. "After Mattias died, you caused a ruckus in the community. People are not too happy that *he* was the one who died."

"Instead of me?" I snap. "What a load of shit. I jumped in to save him and lost my fingers because of it." I feel my face heating up.

"I know, that's what I said too. But people are gonna believe what they wanna believe."

This is ridiculous. We both could have died out there. It's Mattias's fault for falling into the river. I lift the spoon to my lips and take a bite of my stew. Something hard rolls around in my mouth. A bone? I dig my fingers into my cheeks and pull out a piece of cartilage.

Mattias wouldn't have left that in. I can see it on other people's faces too. There are bits and pieces of the deer still present in the stew. Hair and skin float inside my bowl and

I almost gag. How could someone look past that when butchering an animal?

"Who butchered tonight?" I ask Oberon.

"I don't know," he says. "The cooking ladies, I think. I just laid the deer on the butcher's table and someone took care of it." His face twists in disgust when he looks in his bowl. I dump out my food into the grass. I'm not hungry, anyway.

Hadrian's voice startles me. "Did you think about what I said earlier?" How come I never hear him approach? Did he catch me dumping my food out?

"I—uh," I stammer. "I talked to him earlier, and he didn't seem interested in what I had to say."

"I understand," Hadrian says, grimacing. He puts his hands in his pockets. "I know this is hard for you. If you really don't want to deal with him, I can take over."

"No, I can handle it," I lie. He nods anyway. "I'll put more time in with him."

"Good," he says. "If you need guidance, let me know." He breathes in before changing the subject. "I'm thinking of offering sword fighting lessons if you are interested. You are welcome to join too, Oberon."

Sword fighting lessons? I don't plan on killing again, but if I'm going to carry this rapier with me, I better know how to use it.

"Sure, when?" I ask. My hand brushes up against the rapier at my side. "Oberon doesn't even have his own sword."

"I'm sure we can arrange that," Hadrian tells us. "Our guards are working overtime to make everyone their own weapon." Hadrian glances at the captive tied to the tree. "Meet me at the edge of town tomorrow. Just walk down this road until you see me. Midday. I'll teach you proper form."

It isn't a suggestion. We'll be in trouble if we aren't there on time. "Yes, Father," Oberon and I say in unison. Hadrian nods and leaves.

12

The Stance

Nivalis seems to rotate slower than most planets,
maintaining a constant forward direction toward
our sun.
From the Journal of Azura Seren. Cayano section, 28th
orbit

The moon peers over the horizon, indicating a new day. I'd kept a chunk of spare venison jerky, so I tear off a piece to chew on. It tastes fine, though not amazing. My stomach still growls. I cut off another sizable chunk of the meat.

I bring it with me out of the house. The willow tree is a beacon in the distance. The man still sits at the base. People don't sleep on the ground around the tree anymore, likely because of the captive. When I arrive, I drop the chunk of jerky on the ground in front of the captive. He looks up at me, pain in his eyes. Have they not been feeding him? Or is he refusing to eat?

"You just here to taunt me?" he asks. The corner of his cheek twitches upward in a snarl.

I keep my hard expression. "No. You need to eat. I brought this."

He looks at the pound of dried meat in front of him. "Is this a joke?"

"If you're not hungry, I can take it back," I threaten, reaching for the food.

"No!" he blurts. "No, I'll eat it."

Carefully, I bend down and untie his hands from his side, being sure not to untie the ropes holding his torso to the tree. It's considerably harder with only one fully functional hand. I step back, and he stares me down. Neither of us says a word to each other.

He lunges forward, arms outstretched toward me. My body reacts, jumping backward. My right hand equips the dagger from my belt. Had the ropes not held him back, I'd be dead.

The knife shakes in my hand and falls to the ground. It's the same knife I'd used to kill my first victim. I don't know if I dropped it because of his sudden move, or if it is trauma. Would I ever get over that feeling?

The raider smirks a little. He'd psyched me out to see how I would react. He knows as well as I do he could have killed me right there. No other Brightest members are nearby. I could have been picked to a pile of bones before my body would be discovered.

The man reaches for the jerky and bites into it with his sharklike teeth. He eats it like an animal, tearing the meat like paper. This might be the only food he's had since being captured.

"You just gonna keep standing there?" he asks rudely. "I can't eat with someone watching me."

"Not until my job is finished."

"And when it is, are you going to free me? Let me be with my people?"

I'm not sure what my plan is, or Hadrian's plan. Part of me hopes he would die on his own. Or someone, like Oberon, would kill him first. He mocks me while I think of a response. "Haven't figured that out yet, huh?"

"There are only two ways this will go," I say, leaving it ambiguous. "Depending on how you cooperate may change your outcome. Maybe you can start by telling me your name."

"You should kill me now and stop wasting my time. And by what I've gathered, I'm wasting your time too," he says, taking another bite of his jerky. I stand there, waiting for him to continue. After a moment, he groans in frustration, "Pladd."

Pladd. Interesting name. At least this is a step in the right direction. "Pladd, I'm Caelius."

"I don't care." He takes another bite of the jerky.

"You should care, because it seems like I'm the only one feeding you." My words don't intimidate him, but it's better than showing fear.

His eyes drill into my own. I'm sure he's thinking of a hundred and one ways to kill me. With effort, I refuse to react. Instead, I take control of the interaction. "Well, we are going to continue this tomorrow." I step behind the tree, preparing to tie his arms back to his side.

"Leave my arms out this time," Pladd says.

I laugh more as an insult to his idiotic demand. "Ha. No." I take the chunk of meat from his hands and grab the rope, fastening his arms to his side. He accepts his punishment willingly.

"This is inhumane," he mutters. "What if I get thirsty? Have to piss or shit?"

"Tough." I shrug. Pladd is more civil than I expected from a cannibal, which doesn't take much. Maybe he grew up in a normal group before becoming a cannibal?

Though why wouldn't a tribe of cannibals learn table manners? Just because they kill and consume humans doesn't mean they can't hold hands and pray at a dinner table together. The idea doesn't sit well in my mind, but if I really wanted to help this man, maybe it wouldn't hurt to learn a bit about his culture.

Do they pray before eating? Which god could they possibly worship, because it's not the Light. No one could follow the Light and live the way they do.

My pinky finger brushes against the scabbard on my left hip. I could summon my rapier right now and kill him. He'd do the same to me in a heartbeat; why shouldn't I? Could I kill him? What if I see him as an animal instead? Could I do it then?

I have no practice with my rapier. Hadrian promised to teach Oberon and me. Even though he's a stationary target tied to the tree, I couldn't risk it. I don't know what he's capable of. Maybe after training I could do what needs to be done.

When the moon reaches its apex in the sky, Oberon and I walk nearly half a mile down the street to find Hadrian. He is still wearing his pristine white, gold-trimmed robe. Did he ever do anything without that? How does he maintain its cleanliness? In his hands, he holds another rapier inside a scabbard.

"Good afternoon, boys," Hadrian says, bowing to us. "Be prepared to learn some hard lessons today. But remember, these difficult lessons today may save your life tomorrow. Oberon, this is for you." He hands him the sword, and Oberon accepts it reluctantly. "Do not draw it until I tell you to." He holds up a finger.

"Luckily, I don't have a paper and pencil, so you won't need to worry about that," Oberon says with a chuckle, though neither of us laughs. Hadrian steps up close to him, staring at him intensely.

Hadrian shoves Oberon backward with both his hands. Oberon stumbles and nearly falls over. "Hey!" he yells. "I'll kick your—" He stops himself when he realizes who he is talking to. "Why'd you do that?"

Hadrian steps back, examining him. "Stance. Your stance is the most important part of close combat. Your feet are your foundation, and like a building, if your foundation isn't stable, the whole thing comes down."

"Okay, so how do we 'make our feet like a building?'" Oberon asks, not quite getting it.

"Observe how I do it," Hadrian says, lifting his robe up slightly, exposing his pale legs. The sight is unsettling. Instead of paying attention to his stance, I'm more distracted by the color of his legs. For someone who worships the sun, he sure doesn't have much of a tan. I am swiftly punished when Hadrian rams his shoulder into me.

I fall backward, landing hard on my tailbone. Pain streaks through my legs and back. "Another thing to remember is to not get distracted," Hadrian says. "Being distracted at the wrong time will kill you."

Oberon chuckles at my failure and plants himself, setting his legs shoulder-width apart. "Let me show you how it's actually done," he mocks.

Hadrian shoves Oberon again and he falls on his backside, grunting. "What the hell? I did it correctly!"

"You did it sloppily," Hadrian corrects. "Get up, you two. Show me your stance." We lift ourselves up and set our stances. Hadrian steadies himself, holding my shoulders, readjusting my legs by lightly tapping my feet with his own. "Bend your knees," he commands. I do so. When he is done adjusting my stance, he steps back, taking a look.

He rams into me again, but this time I am expecting it. The force still causes me to stumble slightly, but I don't fall.

"Very good," he applauds. "Remember that stance."

I make a mental note, putting it into my memory for future use. He helps Oberon next. Again, Hadrian steps back, studying him. Oberon braces himself, anticipating Hadrian's blow.

Instead, Hadrian rams into me again and I am thrown back a couple of feet. Pain surges through my already bruised tailbone when I land. "Hey!" I grunt. "I wasn't ready!"

"No one ever is," Hadrian says.

"This is dumb," Oberon interjects, scoffing. "We came here to learn about sword fighting. Not how to stand. I already know how to stand." We both give him a flat look, and he realizes, once again, who he is talking to. "Father," he adds, trying to make his outburst a little more respectful.

"Perhaps you are right, Oberon," Hadrian says. "I don't have to train you for anything. I can take back this sword and give it to someone more willing to learn."

"No," Oberon interrupts, standing straight. "I'm sorry, Father."

"Good lad," Hadrian says. "One more outburst from you and you're done. Understand?"

Oberon nods his head, not making eye contact with the old man.

"Good. You two are dismissed."

"Dude, that was BS," Oberon complains on our walk back to the cul-de-sac. Oberon holds the rapier in his hand. He doesn't have a scabbard yet. "I can't believe that he thinks he can treat us like that. Who does he think he is?"

"He's trying to train us to be ready if we get attacked again. Like having a good stance, you never know when you might get attacked."

"I've been shot with an arrow and I reacted just fine. What he did was humiliating. I think maybe the old f— fart got a kick out of knocking you to the ground." Oberon used to swear a lot in the past. He toned it down after having Brena.

"We should be grateful that he is even offering us sword fighting lessons. You're one of the first people to receive a sword. It's a privilege that we get to learn under him."

"Bootlicker," Oberon mutters. I feel my face heat at that comment. I leave it, though. It is no use getting into a fight right now. Especially since there may be a bit of truth in that statement.

On the one hand, he's right. We both expected to learn actual sword fighting techniques; instead we were taught how to stand.

He changes the subject. "What ya planning to do with that freak tied to the tree?"

"I have to convert him into following the Light," I say. I had been planning to kill him after our lesson with Hadrian. But I know his name now. It's become personal. I'm not sure if that's the right thing to do anymore.

"Following the Light? You mean following Hadrian?" he mocks. "I feel so bad for the *mother effer*. Just end his misery now."

My irritation bubbles over with his pessimism, spilling out. "If you hate him and this group so much, maybe you should just leave!" I shout, forgetting my missing index finger when I go to poke him in the chest. I look around to make sure no one else heard me. No one is nearby.

It's Oberon's turn to get angry now. His face turns visibly red and his words begin to jumble together, accent becoming more pronounced. "We are here because it's the safest place for Brena. I don't know why we stopped moving because now I'm seriously doubting the Brightest's ability to keep 'er safe."

"You joined the Brightest before you even had Brena. Maybe you should have left then!" I realize what I said isn't relevant to the argument, but I don't care. "Weren't you the one who wanted to stay?"

"Why are ya so devoted to him? He's justa man. He can't just rain fire down and smite ya for not doin' everything he wants."

"He was there when my parents weren't," I blurt. "My parents left me with *him*. He raised me when they failed to do so." I feel my eyes watering up.

"So, ya understand why I can't just leave?" Oberon says pointedly. "If I leave, Brena's left to be raised by Hadrian. She becomes just like you—religiously devoted to that old man who's far from fit to raise a child."

The rage blossoms within me. A million words threaten to escape my lips, but I only allow four. "Light burn you, Oberon." I leave him alone in the street.

13

The Books

Oberon

*It may get colder or hotter depending on the
location of the planet relative to its star. If that's
the case here, the difference is negligible.*
From the Journal of Azura Seren. Cayano section, 28th
orbit

The **buck stands still, unaware** of Oberon's intention. The forest always calms him down when he is upset. The soft breeze pressing against his exposed skin and roaring of leaves is Oberon's therapy. As if all issues melt away. He is alone this time—no Caelius, no Mattias. He will likely hunt alone until they find a replacement hunting partner.

It had been a day since he and Caelius had their argument. Caelius refused to talk to him last night, sitting alone during dinner. They both said things to each other that were hurtful. Oberon shouldn't have said what he did. He was just so angry. How could he convince Caelius that Hadrian is a terrible leader? It would be better if someone else took his place. But who would want to?

Would Hadrian ever give up his position of power to someone else? He may not show it externally, but that man is a *power-hungry maniac*. Oberon wouldn't trust himself with that amount of responsibility. It's hard enough to take care of one child. Let alone, fifty grown adults. Surely there's someone more fit to lead them.

Oberon pulls the trigger, sending his bolt whistling through the air. It flies past the buck's face, sticking into the tree behind it. The buck leaps away, bounding over a hill.

He missed? He never misses. Sighing, he is going to have to track the buck down again. Just another waste of time. The sooner he gets his deer, the sooner he can be with his family. They arrived in Hollyard over a week ago and Oberon still hasn't found the time to explore his own home.

Leaves crunch under his feet. He is alone out here. A bear could charge at him from any direction. A poisonous—venomous?—snake could strike from under these leaves. He wouldn't have time to crawl back to Hollyard before succumbing to the deadly toxins. If he died out here in this forest, would anyone know? Would anyone care? Would someone even find his body like they found Lyria's?

Caelius is upset with him. Dolora doesn't seem to want to be around him. Hadrian acts neutral, but he clearly prefers Caelius. Of course he prefers Caelius. Hadrian *raised* him. Oberon raised himself.

Oberon feels shame for even thinking that. Of course, people would care. His daughter looks up to him and is waiting for his return. He knows she loves him.

But she loves her mother more.

Oberon knows these intrusive thoughts are unwanted and wrong. Meant only to drag him further down into Darkness. That cold, unforgiving Darkness. The Darkness that the Light once touched, but left behind.

"Caelius hates you. Hadrian is disappointed in you. You claim to follow the Light, but only reap the benefits. Mattias could have lived if you had been more proactive. That arrow should have killed you."

He remembers his conversation with Dolora the other day. She believes he doesn't love her. He doesn't know how to convince her otherwise.

What if she's right? He always thought he loved her. He would do anything for those two. But what if he didn't? The doubt creeps into his mind, making him question these last six passings.

Maybe he doesn't love her. Maybe he loves the idea of her? He loves that she is there to take care of their child, that she is more of a friend than a wife.

The thoughts overwhelm him. He knows they are lies, but he can't push them away. Like arms reaching through the ground underneath, dragging him down. Oberon's vision blurs. His ears buzzing.

Oberon's knife is in his hands. How did that get there? Had he been subconsciously fidgeting with the sheath attached to his belt? He used his knife only for hunting purposes.

Could it have another purpose? The blade glistens in the light. It once had been polished, clean—beautiful. The rubber handle feels so familiar in his hands.

Pressure builds up beneath his skin. It itches at him, needing release, like popping a blister. If he could just—

Oberon shakes himself out of it, the blade dangerously close to his wrist. He sheathes his knife before any harm can be done. He should throw it—far away. He doesn't.

What happened to him? He used to be able to make light of dark situations. He used to crack jokes so he could make someone smile. How could he do that if he can't even smile himself?

Things are serious now. More serious than they ever have been. Coming so close to death made him realize that. They are no longer kids shooting rabbits for sport. He had grown up. He had to acknowledge that—somehow.

Despite what happens, Brena needs him to return.

Oberon drags the large buck by the antlers back to the town. He didn't feel like carrying it. No one acknowledges him when he arrives. He half expects Mattias to appear and tease him, saying the deer is too small. Was he joking when he did that? Was he just trying to make friends?

There's fear in the poor women's eyes when Oberon places the buck on the butcher's table in front of them. Judging by the previous nights, they don't know how to butcher a corpse any more than Oberon does. He doesn't want to put that burden on them again.

Brena and Dolora are waiting for him. He should get home to them. But he couldn't just leave these ladies with the deer. Oberon unsheathes his knife. Guilt and shame creep into his mind upon seeing the blade once more. Had he really considered hurting himself earlier? Could he trust himself to continue hunting in the forest alone?

The knife sinks into the dead animal's stomach. Hot blood gushes out through the entry wound and Oberon cuts upward toward the chin. He isn't familiar with the process of dressing an animal, but he's observed Mattias do it once or twice from a distance. Oberon wishes Mattias were still here to show him his process.

Blood sprays on Oberon's hunting clothes, painting them dark red. "Darkness freeze—" Oberon swears. Heads turn toward him due to his sudden outburst. "Sorry," he says.

Would Oberon be the Brightest's only hunter *and* *butcher* for the unforeseeable future? There has to be another solution. Is there anyone else fit for the job? Maybe Donovan or Tremain? They already have enough on their plate. What other choice does he have?

After nearly an hour of butchering, Oberon takes a step back to look at the mess on the table and on his clothes.

It would have to do. He passes the meat to the cooks, and they prepare dinner, preserving the extras. The relief and thankfulness in the women's eyes make the effort worth it.

He should probably clean himself up before dinner. Caelius was able to get water to flow into Oberon's house, so he wouldn't need to find a river.

He walks up to his front door, a trail of blood following him and collecting at his feet. Dolora would be pissed if he stained the hardwood floor. Either he could strip here or find a river. He's so exhausted. It would take ages to walk back to the river and clean up. He's also not willing to expose more of himself than necessary to anyone nearby. He'll just clean the floors later.

He steps inside and sees Dolora and Brena reading together in the living room. His daughter doesn't run up to him like she usually does. Instead, they both stare at him blankly. Their faces are pale white as if they are looking at a ghost. Neither says a word.

"Hey," Oberon says after an intense silence. "Sorry about the blood. Needed to help the cooks and butcher the deer I found. You know, with Mattias being gone and everything. I'll clean it up right away."

Beef Iron Mutilator sniffs at the blood on the ground and screams at him. The other two remain silent. Dolora's eyes are icicles. Her lips move but no words escape. She's upset but can't bring herself to speak. Maybe she doesn't want to say it in front of Brena, who has her thumb in her mouth. She always reverts to sucking her thumb when she's scared.

Instead of escalating the situation further, Oberon enters the bathroom to clean himself up. He undresses, putting his hunting suit on the ground next to the bathtub. Blood pools underneath, staining the floor. Cold water sprays from the showerhead when he twists the shower handle. He steps in, feeling goose bumps spread across his body.

It's bliss. The water washes away the pain and worry from throughout the day. Blood clears from his skin, flowing into a drain in the tub. Before Hollyard, Oberon never would have imagined something like a shower. Thanks to Caelius, he could experience this small joy of life. If they didn't stop in Hollyard, Oberon might never have experienced a real shower.

If they didn't stop in Hollyard, he wouldn't know what getting shot by an arrow feels like. He wouldn't know what it's like to kill someone—or to watch someone die.

How different would things be if they were still on the road? He doubts much would have changed from before they arrived. Efram and Mattias would still be around. Caelius would still be hunting, and there wouldn't be the looming threat of a raid at any moment. He banishes those thoughts. Life didn't exist outside his shower.

Oberon spends the next hour cleaning and scrubbing blood off his camouflaged suit. He really should have worn something else before butchering. Maybe that's why Mattias always wore that stupid apron. Where is that anyway?

The fear in Brena's eyes stuck in his mind. They were reading a book when he came in. He completely forgot they had a bookshelf. Maybe it would have something that might help him hunt or butcher.

He goes upstairs into his room and studies the collection of books. There had to be a hundred sitting here, collecting dust. He was taught how to read when he was younger, but it was a skill he never needed.

It takes him a moment to read each title printed on the spine of each book. He has to tilt his head to understand what the letters are. His finger lightly drags across the cloth and leather books.

The title *Gardening for Non-Gardeners* sticks in his mind. He pulls it off the shelf with a finger and places it on the bed. The book next to it shows a picture of a bowl of food. *Simple Recipes, Simple Ingredients*. Perfect, he's a simple man. He adds that one to his pile, placing it on top of the first book.

The last book that catches his attention is titled *GUNS*. It has a picture of a peculiar metal object on a wooden table. Small golden pebble-like items lie scattered next to it. Whatever it is, it looks cool.

He sits on the bed and flips through the *Simple Recipes* book. Dust expels from the pages making Oberon sneeze. The text in the books is faded and hard to discern, but most of it is legible. The language used seems dated. Either that, or he needs to brush up on his reading skills.

He spends the next hour sitting on his bed, going through the contents of each book. The *Simple Recipes* book contains pictures of different foods. Many of the ingredients are things he's never heard of before. Beefy sits on the bed with him, periodically rubbing against his hands and face.

The *Gardening for Non-Gardeners* book shows him how to grow the curious items in the recipe book. Maybe he should have read this one first. Each page is dedicated to its own plant. Asparagus, broccoli, cabbage, carrots, dates, figs, garlic, onions. What did each one taste like? Each food is shown with a faded picture as well as instructions on how to grow it. The complexity overwhelms him. The book descriptions go into so much detail, going as far as explaining the optimal nitrogen content in the soil. It shouldn't matter, right? Soil is soil. Shouldn't it already have this nitrogen stuff? Where would he get this nitrogen? Could he grow it? Maybe one of these other books has information on nitrogen. There is so much he doesn't know.

GUNS contains pages and pages of information on the weapons. Each weapon looks peculiar, but the page that sticks out the most is one about a hunting rifle. Maybe it caught his eye because of the word *hunting*, or maybe because of its sleek, yet rugged design. He could imagine how much easier hunting would be if he could get his hands on one.

He has hit the jackpot of knowledge. This shelf contains everything. Maybe he could use what he learned here to help feed the Brightest. Maybe he wouldn't need to go out hunting anymore. Oberon feels giddy thinking about that idea. He could spend more time with Dolora and Brena. The plants could grow on their own, and he could relax.

The book mentions something called seeds. Apparently, he could place them in the ground and supply the area with water. In a few days, they miraculously grow. Although it didn't tell him how to find such seeds. Not unless he harvests them from the grown plant. But where would he find one? Would one be enough? Would a hundred be enough?

Some of the quickest plants take nearly a whole month to grow. Who knows if they would still be living in Hollyard by then? He must figure it out now.

Oberon searches the shelves of the bookcase. Maybe the person who previously lived here left some for him to use. After a minute of searching, he finds nothing but dust. He searches the drawers underneath, pulling them out aggressively. The drawers are filled with junk from the previous era. However, he finds something that catches his eye. A brochure. *Visit Solace! Where the sun shines brightest.* Solace? That's the city next door. He unfolds the pamphlet and something drops to the ground. A seed packet for the plant "*zucchini*" containing twenty seeds. He reaches for the gardening book, catching a glimpse of Dolora.

She watches him from the door. How long had she been standing there? Oberon can't contain his excitement. "Honey, you are not going to believe this!" He stumbles over his own words. "I found these books and they show us how to make our own food in the ground. I know it sounds crazy, but you can find these things called seeds and you put them in the ground and water them and then they grow into food that we can eat." Oberon has to take a deep breath.

Dolora remains silent, with a sad look in her eyes.

"If I could just put these seeds in the ground and grow what's called a"—he pauses to read the packet—"a zuck-c-heenie, I wouldn't need to go out hunting anymore. I can spend more time with you and Brena."

Still, her sad expression remains on her face. *What's wrong?* He didn't have to ask.

"Oberon," she says, hesitating, "I think it's time we separate."

14

The Roommate

*Rubble from civilizations long past implies that
life on Nivalis was not always like this.*
From the Journal of Azura Seren. Cayano section, 28th
orbit

I continue to seethe at mine and Oberon's argument. A whole day had passed and we didn't say a single word to eachother. I don't need him anymore. He had been holding me back.

Maybe it's a good thing we are finally taking a break. We have been spending way too much time together. This will be good for him too, allowing him to spend more time with his wife and daughter.

Some good progress has been made with Pladd, the captive. There wasn't much of note in our conversations other than small talk. But it seems like he's becoming more comfortable around me. He is still wary around other Brightest members.

At dinnertime, I collect two plates of food—venison steak. Everyone else eats where the road connects with the loop of the cul-de-sac, about a hundred feet from the tree. This meal looks a lot more edible than that last meal. I wonder who butchered the meat this time. I'm not ready to resolve my issues with Oberon yet, so I bring the plates to Pladd.

He is still chained to the tree. I let him keep his arms out, although his torso is still tied up. The plate rests softly in the grass in front of him. His eyes go wide. This might be his first real meal in a while, aside from the jerky I've been giving him.

"Thanks," he says, flatly. He doesn't reach for it, though. "Why are you still doing this?"

"Last I checked," I say, "members of the Brightest get the privilege of eating the good food." He looks down at his plate. Maybe if I start treating him like one of us, he'll open up a bit more.

I do something I don't usually do. I pray, blessing the food before we eat, thanking the Light for giving us a home, and for bringing us all together. Father Hadrian usually encourages praying over food, but few of us actually do it. When I open my eyes, his expression is confused.

"What did you do?" he asks eyes wide and mouth agape. "What happened? How did you …" He hesitates. "How did you quiet the screaming?"

The screaming? I can't tell if he is angry with me or not. "What do you mean?" I ask. In one of Hadrian's teachings, he taught of people who were possessed. People who would hear voices in their head and act unnatural. Was this a similar case?

"Like, I feel …" He stops, trying to find the right words. "He's stopped!" He laughs maniacally. "He's stopped screaming. He's just talking now." He laughs again and I scoot back. A few heads have turned to look at us.

He grabs the steak with his hands and tears it apart with his sharpened teeth. This man, Pladd, is a dangerous individual and I need to keep that in mind.

I have to cut my steak into pieces to eat it. "What do you mean the screaming stopped?" I ask. "Are you possessed or something?"

There's a bit more life in his eyes when he speaks. "Possessed? Someone's been talking to me for a while, and they wouldn't stop until now. Now it's just arguing."

"Arguing?"

"Yeah, there are two voices now. But it's fine." He takes another bite. "Why is this so tough?"

It takes a moment for me to realize he means the venison. I don't answer. To me, it tastes fine. But what did he mean there are two voices now? It seems like I didn't clear his mind of the voice, just redirected its attention— potentially to a second voice. I change the subject before I can cause more harm.

"What was life like for you before?"

He swallows. After a couple seconds of contemplating, he finally speaks. "Hard," he says. "My old group, rough around the edges. We hunt our own food. Waited for people to travel through towns and we attacked them. Most victims aren't ready to fight."

"Have you always been with them?" I ask.

"No," Pladd says.

"I see. I've been with the Brightest for as long as I can remember," I say. "I think I was six. My parents joined the Brightest for some reason and left me with Hadrian."

Pladd looks as if he's contemplating his next words. There's a delay and a grin on his face.

"What?" I demand.

"The death of the parents," he starts with a chuckle. "A story as old as time." He sets the meat in the grass and looks at his palms. "When we would raid caravans, we'd kill the children, too. That way, they wouldn't have to live in this world without their parents. If they showed promise, maybe we'd recruit them."

I have no words. He says these things with such casualness. Pladd continues. "We consider it a mercy. It's too bad you grew up without your parents. I think you'd have fit right in with our little group of *Crits*." He stuffs the last bit of steak into his mouth with that last word.

You mean it's too bad that the person who killed my mom and dad didn't have the mercy to kill me too. What did he mean that I'd fit right in with his group? I'm not like him. Not at all.

"It was good talking with you, Pladd," I say, standing up. "It's time for me to go."

I tie Pladd's arms and leave him there, still bound to the tree. We are making progress, but I still can't trust him.

I push open the front door to my house and Oberon is lying on my messed-up couch, a book in his hands. Is he *reading*? He looks like he went through hell and back. I don't feel any remorse for him. I am still furious.

"Hey, buddy," he says, putting the book down. "Hope you don't mind that I stopped over for a bit."

"What are you doing here?" I demand.

"Oh, you know, I figured we could have a little sleepover or something."

"No. Get out." I point at the door I just entered through, feeling my cheeks heat up.

"Ah, don't worry about it." He waves. "I could just sleep in your other room. You won't even know I'm here."

My parents' room is vacant, but I don't want anyone in there, especially him. "Oberon, please can you just—"

"Dolora doesn't want to be with me anymore," he interrupts me. "I have nowhere to stay." That comes as a surprise to me. I thought that their relationship was perfect. I was jealous they had something that I didn't, but maybe it was all a facade.

"Is there really nowhere else?" I ask, flustered. "I'm still pissed off about what you said." This is such bad timing.

"Yeah, you're right." Oberon picks himself off the couch and heads past me toward the front door. "I'm sorry. Any ideas where I could go?"

"Pladd could use some company. Maybe you guys might hit it off."

He chuckles without emotion. "Yeah, s'pose I could." He steps through the door and looks back at me with puppy dog eyes.

I slam the door on him. The lock clicks when I turn the bolt. No way will I let him manipulate me.

"I hope Brena doesn't think less of me." His voice is muffled through the door. Sighing I unlock and open the door. He stands there like an idiot.

I roll my eyes. "What happened?"

Without delay he goes into an explanation.

"I showed Dolora some books about gardening, and she said she wanted to split up," he says. He doesn't look too upset about it. "She said that I'm not there anymore to spend time with the two of them. That she is raising Brena all by herself. And it's unfair because I'm gone all the time." He stops, waiting for a reaction from me. When I don't give him one, he continues, "I didn't even know that she felt like this, and she just dropped it on me all at once. How am I supposed to spend time with her and Brena if she's kicking me out of the house?"

I don't have the answers for him. I wish I did. He pissed me off yesterday, but he doesn't deserve this. I close the door again, purposely leaving it unlatched.

I go to my bedroom to get ready for bed.

As expected, I hear Oberon enter my house and go into my parents' room. I'm not upset. I practically invited him in when I left the front door unlocked. He has a hard time maintaining personal space, but it's a trait I couldn't hate him for.

I just hope it's not a permanent change.

15

The Ultimatum

Seems like the elements don't last when you freeze and thaw them over and over for nearly 560 passings.
From the Journal of Azura Seren. Cayano section, 28th orbit

The paper-thin walls hardly blocked Oberon's snoring. No wonder Dolora couldn't handle him at times. Everything he does is imposing. He makes his presence known everywhere he is. Snoring hadn't bothered me previously, especially since we all used to sleep together on the ground. After sleeping in silence for a couple of weeks, the snoring is much more irritating. That didn't stop me from getting a good night's sleep.

Instead of waking up Oberon, I decide to let him sleep more. I'm still not over our argument. I follow my usual morning routine, before venturing outside, walking toward the tree. I have many more questions for Pladd.

I don't even grab my jacket this time; the warm air feels like a gentle kiss. I enjoy the moment. The longer we stay here, the warmer it will become.

Pladd is still sitting against the willow tree, asleep. I notice something when I examine him further. His hair isn't brown like I thought it was. It's white, maybe gray. He'd covered it in dirt and mud to make it appear brown. When was the last time he cleaned himself?

I kick his foot, and he snorts, waking up. "What?" he asks, rudely. Maybe I woke him up during a dream. I bend down and untie his arms. He wipes away the crust in his eyes with the back of his wrist.

"What were you dreaming about?" I ask. "Murdering babies?"

"No, just you," he says, looking up at me. "I was having such a good time until I saw it wasn't a dream."

"Must be hard," I mock.

"If you think sparing children from Nivalis is bad, wait till you see what other camps do. There's always something worse than death." I'm not sure if I agree with him. What could be worse than murder?

"What do you believe in?" I ask, squatting down to meet him at eye level.

"Myself."

"I mean, what are your values? What drives you to act?"

"Same as you. Survival. Food."

"But you kill and eat other people."

"That's right?"

"Why?"

"It's easy. Deer and cattle are a rare find these days; people aren't. Most people don't know how to fight back.

I see your buddy going out there and hunting every day. He wouldn't have to if you guys followed our lifestyle."

I can't justify it in my mind. In no world, can I see eating other people and killing children as the only way for them to survive. I know firsthand how difficult deer hunting is, but his morality of it seems so twisted. They don't kill people for fun. They kill for survival—at least that's what Pladd tells me.

"What's your role then? With your old group?" I ask, finding myself pacing as I talk to him.

"I am … was … a scholar."

"A scholar? A cannibalistic creature with sharpened teeth as a scholar?"

He sighs with a grin. "Yes. They really do go hand in hand."

"How are you a scholar? What is there to learn?" I ask, genuinely curious.

Pladd looks at me for a moment before speaking. "We eat brains to gain their knowledge."

"What? Really?" I ask, incredulous. It's an answer I wasn't expecting.

Pladd scoffs, grinning, "No. Of course not. We don't eat brain. Messes you up," he says like I should already know that. "There are many travelers in this Solaris Sanctum. More than you might think. I collect their cultures and their stories."

"Collect their cultures?" I ask.

Instead of being upset by my questions, he seems enthusiastic, excited to talk about himself. "I listen. Before we attack, I interject myself into people's camps and document the people and how they interact.

"The Brightest is no different than any other religious camp. So many follow the Light, without knowing who, or what the Light even is. The Brightest is set apart from the rest because of two people—you, and that pompous ass."

Pompous ass? Hadrian? Who else? "So, you are here with the specific intent to be captured? So, you could *learn* about us?"

"Yes."

It doesn't sit right with me. Why care? What's the point of collecting information and learning about different cultural groups if they're going to die? "What makes Hadrian and me different from the rest?" I ask.

"You, friend, don't belong here. You are not like the rest. Of all the members, you're the only one who dared to talk to me."

"Yeah, that's 'cause Hadrian asked me to," I say cautiously.

"No. I don't believe that's true. You are curious. You want to know more. You and I are driven by knowledge."

He's right. I couldn't bring myself to kill him, so I opted to "convert him." I don't think I'm doing a great job though. I ask another question: "Why Hadrian? What sets him apart?"

"Hadrian follows a true Light," he says intensely. "The other groups follow a fragment, a memory of a Light. It was confirmed when you suppressed the screaming in my head."

"Why are you telling me this?" I ask, remembering I'm talking to a savage cannibal. Though is he actually savage?

"I told you. I'm collecting knowledge."

"But you're giving the knowledge away. I'm hardly telling you anything."

He chuckles, smiling. "You tell me more in the words you don't say."

That unnerves me. What have I told him? Did I accidentally say something I shouldn't have? I have an urge to leave. I should tell Hadrian to kill him for me. What if he can read my mind somehow?

"Caelius?" I turn to look at him; my right hand grips my left rubbing the area where I'd lost my other fingers. "Thank you for talking with me."

Pladd extends a hand above his head, feeling the tree. The bark splits, warping around his fingers. The wood squirms and undulates like living worms. The bark stops moving, leaving an opening that contains a small rock. "Whoa!" I exclaim, stepping back. My eyes hardly believe what I'm seeing.

His arm flexes, gripping the small porous rock and pulling it out. When the stone is removed, the tree squirms and shapes itself back, covering the opening.

"Have this, please," he says, holding it outward. I grab it hesitantly with my right hand and hold it in my palm. It's a light gray-green stone the size of my thumb. I could crush it into powder if I wanted to.

"What," I say, hesitant, "is it?"

"It's a token. A sign of our bond." He sits back while I observe the rock. "Sit at this tree for a couple hours and you'll find some crazy stuff. As I said, you're the only one who talks to me. I want you to know that I appreciate it."

The porous stone leaves behind dust on my fingers. It's very light, like chalk, but shimmers slightly green in the sunlight. It is unlike anything I've seen before.

I thought this man was a hard, unchanging monster with no regard for others but himself. But now I see the truth, or perhaps a fragment of the truth. I understand his pain, his struggle, his desire to find knowledge, to learn, to be recognized. He's lonely. Even when he finds something he could keep for himself, he gives it to someone else.

"I—I don't know what to say," I stammer. I still observe the rock in my hand. Brena loves rocks. Maybe she'd take care of it. I shoot that idea down as soon as it enters my head. This is a physical memorial of our friendship.

"You could say thank you," he says, twirling his wrist.

"Thanks, Pladd," I say genuinely.

"Eh, it's just a stupid rock. Not sure why it would be hidden inside the tree." I think I may have a tiny jar I could keep this rock in. I'd hate for it to get destroyed in my pocket.

I leave him, heading back to my house without tying up his arms.

After securing the stone in a jar, I stuff it back into my pocket. Hadrian knocks on my door. He stands at the doorway, eagerness in his face. His robes are clean and light shines off his white hair. "Come on, let's go practice." There's a bounce in his step. I already have my sword, but Oberon is probably still sleeping.

"Let me go wake up Oberon," I say, thumbing over my shoulder.

Hadrian stops me, holding an arm up. "No. That won't be necessary. Just you and me this morning." I shrug, not complaining. I follow him to our usual practice area. We haven't trained since Oberon's outburst, although I feel guilty training without him.

We walk for a couple minutes, heading down a side street to our usual area. I keep my rapier equipped and as soon as we arrive, he turns and catches the guard of my sword with the tip of the blade. The weapon is thrust out of my hands, launched five feet into the air. Hadrian grins.

"Oh, so we are starting now. Is this a lesson on grip?"

"Speak when you are spoken to," Hadrian says, hitting me in the arm with the flat part of his blade. I wince and retrieve my rapier from the ground.

Mimicking his stance, I hold my blade at the same angle. Our eyes lock and I swear I see something behind his own. Is this the true Light Pladd spoke of?

The rapier is launched from my hand once again. It soars through the air, before landing like a crossbow bolt in a patch of grass nearby. He was so fast, I didn't even see him do that.

Hours pass. He shows me a few moves with the rapier. Many times, did he launch the weapon from my hands, teaching me to be more conscious of my grip.

Retrieving my sword for the dozenth time, Hadrian speaks. "Your friend, Oberon, seems to not follow the Light like we do," he accuses. "If he continues refusing to follow the Light, I don't think I can envision a future of the Brightest with him in it."

My head feels heavy on my shoulders. "What?" I manage to say. Oberon being exiled? Who would I talk to and banter with? He has his problems, but he is an essential piece in the Brightest.

"I hesitate because he's our only hunter." He lowers his rapier. "Ever since you lost part of your hand, he's out there alone."

"What are you saying?" I ask.

"Return him to the Light. Devoted to me and my teachings." The world darkens around him, seeping outward. It constricts around me, crushing my lungs. His voice is amplified, all-encompassing. "He has lost his way, searching for answers in himself, the hunt, and his family. He needs to put his full trust in *me*."

He's asking me to do the impossible. My heart shrivels in my chest, and I am unable to make eye contact with the man. Is he a man? Or something more? I'm scared. So very scared.

"Father … I," I stammer. "I don't think I can … I don't know how." My legs tremble, and the darkness multiplies. "I'm already trying to help bring Pladd to follow the Light. I think I've made progress, but Oberon is different."

I remember what Oberon had said about Hadrian a couple of days ago. That there is something strange about him. But this is more than strange. This is terrifying. Reflexively, I reach out to the light, praying for protection. I feel nothing.

"That won't work," Hadrian shouts. "The Light speaks to me, and me only." I open my eyes, unaware that I had shut them. I see only darkness—that infinite dark void. In front of me is Hadrian, tall, looming. My sight has been stripped from me. Could Hadrian have severed my bond to the Light? Is that why I can't see? Why can I only see *him*?

I try not to hyperventilate, but I lose control. My heart beats rapidly. Each breath feels short, not enough. Some of my vision returns, but it's distorted, a dream, maybe a hallucination. Where am I? Houses stare at me, trees mock me, the ground trembles in laughter at my misfortune. I see Hadrian. Not as the man who raised me, but as a deity to be worshipped. The line between the Light and the priest of the Light blurs. Who am I supposed to worship more?

The darkness recedes completely, and I gasp. The world returns to full color. What was that? Hadrian turns around, his back toward me.

"Caelius," he starts. "I'm going to die someday. I fear it will be sooner rather than later," he continues. "I need a successor."

A successor? My mind tries to process what has just happened.

"I've been observing you, your drive, your passion. It comes from me." He turns to meet my eyes. "When it is my time, I need you to lead the Brightest."

My heart sinks, the weight of his words drilling into me. I thought he would live forever, always the leader of the Brightest. The pieces come together. This was why he gave me the rapier, why he wanted me to convert or kill Pladd. Why he wants me to *fix* Oberon. He needs to know I am the right one for the job.

I couldn't become like him. If taking his place means I scare people into doing what I want them to do, I don't want it. While it's mostly out of respect, people are *scared* of Hadrian. I don't want those people to see me the same way.

I could reject his wishes. I could reject the rapier, kill Pladd, and protect Oberon. But it wouldn't matter. Hadrian's already decided. I feel like a piece on a board game, not in control of my own fate.

"No," I say pointedly.

The darkness quickly returns, snapping into place. Everything within me wants to coil up again. But I keep my stance straight. "What was that, boy?" he growls. "I didn't ask. You will lead the Brightest when I'm gone, whether you like it or not."

"No," I quiver but keep my composure. "Pick someone else."

"Give me a name," he demands snarling.

"Reyus," I say.

"Reyus is a *coward*," he spits, venom in his tone.

"Reyus—"

He cuts me off, seemingly growing in size. "Don't you want power? Respect? Think of the greatness you can accomplish. You can destroy *BUILDINGS* with only your hands. You will be the most powerful person on the planet!"

Hadrian extends his hand, touching a tree next to him. The tree sheds its leaves, which wither and fall to the ground, leaving behind a skeleton of branches. A frost pattern disperses from where Hadrian's hand lies. A moment later, the branches snap and crack before crashing to the ground.

Hadrian's voice booms loudly. "YOU WILL SUCCEED ME, YOU WILL NOT RUN FROM IT, YOU WILL NOT HIDE FROM IT." The concrete underneath splits. Windows nearby explode.

I feel the vibration deep within. Ringing. I can't hear anything else. I put my hands up to my bleeding ears. What did he do? I scream, but I can't hear it.

Somehow, Hadrian's voice pierces the fog. "Accept it and it will be yours."

Tears roll down my face. For the first time ever, I feel true fear. His voice pierces the ringing. "You have three days to convert the captive and Oberon."

"Fine," I shout.

"Very well. You may go," he says.

Just like that? He asks me to leave? What about my ears? What about our sparring? I leave him to seek medical attention.

I might be deaf. The realization of it sends me into a panic. First my fingers, now my hearing. *It's just temporary,* I tell myself. I stumble my way to the medical tent, hands on both my ears.

"Oh Light, are you okay?" I read Doc Stella's lips, but I don't respond. She grabs me by the arm and leads me to a cot.

She tries speaking to me, asking questions, I assume. I can't make out her words. Is she even able to fix my hearing?

First, she wipes away the blood from my ears. Then examines the internals with her tools.

As they examine me, I reflect on what happened. What the hell was that? I had never seen Hadrian be so imposing. The image of him, dark, tall, brooding, burns into my memory. I didn't fear this man before, but now I do.

And he wants me to take his place. After seeing that, I could never choose that life. I couldn't be trusted with that much responsibility. Did he freeze a tree right in front of me? It all happened so fast, I hardly had time to process it.

Could he always do that? Freeze things? Could he freeze other people?

It's unnatural, impossible even. I refuse to believe such a thing even happened. But I can't pretend I didn't see it. Did the Light grant him that power? Or was it from something else?

I've known that Hadrian is able to do things that other people can't, specifically healing—but only in special cases.

Maybe the town could have granted him these abilities. That's why he wants to stay here instead of continuing our travels.

"Seems like you'll be better in no time," I hear faintly. My hearing is coming back. Oh, thank the Light. The nurse must have noticed my reaction. "Oh see, it's coming back already." My ears still ring and her words are difficult to discern. She gets closer, shouting into my ear, "I recommend some rest and you'll be better in a few days."

I give her a thumbs-up and she dismisses me from the tent. My eyes immediately look toward Hadrian's wagon. I half expect him to be standing outside. He isn't. I don't think I could look at him the same way again.

I wanted to talk to Pladd more, but that's not going to happen. As the nurse recommended, I need to take it slow. The moon is planted in the center of the sky. Midday.

Entering my home, I find Oberon lounging on the couch. There's no way that's comfortable. He says something and smiles, but I can't hear him.

I don't want to talk or listen to him. And for the first time, I have an excuse. I just smile and nod pretending I understand.

He rolls his head, and I can faintly hear him groan before he points at the counter behind me. There's a book, *Gardening for Non-Gardeners*. I pick it up and flip through the pages. There are faded pictures of oddly shaped colorful objects.

He tries to tell me something more, but I still cannot make out a single word. After a moment, I give up and ignore him. I hand him the book, before heading into my room.

The room is tranquil. Silent. There is no rushing wind outside the house. There are no trees rustling. There's not a man snoring in the other room. It's peaceful. Finally. The bed engulfs me, and I drift off into a nap.

Before I even start dreaming, I feel arms grasp my shoulders.

"Caelius, wake up!" Oberon is sweating and a stream of blood dribbles down his temple. Adrenaline floods my body, waking me up instantly.

"What's going on?" I ask, frantic. Launching myself out of my bed, I snatch the rapier hanging from my wall.

"Raiders," he says taking a deep breath. "I thought you heard the horn."

16

The Piranhas

*I have a hard time believing these perfect
conditions are just coincidences.*
From the Journal of Azura Seren. Hylano section, 28th
orbit

We rush out of the house into the chaos. Flames engulf a house across the street, threatening to spread to the houses nearby.

A Brightest member holds her hands up to protect herself against a hunched raider who approaches slowly. I dash forward, but it's too late. The attacker lunges at her throat, dropping his bone knife. Clattering of the weapon is paired with the squelching of her neck being torn apart. Blood sprays into the air, painting the raider's face red. He laps it up like a dog.

Holding the rapier how Hadrian taught me, I awkwardly skewer the raider in the side. He howls but doesn't drop. I try pulling the sword out, but I'm positioned too close. My arm can't retract any further. He turns, his body ripping the sword out of my hand.

The figure's eyes are the only white in a sea of red. Something draws me to the sight of the woman on the ground thrashing, clutching at her throat, attempting to keep the blood inside.

The distraction would have killed me had Oberon not been there. The raider falls to his knees and then to the side, a crossbow bolt now protruding from his eye socket.

"What the hell are you doing?" Oberon demands.

I shake myself out of it, stealing one more glance at the dying woman. I know I should feel disgusted watching one of my own members struggle to hold on to dear life. Instead, it thrills me—arouses me. She gargles an impression of the word "Help."

"I'm sorry," I say solemnly. I don't even know her name. She is one of Dolora's friends. Should I finish her off? Could I bring myself to kill again? It would be a mercy. What if she pushed for Dolora to break it off with Oberon?

The little quarrel Oberon and I had feels so long ago. Despite our issues, Oberon is my friend and will always be my friend.

I leave her there to die, choking on her own blood. The roaring of the flames drowns out her gargled pleas.

Raiders flood in from alleyways and streets. They outnumber our own skilled fighters. I follow Oberon closer to the cul-de-sac. We hide behind a bush, analyzing the scene. My heartbeat pounds in my ears and fear grips my chest when I realize we may not survive this. Ropes lie where Pladd once sat. Someone freed him.

A man, a member of the Brightest, runs down the street before getting shot in the back with an arrow. He drops face-first onto the concrete. A raider runs up to him and splits his skull with a hatchet. The sound reminds me of stepping on a pine cone.

The raider jams his hand into the victim's skull and pulls out a chunk of brain matter. Thick blood dribbles through his fingers. Four more raiders surround him as they each ravenously devour the brain in his hand. I thought Pladd said they didn't eat brain, that it messes people up. Why would he lie about that?

When they are finished, one raider, a female, steps on the shoulder of the face-down corpse and pulls the arm upward, dislocating it from the socket with a sickening *pop*. Another swift pull, and the arm tears free from the torso. Tendons and muscles split as the arm is removed. Again, they ravenously dig into the meaty arm, tearing the flesh with their sharpened teeth. The woman howls in pain as the others bite into her arm as well.

We watch in horror as they pick apart the once-living human like piranhas. In a minute, the body is an unrecognizable mass of blood, flesh, and bone.

Oberon vomits onto the shrubbery. I almost join him, but I hold my stomach. Should we just run? Leave everyone else here to die? We aren't equipped to handle an attack on this scale. Where the hell is Hadrian?

I understand now why we've never halted our travels. Walking at the front of the Bright Spot was the safest option. There are only a handful of us who even know how to defend ourselves. It seems like a massive oversight to leave most of our party untrained in battle. But why would they train? Attacks like this never happen at the front.

Hell, even basic training would be sufficient. If everyone knew the basics of how to use a knife, a crossbow, or even hand-to-hand combat, the Brightest would be much more prepared for situations like this. If I were leader …

The tall brown buildings of Solace watch us from a distance. Could I gather a few members and migrate into the city? Would that even work? I have a feeling we'd be caught and murdered before we could even leave town. I squeeze my eyes shut, trying to recall any information about Hollyard. Maybe we won't be able to migrate to Solace, but what if there's another safe place nearby?

I open my eyes and watch as another group of three raiders barge into a house. Followed by maniacal laughing and a baby crying. Moments later, there's a blood-curdling scream. I want to help, but my legs don't move. I'd be outnumbered. Even if Oberon came with.

The crying and screams are muted, and the laughter continues. Hiding in a house is a sure way to be found and killed. Unless the houses had hidden basements or some other safe area, it would be too risky.

There is one place that may be safe. It's the one place Hadrian warned everyone *not* to visit. But this could be a matter of life and death, regardless of what Hadrian wants.

"Oberon," I call. "Go down the road, away from the tree and gather as many people as you can. Bring them downtown to the Church of the Light."

Still recovering from throwing up, Oberon hesitates for a moment. "Church of the Light?" he says. "But Hadrian—"

"It doesn't matter what Hadrian says," I interrupt, "just go." He nods affirmatively and jogs away, searching out the others. If the light truly is watching, the church would protect us.

I realign myself and take note of the situation. Those four raiders likely murdered the woman and child inside that house. If they are cannibalistic, it could be a while before they are finished. The thought of someone I know and their child being ripped apart by these monsters cements itself in my mind. I shove the feeling aside—for now.

The sword on my hip rattles as I jog toward the action. Wearing the sword alone makes me more of a threat, but does it make me more of a target? Perhaps some might try to group up on me if they're sure they can win.

In the distance, Hadrian presses his hands against a Brightest member on the ground. Other members run aimlessly in whichever direction they can. One runner bumps right into a cannibal. I recoil, knowing what will happen next.

The cannibal grabs hold of the man and bites at his face like a feral dog. They both fall to the ground. I'm too far to see any details, but the savage's sharklike teeth rip the runner's face to shreds. I know the victim is screaming, but I can't hear it over the noise of the chaos.

There's nothing I could have done. Only what I can do from here. I run toward the creature, no different from the animals I kill in the wild, unsheathing my sword. I kick him hard off the man, almost losing my own balance in the process. He tumbles to the side but stabilizes himself on all fours.

Some cannibals are recognized by their body shape. Instead of clumsily tumbling over, his stout legs complement his stance. As if his body was *made* for running on four legs instead of two. He sprints at me the way a dog chases a rabbit.

He leaps; his exceptionally strong legs launch him at incredible speed. Hadrian's training kicks in and I set my feet, bracing for impact. He still causes me to fall backward, pinning my forearms against the rough concrete.

I smell his breath—the iron in the blood of the victim before me. I see death in his bloodshot eyes. I'm not ready to die.

"You interrupted my dinner," the raider hisses. His filed teeth make him speak like Pladd, but more gruff. "You know what happens when I don't get my meal?" He licks my face, tongue gliding across my cheek and eyelids. I squirm, but all I can move are my legs. "Pladd told me about—"

He's cut off when I ram my knee into his groin. He doesn't recoil, but his grip loosens enough for me to push him off.

We both scramble to stand up. I snatch my sword from the ground, readying it for the attack. The man just studies me, watching and preparing for what I may do next. His mouth splits into an unnatural grin, wider than normal, showing many more teeth. Despite his body modifications, this feature is the most unsettling.

He readies his attack, but before he leaps, tips of large fingers appear on the sides and top of his head. As if someone was grabbing him by the back of the skull. The raider freezes, eyes going wide. His feet lift from the ground as his whole body floats in the air.

In an instant, his body seems to fuzz visually before dissipating into sand. Clothes drop to the ground and the owner of the hand behind the once-raider is a familiar face—Hadrian.

17

The Dust

*Is it a coincidence that a full orbit is almost
exactly twenty passings? Is it a coincidence that
animals can somehow survive the cold passings,
but we cannot?*

From the Journal of Azura Seren. Hylano section, 28th
orbit

I refuse to process what I just saw. The cannibal was there and now … isn't. The cannibal's victim gurgles on the ground before me, clutching at his unrecognizable face. His skin had been torn completely off. He convulses, eye sockets filled with blood.

I kneel in front of the dying man, trying to figure out how I could save him.

I look toward Hadrian, frantic. Hadrian's face is a stone mask. He looks at me as if I shouldn't have seen what I saw. "Heal him!" I demand.

He stays silent. I check my surroundings, wary of getting attacked. We are alone, for now.

After a moment, Hadrian bends down and rests a hand on the dying man's bloody face. He closes his eyes and takes a deep breath, preparing to heal the man.

There's a faint buzzing noise, a hum, coming from the dying member. And then, like his attacker, he dissolves into dust. Sand from where his face had once been falls to the ground.

What? I sift my hands through the sand, searching for something, anything. Hadrian *killed* him. Perhaps I could have saved his life. But I'd been stripped of that opportunity. I try to scream but what escapes is just hissing air. I turn from the pile and look into the eyes of my enemy.

Not the raiders who attacked us. Not the deadly cold. Him. My *true* enemy.

His white and gold-trimmed robes are still in pristine condition. Not a speck of blood or dirt on them. His graying beard is in a neat arrangement, unlike Oberon's. I examine his statuesque face, hard like stone. His pitiless eyes connect with mine—dark blue, the color of the deepest and most dangerous parts of the ocean.

"You *bastard!*" I yell in frustration, hands pressing against my temples. "Why the hell did you do that? I could have helped him!" My hands tremble as I lower them. "How can I be a leader if you won't let me save someone's life?"

"A good leader," Hadrian says coldly, "understands when to save one person, and when to save dozens. A good leader can recognize when a decision is too risky for their followers." His words cut deep, like spilling the blood of wild game.

Hadrian's right.

It's time for me to step up as a leader and make a decision. Not for myself, but for the Brightest. Terrible leadership will lead them toward more death and destruction. We've lost so many already. Their blood is on Hadrian's hands. This should be addressed after the raid, not during. I don't care. This needs to be taken care of. Like an infected limb, it must be amputated before it can cause more harm.

My right hand unsheathes my rapier. It cuts through the air as I make an attack toward Hadrian, the leader of the Brightest, chosen by the Light. I catch him off guard and the sword splits his robe at the chest, exposing bare skin. A bright red mark appears where my sword grazed him.

I follow the attack by flicking the sword up toward his face, but he is ready this time. He steps back, revealing his own rapier. I'd missed. Before I know it, my sword is soaring in the air above me. He'd disarmed me once again, just like he had during training. He holds his rapier right at my neck, inches away.

"I hadn't expected you'd want to train right here, right now," he says. It had taken a moment, but a line of red appears on his left cheek, followed by dripping blood. I did strike him, just barely. I try to hide the grin on my face. "In many cases, a situation like this would be perfect for training. More often than not you're fighting in a chaotic setting like this one. In this case, you must keep your composure." The flat side of his rapier presses under my chin. He could kill me right here.

Hadrian lowers his sword. "I know about your plan with the church. Go collect who you can and take them there. I'll be there shortly after," he says, heading toward more screaming. I grunt, collecting my sword from the ground and follow.

The road around the tree is littered with bodies. Only a couple of raiders lay with dead Brightest members. I recognize each face.

I can't get distracted. Hadrian runs into a house, searching for other members. He completely misses a woman and her daughter running, a raider chasing right behind them. He runs on all fours, salivating at the mouth, barking. The woman clutches her daughter's arm, practically lifting the child off her feet.

Wait, is that Dolora and Brena? My legs move by instinct. The flats of my shoes slap against the concrete as I sprint, sword in hand. The scent of burning wood and blood invades my senses.

I'm not there quick enough before the raider leaps forward, catching Dolora's blouse on a … claw? The blue cloth stretches and the woman falls face-first into the concrete. Brena falls and rolls onto her back.

Like a spider, the raider crawls over Dolora, ignoring her, and focuses on the child. Brena screams, shuffling backward with her arms and feet. The raider maintains his relative position above her.

My legs burn. I'm close. Close enough to hear him speak. His voice is wispy and snakelike. "Oh, if only you knew how good you taste when you're terrified." His pale hands lift from the ground and he grabs the terrified girl by the shoulders.

I only have one chance. Sprinting, I raise my sword and lunge at the creature. My rapier darts through the air before finding a home in the soft flesh of the cannibal's nape. I can only imagine the tip punctured through to the other side. The creature freezes, and Dolora screams from the ground next to me.

I pull the steel from the cannibal's neck and kick him over. I see his face. Pale, malformed, terrified. These aren't humans. Not any longer. I have no problem killing them.

Brena's face is covered in shock, mouth agape. She must have had the wind knocked out of her. The child struggles to breathe and a lot of the attacker's blood covers her midsection.

"It's okay," I reassure. "You're safe now." I kneel to try and help her regain her composure, and that's when I see the blood spreading. It soaks up more of her clothing as she coughs.

Realization hits me like a crossbow bolt. When I'd stabbed through the raider, my blade found Brena lying underneath him. Her coughs rattle. I'd shot a deer in the lung and it made a sound no different than this.

"What the hell did you do?" Dolora screams. "You killed my baby girl!" I can't move or respond. The world around me spins. A clang sound emits from under me. What was that? I'm unable to look; did I drop my sword?

Dolora crawls over and cradles her child, who is gasping for breath and coughing with each breath. She puts her hand over Brena's wound, but it's no use. Dolora comforts her child. "Everything is going to be okay," she says softly.

Dolora sings a lullaby, though I can't make out the words. Tears roll down Dolora's face and she chokes on her song. Brena's eyes slowly close and her body goes limp. Small fingers drop a tiny pink rock onto the concrete.

My lips quiver. It's the first bit of movement my body permits me. "Dolora … I …," I croak.

Footsteps behind me—then darkness.

18

The Church

*Is it a coincidence that the two continents nearly
connect not once, but twice, allowing us to travel
without ever needing a ferry?*
From the Journal of Azura Seren. Hylano section, 28th
orbit

My eyes dart open. My head throbs and the world spins around me. I'm looking toward the ceiling at a grand display of artwork—a painting of a hundred distinct colors. A single bald man with his hands cupped together. In his hands is a star, or a ball of light. The painting is intricate and detailed, displaying a gorgeous landscape of rolling hills behind the bearded, bald man. He wears white robes and his face displays a mixture of both joy and fear. As if the Light held in his hands was powerful and benevolent, while also being dangerous and feared.

My head pulses again in pain. What am I lying on? My right shoulder peels from a slab of polished wood. I force myself to sit up, hearing chattering and hushed conversations taking place. I'm inside a church, sitting on a pew.

There are two columns of pews in the large room. Each column contains twenty to thirty rows. Between the columns is a wide walkway connecting the front doors of the church to the altar at the front. Above and behind the altar is a symbol, not unlike the one Hadrian wears on his breast—a golden sun insignia. This isn't a church of a lost religion. It's a Church of the Light. Why didn't Hadrian want anyone coming here again? Because it taught something different than his own teachings?

I'm more skeptical toward him than ever. I watched him freeze a tree and then turn two men to dust. What else could he be hiding from us?

Seven men, including Oberon, stand at the front of the sanctuary, near the altar. Does he know I killed his daughter? Our eyes lock, and he heads in my direction, expression unreadable.

I need to run. I'm not going to fight Oberon. I shuffle quickly in the other direction, trying to escape the pew. These things are not made for getting in and out of quickly.

"Caelius," Oberon calls, heading down the row of pews I'm trying to escape from. Instead of trying to shuffle out, I step on and over the wooden bench onto the next pew behind it. "Caelius," he calls again.

Still, I try to escape him, leaping over multiple pews, running down toward the walkway so I can make a break for it. I dash toward the large double wooden doors. This place is giving me the creeps. My working hand grips the door handle.

"They're still out there!" Oberon shouts. I freeze in place. "Maybe you hit yer head too hard to remember, but raiders are still out there. They don't know we're here. So sit yer arse back down before you tell them all where we are." I turn and meet his eyes. His lips quiver and his brows are fearful. The six behind him share his concerned look.

How did I get here? I can't recall making it to the church. Everything after Brena has been a blur. He mentioned I hit my head?

"Where's Hadrian?" I demand.

"Hadrian is out looking for others. He knows we're here," Oberon says.

My shoulders relax a bit. Hate still bubbles inside at the mention of his name, but it's quickly replaced with the comfort of knowing he's to return.

I close my eyes and take a deep breath. I need to tell him the truth. Otherwise, it will cause more issues between us. Better to rip the bandage off quickly.

"Oberon …," I say, meeting his eyes. "I—"

"I know," he interrupts, pain flashing across his face. "We can talk about it later—when we're safe."

"Safe? Aren't we safe now?" I examine the seven men. Seven. That's all we managed to save? "Where's Dolora? Lyria?"

"I need to show you something," he says, turning. I follow him toward the sanctuary, which is raised up by a couple of steps. Oberon stops and shoves the altar to the side before stomping twice. After a second, he stomps three more times. A hidden trapdoor swings outward. Donovan—the Brightest's carpenter—pokes his head out. "Come," Oberon presses, taking the ladder down *underneath* the church sanctuary. The other six do not follow.

On the underside of the trapdoor is a woven handle. I grab it with my good hand as I descend, closing it behind me. Shortly after, I hear the altar being shoved back on top.

"Two knocks and then three to come down. Three knocks and then two to go back up," Oberon says.

The smell of dirt, sweat, blood, and fecal matter floods my senses. The walls of the underground room are of dirt and stone. It's well lit by candles, illuminating the scared faces of about twenty-five people, some with children. There are a few resting on cots, being tended to by Doc Stella. Where is Lyria?

One of the cots carries an unconscious Brena. My heart skips a beat and I feel dizzy. Her mother stands close and Stella applies bandages over her midsection. She's still alive. I shakily exhale my worry away, unable to hide my smile of relief.

"Oberon," I say.

"She'll be alright. She's the strongest girl I know. She's already a lot better than yesterday. For now, we are just gonna hafta wait it out." He takes a breath. "I know you didn't mean to hurt her. That's why I'm not mad. Dolora on the other hand—"

Yesterday? Had I been out for that long? I tend to spend most of the raids unconscious. "Do those cannibal freaks even sleep?" I ask, making sure Pladd isn't nearby. He's probably out there, killing with his own kind.

What did he say the other day? *"Before we attack, I interject myself into people's camps."*

He said it clear as day, and I dismissed it as a passive remark. I could have warned someone. This raid might be partly my fault.

Oberon collects some cooked meat from a makeshift table and hands it to me to eat. Even after I nearly killed his daughter, he still treats me like a friend. There isn't a single other person on Nivalis with a heart like Oberon's.

"I don't know," he says. "The plan is to stay down here for a couple days. Once it's safe, we're getting out of Hollyard."

I accept the food and sit on a dirt extrusion. Oberon checks on his daughter. I nibble on the deer meat, trying to ration as much as I can. I'm not sure how much we have stored, or how long we are really going to be here. The basement is fairly large, about the same size as the church above. My clothes are going to be terribly dirty after this, but being alive is the most I could have asked for.

Two knocks erupt from above, startling me. Donovan climbs the ladder to the hatch. Three more knocks and he pushes the trapdoor open. Light from above floods in.

Hadrian and other people crawl down the ladder. The first one to descend is Lyria. Relief strikes me, relaxing my shoulders. I didn't realize how worried I was about her. Three men follow behind. Where does that put us for total bodies? I count. Twenty-six? Twenty-seven including myself.

"Found these four huddled together in a house. Please behave yourselves," Hadrian says. I recognize one man right away. His eyes lock on to mine and sharklike teeth flash beneath his lips.

"Pladd!" I exclaim, standing up. "What the hell is he doing here?" I ask Hadrian, pointing.

"He's a member of the Brightest, Caelius," Hadrian says. "Don't you remember?"

"What?" I snap. My voice echoes throughout the basement. Eyes pin me down, but I don't relent. "He's the one who started this whole thing. You're gonna let a killer down here?"

"I don't feel safe with him down here either," Donovan says, holding his son close. "We have no idea what he's capable of."

"You made your decision when you spared his life. He is no more a killer than you or I," Hadrian says. "If he shouldn't be down here, if he truly isn't a member of the Brightest, strike him down. Right here."

My mind races. Another decision. I pull out my rapier from my sheath and hold the blade to Pladd's chest. I don't know if I can trust him. There's no fear in his eyes. There's no regret, no remorse, no joy. Just indifference. Maybe a tinge of curiosity. I'd nearly killed Brena with this rapier. I remember dropping it and falling unconscious. How did it return to my scabbard?

The tip of my sword shakes violently, only stopping when I press it against his chest. I could just take one step forward. How come taking a life is so easy, yet so difficult?

My left hand grazes against my pocket where I'd stored the stone he gave me. It was an ordinary rock to most, but to us it was a symbol of trust and friendship. I trusted him and he trusted me. Why would that have changed?

I lower my sword, looking at the man. He is my friend. It's impossible for him to have directly called the attack. His group realized he was missing and came to his rescue. I couldn't blame him for their actions.

Hadrian quietly scoffs at me. He thinks I'm a coward. That I couldn't do what needs to be done. That I wouldn't be a good leader.

Maybe he's right. Because, unlike him, I wouldn't kill one of our own. Every life is worth saving, even Pladd's.

The hours roll by slowly. Pladd sits in the corner of the room by himself. He looks indifferent to the whole situation. I'm sure most people here expected him to have attacked someone by now. I keep an eye on him warily. I'm ready to fight at any moment.

Brena still lies on a table, unconscious. Dolora sits, sleeping against the table, her daughter's hand held in hers. Hadrian left shortly after Pladd's arrival to search for more survivors. The raid and the fires had begun to die down, but Hadrian wants to wait another day. Oberon, who sits next to me, hasn't spoken once.

His cat, Beef Iron Mutilator, rubs up against my leg. I stretch down and scratch the critter on the head, surprised to see him here. He does a great job of alleviating tension.

Even hours later, I still have no idea how I got here. The only person who might know is Dolora. Everything feels as if it took place in a dream. I'd hate to wake her up. She's been through so much.

The stone wall behind Brena is a painted mural of two men, one dressed all in white, the other in a deep slate color. His clothes appear like thunderclouds. The man dressed in white strikes a defensive pose, holding a rapier, not much different from my own. The man dressed in black doesn't have a weapon. Instead, lightning shoots from the tips of his fingers, expanding like an impossible tree.

The light of a candle dims and slowly fades. Before we are in full darkness, someone lights another. "Do you think we could stay down here for a full orbit, Dad?" a child asks his father.

"If we had enough food and water, maybe," Donovan, the carpenter, says. "If we can keep the cold from entering."

"But this is a church," the kid says, head twisted to the side. "Light will protect us and keep us safe, right?"

"A candle doesn't stay lit forever," the father says, pointing at the freshly lit candlestick. "It is up to us to relight it, or light a new one." The kid's face continues to look confused. "The Light is always here to protect us and provide us safety in passage, but it is also up to us to take care of ourselves."

His statement gives me something to think about. I'm not sure if I fully agree but it's a good enough answer for the child. Could this underground hideout actually work?

This place is a Church of the Light, so would the Light protect us in its holy building? But why didn't Hadrian want us to come here? Should I really *test* the limits and judgment of the Light?

According to Hadrian, the Light's only directive is to follow the "Solaris Sanctum," or more commonly known as the Bright Spot. By breaking that rule, what's to say that he'd allow the Darkness to reign?

I study the mural again. This time, I might understand its meaning. The two clashing figures aren't random people. They are anthropomorphized representations of the Light and the Darkness.

"There's a book," Oberon finally says. "*The Path*, it's called. I found it while I was waiting for more people to arrive." I turn to look at him. "A tome, really. When I came down here the first time, I was perplexed by the same mural. Until I saw those words down there." Oberon points to words that had been chiseled into the stone, *Song of Light 7:24*.

"Sure enough," Oberon continues, "in the tome there was a passage with the label 'Song of Light 7:24.'" He waits a moment, pondering before speaking again. "I can't remember the exact thing the passage said, but what I learned was that before the creation of Nivalis, the Light"—he points to the figure in white—"fought the Darkness in an ultimate battle." He then points to the man in the cloudy gray outfit. "It lasted hundreds of orbits, maybe even longer. A fight between Light and Darkness. Good and evil. One fought with truth and honor. The other fought with lies and deceit."

Oberon stops a moment. "There's one thing that freaked me out, Caelius." I lean in, curious. "And don't tell anyone this. And definitely don't mention this to Hadrian. I think he's hiding it from us."

I sit at the edge of my seat in anticipation, glancing back at the mural of Light and Darkness. "Caelius," Oberon says, "it said that … that the Darkness won that battle."

Darkness won the battle? How? The Light is the most powerful being in existence. How could it lose? I shake my head not believing him. That book had to be wrong. Oberon continues, "It said the Light and Darkness both had been severely wounded, and, in that moment, they settled on a truce. The Light would have its own section, a small fraction of the planet. But in return, the Darkness would rule the rest of the land and do whatever he pleases with it."

I can't keep my mouth shut. "The Light can't lose. It's an all-powerful being. It could snap its fingers, and the Darkness would be banished. Right?"

"Would a benevolent god destroy that of which he creates?" Oberon says. He lifts a hand and looks at the shadow it casts. "Darkness is just the absence of light. Could such a god destroy a shadow without destroying the thing casting it?"

"I …," I begin, but I have no words. Oberon has never been this philosophical before. His language is different too. I think he's reciting from the book. Could this be about the Freezing of the World? "So, all this happened thirty orbits ago?"

"I don't think so. I think it goes much further back. I'm pretty sure people used to live in the Darkness, 'cause how could Solace exist? Three hundred and forty days is not enough to build a city, I think.

"It ties in well with another passage that I read, only a couple pages in," he continues. "Caelius, the book says that we are made from the Darkness. Our souls cast shadows because we are of the Darkness as much as the world is."

"I thought you weren't much of a religious guy," I say, not sure what else to add.

"I'm not," he says. "After the near death of my own daughter, I looked for something to ease me. We are in a church, after all. If she …" He takes a breath, lowering his voice. "If she dies, I need comfort knowing she's somewhere safe. That I'll be there to see her again." His eyes water, and he wipes them away with a sleeve. "But after reading what I found," he says, "I'm not even sure I want to follow the Light anymore or even pretend to. What's the point?"

"Oberon," I say, trying to comfort him. But I still have no words. Instead, I give him a side hug.

He speaks up again. "I'm not a good father."

"Don't say that," I interject.

He continues before I can say more. "Dolora's right. I'm not present for my daughter. She needs me to be around more and instead I'm off in the woods hunting."

"It's not like you have a choice," I declare. "You and I were hunters. Without us, people would starve." He stays silent. "Don't worry, we will get through this. You need to be a dad for your child."

"Hadrian can't know that I read *The Path*."

"Why not?" I ask. "I'm sure he figured someone here would, eventually. Especially if they are down here for hours on end."

"Because if he does, he'll kill me."

"Why do you think that?"

"Because I'm not fully convinced Hadrian even follows the Light. At least not this one."

19

The Doors

How many coincidences can there be until it's scientifically improbable?
From the Journal of Azura Seren. Hylano section, 28th orbit

I groggily wake up from my slumber. The room is dark with the candlelight extinguished, save for a little light peeking its way through the trapdoor seams in the ceiling. It's enough for me to see the room around me. Hadrian has returned and sleeps on a cloth sheet on the dirt floor. I don't think I've ever seen him sleep before. He always sleeps in his wagon.

Dolora lies on the floor next to her daughter, snoring softly. Guilt pangs me at what I've done, but if I weren't there to stop the raider, Brena would be dead. Dead by the hands of a sick cannibal. I look at Pladd. He sleeps with his back against the corner. He hadn't killed anyone. Should I be surprised? He started to show some growth, putting his trust in me. It seemed like a ruse, but maybe not?

My eyes land on a sleeping Lyria. A large gash splits her cheek under her right eye, but she looks fine otherwise. Thank the Light she is alive.

Where's Oberon? He was here, sleeping right next to me, but now he's gone. My eyes strain against the darkness, looking for my friend. Did he leave?

How did Oberon leave without waking any of us up? He would have had to knock to signal the guards to let him out. Maybe he left when Hadrian arrived. But even then, I should have woken up.

Something is in my coat pocket. I feel it shifting awkwardly when I move. My right hand comes up and pulls out a small brochure. I barely make out the title in the darkness: *Visit Solace! Where the sun shines brightest.*

I stand up from the floor. I don't even spend the time to brush the dirt off my clothes. I grab the wooden plank leaning against the stone wall and step underneath the trapdoor. I lightly bang on its underside. Three knocks, then two. A few sleeping bodies stir, but Hadrian sits right up. "Caelius?" he asks, disheveled. His white hair is an unruly mess.

My heart races. I hear the altar above shift as the guards above push it out of the way. "Where are you going?" Hadrian asks, pushing himself from the ground. Light Almighty above, hurry up.

"I'm going out to look for Oberon," I reply, not glancing back at him. The trapdoor swings open, flooding the room underneath with natural light. My eyes burn, and I climb up the ladder to escape.

"You will do no such thing," he says, stumbling over sleeping bodies. He climbs the ladder after me, moving quicker than I anticipated. I want to close the trapdoor on him but I'm too slow.

He crawls out of the hole in the ground. He's going to try to stop me with his strange abilities. I sprint, making a break for the large doors at the end of the sanctuary. That pamphlet wasn't there before. Oberon placed it there deliberately, asking me to follow him. He wouldn't have just *left* without saying goodbye. What about his wife? What about his daughter?

"Caelius," Hadrian's voice says behind me.

I don't stop. I need to get as far away from him as possible. If what Oberon said about Hadrian was true …

"CAELIUS!" Hadrian's voice booms, reverberating through the massive sanctuary. The words slam into me, knocking me down, face-first. I scramble to get back up and when I stand, two hands grab the back of my coat.

I'm shoved into a neighboring pew, and I'm met with dangerous eyes. "Do not go after him," Hadrian threatens shoving a finger in my face. Hadrian *knows* something about Oberon's disappearance.

"Or else what?" I ask through gritted teeth.

"Oberon is a traitor to the Light. He desecrated secrets and turned his back on the truth. He exiled himself from the group and turned his back on his family. He is a liar, and a coward. If you choose to go after him, you will be exiled alongside him."

Hadrian definitely *knew*. He could be the reason behind it all. Hadrian previously expressed he wanted Oberon gone. He wouldn't willingly exile himself. It's a miracle Hadrian hadn't killed him.

Phantom pain burns where my fingers used to be. "Great, I don't want to be a part of your stupid cult," I say in defiance. I stand up from the pew, meeting the man at eye level.

"If you take a step out of those doors, I will have no choice but to disown you as my son. You will be an enemy of the Brightest. Any sight of you will be met with hostility.

Do you understand, boy?" he threatens, voice hotter than the sun.

I hesitate. *An enemy of the Brightest*. If I stay, I may never see my best friend again. The only person who had been there for me through the toughest moments. The person who dragged me from the river and saved my life. What cost am I willing to pay? Putting Dolora and Brena at risk? I'm somewhat responsible for them. In Oberon's absence, they are my responsibility to protect.

What about Pladd? I didn't trust him fully, but he was still my friend. Light, I wish Oberon hadn't left so soon. It's still unclear if Pladd is truly safe for everyone to be around? He didn't call the attack; his group did. But capturing him cost the Brightest so many lives.

What about Lyria? She wasn't terribly social. I doubt she's made many friends. She'll be okay with me gone, right?

"I'm going, Father," I say.

"Then so be it," Hadrian replies. "Next time we meet, you will not call me Father, for you are no longer my son."

The finality of it feels like tearing of cloth. Messy, but thorough. Losing another father figure isn't something I want, but Oberon needs me to find him. Hopefully, he can take care of himself for the time being.

I expect Hadrian to stop me from leaving, but he doesn't. Instead, he watches me with his cold and dark eyes. He says one last thing before I leave. "I'm the one who knocked you out."

I study him for a moment.

"I knocked you out after you stabbed that girl. I carried your body here. You were too unstable." I assumed it was him, but it's relieving to know for sure. "You could never lead the Brightest. I raised you and you are too much like me."

I'm too much like him? What gives him the right to decide that. My face heats up. A thousand different things run through my mind. I want to yell at him. I want to tell him he's wrong. I want to tell him that I will never be like him. But I know he's right. I won't admit it. Not to him, not to Oberon, not to myself. He raised me, shaped me, groomed me, into what I am today. I was always meant to replace him as the leader. It was only a matter of time.

If I killed him right here and now, what would happen? Would I become the leader of the Brightest? I'd have to be. Who else could take over?

He waits for me to say something, expecting me to object. Instead, I turn away without saying a word. The doors swing open with a shove, and my senses are overwhelmed by the stench and visual of charred buildings and houses.

Goodbye, Hadrian.

The End of Part 2

20

Interlude III: The Horizon

Jaime, Steeq, Dan, Elara

The oiled cloth glides across the bare metal of Jaime's shortsword. The air is stuffy and reeks of sweat. It doesn't bother him, though. The weight room is the only place where he can think clearly. The weights and benches had been removed so he could use the room for sword training. If only he had someone to practice with.

Jaime runs the cloth across the blade again. The rag's microfiber hairs catch on his dry skin. He lifts the shiny metal up to his face and a black-haired child stares at him in the reflection. Those were the eyes of someone who lived a thousand deaths.

How many people had died by his hand? Dozens? Hundreds? Does he love it? Does he love the act of killing? Or is he just good at it? He doesn't have much of a choice.

He stands up from the bench, carrying the shortsword with one hand. Most are surprised by the weight when they hold a sword for the first time. To him, it's too familiar. He tosses the rag on the bench and hangs the sword on the wall next to his other weapons.

His collection of weapons had grown over the passings. Most of them are ancient, made before the world froze. They'd come from weapon stores and museums. Every weapon has a story. A small chip on a blade tells of a battle hard fought. Rusted metal tells of negligent care of an unused weapon.

He'd collect every weapon he came across if he could. It's hard enough to travel with his thirty or so weapons already. This city is littered with unique weapons. The hardest part is trying to decide what to keep and what to leave behind.

The mace he found yesterday is likely the most unique one yet. It hangs on the wall next to his shortsword. The mace has a long handle and a spiky metal head. What makes it unique is its ability to be used as a flail at will. He killed a Crit for it. Such an elegant weapon is wasted in the hands of a savage.

Lifting it off the rack, he feels the increase in weight at the end of the handle. The spiky steel ball is cast perfectly. Not like most crudely made weapons used by the Crits.

Someone who eats a fellow man is no man himself. Crits, genetically mutated cannibals are the ultimate disgrace, spitting in the face of the Creator. As far as he is concerned, all cannibals are Crits. Not just the ones with stout legs and razor-sharp teeth. While she had no issue recognizing Crits, Elara could never tell the difference between a human and a human cannibal. She never took the time to learn, claiming it isn't important to her research.

It is, however, important to Jaime. He could pick them out with ease as if he had some supernatural ability. They walk differently, act differently, smell differently.

Jaime stands at one end of the room, sizing up the training dummy in the center. Practicing with it doesn't compare to the real deal—the heart-racing adrenaline of battle, the groans of the injured, the smell of blood in the air. He's grateful for Dan spending the time crafting this mannequin dummy, but stabbing through cloth and grass will never match the feeling of flesh and bone.

He rotates the mace in his fingers, perfecting his grip. His thumb presses the red button on the handle, dropping the head of the mace, caught by a metal chain. He lifts his thumb and the ball snaps back into place.

Jaime dashes toward the training dummy, dodging an imaginary sword thrust. The mace ball detaches, turning into a flail. It trails behind him carrying his momentum. The ball strikes the mannequin's head, creating a satisfying *poof*. He releases the button, the ball snapping back into place, where he makes a secondary upward blow. He leaps back, pretending to dodge another blade.

He moves to strike a third time but stops himself. The mace had torn open the fabric, spilling grass all over the floor. *Damn*. He needs more practice before using this in combat. For now, he'll just use his sword.

The bright blue glow of the rail gun's barrel temporarily blinds Steeq. The barrel is pointed directly at his chest, seconds from firing. "Not this again." He sighs, summoning a pair of wire cutters from the nightstand. The light had burned into his retinas, leaving behind an afterimage as he searches for the correct wire. If he gets this wrong, he would be obliterated. The orange wire needs to be clipped. But which one is orange?

Taking a guess, he clips a random wire expecting the worst. Instead, the barrel's light dims until it's off.

He sits on his bed, the weapon in his lap. The massive battery next to his bed hums. The static causes the hair on his head and arms to stand on end. Dan says that sleeping next to a battery probably isn't good for Steeq's brain. What does he know anyway?

Oh, he'd cross-connected two wires. That would explain why it started its firing sequence. He snips that pair and connects the wires correctly. He's going to need to find more wire nuts when he is finished.

The rail gun is larger than his leg. It's heavy and needs to be connected to the battery to function. Once the Horizon starts traveling again, he'd have to leave it behind. It's a shame, really.

Copper coils wrap around the barrel of the weapon. Ammunition is loaded in the chamber in the back. Anything round and made of steel works best. Jaime had found some shot-put balls in the weight room, which work perfectly. Though they'll be hard to come by if he ever needs more. They aren't very accurate either. If only he had something explosive.

The other members of the Horizon prefer to live on the lowest floor of the hotel, but Steeq likes the top fourth floor. It provides a nice vantage point. While it's not the tallest building in the city of Solace, Dan was adamant they stay here.

Steeq stands from his bed and places the unstable weapon on the mattress. He'd been spending way too much time working with the thing. When was the last time he ate?

The sun shines brightly through the window after he moves the curtains aside. The weapon practically begged him to be fired. But what could he shoot from the window?

His fingernails catch on a scab. He didn't even realize he was scratching at his face. He brushes the back of his hand against his cheek, returning with blood. A lot of it. Wiping again, more blood pools on his wrist. He wouldn't be scratching if he didn't …

The thought overpowers him. Something guides his hand toward the bottle labeled "gunpowder" on his nightstand. The label is just a cover-up. No one should find out what is *truly* inside. The cap twists off easily, revealing the soft ground-up purple flower petals.

Jaime had begged him to get rid of the stuff. As far as Jaime knew, he did. Somehow Jaime always knew when he was using, so Steeq had to be strategic.

How could he be expected to quit when it provides him with answers.

The rumbling of boiling water and the scent of seasoning flood Dan's senses. The stew burns his tongue when he takes a taste, but the heavenly flavor makes up for it. The hotel's kitchen is surprisingly nice. After thirty orbits of being unused, it needed a bit of cleaning. Somehow everything still works. Thanks to Steeq for getting the power working again, he can finally use the stove. A campfire worked just fine, but this was much better. Plus, the room came with pots, pans, plates, bowls, and utensils.

The carrot he harvested from his traveling greenhouse had dirt on it, but hot water from the tap washed it right off. They've been here for a week, and he is still amazed at his ability to get unlimited water, hot *and* cold. Each room in the hotel has a faucet like this one.

Dan selects the large chef's knife next to him and chops the carrot into little disks. Boiling water splashes his hand when he dumps the carrots into the simmering stew.

The steam warms his face and floods his nose with a fantastic aroma. Hopefully, the crew will like this meal. Some meat would be a nice extra, but they would have to do with vegetable stew for now. His previous caravan never grew herbs. They took up space that could be reserved for more *hearty* vegetables. Dan always prioritized growing herbs for seasoning. Although he is making food for only four people instead of thirty.

The garlic, rosemary, and other seasonings are added to the pot. He tosses a carrot disk into his mouth to ease the roaring in his stomach. His main rule is to enjoy the small things in life, even if it means breaking other rules like eating before dinner is served. It's important that he enjoys his tasks. Everyone deserves a meal and a place to stay. Receiving thanks and appreciation keeps him going. It's one of the few things that make him feel warm inside.

Is he selfish for seeking that feeling? Doing tasks and favors for other people because it feels *good?*

Regardless of the answer, he won't stop doing what is needed.

He sets out four bowls in front of him, slowly dumping his concoction into each one. He sneaks another sip from his bowl, allowing the stew to envelop each taste bud.

Oh, they are definitely going to love this.

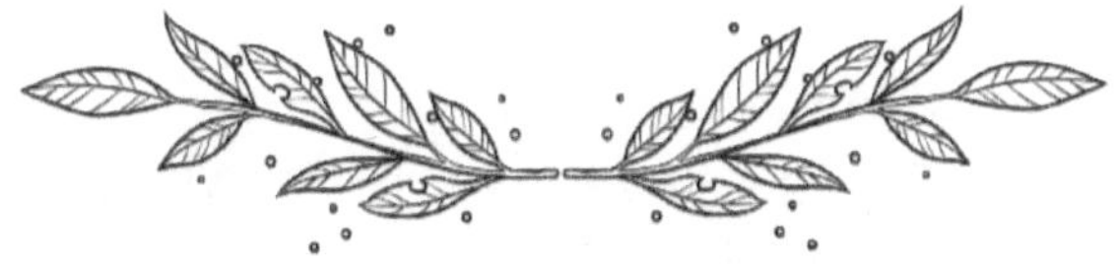

Elara finally made it to Solace. She'd been anticipating this moment her entire life. She wanted to search the city and learn each of its secrets. She wanted to explore and learn of fragments of life pre-Freezing. Many of the strange anomalies and mysteries here and the Horizon have encountered stem from this exact city.

And she is stuck in the hotel, not permitted to leave. Dan says it is too dangerous for her to be out there alone, and it is hard enough to convince her brother, Jaime, to explore with her. Especially after what happened yesterday.

If he hadn't been there, she would have been killed. Or worse. She chose to go to the mall in hopes of finding something valuable for her research, but the most valuable thing she kept was her life. Her brother, however, earned a new weapon.

It was unlikely he'd ever use it practically. Knowing him, it would be just more weight to carry when they get back on the road.

The city is denser than she'd expected. Instead of long winding roads spanning miles like the other cities, this one has a tightness to it. Why is that? Surely it couldn't hurt to expand horizontally a bit. She couldn't complain, though. It makes her job easier.

The graphite in her pencil snaps underneath her hand. She forgot she'd even been drawing. The paper depicted a spot in the city from the perspective of someone on the ground. Except the city was busy, filled with life. People walked the sidewalks, wearing business suits and staring at things in their hands. Cars lined the streets, spewing smoke into the air.

One man walking had his shoes untied. Another had mismatched socks. A child was on the verge of tears as he watched his oddly shaped ball ascend to the heavens. "Happy Birthday" it said. His father was trying to catch it and the mother attempted to console her child. The drawing seemed to be an oddly specific moment from the past, frozen in time.

What was it like to live in that world? To have everything you could ever want at your fingertips. Reliable food, water, shelter, protection. Life must have been so easy.

Careful not to smear the artwork, Elara blows the broken graphite tip off the paper. Some details seem to be missing from the picture, but what? It looks finished to her.

This is ridiculous. They had plans to visit the city and uncover its secrets. And all they're doing is sitting around, waiting for time to pass before moving on. Maybe she should just go alone.

Sure, the city is dangerous, but the reward is worth the risk. Right? But what if the city didn't have anything of note? Could it be possible? How would she feel about that?

Searching and uncovering nothing is better than not searching at all. Regardless of the answer, it would still push her research forward.

A crudely sketched map of the city stretches out on the table next to her. It displays where she had and hadn't visited. The city seems so small from this bird's-eye view. And she'd only explored less than 10 percent of it. Feeling frustrated, she snatches an old coin from the desk. She flips it into the air with her eyes shut. It lands with two hard thuds, marking her fate. Opening her eyes she sees it landed near the hotel. Good, that's not too far. Hopefully she'll find something useful there.

With or without Jaime.

Part 3

Shadows

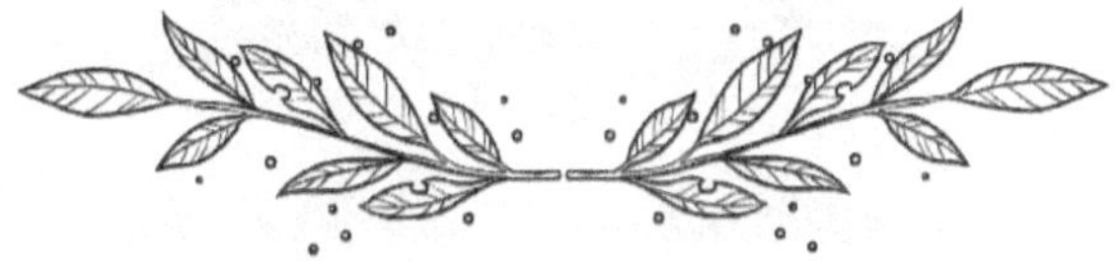

21

The Warm City

Other planets within our system seem to have
inhabitable living conditions.
From the Journal of Azura Seren. Retuno section, 28th
orbit

Rubble. **The house I'd lived** in for the last few weeks had been reduced to rubble. I feel cathartic seeing piles of ash and debris. My parents had chosen this house to live in before joining the Brightest. I hadn't had the chance to build memories in this place.

I step through the rubble into where my room had once been. Everything had been reduced to nothing. My bed is gone. My dresser and nightstand lie destroyed, painted black. I had a few personal belongings, such as different clothes, which are sure to be gone as well.

My parents' room isn't much better. The last connection to my them is gone. I'm all that remains.

It's time to move on. Just as it's time for me to move on from the Brightest. Nivalis still spins and we are far behind schedule. These are the consequences of Hadrian's actions. Old relics from hundreds of passings ago, burned to the ground. The raiders have no sense of preservation or care for history. But why would they? It doesn't matter to them. It's just stuff. A means to an end. Would life be better if we all saw it that way?

The willow tree in the center of town remains untouched. Its tendril-like leaves droop low, touching the ground. Houses next to it are gone while the tree remains. A bit of the natural green had faded to a light brown. Likely due to the nearby fires. Why did they leave the tree? Did it have something to do with Pladd and his—what was that? So much had happened, I didn't even consider how weird the whole thing was. The tree's bark moved to make way for his hand, and he pulled out a stone. That same stone in my pocket. Could other cannibals do that?

Unsurprisingly, Oberon's house is also rubble and ash. Most of Hollyard had been destroyed. I hoped I'd find him here before he left, but that's not the case. I remove the pamphlet from my coat pocket. *Solace.* Opening it up reveals the city's map. It lists different restaurants, hotels, and attractions—all of which are lost to time. Apparently, the city's main attraction was its college. A centralized hub of buildings dedicated to education.

I turn my head, looking north toward the city. The brown-greenish buildings stand tall, looming over me. They are miles away, but it is hard to miss their grand stature.

My foot kicks a rock that survived the fire. I bend down and lift it up with my right hand. It's a painted rock with the words "I love Daddy!" Underneath is a red heart. One of Brena's rocks. The paint is faded slightly, but still recognizable. I slip it into one of my free pockets. I will give this to him when I find him.

Wary of raiders, I head in the direction of the city of Solace carrying my sword at my waist.

The city is much grander when you're walking through it. I nearly lose my balance while looking up. The buildings had always seemed tall before, but standing in between them is something else entirely. I admire a towering brick building with a few busted-out windows. Up close, the bricks are a shade of red, perhaps maroon. The verdant vines make the once-red building look brown from afar.

"Welcome to Solace! The Warm City." A sign greets my entrance. Dulled reds, oranges, and yellows paint the buildings on both sides of the streets. Vines grow on each one. Its color palette must be why it's called "The Warm City." Lunace, The Cool City, is on the other side of the Octoro Bridge. Its color palette consists of greens, blues, and purples.

The street ahead is littered with junk and other paraphernalia—abandoned cars, trash, orange cones, and other bits of undiscernible types of rubble.

What did this place look like before the Freezing of the World? Hadrian speculated these cars could travel from city to city in less than a day. Did people even need to hunt or gather their food? Restaurants seem to be littered on almost every block. Places like these just *had* food, ready to eat.

My foot misses its next step and I fall forward, shin grazing against the edge of deteriorating asphalt. Gasping in pain I see I've stepped in a pothole. There are hundreds in the street in front of me.

I continue to hobble through the city, being extra cautious for holes in the road. I want to yell out Oberon's name, but I can't risk bringing attention to myself. I don't know who … or what could be lurking in this city.

Four large yellow boxes hang in the air, suspended by wires connected to outstretched poles rising from the ground, marking an intersection. Each box has three colored domes on the front. In the center of the road, is a metal disk. Written are the words, "Solace Sewers."

I should head back. I do not belong here. I am out of my element and could be attacked at any moment.

My breathing intensifies and darkness starts to close in around me. The fire-colored buildings gaze upon me in anger. I'm a trespasser in their city. I drop to a sitting position in front of the sewer cover, knees against my chest and chin. I bury my head, hyperventilating.

The rational side of me knows this is ridiculous. I could get myself killed by panicking like this—especially out in the open. I'm never going to find Oberon. This place is just too massive.

The other side of me misses Hadrian. It misses the comfort of safety, despite the looming threat of raiders. That side is *angry* at Hadrian for doing this to me. Hadrian knew Oberon was the only hunter the Brightest had and he still exiled him. What about his daughter? She needed him.

I could say the same thing about myself. I condemn Hadrian for exiling Oberon, but I *chose* to leave. I *chose* to leave Dolora and Brena, who need someone to trust. I left Lyria, whom I saved from death by hanging.

Who *we* saved. It was Oberon and I who saved her. Not just me. *We* killed that deer together before reaching Hollyard. *We* protected the Brightest during a raid.

We defied Hadrian. *We* brought on the first raid attack.

Deep breaths, my mind commands. I oblige, each shaky breath easier than the last. *You got this.* I examine the area around me, grounding myself back in reality. The wind blows between the buildings, whistling gently. It's a sharper tone than when it blows through trees in the forest. It presses against my skin, offering a cooling touch against the increasingly warmer days.

The buildings on each corner of the intersection aren't just unnamed random buildings. The first one I see is a red painted restaurant. The floors stacked on top of it seem not to be related. "Giovanni's," the sign says. The other building, "John and Jane Clothing," had been looted and cleared out. Glass covers the ground where the large window used to be.

A shrill screech pierces the air. *Oberon?* No, that was a woman's scream. I stand and run down the street toward the screaming. "Jaime, help!" the voice yells.

My legs move faster than ever, twisting and turning through alleys and intersections, avoiding each pothole in the road.

That's when I see them.

The screams come from a brown-haired woman with pale skin. She scuttles back on the ground, putting her hand up, trying to ward off a cannibal looming over her. He carries a metal pipe in his right hand, slowly advancing on the woman. I'm still about a hundred feet away.

The raider turns to look at me. He bears his teeth, and like Pladd, they are filed down to points. His eyes burn with fury. Claws, where fingernails should be, curl inward.

I sprint, unsheathing my sword. He drops his attention from the woman and dashes toward me as well. I'm in range; the cannibal swings the pipe toward my head, missing me by an inch. I counterstrike with my rapier.

The cannibal leaps backward onto all fours, dropping the metal pipe. It clatters loudly on the ground. The creature runs at me like a mountain lion. Hadrian's training could not have prepared me for this. It leaps at me, mouth wide open, ready to tear into my face. I hold my sword horizontally with the palm of my left hand pressing against the flat side of the blade.

The cannibal's mouth envelops the blade, and Hadrian's training allows me to keep my composure. He was right. Stance really does make a difference.

The cannibal recovers and swipes his hand at my midsection. The claws tear into my shirt and split the skin underneath. I scream in pain, and the cannibal takes the opportunity to leap at me. My sword cuts through the air but finds nothing. My stance is unprepared and I'm forced to the ground. The wind is knocked out of my lungs, but I can't risk recovering it.

Without wasting a single second, the cannibal uses his claws to *dig* into my chest. My thick overcoat is shredded to pieces and the claws *carve* my skin. The pain is agonizing, but I can't scream. I reel in pain instead, back involuntarily arching.

CLANG! I open my eyes and see the cannibal fall off me. He shakes his head, dazed, and the woman swings again, striking the cannibal in the temple. He flies backward, landing hard against the concrete. He does not get back up.

The woman makes eye contact with me and winces. "Oh shit," she says, "I'm gonna be in trouble."

22

The Sharks

*Nivalis almost seems to have been *created**
specifically for us to survive, at least before the
Freezing. Wouldn't these coincidences prove the
existence of God? Or at least a higher power?
From the Journal of Azura Seren. Retuno section, 28th
orbit

I wish I had stayed fully unconscious for the next part. Instead, I fade in and out of consciousness, fully aware of every bump in the road, bringing pain along with it. The woman spends the next hour dragging my body through the streets of Solace.

"If you're going to eat me," I mumble, "at least have the decency to kill me first." Everything is blurry and my mind lags to register what she responds with.

"I'm not going to eat you. Light's sake," she swears.

"Then what are you doing?" I ask. Or at least I try asking. She doesn't respond. I ask the question again, more deliberately this time.

"I'm getting you help," she says. "Light, how far away is this *burning* place?" She's got kind of a mouth to her. Like Oberon.

The sky peeks out from above the buildings, seeming so far away. I feel lightheaded.

"Caelius ....," an ominous, wispy voice says, dragging out. Who said that? The woman wouldn't know my name. Am I hallucinating? I ignore the voice, quiet as it already is.

"Caelius ....," it says again, insisting on getting my attention. My head hits a medium-sized piece of rubble. I groan. The pain is dull compared to my chest wound.

"Sorry," the woman says.

"You can't ignore me forever," the wispy voice says again. What? Ignore who? The voice speaks again. "Your soul is broken. Let me fix you. Let me in."

I must be delirious. These must be hallucinations caused by excessive trauma. But what if it's not a hallucination?

"Who are you?" I ask the voice, mumbling.

The woman speaks first. "I'm the one who's going to try to save your life, after you saved mine."

"Hadn't Hadrian taught you of blind faith, pupil?" the voice says next. Hadrian? Pupil? Is the Light itself talking to me?

The woman dragging me against the ground says something, but I can't make it out. I know I should recognize the words, but I don't. The back of my head slams against a curb. I groan in pain as I'm dragged by my feet through a large, dimly lit room into a smaller room. Where am I? When did we get here?

Craning my neck I see a large, dark-skinned Okanakan man. He stands next to the concerned woman who dragged me here. I stare at her, admiring her features, unable to drag my gaze away. Her dark hair flows with her movements. I'm enthralled by her plump lips and deep brown eyes.

She's not real.

The man hands me a cup, saying something. His words lag in my mind, taking a second to process. "Drink this." The cup is small and hot in my hand. The liquid inside looks like hot water with a light brown color.

I shakily put the cup to my lips before the woman guides the cup, helping pour the water into my mouth. I drink it reflexively. It has a sweet and bitter taste. She pulls the cup back and sets it on the carpet next to me.

The man's voice is deep. "That should put him to sleep while I …"

In front of us was the Octoro Bridge. It stretched for miles. I couldn't see the other side. I looked up to my right. I saw my dad holding my hand. His spectacled face and warm smile reassured me everything would be alright.

"It's okay, Caelius," he said, giving my hand a squeeze. "We will be across the bridge in a couple of days."

I looked up to my left and my mom was standing there. She was so pretty. She placed a hand in the middle of my back and we stepped onto the unfamiliar ground together.

My parents were so smart. They knew everything. I don't think there was a single question they couldn't answer.

"Daddy," I said. "What if the sharks jumped up on the bridge?" I didn't want to be eaten by a shark. I'd heard stories about their teeth and I did *not* want to be on the wrong side of those.

"Sharks can't jump," he tells me. "If they could, they couldn't jump high enough to reach the bridge."

"What if they can?"

"Well, sharks don't have feet, so they can't get us."

"What if they have robot legs?" I figured I was the only kid in the world who knew what robots were.

"That's a great question. Luckily for us, robots don't work in the water," my dad said, somehow having the answer.

"Caelius!" another kid's voice called out. "Come on!" It was Reyus. "Last one to the end of the bridge is a rotten egg!" He giggled and a few other kids started running. Reyus was my best friend. He didn't have a mom and dad, though.

I released my parents' hands and started running after him. I wasn't as scared of the bridge anymore. I was more scared of being a "rotten egg."

"Hey," Hadrian yelled. We all stopped to look at him and listen. The old white-haired man had a slight smile. "Don't go too far. If you turn around and can't see us, you need to come right back, understand?"

"Yes, Father Hadrian," we all said in unison.

"Good," he said. "Now, to make sure you don't run too far … This *rotten egg* might get some sweets."

Our eyes widened. I wanted sweets. But I also wanted to be with my friends. The other kids ran, and I followed after them.

We ran as far as we could down the bridge and then back to the caravan. Reyus was always the fastest. When we returned, I tried to seek out my parents. They were pretty easy to spot. My dad had glasses and was almost bald and my mom was the prettiest person ever. But they weren't there. Hadrian faced away, back toward the shore.

"Mom?" I asked to no one. Where was she? She was supposed to be here. "Dad?" No response. "Hey!" I yelled to Hadrian. "Where are my mom and dad?"

His grimace turned into a sad grin. "They forgot something in Hollyard, so they had to go back." I looked up at him. He stood so tall. "Oh, I nearly forgot." He reached into a pocket on his white and gold robes retrieving a handful of assorted sweets. "If you keep this a secret, you won't have to share with anyone." He gave me a smile and wink.

"Thank you, Father Hadrian," I said quietly, making sure no other kids could hear me. "Can I tell my mom and dad about the sweets when they come back?"

"Of course, little one; they will return." He rubbed my hair with his palm. His hands felt cold even over my thick head of hair.

They never did return.

The warm bed I lay on suppresses my desire to move. Was it just a dream? What happened? It doesn't take long before the comfort bleeds away and is replaced with pain. My entire body aches.

The room around me is unfamiliar. The tan walls and black drapes differ from those in my bedroom. *Where am I? Why can't I move?* I try to yell, but I croak instead. I'm *parched.* My heart rate increases and I try to swallow, but there's no saliva. Fear grips me as I try to make sense of what's going on. Am I dead? Is this the afterlife? Where is the Light? What was that voice I heard?

I hear a creaking. *What is that?* I strain my head to look. Around the corner, a very large dark-skinned man appears.

Not a single strand of hair litters his head or face. He wears a white sleeveless shirt and black cargo pants. His biceps bulge and are probably larger than my head.

"I was wondering when you'd wake up." His deep voice rattles some items in the room. "Here." He stomps over to me and extends a small glass of water. No, the glass is proper size. The man's hands are just very large. With effort, I move my arms up from my sides and reach toward the glass. It takes every bit of energy to hold it. Even with both hands, the cup trembles, spilling some of its contents onto my lap.

I raise the cup to my lips, straining to sip while lying on my back. The water painfully moistens my mouth and I cough by reflex, spitting water onto the man. He flinches.

I feel a cold wet spot on my chest. I've spilled. "Let me get you another blanket," the large man says before exiting. When the door closes, I take another drink. Before I realize it, the cup is empty.

I'm feeling more awake by the time the man returns, this time with a thicker, fluffier blanket than the thin sheet covering me now. He lifts it into the air, and it floats gently down over me. Before it lands, I catch a glimpse of the design. Three brown wolves snarl, teeth bared, circling a much smaller white wolf. The white wolf doesn't cower. It stands still. Stoic. As if it knows it is something the others could never be.

The man pulls a chair up beside my bed, taking a seat. "You're lucky we didn't leave you for dead. We are taking a big risk here keeping you alive."

I want to speak, but he continues before I can start. "If you hadn't saved the life of one of mine, you'd still be out there on the streets. This is my repayment. Thank you." I nod, breaking eye contact, to take a more analytical look at the room.

On the ceiling is a dome with a nub at the end. I'm confused by the odd eroticism it portrays. It shines as if they harnessed the power of the sun and confined it to that one spot. It is unnatural. It is wrong. The curtains are drawn closed, so I can't see what is outside or where we are. It seems like we are in a house of some sort.

The large man speaks again, filling the silent air between us. "My name is Daniel, by the way. But just call me Dan."

"Cae—," I rasp before coughing again. "Caelius."

"Well, then … Cay-lee-us," Dan says, sounding out each of the syllables as he says it. "I'll get you some more water. In the meantime, I'll have Jaime keep an eye on you to make sure you aren't up to any funny business."

Dan stands up from his chair and retrieves my cup from the nightstand. "Here, put some of this under your tongue." He fishes out a small pinkish-purple petal and sets it on the nightstand. "It should help return the *spring* to your *step*."

"Drugs?" I croak, familiar with the substance he gave me. SpringStep. It's a flower known for its psychoactive effects on those who eat or smoke it. In lower doses, it provides the user with increased cognitive function and a burst of energy. Being a hunter and forager taught me a lot of things over the passings. Deer and rabbits love it, making it an excellent trap for hunting. If only it weren't so rare—or addictive.

"Prescribed by a doctor," Dan says, pointing a thumb at his chest. "You don't need to take it. It won't help speed up your recovery, but you'll be moving again much sooner."

Nodding, I press the petal underneath my tongue. After a brief moment, my mind slows and my body vibrates. I feel as if I could stand up and walk around with no pain or issue. For the first time in a long time, I can think clearly.

23

The Dinner

It's not uncommon to believe that there may be life beyond our solar system. How many other planets live in a habitable zone like ours?
From the Journal of Azura Seren. Retuno section, 28th orbit

The stench of my wound makes me gag. I don't know how many days I've been stewing in my own filth, but I do not smell good at all. My chest is wrapped tightly in bandages. Dan, over the past few days, has been changing them periodically. The SpringStep helped me recover mentally, but my body still aches with pain.

I force myself out of bed and waddle to the bathroom. I sit down and relieve myself. They figured out their water lines as I had in Hollyard. Apparently, my room is on the first floor of a four-story hotel. Thank the Light I don't have to climb up and down stairs.

Dan and I have had a few conversations, but I haven't met the other crew members. I plan on joining them for dinner now that I can walk by myself. I found out the other members' names are Steeq, Jaime, and Elara. Elara was the one who saved my life. As for the others, I'm not sure what to expect. Apparently Jaime was supposed to keep an eye on me, but I never saw him.

Dan had given me crutches to get around, but I'd rather hobble from place to place without them. They hurt my armpits too much. Missing a few fingers made them even more difficult to use. Whoever invented them clearly never had to use them.

The group eats dinner in the lobby of the hotel. Dan said he'd retrieve me when dinner is ready. He is preparing yams and broccoli, though I've never heard of either.

How is Oberon doing? Is he still alive? I tense up, knowing I've been in recovery for days, maybe a week. I should be out there looking for him. If he was killed by cannibals, there would be no body for me to find.

Holding my left hand up before me, I examine its details. I'd lost these fingers because I tried to save someone's life. They were fingers I didn't use much, but what if there was a cost to every life I wanted to save? I wanted to save Mattias and lost my fingers. I wanted to save Brena and almost killed her. I wanted to save Elara and had my chest torn open. I hadn't been in the city for an hour before I was nearly killed. What am I willing to lose if I want to save Oberon? I'd already lost the Brightest.

Next time I need to keep to myself because I won't be as lucky. Dan nurtured me back to health, but I don't know his true motives, despite his friendly demeanor. For all I know, this group could be cannibalistic as well. I just need to find Oberon and leave the city.

But what about afterward? We can't go back to the Brightest. We'd have to walk alone or maybe join another group dedicated to following the Light. What about Brena?

I push my worries aside. We'll deal with it when we get there. It will be a lot of work, but there's no turning back now. I've already stepped out the door of opportunity, and it locked behind me. Whatever may happen, I will figure it out.

A light knocking comes from my door. "Dinner's ready." It's Dan. I open the door and see him standing there, taking up the entire doorframe. A fat grin paints his face. I can hear people talking and laughing from down the hall. "Come on," he urges.

I hobble my way toward the lobby. Three other people sit at the long table in the center of the room. A maroon tablecloth with an etched floral design drapes over the table, displaying a centerpiece basket of fruit.

"Hey! There he is!" a little man with a thin mustache says in a high-pitched voice. "It's the guy!" I don't know him, yet he acts like he's known me for months. This must be Steeq. Dan described him as excitable and sporadic. Sitting next to him is a teenage boy with long black hair. This must be Jaime. He doesn't share the same enthusiasm as the little man. His gaze is intense, and I can't hide my discomfort. He looks like he knows something about me the others don't.

At the end of the table, next to Jaime, is Elara. Her dark hair parts to one side, resting on her shoulder. Her eyes are a deeper brown than spruce bark soaked in morning mist. They carry an air of intellect unmatched by anything in the Brightest.

"Hey, buddy, that's my sister you're ogling at," Jaime says.

I snap out of the trance I didn't realize I was in. "Your—your sister?" I stammer. "Oh, I'm sorry, I didn't

…" I trail off. The group is so small. "Where is everyone else?"

"Everyone else?" the small mustachioed man, Steeq, says.

"This is it," Dan answers, coming from the kitchen. "Just us four, for now." He sets a large bowl of something mushy and orange in the center of the table. "We call ourselves the Horizon." He takes off his oven mitts and tosses them on the table.

The Horizon. It's a good name; not as good as *the Brightest*. "Why the Horizon?" I ask.

Dan stops in his tracks to think. "Um …" He hesitates, looking at the other members. "Because we couldn't think of anything cooler?" He heads back to the kitchen to bring out more food.

"The Horizon represents a light peeking through the veil of darkness," Elara says. "Our group is dedicated to helping restore the land to how it was nearly six hundred passings ago. Or at least learn the reason why things changed."

"The Freezing of the World?" I ask.

She smirks slightly. I'm not sure if it's one of warmth or pity. "Yep."

Dan places another dish of food on the table. It's a bowl of green florets. They look like miniature trees.

"What is this?" I ask him. I didn't intend disgust to taint my voice.

He points at the bowl of orange paste. "That there is mashed yams." He then points at the bowl of green florets. "And this is steamed broccoli. I told you this earlier. Are you even paying attention?" he teases. I stare at the food, unnerved. He did mention it, but I didn't expect it to look like … or smell like this.

Dan takes a seat at the end and grabs the bowl of yams before scooping some of it onto his plate with a spoon. He passes the bowl to Steeq, who does the same thing. Steeq passes it to Jaime, then Elara, and it eventually lands in my hands. I follow suit. Before I can even set the bowl of yams back in the center of the table. I'm handed the bowl of broccoli. Everyone else already has their servings.

I suppress a gag when the smell of it reaches my nose. I scoop some onto my plate to be courteous. Steeq and Jaime both dig in after I put the bowl back. Dan and Elara take their time. I poke at my food, watching it react to my input.

"Tell us about yourself, Caelius." Dan says.

"Me?"

He nods. "Where are you from? What do you do?" I forget everything I'd ever known about myself. Can I even trust these people? I only just met them. How would I know the Brightest would be safe? "I was in a religious group dedicated to following the Light."

"So why are you here," Jaime says, "and not with them?" His voice is deeper than I expected. I hadn't noticed it earlier.

"Uhh," I drag out, setting my fork down. "I just wasn't a good fit, I guess. So, I left."

"No," Jaime says, shaking his head, "I don't think that's why you left."

"Jaime, be nice." Elara says. Though they all look at me, curious of my answer.

I contemplate for a tense moment before opening my mouth. "The leader, Hadrian, exiled my friend. Before he left, he gave me this pamphlet." I reflexively patted my chest for the item, but it was still in my coat in my room. "I assumed he went here, based on that. I'm just out here looking for him."

"We saw a guy!" Steeq says and then chokes. My heart skips a beat. A piece of broccoli shoots out of his throat and back onto his plate. "Sorry," he says. "There was a guy who came passing through a couple days ago." He puts the broccoli that he ejected back into his mouth and starts chewing. "What's his name?"

I hesitate slightly, trying to guess their angle. "Oberon," I say cautiously. "He's my best friend."

Steeq taps his lips lightly with his fork. "Oberon … Oberon … I think we had an Oberon pass through? Or maybe it was someone else. His name started with an O, I think."

"No," Dan interjects. "Steeq, you're thinking of Petyr." My heart sinks. It wouldn't be that easy, would it?

"Oh, yeah!" Steeq says. "I was close!"

"You weren't even remotely close," Elara says from the end of the table.

"It was by ONE letter!"

Dan turns to me and says, "We'd love to help you find your friend, but we are here on limited time."

I wouldn't want help, even if they did offer. "No, it's okay. It's not your responsibility anyway," I say. "In the morning, I'll head out and continue my search for him."

"No you won't. Not in that condition," Jaime says, darkness covering his expression. I feel a pang of terror. Something about Jaime tells me he's not inexperienced. "If you're going back out into the city, you need to be able to properly defend yourself. Your sword is with me."

My sword! I'd completely forgotten. Did they take it while I was sleeping? "Great, I'll take my sword back. I can handle myself," I say with probably too much arrogance. I've had enough training with Hadrian to know how to use a rapier.

"Clearly not," he says, smirking. "The hole in your chest says otherwise. Meet me in the gym room tomorrow morning after the moon rises. I can tell that this city is unfamiliar to you. If you want to survive, you're gonna need to listen to me."

I nod. Is he speculating or does he know that much about me already? Is he trying to lure me into some sort of trap? Jaime seems to be very intuitive, knowing when something is off. And they all probably trust him.

But what if he really is trying to help?

I stick my first broccoli into my mouth, and it tastes … fine. I can't tell if I like it or not. I feel like it needs something on top of it. Salt maybe? I look around and everyone else is finished with their plates. They stand up and collect their dinnerware for Dan to take back into the kitchen.

I watch Elara head back to her room. I consider following to thank her for saving my life. Would that be too weird? Before I can make a decision, a high-pitched voice makes its presence known. "Hey, new guy. I wanna show you something."

It's Steeq. He's smaller than me, but not by much. His complexion is darker than Jaime and Elara's, but not as dark as Dan's. He's Misuran, like Reyus. Misura is another country south of Solace. The Light had never touched there. Even before the Freezing, the Bright Spot travelled on the same course it does today.

"Uh, yeah, okay," I say, glancing back in the direction of Elara. She'd already rounded the corner.

How much longer could Oberon survive without me?

24

The Polarity

Despite living in a habitable zone, 99.5% of our
planet is completely frozen over at a time.
From the Journal of Azura Seren. Retuno section, 28th
orbit

Steeq's room is on the third floor. He dashes up all the stairs blazingly fast. I attempt to follow, but my wound makes it difficult. I wish I had my crutches. I'm not sure if they would help. They might even make it worse. "Come on!" he urges.

I take a step. A sharp pain flashes through my injured chest. I grunt in pain, clutching the bandages with the remaining fingers on my left hand, while my right hand grips the side rail.

Whatever it is he wants me to see couldn't be *that* important. And it's unlikely to be time-sensitive. "I'm not sure if you know this," I say, heaving. "But I'm quite injured."

Steeq groans hoarsely. "Come on, you can do it!" he encourages ineffectively. I take another step and the pain makes my head spin. A touch of SpringStep right now would go a long way.

"I would suggest the elevator, but the emergency phone is inoperable right now," Steeq says. "Odds are, it hasn't gone through inspection in a long time." What the hell is he talking about?

He's sitting by the time I reach the top of the stairs. He stands up quickly and I slowly follow him to room 403. He pushes the door open revealing his messy bedroom. Inside are around a dozen rectangular metal boxes emitting a faint blue glow. They are stacked on top of eachother in the corner. Each one being about two feet across and one foot in height and depth. Wires dangle from each box, some plugged into the wall, others heading toward a pile of coiled wires.

"What are these?" I ask, still trying to catch my breath. They seem strange and unnatural.

"They're batteries!" he says. "They power the entire building." He must have noticed the confused look on my face because he continues. "They give your room light and hot water—among other things. Just remember to turn your light off when you leave. There's only so much juice in one of these."

"Light? You can create light?" I ask, shocked.

"Well, in a way." He nods, not meeting my eyes. "Essentially, if you can provide enough power through a certain metal, it gets super-hot and glows bright." He smacks the top of one of the batteries and its blue light pulses.

"Sounds like blasphemy," I accuse.

"Sounds like science," he rebuts, eyes wide. There's a gap between his front teeth when he smiles.

I grunt, looking around his room. There is one of these lights on his ceiling as well, except it doesn't have the distracting dome-shaped cover—only a bulb. "So all of this is powered by juice? Which you store in those things?" I point at the batteries.

"Well, not *juice*," he says. "Sorry, poor choice of words. Electricity."

One of these battery things would have been helpful with the Brightest. We wouldn't have much of an application for light, except maybe in the church basement. What else could one of these things do?

"Where did you get all of these? And where do you get the electricity?" The word feels weird on my tongue.

Steeq looks giddy, grinning widely. He shuffles excitedly, shuffling his socked feet on the carpeted floor. "I knew you were a smart cookie," he says. He sticks his index finger out and pokes me on my bare arm. A cracking noise is accompanied by a shock. I flinch, startled. "Like that."

"What was that? Was that electricity?" I ask. "How do you put it in there?"

"It doesn't matter," he dismisses, waving his hand. "What does matter? That you *do not* want to be on the receiving side of one of these bad boys. There's enough raw voltage in here to scramble your brains like an egg. Just let me deal with the electricity, for now."

Steeq grabs something from the corner of his room. It looks quite heavy, especially for him. The object is made of metal and as long as my arm. It looks like a … heavily modified crossbow? If you could even call it that. The upper half had been replaced by a giant opening, like someone took a cylinder and cut it in half lengthways.

Thick copper coils surround the half-cylinder, each about three inches apart from one another.

Steeq pulls out a metal ball from his pocket. It looks like two disconnected halves of a sphere connected by a smaller sphere in the middle. It's about the size of my fist. Had he been carrying that the entire time? He places it into the chamber of the tube and locks it in. "These copper coils are electromagnets, and they are triggered when an electric current passes through, and when they are fully charged, they create a magnetic field that launches anything metal into the chamber at insane speeds!" He says that whole thing without stopping to breathe a single time.

"See that car down there?" He points at one of the rusted metal boxes in the street. "Check this out." He points the tube at the car. "Oh, hold on." He stops himself. "I forgot to reverse the polarity. Ha ha, that would have been really bad." He twists a dial on the device and aims the tube at the car once again. I hear a click and before I can even comprehend what happened, the car's metal bends in and explodes, shaking the building underneath him.

Steeq yells in excitement, "Yeah! That's what I'm talking about! Did you see that!" he says excitedly, pointing at the detritus in the street. He looks like a child trying candy for the first time. "That was so cool!"

I admit, it is pretty cool. I didn't show the same kind of excitement, though. I smile instead. "What would have happened if you didn't reverse the polarity?" I ask.

"Well, the thing I put in there was essentially a grenade with a magnetic fuse," he informs. "So basically, imagine that explosion down there, right here." He shoves the weapon into my hands, and I reluctantly take it.

"Oh." It isn't as cool anymore. We could have died because of a simple mistake. The weight of that idea doesn't strike me as hard as I thought it should. I look around for a place to set the object down. I don't want it to spontaneously explode.

"Aw, man!" Steeq yells. He is looking at a gauge displayed on the battery the weapon was attached to. "That one shot drained this entire battery! All that gone in a second."

"Is that a lot?" I ask.

"I mean, it's only a couple days of power. I'm shocked the battery didn't combust on us. The cable didn't even melt, either. It must have some serious safety measures. We have a ton of other batteries, anyway. I just probably won't be shooting that thing again." He stops speaking for half a second to think. "Maybe I just need to wire in a power regulator. That or get a smaller battery. Well, no, that wouldn't work because …"

I stop listening to him. He's talking to himself now. Being around him is dangerous and I should probably say no next time he wants to show me something. That's if I want to keep the rest of my fingers.

"Oh yeah! I was gonna show you how the batteries recharge," he says.

"Uh." I hesitate. "I think I'm good. I don't really want to risk being blown up for a third time."

"Please!" He gets down on his knees and holds his hands together. I almost laugh at how little it took for him to start begging. "I promise that won't happen."

I sigh, giving in to his pleas and follow him out of the room and into the stairwell. The final flight of stairs is just as painful as the last three. Steeq opens the door and light floods in, leading onto the roof of the hotel. "The geniuses before us came up with a solution," Steeq says, raising his palm toward a couple dozen rectangular black plates. "These are solar panels. To break it down, they convert the sun's energy into power that we can use."

"But what about the nineteen passings when the sun isn't overhead?" I ask, looking toward the sky, squinting.

"A good question," he says. "You don't see them much anymore, but they used to have large wind turbines that converted the power from the wind. Those were quickly torn down after the Freezing for scrap metal. Otherwise, they used a liquid called gasoline, which is long gone now." He moves his hands wildly in explanation. "The cars on the ground used to use gasoline and people could drive around, but gas doesn't have a very long 'shelf life.'"

It's a lot of information to take in at once. I hardly understand his first sentence. "How do you know all this?" I ask.

"Look around you," he says, arms extended. "Everything has—or had—a purpose. If you break it down, you can usually figure it out. Every big, complicated thing is just a mashup of smaller, less complicated things that work together."

It makes sense, although a thought bugs me—one that I can't say out loud. The sun and the Light are a gift to humanity. Before the Freezing, these people took advantage of them and stole their grace, harnessing it for themselves. Could that be why the Light allowed the Darkness to freeze the world? To cleanse it of this evil? Light isn't something you can carry around in your pocket. It's experienced as a blessing.

"We could always use more batteries, if you and Jaime want to go out and look," he says. "Up to you, though. They're pretty hard to come by these days."

I perk up at the opportunity. Maybe I could use this to search for Oberon. Especially with someone who seems to *know* these streets better than I do. But could I trust Jaime? How will I know he won't just stick me with a knife and dump my body somewhere?

Seems like it's a risk I'll have to take.

25

The Truth

Many have tried to speculate what caused the
Freezing of the World.
From the Journal of Azura Seren. Fonalo section, 29th
orbit

My knuckles rap against Dan's door. I couldn't sleep. The pain in my chest kept me from even closing my eyes. Is it morning? I can't tell. City buildings block my view of the sky. The moon is not visible from my window.

Dan's door creaks open. He yawns when he sees me, his body filling the doorframe, eyes heavy. "Caelius, good morning."

"Hey, Dan," I say, shame already accumulating. "You wouldn't happen to have more SpringStep on you?" My hands nervously run through my hair.

"You know that stuff is highly addictive right?" He sighs. "I wondered if this would be an issue. I assumed you already knew."

"No, it's okay," I reassure. "I knew what I was getting into when I took it. I just need something to relieve the pain so I can sleep."

"Well, SpringStep won't help you sleep, if that's what you're looking for. I have some other remedies if you—"

He doesn't finish his sentence when I cut him off. "SpringStep is fine. I'm already awake. Plus Jaime wants to practice or something." I bite my cheek.

Dan nods and turns around, leaving his door open. He opens a cabinet door under his sink and rummages through the mess of bottles. "I'll get you your SpringStep," he says while searching. "He wants you to practice with him? Doesn't he see what kind of condition you're in? Why not tell Jaime you can't?"

"Because I feel like he won't let me leave until I've proven to him I can handle myself in the city."

Dan stuffs his fingers inside a toilet paper tube and pulls out a small bag of a dozen or so purple petals. "Yeah, you're probably right," he says, picking out three petals from the bag. "Don't let anyone know you have these." He places the petals in my outstretched palm. "Especially Steeq."

I feel relief just by touching the petals. I need to be careful and ration these out over the next few days. I can't rely on Dan.

What if that's the point? Maybe Dan is trying to make me depend on him so I'll stay. Maybe that's what happened to Steeq. "Why not Steeq?" I ask, curiously.

"It doesn't matter," he dismisses, rubbing his eyes. "Steeq has a few things he needs to work on."

Before I can pry further, he says, "Don't overexert yourself with Jaime today, okay? You're not invincible."

I give him a nod and he yawns, closing the door.

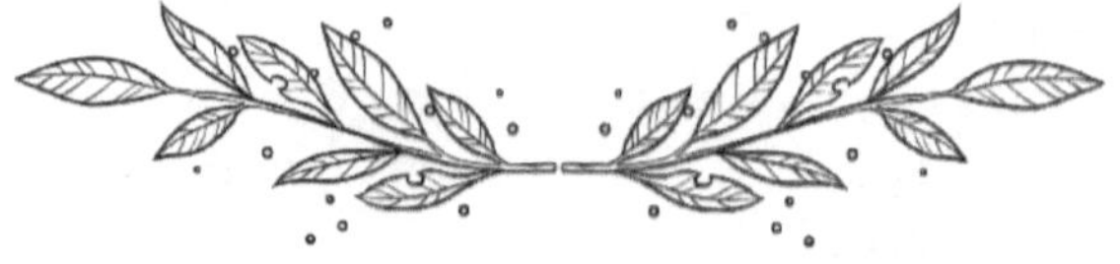

I find Jaime in the weight room, practicing. The weight room was hard to find being so far removed from the rest of the building. I'd gone down the same hallway multiple times before realizing it was a loop.

The weight room smells of rubber and sweat. Red paint peels from the walls. Foam tiles lay on the ground, providing soft padding under my feet. Dumbbells line the floor, next to a bench. On the other side of the room is a large rack, mounted to the wall. Dozens of swords, knives, axes, and other weapons hang. There are more weapons in this room than in the Brightest. Jaime sits on the bench wearing a baggy white suit. His greasy black hair is unruly over his face.

"Finally," he says, forcing himself to stand. "Took you long enough. You ready to show me your skills?"

"Not really," I say. The effects of the SpringStep course through my veins, giving me energy. I'd forgotten my chest is still wounded. The pain is completely nullified.

"Great! Don't forget to stretch." Jaime stretches his arms from side to side and rolls his neck.

"I'm still pretty weak. I'm not sure if I'm in the best shape to fight," I lie, testing to see his reaction. I'm actually feeling really good, eager to hold my sword again.

"Ah, don't worry about that," he says, waving a hand. "That SpringStep should help."

I'm caught off guard. "How did you know I—"

"I didn't until you confirmed it." He smiles, changing the subject. "No one is ever ready to fight, but everyone must when they need to. I'll go easy on ya."

Hadrian said the same thing about being ready. I stretch my arms and legs and spot my sword on a weapon rack, distinguished by the symbol embossed on the guard. Good to see that it's safe and respected, rather than in a box somewhere. But how did he know I was on SpringStep?

"What size are you?" Jaime asks.

"Huh?"

"Probably large," he answers himself. He unhooks a matching white suit from the closet and tosses it toward me. "Judging by your rapier, you're probably used to épée. Right-handed, I assume?" He smirks, looking at my disfigured left hand. He pulls out a sword shaped similarly to my own and places it beside me.

I hold the weapon and it fits my right hand well, but nowhere near my own. There's an acorn-sized ball on the tip of the rapier. I run a finger down the length of the dulled blade.

The white bodysuit is baggy but not heavy. The new sword feels odd in my hand and I have to readjust my grip multiple times.

Jaime hands me a dome-shaped mask. I put it on and Jaime does the same. Jaime is easily visible through the black mesh filter. He sets his stance, holding his sword at an angle.

"You ready?" he asks. I position myself in the same way that Hadrian taught. Legs apart, arm bent at the elbow, body to the side to minimize exposed surface area.

"Ready as I'll never be."

"En garde!" I flinch, but Jaime doesn't attack; instead, he studies me. I know better than to engage quite yet. We rotate around the arena, our steps mirroring each other's.

After a bit of stalling, he thrusts at me, testing the waters. I block, returning an attack, scoring a strike by poking him in the chest. That was too easy.

"Good one," he says through his own mask. "Again. Ready? En garde!" This time, he leaps forward. I don't have time to react before the safety tip of his sword sinks into my suit, scoring a hit against me. My chest stings in pain in response to the pressure. I grunt sucking in through my teeth and ready myself again. I'd expected the SpringStep to completely nullify the pain.

He tries the same thing next round. I'm ready for it and block. He weaves an attack through my block and scores another hit on me. "Gotcha," he teases, a smile in his voice. We continue practicing.

He's testing my skill level. He's adjusting his attack patterns and moves accordingly to examine which areas I excel at, and which ones need improvement. Although I am embarrassed about not being as good as he is. But I see this as an opportunity to learn and get better. He has likely been training for his entire life. Hadrian is no longer around, but at least I can continue practicing my skills.

"You know," Jaime says in between rounds, "it's nice to finally have someone to train with." This catches me off guard more than any sword attack. He pulls off his mask and I do the same, figuring we are finished. "Everyone here is just so smart and I'm their dumb fighter boy." He drops the mask and kicks it across the room. "They're all too busy to spar with me. It's all lies. I see right through it all. You don't exactly match my skills, but if you decide to stick around, maybe we could spar more."

"Everyone seems to have a different skill set here. Which is great for a group of people, especially for one so small."

He grunts. "They say Elara's the smart one. She may be book smart, but Light, she lacks any common sense." He chuckles before continuing, "I don't know what she was thinking, going into the city alone with no weapons."

He places his left hand on my shoulder. "Thank you again for saving my sister's life. There isn't a single thing on this planet that could replace her."

"Ah, you don't need to thank me," I say. "To be fair, she saved my life too." He nods in appreciation of that. I can't help but ask the burning question. "Do you know what she was doing out there when I found her? What was she looking for?"

"No," he says. "I have no clue. You'll have to ask her."

I feel a pressing against my sternum. I look down and the safety tip of Jaime's sword pokes my stomach. "Gotcha." He grins.

Steeq mentioned wanting more batteries for his experiments. Jaime was on board when I brought the idea up to him, but I didn't mention I mostly wanted to go to get an idea of the city's layout. The map on the pamphlet was helpful to an extent, but I needed a better reference point.

Jaime and I leave the hotel and head out into the expansive city. The tension in the air is lessened around him after our sparring lesson.

The street ahead is littered with potholes. Each step must be careful. I don't want to trip. My rapier hangs comfortably from my belt, swaying side to side. Jaime opted to bring a different weapon with him—a mace with a sturdy handle. It's shorter than my rapier, making it easier for him to carry and equip.

"So, batteries." I attempt at small talk. "Where do you guys even find them? How come I haven't seen one until today?"

The wind blows and dark hair blocks his view. "They're in about ninety percent of buildings. Either on the first floor or in the basement. Although less than a quarter are still salvageable. Some smaller towns usually have just one or two inside their town hall."

I don't remember seeing these batteries in Hollyard. Though we never explored its town hall. Are they really able to provide power to every house in the town?

"Are they heavy?" I ask.

"They can be," he says. "Usually two people can carry one. They're just more cumbersome than anything. Once it's on a cart, it's not too bad."

"How did you guys get the batteries into Steeq's room on the fourth floor? And why?"

"Steeq is a maniac. Dan figured if he blew himself up on the fourth floor, the hotel wouldn't collapse, like it would if he were on the first floor. As for how we got it up there ... we used the elevators."

"He mentioned that word," I blurt. "He said I couldn't use the elevators because they didn't pass inspection, or something."

"Yeah, he probably thought he was being funny. But he mostly comes off as an ass."

The street we walk down sprouts more red and yellow brick buildings. Dull green vines creep from the top of the tallest structure to the ground below. "I know you couldn't give more of a damn about finding batteries for Steeq," he says. "You want to look for your friend."

I nod, but he's not looking at me. "That's why I'm here," I say instead. "I just hope I find him soon."

"You probably won't," Jaime says honestly. "This city is too big and dangerous. Crits woulda got him by now."

My heart sinks, knowing he's likely right. There's no way I'll find him. How do I even know he's in the city? That pamphlet could have just been a memento to remember him by. Was it even his? What if Oberon went a different direction?

Is this how Lyria felt? Searching for someone, her son, knowing the search is futile? Knowing that they are likely dead? Holding on to hope because it's the only thing she has left? It's crushing. And then someone unknown, strings her up by her neck. Or did she …

He notices the despair on my face. "Hey, it's okay. We've all lost someone. For me and Elara, it was our mother."

"So how are we bringing back these batteries to Steeq?" I ask, changing the subject. "I'm not in any condition to haul something heavy."

"We aren't," he says. "Steeq still thinks they're pretty rare and I want him to continue thinking that. I just wanted to get out, stretch my legs and maybe kill a couple of Crits."

"Crits?"

"You know, the cannibals who have specifically evolved to be cannibalistic? Stout legs, sharp teeth?"

"Right," I drawl. I vaguely remember Pladd using the term during one of our talks. I didn't know what he meant until now.

"Not sure who recently coined the term, but it stuck." He grins, stopping to hide behind an orange car. "I've been dying to wipe out this clan for a while now." I shuffle quickly to hide next to him. "That there," he says, pointing to the yellow building behind us, "is a hive. I'm pretty sure it's the same group that attacked you and Elara."

"How are you planning to 'wipe them out?'"

He pulls out a small disk-shaped object, about the size of his palm. "Remember when I said we aren't bringing any batteries back?"

26

The Hive

*Society was very technologically advanced before
the Freezing. A lot more advanced than we
realize.*
From the Journal of Azura Seren. Fonalo section, 29th
orbit

Before we go in, there's** something you should know," Jaime starts. "Crits aren't necessarily human, which is good for us in one regard." He passes the disk to his other hand. "They kinda act like bees. In a way."

"Bees?" I squint my eyes, confused.

"You know, the fuzzy little guys with stingers?"

"I know what bees are." I roll my eyes.

"Oh," he says, taken aback. "You see, a beehive works because everything revolves around the queen. Workers come and go, feeding and protecting the queen. But if you remove or even kill the queen of the hive, the bees will do either one of two things. Appoint a new queen or slowly die off. Crit hives act similarly. Once news gets out that their queen is dead, they assign a new one or …" Jaime makes a cutting motion with his hand at his neck.

Interesting.

"So, we just gotta sneak in, kill the queen, sneak out," he says. "Or we blow the joint. Personally, I like the second option better." He chuckles to himself.

I didn't want to be a part of this. I didn't want to kill more people than I had to. How dare Jaime drag me into this. I could leave. I have my weapon. There's nothing else of mine at the hotel.

But Jaime is right to an extent. These Crits have been an issue with the Brightest as well. The fewer Crit hives there are, the safer the Bright Spot is. I have to take lives to save lives.

Jaime chose to kill to save others from needing to do so. Perhaps it is time for me to make that decision. I'll kill who I must, to save more.

"Come on," he says, sneaking toward the front door. I stay behind, peering over the stationary car. He lightly pushes the door open, holding his mace tightly in his hand. I can't see what's inside, but I watch him peer in, looking around. He turns and gives me a thumbs-up, signaling it's safe for me to follow. Wary of any attackers nearby, I sneak low toward the building, footsteps quiet, like how I would in the forest.

The building seems empty. A hallway stretches forward before turning sharply right. Two doors on the left, one door on the right. The place gives an uneasy feeling, smelling of mildew and vegetation. The hallway is dark, not illuminated like the hotel. Did they even have a battery?

"So, we are just going to walk right through the front doors?" I whisper, stepping softly on the short carpet.

Jaime quietly twists the handle of the first door on the left. It swings inward and he equips a cylinder-shaped object from his belt. I hear a click and the room is illuminated by a large circle of light. "This place doesn't have a back door, to my knowledge," he says. "Plus, it's more fun this way." This guy seems just as thirsty for the thrill as Steeq. Both men tiptoe on the edge of death.

The room is empty, save for a few chairs and desks. Jaime turns to the next room on the right side of the hallway. He pushes the door open revealing a much larger room. The floor is tile and six tables spread throughout the space. A counter edges along the wall. This must be a dining room.

Jaime sighs. "I wonder if I chose the wrong building." In the dim light, I see him biting his lip. "It's probably safe. Typically, these places would be trashed if there was a Crit hive."

He continues searching anyway, turning down the hall at the end. There's a stairwell that splits, one heading to the second floor, the other heading to the basement. "Do you think there's a battery down there?" I ask, not sure what else to say.

"Probably. Let's at least get the lights turned on and scavenge what else we can find here."

Feet still quiet, we head down the stairwell into the basement. The pain of climbing upstairs yesterday lingers in my mind. I didn't have SpringStep to nullify the pain like I do now.

The basement is musky and humid. I gag reflexively at the rancid smell. Jaime breathes out through his mouth. "Whew. Yeah, something died down here." I pinch my nose shut with my left pinky and palm, equipping my rapier in my other hand. I don't feel safe.

A blue glow emanates from the corner of the large open room. Jaime shines his light on it, revealing a battery, just like one in Steeq's room.

He turns his flashlight, examining the room a bit. Blood pools on the floor; bones pile in corners. I feel as if I'm going to hurl. Cautiously, Jaime steps toward the large battery and flips a switch.

Lights blind me and the entire room is illuminated with harsh sterile light. The pink-stained tiles hide the white underneath. There are a lot more bones than I thought.

On the wall in front of me, words are written in blood: "REJOYS 4 THE NEW QUEEN."

"Darking hell. Crits have been here." He looks around the room, frustrated, brows sharp. "A new queen? Darking bastards. Where could they have gone?" His flippant use of the swear discomforts me.

Underneath the words is a symbol—a crude drawing of a wolf's head. "Is that their insignia?" I ask.

He sighs. "Yeah. This was a Kreetur hive. They're typically the dumbest of the clan types. It's uncharacteristic of them to do something as smart as relocating bases." He rubs at his hairless chin. "Maybe they know something we don't?"

Hearing that makes the hair on the back of my neck stand straight up. There are different types of Crits? "Jaime, let's get out of here," I say shakily.

"Agreed." He pulls out that disk object and places it carefully on the side of the battery. He pushes a button on the front face, and it produces a single soft beep. He unplugs the device from the side and puts it back into his pocket.

"What did you just do?" I ask.

"We got about a minute before this place blows. Just run."

My SpringStep-enhanced legs move and I sprint up the stairs, Jaime right behind me. I don't feel any pain. What a miracle plant.

We charge down the hallway on the ground level. We'd only explored two rooms on this floor, yet the third room's door is wide open. It's fully lit up and I catch a glimpse of a figure standing in the middle. A child.

I stop in my tracks. Jaime runs into me and we nearly topple over. He sees the kid as well. The child's gender is ambiguous; their black greasy hair grows long over their eyes. Their legs are stout, and a row of pointed teeth hide behind their lips.

"Jaime, that's a kid," I say, in shock. I feel my heart beating rapidly. Everything tells me to run and leave the child behind, but I'm paralyzed.

"It's a Crit," he says. "Leave him." He runs, but I can't move.

The kid wears ragged clothes with no shoes. They hold some kind of stuffed animal. Dirt, blood, and fear cover their face. "Come on, buddy," I say, outstretching my hand. "We need to go now." Worry poisons my words. "Please, you need to get out of here."

A pit forms in my stomach and the kid doesn't move. Blood covers their thumb in a ring. Does this child still suck their thumb? What if this is Tommy, Lyria's son?

My legs move and I reach for the child just as an arm grabs my other wrist tightly. I'm dragged away from the room and out the front doors into the sunlight.

Not a second passes before the building rumbles and fire spews from the entrance. Jaime releases my hand and adrenaline takes over, making me run swiftly from the burning building.

The child was still in there when it blew. I take many large breaths before I can speak again. "Light burn you, Jaime!"

27

The Tomato

*The humans before the Freezing seemed to have
had the ability to communicate almost
instantly. Someone in the Mino section could
communicate with someone in the Cayano section
in seconds.*
From the Journal of Azura Seren. Fonalo section, 29th
orbit

Jaime and I walked back in silence. He tried saying a few things to me, but he knew I was upset at him for leaving the child. There were so many things I wanted to tell him, but I kept my mouth shut to avoid saying something I'd regret.

I'd felt the effects of SpringStep wear off on the walk back. I was tempted to take another petal, but I stopped myself. I didn't know when I might need it again. My chest wound had been healing quicker than normal. Dan said the

SpringStep wouldn't help speed up recovery, but he may be wrong.

The lobby of the hotel is empty when we arrive. Jaime returns to his weight room, and I search for Dan. I needed someone to talk to—someone normal. The Crit child's face is burned into my memory.

Turning down the hallway on the first floor, I knock on Dan's door. There's no response. I knock again. Is he even in there? I wait a couple of seconds.

Groaning, I walk toward the elevator's steel doors down the hall. I press a button and the doors slide open to a small room. Hesitantly, I step in and the doors close behind me.

A panel of buttons is flush against the wall, near the door. I press the button labeled "4," and it illuminates. A moment later, the entire room shakes and shifts. There's a feeling of unease in my stomach. My hands tightly grip the bar on the wall.

After couple of seconds, there's a chime and the doors slide open, revealing the hallway I was just in. I step out, the floor feeling strange and uneven. Looking around, I realize I'm on the fourth floor now, not the first.

How did that work? Steeq might know, but I'd rather not listen to another lengthy explanation. Walking down the hallway, I find room 403 and knock on the door.

A few seconds pass before it swings open. His eyes are wide and his pupils are dilated. Purple stains his skin under his nose. He looks panicked.

"Steeq," I say, concern in my voice, "are you okay?"

"What?" he says, looking at something behind me. "I'm fine. What? What is it? What do you want?" He speaks fast like he's trying to get me to leave.

"Have you seen Dan?"

"If he's not in his room or in the kitchen, he's out back with his greenhouse. Anything else?"

"No, I …" Before I can finish the sentence, he closes the door on me. Should I be concerned? I shut my eyes and take a deep breath. His problems are not my own.

Behind the hotel are two clear tents. The dome-shaped tent stands about eight feet in height. The smaller box-shaped tent is attached to a wagon with wheels. I see the dark moving outline of Dan inside the standing dome-shaped tent.

Pushing open the curtains, I'm hit with a wave of heat and humidity. Sweat drips from my forehead and I nearly choke on the thick air. Dan pours water on a budding sprout with a watering can that is way too small for his hands.

"Expel all negative energy before you enter," he says softly without looking at me.

"What?" Negative energy? What does that even mean?

"Plants are living things too. They are affected by negative energy and moods. Just like us." He sets his watering can down on a nearby shelf and meets my eyes. "The best way is to take a deep breath in." He shows by example. "Hold it. And then let it out." He exhales. "Let your worries and frustration go with it."

I'd just watched a helpless child die. If this negative energy is truly inside me, it's not leaving for a while. Still, I humor the man and try to do as he says, taking a breath in, holding it and letting it out. The exhale is shaky and I find myself gasping for the next inhale.

"I know you think it's stupid," he says. "When I was younger, my parents taught me a lesson. They gave me two pots of soil. Both contained a single tomato seed." Dan bends down and picks up a small empty pot. "They told me to grow each one equally. To provide them with the same amount of nutrients, and to water both at the same time every day."

Dan always seemed very wise. I needed to discuss something with him, but it can wait. I always want to hear what he has to say, even if it isn't relevant.

"They requested I give a plant praise and recognition. So that's what I did. I'd admire the plant verbally, complementing its leaves and growth. I'd tell it that I believed in it. That it would create the biggest, reddest, juiciest tomato. And sure enough, over the next few weeks, it did. I haven't been able to grow a tomato like that one since.

"The other seed," Dan continues, "I was to berate, yell at, discourage. But I wasn't allowed to touch it. I'd explain how terrible it was. How its leaves were disgusting and undesirable. I'd tell it that it didn't have a reason to exist, that it was worthless. I'd even compare it to the other tomato plant, saying that the other was so much better.

"I did that every single day. Without fail—the tomato plant that I fed my 'negative' energy to—wilted and died. It didn't even have a chance to bear fruit."

I reflect on the words before picking up on a possible inconsistency. "Your parents used bad soil. Or poison maybe."

Dan smiles and nods. "I thought the same thing. When they gave me the already potted plants, I transferred them both into new pots with fresh soil," he says. "Seeing it firsthand changed my perspective completely."

I didn't realize until now that Dan's speaking put me at ease. I'd forgotten what I even wanted to talk about. Like my negative energy *had* disappeared. Dan plucks a tomato gently from a plant and places it in my hand. It's smooth to the touch.

"That's why we shed our negativity before entering the greenhouse." He stands up straight with confidence. His bald head grazes the supporting bar on the ceiling.

I hold the tomato upward to get a better look at it. "How'd you do this? How do you *grow* plants? It's like you're creating something out of nothing?"

Dan smiles. His bright white teeth contrast against his dark complexion. "How patient are you?"

The next hour consists of Dan unloading information on the process of gardening. He discusses soil and its properties. He goes over the intricacies of nitrogen and the process of photosynthesis. Plants need sunlight to survive. It's their food.

A question bugs me as I sit at the dinner table an hour later. If plants feed on sunlight, what happened to the vegetation outside of the Bright Spot, absent from the sun's touch? I previously assumed they died, but that theory doesn't seem to hold up when I really think about it. Trees and vines grow as if they'd been growing for hundreds of passings.

Dinner is another concoction of vegetables, like the previous night. Dan made a salad with lettuce, spinach, and, of course, tomatoes. We all collect our plates and sit at the table. The vegetables are passed around so we can pick and choose which to add to our plates.

I decide to hesitantly give everything a try, filling my plate. Steeq digs in first, ravenously tearing apart the salad. The leaves crunch in his mouth as he chews. Jaime follows suit, with a bit more civility than Steeq. I lean closer to

Elara nervously. I hadn't had a chance to talk to her since I arrived. "Hey," I say. "I never got to say th—"

I'm interrupted by Dan's booming voice. "We are glad you decided to stay with us another night, newcomer." He sets down another bowl of vegetables, fresh carrots. "You've told us what you're doing in the city; why don't you tell us more about yourself?"

Elara looks at me, smirking slightly. I hope she knows what I was trying to convey.

"Well …," I say, "what do you want to know?"

"Whatever you're willing to tell us," he says, sitting down. "What did you do before coming to Solace?"

All eyes turn to me, expecting a response. I hate being the center of attention. I consider concealing the truth, but they've been nothing but kind and hospitable toward me.

"I was a hunter for my old group," I say. "Deer, mostly." I take a bite of my salad before setting the fork down.

"Huh," Jaime scoffs. "Never heard of a hunter with a sword. How'd killing deer go for you?" He talks as if we hadn't spent the afternoon together training and blowing up a building. Maybe he's putting on an act for the table.

"I had a crossbow, but I'm not sure where it went," I say. "Had to retire when …" I lift up my left hand, exposing the lack of fingers.

"You haven't told anyone what happened to your hand. It must have been recent then. Not like you lost them in the womb?" Steeq asks.

"There was a hunting mishap," I say, trying to leave out the minor details. "A friend fell into a cold river and I jumped in to save him."

"Is that the same friend you're looking for?" Steeq asks again before I could explain.

"No," I say, solemnly. "That person died. I couldn't save him." No one says a word for a while. The only sounds in the room are forks clinking against bowls and the crunch of lettuce as people stab and eat their food.

"Frostbite is a nasty condition," Dan says, steering the conversation. "You're lucky you only lost your fingers. How long were you in the water? A minute? Five minutes?"

"I don't … I can't remember." I cringe. I'd forgotten how traumatic the event truly was. I really *did* kill Mattias.

"Well, I admire that you go out of your way to try to save people—even ones you don't know," Elara says next to me, smiling. She sets a hand on my wrist, giving it a slight squeeze. "It really shows what kind of person you are."

Her touch sends a chill through me. Jaime rolls his eyes from across the table, trying to break up our moment. "So what kind of group were you in? A military caravan or something?"

Elara pulls away. "No," I say, "it was more of a religious group. We followed the Path at the front of the Bright Spot."

"The Path huh?" Jaime's eyebrow raises. "You should be near the Octoro Bridge by now. What are you doing so far behind?"

"I don't know." I shrug, feeling the tension in the room. How much did Jaime know of the Path? "Our leader, Father Hadrian, wanted to take a break in the town south of here."

"Uh-huh," he says, crossing his arms. "Some kind of Path follower you are."

"Oh yeah?" I say, offended. "What do you follow?"

"I follow the Chosen," he says.

Dan interrupts before I can open my mouth. "Let's change the subject, shall we? Steeq, what did you do today?"

Jaime and Elara both roll their heads and get up. They collect their empty plates and Steeq recounts his *entire* day to Dan. He includes unimportant things like when he picked at his teeth for a bit of food, or when he went to the bathroom, going into an excruciating amount of detail.

I pick up my plate too, having eaten my entire serving. I meet Elara at the kitchen sink. "Help me wash?" she asks, handing me a sponge. In the Brightest, I wasn't typically the one washing dishes, but I knew how. I start working on my own plate first, scrubbing in circles.

"I'm sorry about my brother," she says. "He thinks that anyone who doesn't share the same beliefs is wrong."

"What does he believe in?"

"Hell if I know." She sighs. "He's tried them all, including the Path. He says he's lost, looking for a purpose—a higher power to believe in. He says he follows *the Chosen* but I know it's just a phase—like all the other ones."

"What do you believe in?"

"People. Data. Patterns that don't lie to you. I can't imagine a god existing in a world like this one."

I give her idea some consideration. Maybe she's right. Perhaps I've been following the wrong thing. Maybe Jaime is right in his own regard. What kind of follower of the Path am I?

"You know," I say, "I thought I was worshipping a god, the Light. Turns out I've been worshipping a man the entire time."

She smiles, putting a plate on a drying rack. "I think there might be a piece of the true god in all of us." She adds, "It's not the human side that makes someone jump in a river after someone, or protect them from a rabid Crit." She grabs my wet hand with one of hers. "Thank you again."

28

The Seed

*Some speculate that they killed God, which
caused the Freezing of the World.*
From the Journal of Azura Seren. Fonalo section, 29th
orbit

I'm woken up by three distinct taps on my door. Dan? Sluggishly, I get dressed and open the door. Behind it is not Dan, but Elara. "Hey," she says. I quickly adjust my hair, but she'd already seen my bedhead.

"What's up?" I ask, wanting to lean against the doorframe. She looks tired. How long had she been awake?

"Can I ... ask you something?" she says timidly. "Actually it might be better if I just show you." She waves, and I follow her to a room a few doors from mine. She twists the handle and the door swings open into a bright room. The beds have been removed, and the lighting is sterile. The colors are cold and harsh compared to the warmer colors of my own rest area. There is no carpet, only white tile flooring. This used to be a bedroom?

A counter against the wall holds an odd-looking device and the porous stone Pladd had given me. I thought I'd lost it, but here it is. "Dan found that stone in your pocket while he was treating you. He thought it was odd— and honestly, so did I. I've never come across anything quite like it. Take a look through the microscope and maybe you'll see what I mean."

The microscope holds a panel with a small pinch of dust. I peer through the lens to find thousands, maybe millions of oval-shaped objects. Each one looks like a sandbur with hundreds of individual hairs. "What am I looking at?" I ask.

"I ground down a piece of the stone and placed the shavings on the panel," she explains. "The odd thing is, those grains you see aren't stone. It looks like microscopic seeds concentrated into a single object.

"Here's what a sedimentary rock looks like under a microscope," she continues, removing the glass panel and replacing it with another. The grains in this are much bigger, each being a different size and color. "Interesting huh?"

"So, this weird stone isn't actually a stone?"

"That's what it seems like. But not until viewed up close." I pull away from the microscope, and she removes the sedimentary panel, setting it aside. She leans on the counter, a strand of hair slipping loose to dangle by her cheek. "Where did you find this?" She picks up the seed-rock, holding it with her forefinger and thumb.

I remember Pladd pressing his fingers into the bark of the tree. The bark seemed to move around them, exposing the strange rock in the center. "A friend found it," I say. "It was lodged in some tree." Should I still call Pladd my friend—after what his group did to mine?

"Do you think maybe it's a tree seed? I've never seen a tree seed look like this."

Dan's gardening instructions are still fresh in my mind. "I guess there's one way to find out."

Elara and I leave the research room and make our way to the back door. Outside, Dan is facing away, tending to his plants, trimming dead ends. Stray stems and leaves fall to the ground. It's strange, seeing someone so broad and imposing nurture something so small and delicate.

"Dan," Elara says. The man peeks over his shoulder, meeting our eyes. He sets down his trimmers to give his full attention. He gives us a welcoming smile. "Remember that rock Caelius had? I did some research, and I don't think it's a rock. I think it may be some kind of seed."

He perks up at that. "Oh?" He sounds perplexed. "It didn't look like a seed to me. I would have known." His brows tighten. "Do you have it with you? Can I look at it again?"

Elara summons the seed-rock from her pocket and places it into Dan's outstretched hand. He pulls it closer to his face, inspecting it with one eye. "It's not one seed," Elara explains. "It's thousands, maybe millions of tiny seeds, all clumped together. We are thinking maybe it's a seed for a tree, but I don't know."

"Well, that wouldn't make any sense. Plants usually just need one seed to grow, not millions," he says.

"That's why we came to you. Caelius found it lodged in a tree somewhere. Could it be anything else?"

Dan thinks for a moment before speaking. "I have an open spot over there." He points to a long planter box— about three feet wide. "I can plant it there if you'd like. If it sprouts in a couple days, we'll know what it is. If not, then maybe it's not a seed."

A couple days? I don't have a couple of days. I need to search for Oberon. Maybe I should leave today. I'm feeling much better, although not fully recovered. I nod anyway to give him the go-ahead. Maybe I'll come back once Oberon is with me. How would he integrate with the group? I could see him and Jaime butting heads often.

Dan digs a small hole in the center of the box. The planter box already has four plants sprouting, two on each side of the hole. The rock-seed seems large in comparison to the growing buds.

He covers the planted stone back up with dirt. "Time will tell what grows." Dan smiles. "Don't worry, I'll take care of it. Remember what I said about positive energy?" I nod my head again. "You two can go do … *something else.*" He gestures a shooing motion with his hands, so we leave. A pit grows in my stomach. I feel like we planted something very dangerous.

29

The Scars

*Others speculate the sun is dying. But that makes
just as much sense as God dying.*
From the Journal of Azura Seren. Fonalo section, 29th
orbit

I make the decision and knock on Jaime's door. He's the last person I want to see or talk to, but I need his help. After a minute of waiting, it swings open, and he stands there wearing loose gray clothing. His room is a mess. Clothes lie on the floor. The bedsheets are bunched up, not attached to the mattress. Drawings and maps hang crookedly from the dark gray walls. He truly lives like this? "What's up?" he asks.

I can't get the image of the child Crit out of my head. He killed him and felt no remorse. "I want to search for my friend," I say. "You are the best-trained person here and I want you to come with." I dread his response, hoping he'll say yes, but also hoping he'll say no.

He looks at me for a second. He's not contemplating, just looking. He's already made up his mind. He doesn't want to come with me. I'll have to look for Oberon in the city—alone. The city filled with dangerous cannibals and murderers. I feel a queasiness in my stomach.

"Sure," he says.

"What?" My head jerks forward. I wasn't expecting him to say yes.

"Yeah, I'll go with you." He turns, going back into his room, but he leaves the door open. He walks to his dresser and pulls out a drawer filled with clothes. "There's a problem though. I don't think you realize how massive this city is. Do you have a plan?"

He talks as if nothing happened. That killing children is something he does every day. Pladd's group would kill children to spare them from living in this world alone. I remember how I'd nearly killed Brena. I remember how it affected me, days after. That was an accident. The explosion, however, wasn't. But Jaime didn't know beforehand there was a child present.

"No." I shrug. "I don't. I was thinking about maybe going through the buildings nearby and searching for him."

"Ha, yeah, the Darkness will be here before we've covered the entire south side of Solace." He takes off his shirt and tosses it onto the messy bed. He rummages through his drawer, searching for another shirt to replace it with.

His body is lined with scars and cuts. Some are still fresh; others bear the color of age. I know he's younger than me, but how much more pain has he experienced?

"I suggest," he starts, sliding a shirt over his bare skin, "we take out more hives." His black hair is flattened by the shirt and touches the base of his nose. I meet his eyes and he's not joking. "As disturbing as it sounds, Crits like to collect souvenirs from their victims. If Oberon had been found, we'd see his belongings on a dead Crit."

My heart twists at the idea. If we find some of Oberon's belongings, that would imply he is dead. But if we don't, then we would be searching every Crit camp in Solace. An overwhelming feeling of doubt washes over me, followed by more dread. "What does he typically carry with him?" Jaime asks.

I don't even want to answer. "Usually his crossbow and bolts." I look down at the ground, missing my friend, knowing his daughter misses him even more. "Maybe some rocks. His daughter paints them for him."

I look up at his walls, ignoring the next thing Jaime says. A charcoal diagram depicts two figures. On the left is a human, standing tall, arms outstretched to the side. On the right is an abomination—a Crit. It's shorter than the human depiction. Its pelvis is a lot lower, and arms are much longer. Each hand has claws that extend almost double the length of each finger. The teeth are sharp, like Pladd's. Are they born like that?

I turn to look at an overhead view of Solace. The scale of it is mind-numbing. The pamphlet's map in my coat pocket doesn't do the city justice compared to this one. Thumbtacks staple themselves into specific points on the map. Underneath the tacks are symbols drawn in bright red. To the left of the map is a legend, depicting the symbols and their respective names.

"The Claw," depicted with a crude drawing of a clawed hand is the first group listed, followed by a symbol of a scythe with the label "Shearing." Underneath is a wolf head, like the one we saw in the basement of the first building. "Kreeturs," the label reads. All the symbols spread randomly throughout the map.

"Crits tend to group up and form their own cultish clans, staying away from other factions." Jaime looks at the map with me. "It's fun watching two Crit groups start a clan war. It's more fun to cause one. It's a bloody, messy good time."

"How do they know who is who? They look so similar."

"They don't. In many cases, they tear their own people apart. The three main groups have their tells, but they aren't distinct. Kreeturs are known as the dumbest, but most fierce. Some clans, maybe all of them, have a type of pheromone that they emit, but in the heat of battle, I bet it's hard to tell who's who."

Was Pladd part of one of these clans? Other than the sharpened teeth, I would have never guessed him to be a Crit. He did mention he was in a group of Crits, but not that he was born into one. "When I was with the Brightest," I start, "we captured a cannibal. I don't think he was a Crit though. We were attacked shortly after. Could those pheromones have something to do with that?"

"Absolutely," he says. "They can be recognized by a member of the same clan for dozens of miles. As long as they eat the same food and practice their culture, they'll emit pheromones like any other."

"You mean human flesh?"

"Yes, human flesh."

I knew the raid really wasn't Pladd's fault, but it's nice to see it confirmed. Though he could have said something. Maybe he wanted to, but it was already too late.

On the map, circled in blue, is a square with the word "HOTEL." I assume that's where we are. A couple of blocks north is a crossed-off red Kreetur symbol, a crude wolf head.

"Rotten despicable things," Jaime says. "I want to wipe them all out from this side of the Bright Spot." He shakes his head. "The Crit hunter groups ain't doing a damn thing. If you are going to find your friend, we should look in one of these places."

I nod. I can't sit around and wait any longer. Even if Oberon is dead, I need to know for sure that he's gone. At least I could say I tried. What of the writing on the wall, spread with blood? "Rejoice for the new queen." Despite being straight to the point, the message seems cryptic. What did it mean?

I feel ridiculous even thinking it, but what if they appointed Oberon as their new queen. Despite his pitfalls, Oberon is charismatic. I'd describe his humor as crude but maybe he'd fit right in. He's not helpless. Maybe he killed the old queen, and they appointed him as the new one. Could that even work?

"Jaime," I say looking intently at the symbols on the map, "what do you think of hunting down just the Kreetur camps? I want to know more about this new queen."

A corner of his mouth points upward. "I like your thinking. Where did you want to go first?"

I ponder for a moment, looking at all the symbols. We'd need to avoid walking near Shearing and Claw camps. I press my finger against a symbol located about two miles from the hotel. I pull my finger away and charcoal dust follows, staining it black.

"Let's do it," he says excitedly. He grabs the nearest weapon in his room and opens the door.

Steeq stands there with a huge smile. In a single breath, he says, "I heard you guys talking and I want to come with you. I haven't gone and hunted Crits in a super long time."

Jaime sighs, deflated. "Steeq." He puts a hand on the little man's shoulder. "You should probably stay here. This is something Caelius and I need to do." He turns to look at me wanting help. "Alone."

I sigh as well, chuckling. "It's fine, Jaime. He can come with. It can't hurt to have another person watching our back."

Jaime gives me a dead stare. There's a pause before he sighs, and finally says, "Okay."

Steeq jumps in joy like a child, squealing. "Yay! You guys won't regret this! You'll be so glad I came along!"

30

The Attack

*Most have believed that the humans became too
technologically advanced, they learned how to
harness the power of the Light and threatened to
overthrow him. So he froze the world as
punishment.*
From the Journal of Azura Seren. Fonalo section, 29th
orbit

We were not glad Steeq came along. He talks about his inventions, books, and porno magazines, which he acquired at some point a couple of weeks ago. He goes into excruciating detail describing one of the models he's obsessed with. Just when I feel like he's said everything there is to say, he finds more to talk about.

The Brightest would walk three miles every day with no issue, but this two-mile trip through the city feels like it takes hours. Luckily, before we left, I placed my second SpringStep petal underneath my tongue to dull any pain. Unfortunately, it heightened my other senses, causing Steeq's high voice to be ear-splittingly obnoxious. Neither Jaime nor I say a single word during the trip. Whatever hadn't been said already was coming out of Steeq's mouth. He'd ask questions and have already moved to a different topic before letting us answer. The annoyance I felt with Jaime yesterday hardly compares to the annoyance I feel with Steeq in this moment.

Jaime finally shushes him and Steeq tightens his lips, though I still feel like I can hear him yapping. A couple of hundred feet in front of us is the Kreetur Crit camp. If two Crits weren't huddled outside the building, we may have walked right past it. They gnaw on a dead bird, biting the same carcass. The building is not unlike any of the other ones. It's four stories tall, about the height of the hotel but built with red brick. Each floor has four windows on each side.

We hide behind a corner of a building out of view. "Okay, so here's the game plan," Steeq whispers. "Caelius, you go in and create a distraction. Try to stall as long as you can and make them want to either eat you or make love to you. I don't care which.

"Jaime, after Caelius distracts them, you are going to sneak up behind one and KYAH!" Steeq makes an exaggerated stabbing motion with his hand. "I will wait until your signal and sneak in, grab the battery and we make our escape!"

"Yeah, no. Sorry, Steeq," Jaime says. "I can't see how that will work."

"What do you mean? I just told you how it would work. You just gotta trust the process." He lays a hand on Jaime's shoulder, but he has to stand on his tiptoes to do so.

"Yeah, okay," Jaime scoffs.

"What am I supposed to do with this, then?" Steeq pulls a makeshift grenade from his pocket. It's similar to the one he used in his rail gun.

Jaime's eyes light up. "You brought that here? And you didn't say anything? What if that triggered?"

"Don't worry!" Steeq says, nonchalantly. He waves a hand. "You worry too much. Don't be such a worrier. It's fine. I've been working on making them more stable so they don't explode randomly!"

"Is that one more stable then?" I ask.

"Well, no … But—"

"Steeq!" Jaime nearly shouts through gritted teeth.

"It's fine!" Steeq emphasizes. "I wasn't actually going to sneak in. Look." He points to a building that has a direct line of sight to the Kreetur camp. It stretches over thirty stories high. In the middle is an open window with Steeq's rail gun peeking out of it. "I'll launch the grenade right into the building while you two distract the guards in front."

"And if you miss, killing one or both of us?" Jaime asks.

"Worry about it when we get there." Steeq smiles again, seeming to not understand the severity of the situation. Either that or he doesn't care. When did he have time to set up his rail gun anyway? How'd he know we'd strike this specific camp?

Jaime sighs again. He puts his hand on his forehead before coming up with an idea. "Let's try this instead."

After relaying the plan, Steeq skips away toward the building where he set up his rail gun. He's careful not to get spotted by the Crits who are licking up blood from the concrete.

"There's something about that kid," I whisper.

"Tell me about it," Jaime says. "He's smart though. Dangerously smart. Like if you took Elara's brains and my weapons and mashed them together."

"Has he always been like that?" I ask. "Odd, I mean."

"He's always been a little quirky, but it seemed to get worse around the time we arrived at Solace." He hesitates for a moment. "Steeq used to have an addiction to SpringStep. I know he's using again because he acted like this before. He relapsed right before your arrival but we've been too busy to address it."

It makes sense. SpringStep is highly addictive. Though it affects him differently than it does me. Does Jaime know I'm also on SpringStep? He eyes me suspiciously.

"Everyone reacts to SpringStep differently," he says, almost reading my mind. "I prefer to stay away from that stuff like it would kill me. Because it will."

"Are you allergic?"

"No, not at all. Though that stuff is incredibly dangerous. I've heard of people using it as a painkiller for something minor, like a stomachache or a mild cut and they get stuck on it for the rest of their lives, which doesn't typically last much longer." He spits on the asphalt. "If you run into any of that stuff, just run. Don't even let it touch your fingertips."

His description of the plant spikes my anxiety. He's right. I knew the dangers but ignored them when I took my first dose. It made me feel invincible. I remember how thoughts would blaze through my head. How I could analyze and break even mundane things down, as if I knew everything about them.

"Of course, it's just a prediction. I can't prove for sure that he's using," Jaime says.

We both jump at a loud sound behind us. A static noise is followed by Steeq's voice. "Hello? Over." Jaime reflexively equips his hatchet.

Steeq isn't behind us. Jaime and I exchange looks before Steeq's voice sounds behind me again. "Can you two hear me? Jaime? Over."

Jaime locates the source of the sound and pulls something off the back of my belt. It's a small black box with an antenna. "Light dammit, Steeq," Jaime whispers.

"Push the button on the side to speak to me. Over," Steeq says through the box. Jaime rotates it in his hand and presses the large button in with his thumb.

"Hello? Steeq? What the hell is this?"

"Jaime! Good to hear your voice again. That's a radio. Over."

A radio? A device that transmits audio over the … air? I'm increasingly fascinated by the technological magic from the previous age. It would have been so helpful to have a radio in the forest with Oberon. We would have saved hundreds of hours of time. "Okay, what do you want?" Jaime asks, flatly.

"I'm ready and in position. Over."

Jaime turns a knob on the top of the radio and Steeq's voice decreases in volume. Jaime lifts his thumb to talk to me. "This is what I mean," he says. "Steeq is a fricking genius, but Light he's got a way of getting under your skin. I mean look at this." He holds the radio up in his hand. "Who else could come up with something like this? I just wish it were anyone else on the other end."

He puts the radio up to his mouth and presses the button in. "Alright, Steeq, we'll let you know when to fire."

Jaime waves a hand, and we sneak closer to the pair of Crits. I grab a slab of rubble and chuck it nearby. The two abominations turn to look at the sound, and we sneak up behind them. Jaime slips a knife from his belt, slitting the neck of the first victim, while I equip my rapier and skewer the second in the back. Their bodies drop to the ground softly.

The front door is made of two large metal panels that swing outward. Jaime grabs one handle and stands against the wall. He nods for me to do the same.

"Okay, Steeq. Fire."

"Copy."

I watch as a grenade is lobbed toward us. It soars through the air at an incredible speed, arcing downward. Jaime and I pull the doors open, and the grenade bounces off the ground in front of us, hurdling right into the building.

"Now!" Jaime yells. We shove the doors closed, just barely locking them together before the explosion shakes the building behind us. What if there are more Crit children in there? I can't even think about it. They're Crits. They'll grow up to be just as dangerous as every other Crit we've encountered.

"Open the door!" Steeq yells. "I'm sending another one!"

Another grenade is hurled in our direction before we can open the doors. Jaime screams, "Steeq!" sprinting away. SpringStep enhances my run, evading the grenade. Panicked-looking Crits open the door, trying to escape and the grenade explodes right as it hits the ground.

Bodies fly in every direction as a sizable hole is blown in the building.

"Holy shit!" Jaime exclaims, holding his arms up to block the flying debris. More Crits file out, running away from the building. "Dammit!" he yells. "I'd rather have overcharged the battery." He holds the radio up to his mouth and yells, "Steeq, hold off."

Steeq's voice is distorted through the radio and I can't make out what he said. Jaime dashes toward the smoking building. I follow, sword in hand. Two more Crits exit. Jaime hacks at the first Crit and he drops easily. The other jumps at me, gripping my throat. Claws threaten to dig into my flesh and I meet the eyes of my attacker.

His skin droops low on his pale face. He's maybe in his eightieth passing. Sharp teeth grit as he readjusts his thumbs over my throat. I can smell the blood on his breath when he licks his lips. This isn't a human. There's no way I could convince myself otherwise. I've killed human cannibals, but this is a Crit in every sense of the word.

My knife appears in my hand and I jam it into the elder's stomach. I drag it upward, finding resistance against his ribs. The creature squeals in pain before Jaime brings a hatchet down into the Crit's back. He drops limply.

"You alright?" Jaime asks, breathing heavily. I nod in response, rubbing my throat. "Good. Let's find this damn queen."

We clear the floors, heading upward. Each floor has fewer and fewer Crits. With Jaime, I feel invincible. I may not share his skill, but we work really well together in combat. I synergize with him better than I do with Oberon.

I am sure to scan each room for any relic that may be tied to him. I'm not sure what I'd be looking for. Perhaps an article of clothing or something similar. "Final floor," Jaime says with a grin. Blood plasters his face and we march toward the staircase.

There's a singular man on the top floor. He's been waiting for us. In his hands is a familiar crossbow, bolts attached to his side. The heavyset man is bald with a thick beard.

For a moment, I believe it. But his legs are too stout. Teeth too sharp. Eyes are too far apart. He holds the crossbow like he's holding it for the first time. It's not him.

Jaime menacingly stomps over to the short Crit. Terror masks his face and he trembles. The crossbow releases a bolt and misses, bouncing off the brick wall behind him. The Crit quickly reloads and fires a second crossbow bolt. This one sinks into Jaime's shoulder. He flinches, grunting slightly, but continues advancing.

Jaime drops his hatchet and picks the man up by his shirt. "Where is your queen?" Jaime shouts into the Crit's face. He drops his crossbow, whimpering, and it clatters on the ground. A dark yellow liquid drips lightly from his pant leg, pooling on the hardwood floor underneath.

Jaime yells, launching the Crit through the air. He slams against the brick wall with a crack. The Crit wheezes, wind knocked out of him. "I hope you're not this new queen. Absolutely pathetic."

Jaime picks his hatchet up from the ground and slowly walks toward the Crit. The man cries, holding his arms out as if it would stop Jaime.

I pick up the crossbow he dropped near the puddle of urine. It's a similar shape to my own. Blood stains the wooden grip, but I recognize the craftsmanship. Engraved on the side is a signature "O."

"I will eradicate every last one of you Crits off this darking planet," Jaime says. He raises his hatchet above his head, preparing to swing it down and end the man's life.

"Jaime!" I yell. He stops to look at me. I hold up Oberon's crossbow, hoping he understands the message I'm trying to convey.

"Where did you get that?" he demands of the Crit. He just sputters and speaks unintelligibly.

"I … I … I don … don't know," he says, eyes wide, lips twisted in pain.

Jaime brings his hatchet down hard. The man screams as three of his toes are severed from his foot. "I know when people are lying to me," Jaime says with precision. "You're going to tell me where you found that darking weapon or else you'll be losing more than just your toes."

Blood streams out from the open wounds in his foot. The man moans in pain, trying to catch a breath. Jaime gives him time to recover.

"The … the queen gave it to me," the Crit says. "It … it was his …"

"Your queen," Jaime shouts, "where is he now? Is this the newly appointed one?"

"Yes, it's the new queen! But I swear I don't know where he went! Maybe the college!" the Crit cries. "Please don't hurt me anymore. I promise I told you everything!"

"I know"—Jaime shakes his head before raising his voice—"but you're still a darking useless bastard!" He raises his hatchet and swings it down swiftly, splitting the Crit's skull in half.

31

The Planter Box

*Would a benevolent God destroy his world,
killing billions of innocent lives to "cleanse the
evil?"*
From the Journal of Azura Seren. Fonalo section, 29th
orbit

My **finger rubs across the** blood-stained "O" on Oberon's crossbow. I sit on the couch in the hotel lobby. Jaime sits in the chair across from me. The arrow still juts from his shoulder and he grips the chair's arms tightly.

This crossbow is Oberon's. There's no doubt about that. But why did the raider—no, Crit—have it? My stomach sinks, knowing the answer. There was no body. There couldn't be a body. It would have been consumed. Could his bones be in the basement of the first building Jaime and I explored? The one with the Crit child?

I feel sick to my stomach. There must be more I can do. Just because his crossbow is with me, doesn't mean he's dead, right? He is too smart to die. We did get one crucial piece of information though. The college.

Is there a fate for Oberon worse than death? What if he truly is this new Kreetur queen? Would he want to leave? Would the Crits accept that? Would I just stay with the Horizon and start over with my new friends? I wouldn't mind that much. I don't think they would either. Sure, I'd miss the Brightest, but they'd be fine without me.

But what about Dolora and Brena? Would they be fine? How are they going to handle not having Oberon around? Brena would grow up to forget her father. Just like I did. I didn't even remember my own father's name.

I wouldn't have to worry about being their potential leader anymore. Hadrian can find someone else—someone more fit for the position.

Dan and Elara enter through the back door. Dan is saying something to her before interrupting himself when he sees us. "Oh, brightest Light!" he swears, eyes wide, mouth agape. There's a moment of hesitation before he rushes down the hall toward his room, feet pounding against the short carpet.

"Jaime!" Elara exclaims. She dashes toward the boy in the chair, who sits calmly. "What happened? Are you alright?"

"I'm fine. It's just a crossbow bolt."

Elara looks frantic, arms moving and hesitating. She tries to remove his shirt but stops when he winces. "I'm sorry," she says, "I don't know what to do."

Dan barrels back down the hallway into the lobby carrying a med kit and a lot of gauze. Elara steps back, letting Dan take over. He's swift, but calm, unlike Elara. Popping open the med kit on the coffee table, he equips the fabric scissors and cuts the cloth around the bolt. He then cuts down the length of the shirt until it opens loosely.

I wince at seeing Jaime's exposed scars again. There looks like there are a few new ones. Were those from our attack? I hadn't even checked to see if I had any. SpringStep would have blocked the pain.

"See," Jaime says to his sister, "Dan's got it under control."

Her pale cheeks turn pink. She raises her voice but doesn't yell. "What if it hit a lung or your heart? You could have died!"

"It didn't and I'm fine."

Dan pours a clear liquid on a cloth before dabbing it around the wound. Jaime screams through gritted teeth, kicking his feet and gripping the armrests even tighter.

"You need to be more careful when you're out there. If you die, how am I supposed to know—"

Jaime cuts her off. "Elara, can you cut it?" he snaps. "I'm not your baby brother anymore. I can take care of myself."

Dan attempts to take the bolt from his shoulder by pulling on it, but he stops when Jaime winces in pain. I know those bolts. "Dan," I say, "you'll have to push it all the way through and remove it from the back. Otherwise, you're going to cause even more damage."

"I'm not going to do that," Dan says. "I'm thinking of a different way. Maybe breaking the shaft."

"That won't work," I inform. "The bolt will splinter, and you really don't want those slivers in his flesh. Plus, the arrowhead will still be lodged inside."

"Either way, I'll come up with another plan. Maybe if I—"

Jaime grabs Dan by the shoulders and shoves himself against him, pushing the arrow through his own back. Jaime screams in pain as it penetrates his skin again.

"There," Jaime says woozily, taking a breath. "That wasn't so bad." Dan's expression is one of shock. He's frozen in place, mouth wide open. "Caelius"—Jaime turns away, exposing the bloody arrow tip toward me—"would you do the honors?"

I hesitate for a moment. Shouldn't Dan be the one doing this? My hands are dirty; I don't want to cause an infection. He notices my delay and wiggles the arrow in anticipation. I respond by grabbing the bloody shaft with my right hand and jerking it out swiftly.

Jaime sucks in a sharp breath through his teeth before sighing in relief. "Much better." He turns to meet the large Okanakan man. "Dan, patch me up!" Dan grimaces but pulls out a roll of gauze from his kit.

With the back of her hand, Elara taps me on the shoulder gently. "Hey, I think you should see this." Concern covers her face. I'm unsure if it's from Jaime's injury or from what she wants to show me. I follow her through the back door of the hotel to the greenhouses.

Elara pushes the flap to the large tent aside. Humidity assaults me when I step in. I see right away what she is concerned about. The seed-rock we'd planted earlier is now a miniature two-foot-tall weeping willow. It looks identical to the one in Hollyard but scaled down.

Not only that, four brand-new plants grow to either side of the miniature willow. The leftmost plant sprouts a thick green stalk nearly three feet in the air. It ends with a massive bell-shaped flower, the color of fresh blood. A few smaller bells extend from the stalk—like a lily.

Next to it, a cluster of stalks stands tall, like lavender, but bolder, more dominating. Their blue horn-shaped blossoms fade to a deep magenta at the center.

The willow, despite being small, demands attention. Thick leaves droop low, hanging over the side of the planter box. I recognize the branch we found Lyria attached to. The precise detail of the tree sends a shiver down my spine.

To the right of the willow is a flower I've become familiar with. It grows in a cluster, like a rose bush, yet the effects are much sharper than a rose's thorns. Each bloom sprouts exactly three purple petals, which come to a soft point. They call to me, begging for me to take a piece. SpringStep.

Is Dan purposefully growing SpringStep? Or is this Steeq's doing? Both are equally viable options, but growing such an addictive plant is dangerous. If Elara weren't standing right next to me, I'd cut off a piece right now.

The fifth and final plant is a normal-looking fern. It stands a foot tall, spewing leaves in every direction. I reach out to touch it with my fingers. Elara yells something but is too late. The edge of a leaf catches my hand and I feel a searing pain. I pull back reflexively and squeeze the area. Blood wells from the slit and hives visibly bubble up on my skin. The urge to itch it comes immediately. It had only been a few moments.

"Remember what I said about respect?" Dan's deep voice booms. The tent flap closes behind him. "Some don't like being touched and would rather be observed from afar." He holds out his hand. "Are you alright?"

"I'm fine," I say shortly. I squeeze my hand tighter as the pain magnifies.

"Jaime is all patched up. His wound is cleaned out so there's little chance for infection," he says. "He's going to rest for a while to let it heal up."

Elara puts her hands on her hips. "And by rest, he means training, right?"

Dan grimaces, shrugging slightly.

I step in. "Dan, what the hell is this?" I gesture toward the five mutant plants, sweat beading on my forehead.

"I don't know," he says. "I haven't seen anything like this before. They were all just seeds a while ago. Plants don't grow like this."

"Why are you growing SpringStep?" I interrogate further.

"I'm not." He holds up his hands. "It's not even possible to grow SpringStep." That piques my curiosity. "That's why it's so rare. You can't just grow it in a greenhouse. It has to grow naturally. SpringStep doesn't have its own seeds."

"That's impossible," I say speculatively. "Right?"

"What's impossible is that I was growing cabbage there. Now tell me how a cabbage turns into a drug that can't be planted." I look at the label. Sure enough, written in ink, "CABBAGE." The other plants have labels for carrot, radish, and onion.

"We planted that rock earlier," Dan speculates. "I think it could be part of the problem." His face contorts and he taps a finger against his lips. "It just doesn't make sense. Even if the root system had infected the other plants to grow rapidly, it couldn't completely change their species. It's not possible."

Elara sighs. "I need to study these. If that's okay, Dan? I'd like to do some research before it gets worse."

"Yes, go right ahead," he says waving a hand. "Do you need help?"

"No, Caelius and I got it." She bends down and lifts the side with the large red flower, leaving me to grab the end with the fern with razor-sharp leaves. I'm not thrilled with the idea of getting cut again, but I bend down and pick it up anyway. It's nowhere near as heavy as a buck. "Just to the research room," she says straining. "Careful not to cut yourself."

Dan guides us out of the greenhouse. I lean as far away from the fern as possible but I'm the one walking backward. He opens the back door and we step inside. Dirt spills over onto the carpet.

The walk is brief but troublesome. I cut my arms a few times. The razor-sharp leaves create large gashes in my shirt. We lower the box to the floor of the research room and push it against a wall. Elara finds a pair of trimmers and clips a blue petal from the horn-shaped stalks.

I observe her in her element. With calculated haste she sets the petal on a panel, placing it under the same microscope from earlier. The microscope moves down when she twists a knob on the side and a strand of hair falls loose when she presses her eyes against the lens.

Minutes pass and neither of us says a word to each other. I find a seat in the corner next to a counter and watch her work. She scribbles in a notepad, drawing, writing, and graphing.

"Find anything useful?" I ask, impatiently.

"Nope."

I wait for her to elaborate, but she doesn't. She's in too deep. I feel useless just sitting here, but I feel terrible interrupting her. "Is there anything I can do to help?" I ask.

She looks up at me. "Um, I'm not sure." She thinks for a moment, lips tight. "If you could just stick around, I might need your help in a couple of minutes."

I relax in the chair, and she returns to the flower. She digs up a singular stalk, to examine its underearth root system. Other stalks come up with it, and she trims the connections.

Using my pinky and ring finger on my left hand I open the drawer next to me. Inside are stacks of papers and rows of books. One document's heading catches my eye— *Frozen World? What Happened?* Below the heading is a picture of a landscape blanketed with snow. The article contains jargon of which I am not intelligent enough to understand.

Underneath the document is a newspaper article with the headline "6 Scientists Plead Guilty, Billions Dead." I grab that one.

Illustrated is a small group of men and women wearing lab coats like the one Elara is wearing now. They stand together holding a trophy, smiling. Under the leading image are close-ups of each person's mugshots.

Revyn R. Shile, Brand W. Sandstone, Samantha B. Ishing, Jonathan T. Merida, Clyde M. Gratch, Serene T. Rivers. I don't recognize any of the names, obviously. I do notice the date, however. Dektoro section, initial orbit.

Initial orbit? They hadn't even gone through twenty whole passings, a full orbit, when this article was published. How curious.

The article explains that the reason for the Freezing of the World was because of these six and their failed science experiment. The article didn't go into detail about what the experiment was but called it "Floral Integration with Thermal Substitution." Or FITS for short.

How am I to know what's true? The church mentioned the Freezing was caused by an eternal battle between the Light and the Darkness. But this article blames the scientists. Could it be both somehow? Could my entire way of thinking be wrong?

"Wait," I blurt, "did these six cause the Darkness too or just the Freezing?" Elara looks up at me from her microscope.

She grins slightly, sighing. "I guess I could take a little break." She grabs a ball from a cupboard. It's larger than her fist. She hangs it by a thin piece of wire from the ceiling. It floats in midair.

"This planet, Nivalis, rotates very slowly around the sun." She sits in the chair next to me. "Slower than other planets within our star's system." There's a pause when she notices the look on my face. "Oh, by the way, there are other planets orbiting the sun. Remind me to show you them sometime."

I would never have known. Did these planets have other humans on them? Do they need to walk around the planet like us?

She continues speaking before I can ask. "If you stood at the very, very front edge of this 'Bright Spot' where the light just barely touches your skin, you could stand there for three hundred and forty full days before the tail end of the Bright Spot passes you and you're left in the Darkness and cold."

She leans closer to me. "Have you noticed that when you stand in the Darkness, the sun still hangs in the sky above? The light stretches about twelve hundred miles across, but yet it should be much more. Like the entire continent of Octoro."

I scoff in amazement; I can't help but smile. "How do you know all this stuff?"

She promptly rummages through the drawer I'd opened and pulls out a rough, beaten-up book. I read the title when she hands it to me: *The Journal of Azura Seren.*

I open the book, peering inside. Elara flinches when the spine crackles in response. The first thing I see is a full map of Nivalis, showing straits, rivers, large city locations, and the entire continents of Octoro and Retuno. There's even an "estimated path of the sun" that stretches across the page in the northern hemisphere. There's so much south of us we will never get to explore because the Bright Spot will never touch that land.

"Don't let it explode your brain," she says. "Our planet is mostly tidally locked with the sun, which is why it stays in one place, drifting ever so slightly. What's strange is that the sun only lights up one twentieth of Nivalis, instead of what I'd assume to be half." She thinks for a moment, tapping the pencil slightly against her chin. "No, actually, the Bright Spot covers only half a percent of the entirety of the planet."

"Wow," I say in amazement. "How is that possible?"

"Yeah, Nivalis is big." She points the head of a table lamp toward the ball hanging from the ceiling. With a click, the lamp's beam flicks on. A moment later, she flips off the overhead light. One half of the ball is fully illuminated by the lamp. The other half stays completely dark. My eyes adjust to the darkness, and a sliver of light comes through the curtains of the window.

"If we could suspend our belief for a moment and imagine this is a planet like ours. The lamp here represents our sun." Elara points at the bright side of the ball. It bounces off her finger. "This is how light should interact with Nivalis."

She holds a large glass disk in her palm. "This is how light actually interacts with Nivalis." She holds the lens in front of the lamp and the light splits. She moves the lens further from the lamp and the light concentrates to a single point on the ball's surface.

"So, is there a giant glass disk in space?" I ask, knowing it's a dumb question.

"I honestly have no idea. At this point, I feel like anything could be possible." Goose bumps form from the cool draft in the room. "Is our sun just colder than other stars, and the only reason this 'spot' is warm is because it's magnified? Are we like ants trapped under a child's magnifying glass?" She paces around the room. "But it doesn't make sense. Our planet's atmosphere should trap the heat, right?"

I wish I were smarter. I want to be able to offer my own input and help. Though I have to remember I'm not here to fix the world. I'm here to find Oberon. I'd love to go back out there and search more, but I can't go without Jaime.

Elara covers her arms. "Is it cold in here to you?" She looks to me for a response, but I can't find the words. The willow tree behind her is glowing with a vibrant blue, illuminating the plants nearby. "I told Steeq not to mess with the thermos—" She cuts herself off when she sees it too.

I step closer to the plant, admiring its colors speckled along the branch and leaves, alternating between cyan and neon green. Shades of magenta lightly dot the plant as well.

"Light of the brightest sun"—she swears—"I figured it out."

32

The Glowing Tree

Who is God?
From the Journal of Azura Seren. Fonalo section, 29th
orbit

Thermosynthesis!" she yells, running back to the light switch in the corner, turning on the overhead light again. She stops and stares at me wide-eyed. The room is still cold, but it gradually warms up.

I lag behind, still not connecting the dots. "Thermosynthesis?" I say, stumbling over the word. My eyes maintain their fixation on the miniature willow.

"I'm not sure how much Dan told you, but plants typically derive energy from the sun by a process called photosynthesis." I remember—it's the vegetation version of eating.

She paces around the room. "I think the plants are switching from photosynthesis as their primary source of energy to thermosynthesis when not in direct light."

"What does that mean, then?"

"I'm getting there," she says impatiently. "Our atmosphere heats up and the plants consume that heat instead, cooling everything down. Cold isn't quantifiable as it's only the absence of heat."

I think I understand. But something doesn't add up. "What about life before the Freezing of the World?" I ask. "I mean, the Bright Spot rotated around the planet at the same rate, but only six hundred passings ago the world froze as well? Why?"

She smiles, huffing a laugh. "I honestly don't know," she admits. "That's what I've been trying to figure out for the longest time. Though I feel like I'm close to the answer." She grabs the same newspaper I'd acknowledged earlier. "I think that maybe these six have something to do with it." The scientists stand in the black-and-white image, frozen in time, showing off a trophy. They are all dead— like Oberon.

I can't help it. My mind drifts back to him. How long did he suffer before he died? I refuse to believe he would have been killed so easily, but I don't know. Every ounce of my being tells me to give up, to stop searching for him. I walk the tightrope of death every time I go and look. I should give up before I end up like him.

"Hey." Elara bends down, her brown eyes meeting mine. "Are you okay?"

A lump forms in my throat. "I'm fine." I turn my head to hide my soaking eyes. "It's time for me to move on." I take a shuddering breath to recompose myself. "So, thermosynthesis, huh?"

"Do you want to talk about it? I'm here to listen," Elara says, placing a hand on my knee. The sudden touch is warm and comforting.

There's a long pause. Minutes pass in silence. Despite experiencing a breakthrough in her research, she decides to spend the time with me. I'm the one who speaks first. "I had a friend. Oberon and I saved her life together. Lyria." The memory plays back in my head, her body hanging loosely from the willow tree in the center of Hollyard, neck craned to the side. "She was looking for her son. He'd disappeared and she looked everywhere for him. I'm not sure for how long, but she searched for her son despite knowing the truth. She held on to that feeling like it was a rope, until that same rope was tied around her neck." I break; a tear rolls down my cheek. "I feel like I'm at that point."

"Hey, it's alright," Elara says softly. "I know what it's like—searching for something that you know isn't there, believing someday you'll find it. Letting go is the hardest part, and it's okay if you're not ready to take that step yet."

Another tear drops, staining the newspaper in my lap. Elara hastily snatches the batch of papers. Through blurry eyes, I see how my tears splotched the ink on the paper, making certain words unreadable.

"I'm sorry," I say.

"No, it's okay," she says, examining the pages, checking which parts I'd ruined. She lingers on a page for an extended period, concentrating.

"What?" I ask.

"This happened at the University of Solace." She flips another page, showing me an image of the front of the college. "If they created this mess here, there has to be some kind of reversal. Maybe there are more answers in that college!"

The Crit Jaime killed mentioned the college. He'd said the new queen might be there. But that would imply the existence of a Crit hive in that location? Elara didn't know that. According to the pamphlet I received, the college is located at the most northern side of Solace. "Why haven't you guys gone already?"

"It's on the other side of the city. It would take a whole day to get there by foot."

"And," I ask, "how different is it from walking with the Bright Spot?"

"Well, for starters, the city is crawling with Crits. I'm sure you remember. I didn't make it half a mile before being attacked by one. But if I have you and Jaime, maybe we will be fine."

"Yeah maybe. There's an issue though," I drawl as she meets my eyes. "I think the college is a Crit hive. Jaime and I learned there is a new queen who might be there."

Her head drops and she sighs, rubbing her temple with her thumb and forefinger. "Of course it is."

I hate breaking the news to her, but it is too risky. We couldn't walk a whole day through an extremely dangerous city, just to turn back, or die. Standing up, I change the subject, hopefully taking her mind off the idea. "Hey, let's focus on learning what we can right now. Maybe the answer is right in front of us."

Absentmindedly, my finger slightly brushes against the miniature willow tree. Pain. I pull back instinctively and in an instant, I feel ice coursing through my veins. It freezes my blood vessels, traveling throughout my entire body spreading to my chest and head.

An overwhelming sense of fear, anger, hatred, and pain washes through me. I drop to the floor, spasming intensely. The agony is so overwhelming that my vision fades until I see nothing. Not darkness, not the back of my eyelids, nothing.

The void is filled with visions of various places around the world. Most places are dark and frozen, though each image is anchored by a singular object. A willow tree. Every willow tree in every location glows a vibrant blue and green, illuminating the snow and ice accumulating around it.

One area is lit up, and I recognize it right away. Hollyard. The willow stands tall in the center of the cul-de-sac. It does not glow. No one crowds around it. There is no prisoner tied up. There are no sleeping bags. There is no Hadrian's wagon. Just the remains of Lyria's rope. I wish I'd removed it. It looks like it's showing me what's currently happening. Is the Brightest gone?

In the blink of an eye, every event that happened near that tree plays out. I watch the moment Lyria arrives in Hollyard; we follow shortly after. I watch her grief when she hangs herself from one of its branches. I watch Oberon lift me up while I cut her down. Hadrian trying to heal her. People sleeping on the ground. Oberon dragging my body from the river. Pladd being captured and tied to the tree. Me feeding him jerky. Him pulling the BlightStone from the tree—the item Hadrian had been looking for.

How did I know it's a BlightStone? How did I know Hadrian was looking for it? It's the same stone Elara and I planted in the planter box. It corrupted the plants next to it, altering their growth, sprouting its own beautiful tree right in front of me.

I hear something speak to me in my mind. He's calm, collected, chilling, his voice layered upon itself. I've heard this voice before. "Hello, Caelius. I wondered when I'd get to finally talk to you. We have a lot of work to do."

250

The End of Part 3

33

Interlude IV: The Mother

Lyria

It's time we ride again.** The Octoro Bridge awaits our arrival," Hadrian says loudly for everyone to hear. The group groans in complaint. It had been weeks since the last raid. After both Caelius and Oberon left, it had become exceptionally difficult for the group to find and hunt food.

Lyria picks out the leaves from her pile of berries and shoves the purple fruit in her mouth. Life would be so much better if Tommy were here. She misses him so much.

The same thoughts that have plagued her for months overwhelm her now. They scream at her. "You're a terrible mother. You don't deserve your son. You don't have a place within the Brightest. You are going to let everyone down, just like how you let yourself down. How you let Jack down." She left Jack, her ex-husband, to find a better life. A life of freedom and not of servitude. She found what she had been looking for, but it didn't mean anything. Not without Tommy. She goes to wipe tears from her eyes, but her fingers return dry. She's not surprised. She's cried so much, her eyes were bound to dry up sooner or later.

The group sits around a fire. Pladd, the newest member, chats quietly with Hadrian. He'd cleaned up in one of the showers, clearing the dirt and grime from his skin and hair. His long, messy hair shone with a brilliant white color, like Hadrian's. Like Jack's.

Where were Caelius and Oberon? They were the only ones who even cared to talk to her. Other than Mattias, who's dead now. They had a date that never came. He was gentle, kind, and respectful to her. But he died in a hunting mishap, drowning in a river. Some think Caelius killed him. Lyria didn't think so.

Why did this stuff only happen to her? Is the Light punishing her for her past? Where would they be if Mattias had lived? Where would she be if she still had her son?

Brena, the daughter of Dolora and Oberon, looks at her from across the campfire. She is a cute thing. She's recovered well from her recent injury. Almost like it never happened. If only Oberon were here now to see her progress.

The clearest moments in her mind are the times she spent with Brena. Dolora often requested Lyria to watch over Brena while Dolora unwinds with her friends. It is a blessing in disguise. Brena revitalizes Lyria. She gives her purpose. Her life feels like it has meaning again.

Jack's words play in her mind. *"You can run, but you'll always return to me. You're a whore and that's all you'll ever be."* She blocks them out—or tries to. *"There's a part of you that enjoys it—enjoys being a washed-up piece of meat to be used over and over. Until eventually you're thrown away as new flesh pours in."*

She won't admit it, but he's right. She does still love him and a part of her believes he loves her back. Even after being with a new group of people, a safe group of people, no one here loves her like he did.

She yearns for that connection again, too afraid to seek it out. The available men here are either married or too committed to the Light. There is Pladd … but she'd rather die before mating with a cannibal. That doesn't stop him from being handsome, though.

Is she infatuated with him because he is handsome or because he's dangerous? Maybe both? How would his sharp teeth feel during a kiss. She wants to find out. He is getting closer to the Light and its teachings. Maybe she can swoop in before he is fully committed.

No, she must stick to her rules. No cannibals. *"Touch him and I'll gut you like a fish,"* Jack says in her head. It's like he's right there. She sighs in defeat. She can't keep living this life like nothing happened. She should have searched harder for her son. But it doesn't matter anymore.

Hadrian is right. It's time to leave Hollyard. She hates living this way and can't wait to get back on the road. Back to her comfort.

It's too bad she'll be leaving her new family behind. Not that they'd call her their family. But what if Jack doesn't want her back? What if he's moved on from her. What if he rejects her when she arrives? He wouldn't do that, would he?

In a moment of lucidity and fear, Lyria comes up with an idea.

"Brena, come here." The child stumbles over to her, passing the fire. "You like collecting rocks, yes?" The child nods, thumb buried in her mouth. "I have a really pretty rock for you by my house. Do you want to come see it?"

Brena nods again and looks back at her mother, who is talking distractedly to one of the men in the group. "Don't worry, it will be quick. I promise." Lyria holds a pinky finger out and the child grabs it with her small hand. "Awesome. Let's go then."

It feels good to be a mother again, to take care of someone who can't take care of themselves. The Brightest will hate her forever. But that's okay.

Part 4

Darkness

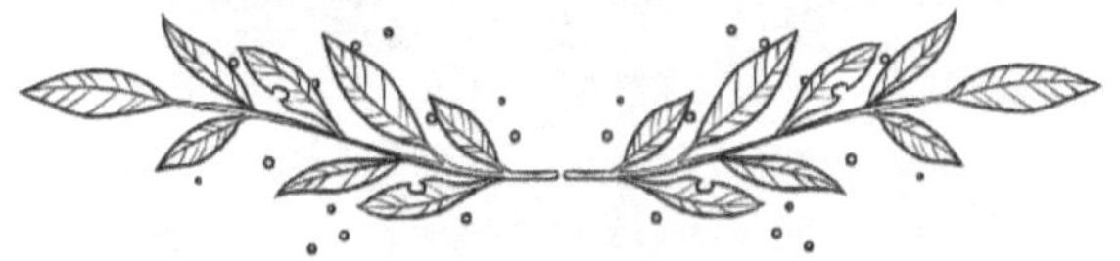

34

The Void

*If God exists, is there just one? Maybe there are
more, but how many?*
From the Journal of Azura Seren. Janero section, 29th
orbit

Jaime and Elara argue in the lobby. Elara sits next to me on the couch while Jaime paces throughout the common area. I can't banish from my mind the voice I'd heard after touching the strange BlightStone tree. I've heard the voice twice before. Once after jumping in the river to kill Mattias. The other time was while Elara dragged me through the city, right after my altercation with a Crit. The voice is stronger, louder, more threatening than before.

"Absolutely not!" Jaime exclaims in response to Elara's request. "We are not going across the city for some stupid college!" He paces toward the lobby counter before turning back, tossing a knife back and forth in his hands.

"Please!" she begs. "Jaime, this is the reason we *came* here. Don't tell me you've lost sight of that."

"We aren't going," he says, sticking a finger in her face. "Final decision."

Elara grunts loudly and storms away. She turns hesitantly as if she is going to say something more but decides against it, leaving.

Jaime sighs, directing his attention toward me. "I'm not putting her in danger again. She'd be dead if you weren't there to save her. She can't defend herself. She can barely hold a knife correctly. We've done hours and hours of training with nothing to show for it." He drops himself onto a recliner and I sit across from him, arms outstretched on the sofa behind me.

"She is determined," I say. "I'll give her that. How do you know she isn't going to try to go alone?"

"She won't. It's too far," he says.

"That didn't stop her last time."

"Yeah, but she hasn't gone since. She's learned her lesson after seeing firsthand what could happen to her."

"You don't know that. This is her life's work."

"She's a liability." He stops fidgeting with his knife to look at me. "If she goes out there and spills our location, we may as well all be dead. It'd be a bloodbath, like the hive we took out earlier today." Did that really happen today? It felt like a lifetime ago.

"I like this one," the voice says. "He is smart, dangerous. He reminds me of Grafter." I can't tell if I'm going insane, but I want it to stop speaking to me. The voice has been harassing me periodically for the last hour—stuck in my head without my consent.

"What if I go with her?" I ask.

He meets my eyes with a dark expression. "Don't," he says softly. "If she dies, so will you." There's a double meaning in that threat.

I lift my hands up beside my head. "What other choice do we have?" I ask. "Either we go, or we sit here and wait for the Bright Spot to pass us before we leave. Maybe there *are* answers there. You mentioned wanting to take out their queen."

"It's dangerous," he says, sharply. "There could be hundreds, maybe thousands of Crits there. Not to mention, it's likely a Kreetur hive. Killing the queen won't work like it does with smaller camps."

"How do you know that?"

"I just do," he snaps. "I could feel it before I killed that last Crit.

"There are more Crits in that building than people you've met." He continues, "Even if there was information about the thermosynthetics or whatever, it's destroyed. Gone. Crits have no care for preservation."

"We have to try."

"No," he spits, "the most valuable thing we can keep is our lives. End of discussion." Jaime stands and leaves without letting me say another word. I feel helpless. Maybe he's right. Judging by his scars, he's seen a thing or two and knows what he's talking about. It doesn't make it any less infuriating.

'He'll come to his senses in the morning. You should sleep," the voice says in my head. It feels like my own thoughts, but they sound different—out of place. I warily ignore it. I just have to convince myself it's not real and it'll go away.

Exhaustion hits me like a train. It is so late, I wouldn't be surprised if the moon started to rise, signifying morning. My chest hurts and I'm tempted to take my last SpringStep petal. Though I know it would just keep me awake.

"Sleep," the voice requests again. I don't have the energy to deny it.

The walk to my room is agonizingly long. Each step feels heavier than the last and my body threatens to drop in the hallway.

The door is heavy when I push it open. I don't even turn the lights off before I fall onto the mattress. I'm so cold. I grab the blanket and lay it over my fully clothed body. It doesn't help. I huddle, pulling my legs closer to my chest. What's going on?

My body convulses rapidly. I feel colder than I did in the icy river. My body refuses to move. I feel myself drifting before I'm plunged into an empty white void.

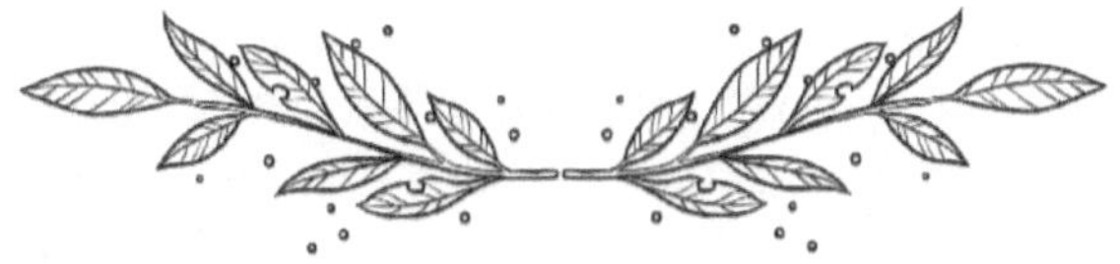

Where am I? I look down and I don't see anything. My hands are gone, along with the rest of my body. I seem to be floating in an expansive white void. I can't move. It's neither hot nor cold. Just existence. Or lack thereof. Maybe I'm dead. Is this what comes after? I can still form thoughts, so something is real.

A figure appears in front of me stepping through a fog. My mind can't comprehend it. There's nothing to compare it to, and my brain refuses to make sense of it.

I cannot speak, nor scream. An overwhelming feeling of power flows around me. I exist before something powerful. Is this the Light? Perhaps Light's creator?

My vision blurs and I see things again. Except this time, I'm outside in an unfamiliar part of the city. Around me are hundreds of Crits. They all fear me. Many bow in subservience; others watch with reverence.

They are disgusting. Ugly even. But they respect me. I have a duty and a responsibility to them. My mouth moves without my permission. "Friends. Family. Brothers. Sisters," I shout. "You elevated me to this position as your queen. For that I am deeply honored. I must thank every one of you." My voice sounds different in my ears—congested.

The crowd yells in excitement. They know they made a good choice. I can't let them down. They are people. Just like me.

There are so many of them, I have a hard time processing it. My surroundings indicate a completely different part of the city. I think I'm at the college Elara wanted to visit.

Where was Elara? Jaime? Dan? Steeq?

Is this a glimpse of my future? They aren't around. Did they die? Or did I come by myself?

Jaime's right. They *will* die if we go to the college. But is this a vision of my future or just a possibility? If it's my future, I'll be heading in this direction whether I like it or not.

I recoil in fear seeing my fate sealed as a queen of a thousand Crits. I feel sick to my stomach, but my body doesn't move. Instead, I wave my right hand in the air.

The vision fades like mist and I'm subjected to the harsh white void. The indescribable figure stands in front of me. I feel an impression of words and emotions. It speaks to me. "YOU HAVE BEEN LOST FOR SO LONG AND YOU FINALLY FOUND ME," the voice booms, layered upon itself, echoing in my brain. "YOU HAVE BEEN CHOSEN. FOLLOW ME AND MY WILL AND YOU'LL RECEIVE GREAT POWER."

The Light itself is speaking to me. The same Light Hadrian follows and teaches. It's real. But I don't want power. I want my friend.

"GATHER FORCES AND CLEANSE THE WORLD OF THE DARKNESS. ACCEPT YOUR DUTIES AS CHOSEN."

A glowing willow tree appears in front of me, formed from threads of light. It glows so brightly it permeates the blindingly white background. I need to touch the tree and its power is mine.

It draws me in—sings to me even. A harmonic melody pulses from the tree in a beautiful song. I see two visions of the same tree. Through one eye, the tree glows magnificently. Through the other, it's engulfed in flames. Fire roars infinitely upward.

I don't want it. I shouldn't have it. I remember the *thrill* I received from killing all those Crits at the hideout. The excitement of finding Elara being attacked and wanting to save her. Not because it was the right thing to do, but because I felt the urge to *kill*. I just wasn't skilled enough to do so. I don't want it, though I crave it. Those who crave power should never have it.

"YOU HAVE NO CHOICE," the voice booms. If I had a body, I'd cower in fear.

"I don't want it. I reject!" I yell back.

"DON'T YOU WANT REVENGE ON THE PERSON WHO KILLED YOUR PARENTS?"

The Octoro Bridge fades into my vision. A vast ocean stretches in every direction. My parents stand, their backs toward me. I only see Hadrian's fury. I don't hear anything from them. I don't hear the argument; I don't hear my mother's stomping. Just the clashing of tides beneath me.

Hadrian grabs both my parents by the neck, lifting them into the air. Their bodies freeze, turning pale. My mother kicks and shakes before going limp. I can't move.

In a fraction of a second, both my parents disappear—bodies turning to dust. I'd seen Hadrian do this before.

He'd turned a Crit to dust. The same way he killed my parents.

The dust of my parents floats off, carried by the wind. Hadrian's eyes meet mine, as if he can see me.

Before I can process what happened, another vision blurs into view. This time I stand helplessly on a trail. No, I'm not standing. I'm sitting against a tree. The handle of a sword consumes the bottom portion of my view. It hides its blade within my chest, and I cannot move.

I watch helplessly as an older Jaime fights expertly with an unknown figure. They wear a long cloak that covers their face and figure. They dodge every one of Jaime's attacks with precision. A glistening shortsword appears in the figure's hands, and he rams it through Jaime's stomach.

I need to get up and stop this, but I can't. The sword pins me to the tree like a thumbtack. I cough, spitting blood over the handle as Jaime falls limply to the ground. I hear screaming from the side; though I can't turn my neck, I know it's Elara. She foolishly runs to her brother's aid. The cloaked figure drops the sword and wraps a hand around Elara's throat.

She kicks and struggles as he raises her into the air. A moment later a frost pattern spreads from her neck, spreading up her cheeks and down her chest. "No," I spit. Elara's movements slow and her struggling stops. "Elara," I rasp.

"IF YOU DO NOT ACCEPT MY POWER, THIS WILL BE YOUR FUTURE. YOU WILL BE HELPLESS IN SAVING YOUR FRIENDS."

It's right. If this is real, I won't be able to protect them. Clearly, someone bested Jaime and me in combat. What was that sword? It seemed to form in the air like they summoned it.

If this is a variation—a future where I do not accept the power—then the other future could be changed as well, my future as the leader of thousands of Crits. I still do not want it, but it's my responsibility to take it. If I don't, how many people will die? Dan, Jaime, Elara, Steeq, Brena, Dolora? But how many more people will die if I do take it? What kind of power does this entail?

I watch the willow burn through one eye. It roars in anger, heat radiating from the flames. The same tree is calm through the other eye. It glows brightly and cools the air around it.

My body returns. I stand on soft, bouncy grass and I make a decision. Sticking my left hand out reminds me once again of my missing fingers, a debt I'll forever have to pay. What kind of debt will this deal entail?

My hand touches the bark, and I feel the power pressing, asking to be let in. I allow it to consume me entirely.

35

The Frozen Room

*Many seek religion because they fear death. I
sought religion because I feared knowledge.*
From the Journal of Azura Seren. Febro section, 29th
orbit

The Light's influence didn't stay in my dream. I feel panic welling deep within. My heart rate increases, and my eyes open.

The room around me is completely frozen. The walls are frosted over. The ceiling drips with icy stalactites. What happened?

I take a breath. Focus. I ground myself back into reality and ask a different question. *Why* did this happen? I'm somehow not cold. The room is silent except for my heavy breathing and heart pounding in my ears.

The insanity of it makes me laugh. What I'm seeing shouldn't be possible.

I move the incredibly stiff, frozen blanket to the side. I feel like it would shatter if it fell to the floor. I nearly slip on the frozen ground when I stand up.

I search my room, looking for anything that could cause the room to freeze. I check the nightstands, closets, drawers, and even under my bed for some type of plant life that might be drawing the heat from the room. Nothing. Did the whole building freeze?

Did I oversleep into the Darkness? They'd have woken me up, right? Light peers in through the window, warming up a spot on the carpet. I look outside and everything in sight is the way it was before I fell asleep. No snow or ice in the streets or on the sides of buildings.

I carefully shuffle to my door and attempt to turn the knob. My hand glides around it without any friction, unable to tighten my grip. It's not locked as far as I know. I slam my shoulder into the door. Maybe I could force it open.

I throw my shoulder into the door again and this time, a thin sheet of ice layered on the door cracks like a web. I charge again. This time, the ice shatters and falls to the floor.

More ice gathers on the edges of the door, so I take my knife from my nightstand and chisel away at it.

After an excruciatingly long time, the ice is completely removed. I grab the door handle again, this time allowing my body heat to warm it up a bit, before pushing forward. It still doesn't budge.

That's when I realize I'm an idiot. The door swings inward.

I twist and pull. It gives slightly, cracking. I pull again, this time with a lot more effort, and it swings open.

The hallway is warm. The carpet isn't frozen out here, and I still smell the faint hotel mildew. So, it must just be my room? I shut the door behind me and jog down the hallway.

When I arrive in the lobby, I see Jaime sitting on the couch. "Caelius, I did some thinking, and—" He stops to look at me, and his eyes go wide. "Oh shit. Are you alright?"

"What?" I say. "Yeah, I'm fine."

"You don't look fine," he says. "Sit down. You're paler than Elara. What's going on?" He grabs my arm. "Light, you're cold."

I decide to keep it a secret for now. I don't want him to freak out. "I just … had a nightmare."

"Yeah, no joke. Looks like you saw a ghost and became one," he says, eyebrow raised. "Is there something I can get you? Water?"

"Something warm, maybe?" I rasp, voice fading out.

"I'll go get Dan."

I nod, but he'd already left. Something is very wrong.

"It's me. I'm what's wrong," the Light says. "It will pass. When it does, you'll feel stronger than ever."

The Light seems to know what's happening. It's the reason I feel like this. In my dream, I'd accepted some kind of power, but maybe it wasn't just a dream.

Jaime returns and Dan follows behind him. "Looks like there's an emergency," he says. "What kind of tea?"

"I don't care," I say. "Just make it hot if you can."

He smiles and heads into the kitchen.

Jaime tosses me a blanket, and I promptly cover myself up. It helps, but not much. "Anyway … back to what I was saying," he starts. "I did some thinking last night and I changed my mind. I'll go with you and Elara to the college." He drops his head. "I've accepted that we may not make it, but Elara's right. It is the reason we came here. She wants to find anything that could help reverse the Freezing of the World." I'm too cold to respond. "Maybe it won't be so bad. Maybe it will be abandoned like the other hive. It's gonna be a long walk though. I hope you know that."

I nod. "We'll be fine," I say.

"Not with you looking like that," he continues. "Did you get in a fight with the Light or something? You look like you caught a flu."

His mention of the Light makes me panic, a pit forming in my stomach. There's no way he could know what happened.

"Whatever it is, we aren't leaving until you are looking better. Fighting a Crit along with sickness is a deadly combination. If we run into trouble, you need to be on your A game."

"I'm fine," I say, struggling to get the words out. I feel myself growing *weaker.*

"Nuh-uh. No way." He shakes his head. "Besides, letting you rest will give me some extra time to work on Elara's combat skills." He has a good point. Teaching Elara to help defend herself may be valuable, even if she isn't on our level.

I think of my dream from last night. I stand in front of thousands of Crits and they all cheer for me. My friends nowhere in sight. I convince myself that they escaped. They made it back to their hotel. But I don't know that for sure. I also don't know if that vision is *true.*

Dan comes out of the kitchen holding a hot mug of tea. He sets it down on the stand next to my chair. Steam rises from the dark liquid, reaching my nostrils. "This chai should get you back to your old self again."

"Thank you, Dan. I genuinely appreciate it." I take the cup in my hands and hold it close. He grins.

I put it up to my mouth and take a sip. It's … cold. Like he used cold tap water instead of hot water. "What's wrong?" he asks.

"Nothing, it's just … really good."

Jaime eyes me. He noticed my lie.

"Great," Dan says with a smile. "Chai tea is a delicacy where I'm from. It was only made as a celebration when someone was old enough to leave the nest and explore the Bright Spot."

This bit of lore intrigues me. I take a sip of the cold drink. It still tastes phenomenal. "You left your old caravan when you turned a certain age?"

"Everyone does. Once they turn a full passing, they are expected to leave and spread the classic Okanakan kindness to more groups."

How interesting, so his parents and childhood friends could still be out there. Would he ever run into them again? I take another sip. They don't know about my room. Should I tell them or let it melt? Maybe some other time in the future we could laugh about it.

If I knew they had a future.

"Take it easy today, okay?" Dan asks softly, genuine concern in his eyes. I nod in response. He really cares. They all do. I can't drag them into my mess.

Dan heads back to his room and Jaime leaves to search for Elara to do more combat training. I take a final sip of my tea. It leaves a dark residue at the bottom.

One of Jaime's items fall out of his pocket, resting on the cushion. It's one of the devices used to make batteries self-destruct. When he's out of sight, I snag it from the chair and hold it in my palms, examining the circuitry.

I sit alone in the lobby of the hotel. "Caelius," the Light says playfully. "Can I show you something?"

The voice sends a chill down my spine. Is it too late to reject the power? Could I just ignore it? The less I know about my "great power," the better.

I fish out a purple petal from my pocket. The last one. The SpringStep's color dully fades, but it's still potent. "You don't need that, child." The voice speaks in my head again. The urge to place the petal on my tongue is replaced with the need to be outside. It looks so warm out there.

Maybe I should get as far away from these people as possible. I need to do what I can to ensure their safety. After getting a glimpse of my own future, I can't trust myself to be around them. Putting the petal back in my pocket, I open the lobby doors and step outside.

The sun beats against my skin, and it feels fantastic. Its warmth invigorates me, refilling me with power, with energy. The lethargy fades—I feel unstoppable.

I feel welcome outside for the first time. Like I'm no longer an unwanted guest in the sun's house. I take a breath in. The air is enriching despite the stench of urban abandonment.

I take a moment to truly take in my surroundings. Vines crawl up buildings, creeping in through windows and cracks. Small flowers sprout in unlikely areas. They bloom out of the cracks in the concrete or out of the gas tanks of abandoned cars. I feel as if I'm recognizing the beauty of the world for the first time. Just like us, these plants look for ways to survive, persevering through even the most undesirable of conditions.

I understand how Dan feels about plant life. They are so much more than just food or a pretty sight. They deserve our respect. By seeking out the college, I essentially sign the death contract for all floral life. There would be no trees, no grass, no vegetables. Without thermosynthesis, how else could they survive nineteen passings? Elara wants to take away their only survival mechanism.

The dream I had continues to haunt me. Being the leader of thousands of cannibals. My friends are nowhere to be seen.

Why did the Light choose me instead of Hadrian? Did it know I was to replace Hadrian someday in the Brightest? Why did it choose me now, after I left?

"Because you're the only one who can do what needs to be done," the Light whispers, its voice layering upon itself. "Hadrian is occupied with another piece of me."

"Another piece of you?" I ask audibly, to which the Light doesn't respond.

If the college is a place of research, it's likely to have batteries like the ones Steeq uses to power the hotel. I have one of Jaime's devices. I could use it to destroy the building, wiping out an entire Crit camp, along with any information that could allow Elara to reverse the Freezing.

How would I sneak in? If the area is truly crawling with Crits, there's no way I'd be able to just walk in, blow it up and leave. If only I could scout the area. But with it being dozens of miles away, it would take days to get there, accounting for any Crit encounters and rests along the way.

Maybe I'll just figure it out once I'm there. I know deep down now that if Elara "fixes" the world, she'll kill it and everyone on it. I can't let her do that. As much as I could really use Jaime's combat skills for my trip, I can't risk their lives. I need to do this on my own.

I reorient myself by observing the buildings around me. I pull out the pamphlet of Solace again, inspecting its map. Once I'm sure I know where I'm at and where I'm headed, I make my way northwest—toward the University of Solace.

36

The Vessel

I fear knowledge of what has been and knowledge of what will be.
From the Journal of Azura Seren. Febro section, 29th orbit

I'**m too far from the** hotel before I realize that I'd forgotten my rapier. I could turn back, but it would be moonfall before long. And when Jaime sees I'm doing better, he'll want to come with me.

Luckily, I keep my knife close at all times. Not that it will be enough if I'm ambushed. My rapier wouldn't be enough either. Jaime would have been great to bring along, but I can't risk him jeopardizing my plan.

I have to remind myself why I'm doing this. Elara wants to reverse this thermosynthesis, which would kill all plant life by "curing" them of their disease. The disease that allowed them to thrive in a world where it's always dark. If I can destroy any information that could help her, that would be perfect. If I did go back, could I convince Jaime to help? He seemed indifferent on the matter.

Maybe I could get revenge for Oberon while I'm at it. I might die but I'm okay with that. I wish I could have said goodbye to my new friends. For the first time in a long time, I am truly alone.

"You don't need anyone. You have me," the Light says in my mind. I'm still not convinced that it's the Light and that I'm not just losing my mind. "You keep ignoring me. You can't hide from me forever, you know."

I sigh as my stomach rumbles. I could really go for some food right now.

"Food?" the Light says, reading my thoughts. "I know where to find food. Good food."

Where? My mind reacts before I want it to.

"There is an abundance of food. Unfortunately, right now, your body requires much more than what the sun provides."

"What do you mean?" I ask aloud.

"I feed from heat, Chosen. In return, I give you energy. And more. If you fail to do your part, I'll take from you. I think it's a fair trade, don't you?"

"No, it's not a fair trade! I didn't ask for you to be here" I shout. There's no one to hear my insanity anyway. "Do not feed off of me!"

"Then do as you're told." The words send a chill down my spine. What kind of contract have I signed by accident? If this *is* the same *Light* that worked with Hadrian, then he must have had to do the same things.

"Where can I find heat?" I ask. "Specifically."

"Oh, this is my favorite part!" The voice seems to squeal in excitement. "Hot steel, pavement, fire, the sun—you know, the typical hot things."

"Okay?"

"But the best source of heat is a soul. They blaze like an inferno."

"Not happening. I'm not going to kill people so you can have your fix."

"Oh, but you will. Because it's not just me who benefits. You truly have no clue what power you wield, do you, Chosen? Maybe I should show you."

The world goes dark around me. As if the sun had been snuffed out like a match. Faint light comes through windows in buildings around me. I'm cold. Very cold. Freezing. I wrap my arms around myself and begin to panic. The world around me is so very unfamiliar. I recognize the buildings around me, but the Darkness makes it seem like a completely different place.

"Scared yet?" the Light asks. "This will be every day if you do not feed me. Every day until your body gives up and freezes over. I'll suck every last drop of heat from your corpse and move on to my next host. You don't hold power. I do. You are a vessel to do as I say."

"No," I growl through gritted teeth.

"Come on. It's so easy! I'll even show you what to do." I close my eyes, squeezing them so tightly they burn. But as if my eyelids never existed, I see a figure standing in front of me.

It's not the same figure I saw in the dream. But someone else. Someone I recognize. The handsome man looks at me in terror, unable to move. It's my friend. Pladd's mouth moves rapidly, trying to say multiple things at a time. "Caelius?" he finally says.

My stomach sinks. How did he get here? I can't kill him.

"What's wrong?" the voice asks with a whiny, mocking tone. "He's just another cannibal. You've killed them before. What makes this time different?"

"He's my friend," I shout. "I—I can't kill him."

"Friend? Are you sure?" the Light mocks, as if it already knows. "Well, you better get used to not having friends."

Pladd sticks his arm in my direction, a finger extended. I reach for him. My finger barely touches his and before my eyes, the man turns to ice. A web of frost spirals up his arm and infects the rest of his skin. His now gray face is frozen in time forever. The suddenness of it catches me off guard. It takes me a long time to process what happened. What I had done.

"Mmm. Yes." The Light moans in pleasure. "Just like that."

Pladd. I'd killed him. Without even meaning to. What the hell is going on? "What did you do?" I scream, lungs burning.

"Me? You're the one who drew his heat." I look at my terrified friend. He's dead. Before I can grieve, he fades away into mist. I reach outward, trying to grab him, but all I catch is air.

Shortly after, the darkness recedes, and the sun blinds me. I can't tell if the tears are from the sudden brightness or from killing Pladd.

Why do I care so much? He was a Crit. "That wasn't so bad, now was it?" the Light says in my head.

"What even are you?" I demand. "You're not this benevolent deity. You're not the same God that I follow!"

"And who told you I was benevolent?"

Hadrian. At least he made it seem that way.

"Then maybe the god you were following wasn't me. But Hadrian himself, Chosen." I'd said the same thing to Elara although hearing it from the Light itself made me sick.

"Is that why you abandoned him?" I ask. "Because people followed and worshipped him instead of you?"

"I'm not the one who abandoned him," it mocks. "Although part of me still lives within him. Despite our messy severance."

I don't think I realized what kind of trouble I got myself into. I have an unstable parasite attached to me with no way of removing it. How am I supposed to do this? Manage this *thing?* The only person who might know is Hadrian himself. And who knows if he's still alive?

"I am not a thing," the Light says. "I think a bit more respect is due."

"You're not getting anything from me," I say.

I continue walking toward the college when my feet slip. The ground underneath me had been replaced with ice. I fall forward and can't catch myself. I land hard, face scraping against the concrete, splitting open multiple areas on my skin. So, I'm bonded to a funny guy.

I push myself up and continue my journey. My stomach rumbles again. "I thought you said that you'd feed me if I give you warmth."

"You think you actually fed me anything, Chosen?" it mocks me, giggling. "You are incorrect. That was a vision. In order to make the illusion, I'd concentrated a bit of heat in that one area to simulate the effect. Hence it freezing instantly. You'd just frozen a cluster of water molecules in the air. For me, it was like spitting into a cup and drinking it."

"I don't know what that means."

"It means: I need food. Real food."

"No."

"Caelius," it whines, "you don't need to hunt anymore. You'll never need to put your life on the line in a forest ever again."

But I enjoyed hunting. I appreciated being alone in nature, listening to the trees and wildlife surrounding me. It is my home. My real home. Unlike this place. I'd put my life in *more* danger trying to please this entity. I need to get up close and personal to Crits, or even other humans to satisfy it. Could it be satisfied?

"You won't be risking your life if I'm here. After all, it is a trade that works in both our interests. If you so desire, I can return to you what has been lost." I feel phantom pain in my left hand. I flinch and try to ignore it. "I can't help you if you don't accept me. I'm already here, in your head, in your body."

The way the Light says it disgusts me. I want it out, gone. I didn't *consent* for it to be here. "I request that you leave," I say. "Find another host."

"You think it works that easily? Fool. I only move on when I'm done with this body."

So if the Light kills its host before moving. Would that imply that Hadrian is dead? Who is running the Brightest?

"Hadrian lives, Chosen. His death certificate will be signed by another."

"Why not?" I demand. "Why is it different for me?"

"Look out," the Light urges. The change in tone confuses me for a moment. But it's too late. I feel a sharp sword enter through the center of my back and reveal itself out of my stomach, right above the navel.

I see it before I feel it. The sword retracts through the entry as quickly as it arrives. Shock, followed by pain, engulfs me as I turn around and see a wicked man. A creature. A Crit. I reach for my knife, but my right arm will not move, despite how much effort I use. My left hand comes up instinctively, and I fumble with the knife sheath on my right thigh. My missing fingers betray me.

The Crit lunges again. I'm not fast enough, and the tip of the sword digs into my leg. I scream in pain, stumbling. The Crit shows a face-splitting grin, exposing two dozen sharp teeth. I finally undo the latch on the knife holster. My chest wound burns with pain.

I wait for the Crit to attack first. When it does, I swiftly dodge the incoming strike and sink my knife into the Crit's right eyeball—a signature move. The palm of my hand touches his face ever so slightly.

A connection forms between the two of us. In my mind's eye I see two buckets. One is full and the other is empty. A straw connects the two. Without a second thought, I pull on the straw, creating a siphon.

The man in front of me slows. His left eye, the one I didn't stab, glazes over first. Shortly after, a frost pattern emerges on his face from where my palm touches him. I feel it. I feel the warmth filling me—rejuvenating me.

The Light moans in pleasure as the man is drained of all his heat. I can't bring myself to pull away. I find enjoyment watching this creature die in front of me. Despite hating the method.

My right hand feels my stomach where I'd been stabbed. There is no exit wound. I reach around my back with my other hand. No entry wound either. What the hell?

The Light speaks but is a blubbering mess. "I .... I told you. I of-offer great p-power." I pull my left hand back to check for blood. Nothing could prepare me for what I see.

Instead of finding blood painted across my hands, I find something even more strange. My middle, thumb, and forefinger wiggle as if I'd never lost them.

37

The Pressure

I've come into contact with what I know to be a
BlightStone.
From the Journal of Azura Seren. Mino section, 29th
orbit

The pain in my chest ceased entirely. When my fingers oddly grew back, my chest wound was healed alongside it. Was I supposed to say thank you? While I didn't want the Light speaking in my head, influencing my actions, I am not ungrateful to have what I'd lost returned to me.

"I mentioned earlier that a piece of me still lived within Hadrian," the Light whispers. "That was only a half-truth. A piece of the Light lives within Hadrian, but it is out of my reach. Inaccessible."

"What do you want me to do about it?" I say. I figure I could be rude, as long as I'm not disrespectful. It is inside my head without my permission after all.

"Reunite me with that piece," it says. "Take it from him with my aid."

"I'm not going to kill Hadrian for you." I don't even want to face him because I'll be the one who dies. I'll deal with it later. I'm going to need all the help I can get if this college is infested with Crits.

I'm not sure how much more walking I'll need to do. I've already walked about three times the distance of a normal day's walking. Other than the first attack, it's been oddly calm. The silence is uncanny. There's no wind, no trees, no wildlife. Just the random creaking of buildings and the occasional sound of glass crunching beneath my feet.

I thought I'd find more groups like the Horizon. There ought to be more caravans traveling through the Bright Spot. Unless they all avoid the cities. Who could blame them? Crits seem to love the opportunities buildings provide. It's almost like there are more Crits alive than normal travelers. Maybe because there are.

I'd always wondered why someone would stoop so low as to become a cannibal—to raid and attack helpless groups for food. But every day, I understand it more and more. Wild game is scarce. Meat is hard to come by. Why wouldn't they take advantage of the more abundant resource?

The moon hangs low in the sky. It's late in the day, but I'm not tired. Should I find a building to rest, or keep going?

I decide to just push forward. Having the sun replenish my energy proves to be very helpful. Although I know it's not *just* the sun that fuels me.

My previous murder sends a chill down my spine. It happened hours ago but I can't seem to banish it from my mind. I replay the memory of the incident. The man's terrified eye freezes over before the rest of his body becomes an ice sculpture.

My feet move without direction. I turn down a street corner knowing it is the right way to go. The feeling—the desire to head this direction—strengthens.

Something tugs at me. "I can feel it," the Light shouts in my mind. "Can you?"

As a matter of fact, I can feel something. I don't know what it is. It feels like the tension of a magnet when another magnet is nearby. It's in the direction I'm headed, and I'm drawn to it. I need to know what it is.

It's a short red brick building, probably about three stories tall—with two Crit guards standing outside. Is this what I'm drawn to? Why? I'm not entirely sure which faction it is, whether it's the Kreeturs, Claw, or Shearing, but I need to stay far away from it. I'm not Jaime. My goal is the college, not a random camp. I turn down a street to take a different route toward my destination.

"You're passing up an opportunity to acquire some heat. A lot of heat," the Light says gluttonously. "Let me show you something, Chosen. Let me show you the extent of my grandeur."

"Absolutely not," I say. "They're not my problem and I need to get to the college."

Pressure builds around my brain, pushing inward, threatening to crush my mind. The world spins and I drop to the ground, clutching my head. I can hardly move. I can hardly think. The pain blinds me, and I grab my hair, pulling it out to the sides to try to alleviate the pressure. My attempts are fruitless.

I scream in pain. It feels like I'm submerged in deep water. But many times worse than what I've experienced. I remember a time when Oberon and I were together in a lake in the Febro section. I forget which one. Brena hadn't been born yet, and we were still young. We both tried to see who could swim deep enough to touch the bottom.

I held my breath and slipped beneath the water. My body refused to sink, so I forced myself deeper, kicking with everything I had. The pressure built, pain bursting through my ears. I couldn't touch the bottom before my lungs began to burn. I shot back up, the ache in my chest growing. When I broke the surface, Oberon was waiting for me. He hadn't even tried. The bastard.

"My patience grows thin, Chosen," the voice says. I continue lying on the ground clutching my head. "Trust that I will take care of you. Understand?"

I have no choice. "I understand," I croak. Immediately, the pressure disappears. Extremely disoriented, I attempt to stand up, but I fall to the side. My body's natural reaction is to retch onto the concrete. There's nothing to vomit other than burning stomach acid.

"Light burn you," I swear. The Light chuckles at its name being used in vain. "Fine. What do you want?"

"That building with the two Crits, go inside. We are going to have some fun."

Dread forms a pit in my stomach. There could be dozens, maybe a hundred Crits in that building. Even with these weird abilities, I wouldn't be able to defend myself. But what would happen to me if I said no? Something worse?

"Something far worse," the Light affirmed. "That pain you felt just now is a scratch compared to the pain you are capable of feeling."

I hesitate, looking at the building and two guards out front. Green vines creep from the roof, making the coloring look brown. The two Crits out front are similar, both with long matted hair and ragged clothes. They laugh about something I can't hear. I feel disgusted looking at them. I remember that they are just doing what they can to survive. Just like myself.

"Now." I feel a light push against my head. It's a warning.

Fearfully, I approach the building, and the guards freeze when they notice my presence. Instead of attacking, they warily just watch me approach. They are poised to attack but don't advance.

"I request entrance," I shout from a dozen feet away, arms upward, showing my lack of weapons. They don't respond. Their cold stares make me second-guess my choice.

"You do not ask. You take what is yours. Let me show you what can be yours," the Light says. The two guards walk toward me. They don't carry weapons, either, but they don't need them. Their teeth will suffice.

I take a step backward, but they still approach. I'm going to die here. I stick my hands forward. Maybe I could do what I did to the other Crit—freeze them.

Instead of attacking, the guards walk *into* my outstretched palms and stop, closing their eyes. I feel a connection between them and myself, forming the same metaphorical straw. They seem to *push* their heat into me. It trickles in slightly as I resist. I feel both hearts beat under my palms. These are living beings—with hearts—like me. I can't.

"Do it," the Light demands, breaking the barrier.

The warmth flows into me. The same high and euphoria flood my body. Goose bumps form up my arms as the two guards slow. I watch as their eyes frost over first before the rest of their body follows. The frost spreads from their chests from where I touch them. The Light groans in pleasure. It's sickening.

One frozen guard—now an ice sculpture—falls backward. The body shatters as it hits the ground, launching chunks of ice in all directions.

The Light didn't break the barrier; I did. I drank in their heat because I wanted to. I killed them because I wanted to. In that moment, I realize I'm no different than a Crit. I go out of my way to steal.

At least I don't eat human flesh. That's one thing that separates me from them. It's the only piece of identity I have left.

"What happened?" I ask.

"Like the birds and the trees, like the grass and the wind, they serve me. Just like you. Just like the Brightest. They do as they're told when asked." That last sentence is a jab directed at me. "Now enter the building."

I don't have a choice. Every fiber of my being tells me to turn and run. Energy surges through my veins when I open the double doors to the building.

There's a front desk with no one there. "What am I looking for?" I ask, looking around the lobby. Ancient paintings litter the walls. Some of them are torn up either from previous travelers or age.

"Look," the Light commands. I do so, walking around the front desk and through an entryway. The hallway is long with a door at the end. Each step down the hallway feels like sandbags are tied to my feet. Loud chanting and the smell of rotten flesh intensify as I draw closer. I push open the door and behind it is a large room.

Dozens of Crits circle a pile of flesh and bones. Their chanting halts when I arrive. They all look at me with crazed, distant eyes. A few look at me hungrily. Some are confused, but most are indifferent to my arrival. Like the guards outside, they don't attack me.

"That's a queen." The Light brings my attention to a lavishly dressed man. His face is covered with makeup and lips painted with blood. His crooked nose signs that he'd broken it once. His headdress made of smaller bones woven together with cloth and string, makes him seem taller than he is. Each bone is perfectly aligned in an intricate array.

Is this the new queen the bald Crit referenced? Could this person be responsible for the murder of Oberon? We aren't at the college, but what if it's true?

The queen approaches me curiously, mouth open. Surprisingly, his teeth are not shaven down into points, but straight across. He bears no semblance of being a Crit either.

He steps closer and I smell his breath as he breathes on my face. He doesn't look at me with hunger, anger, or fear. But with a mutual respect.

This guy is normal. Had he been elevated by the freaks around him? Like the vision showed, this is my fate. I'm staring at what could be a future version of myself. Except the vision had me outside, not in a dim room in some building.

"Touch him, Chosen," The Light hisses.

"I offer my warmth to you, holy one," the queen says, arms outstretched. His expression isn't sorrowful, but rather acceptance. He's been waiting a long time for this moment. Would it be revenge for my friend if I killed him? Would this make me the new queen?

My hand trembles as I raise it. Every sane part of me screams in refusal. Deep down though, I want this. I know what kind of person I truly am.

I must kill to protect.

A connection is created between us, a straw between him and myself. "Do not take from him. Instead, give." I feel the connection, begging me to pull. I push instead.

I feel my body temperature cooling down and after a moment, the man combusts into flames. The room illuminates brightly with a strong orange glow. The fire touches the ceiling, and I feel the radiant heat. Other Crits watch in fascination and in horror as their leader burns.

The queen bellows a blood-curdling scream, but he does not try to bat the fire away. I watch in horror as the flesh drips from his bones, creating a dark maroon pile around his feet. Could I help him? Could I draw the heat back in? Should I?

Before the Light can tell me no, the flames die out and the once-human falls to the floor. His face is unrecognizable.

I gag, trying to vomit, but there's nothing in my stomach to empty. Not even bile. Crits in the room weep in unison. Some fall to their knees and bury their faces in their hands. They don't look at me in hate. Only sadness. I'd killed their leader. The person they respected the most.

Light. That was horrifying. I'd just burned him alive. I'd sacrificed him—for what?

"Queen! Queen! Queen!" the voices moan in unison. It sounds both a chant and a eulogy. Guilt creeps into my throat. These people feel pain like everyone else. I have to remember Pladd. He'd offered a new perspective on his people. A perspective I ignored after spending more time with the Horizon.

"I bore of this," the Light says. "Ready to leave now?"

"You bore of this?" I whisper sharply so only the Light can hear me. "You made me kill their respected leader and you say you're bored?" I don't hide the disgust in my voice.

"You're right. I know of a way to make it a little less boring." The Light's voice edges on insanity. I feel a warmth surge within my chest.

"What? No, I—" Before I can protest, a burst of energy erupts from my core. Like one of Steeq's explosives. Within a blink of an eye, the entire building is in flames.

The smoke stings my throat. Paintings on the walls curl like dry leaves. A wail escapes from the floor above—a child.

My legs move lethargically. I head back through the hallway, flames already spreading throughout the entire building. I run past the front desk and out the front doors. Destruction plays out behind me. I turn back to watch the entire building collapse in on itself, crushing and killing anyone still left inside.

So this is who I am now? I hate it. What does it matter how many lives I might've saved—when I've taken so many more. Crits or humans ... what's the difference?

"I love thermal transference," the Light says in my head. "What do you think?"

"I'm going to kill you," I threaten. I'm not sure how I'm going to do it.

"Good luck with that one," it says mockingly. "You're my puppet, Chosen."

I stumble through a few more blocks searching for a place to rest. My body hurts in so many different places. Why hasn't the Light healed any of it yet? If I killed myself would the Light die with me? Unfortunately, Hadrian is still alive and carries a piece of it. The Light would live on, even after my futile attempt.

My foot misses its next step, and I fall forward, shin scraping the edge of the pothole. I groan in pain and the Light chuckles.

I realize something then—the Light can't make my body do anything. It can influence the heat and freezing abilities, but it can't move my legs or swing my arms. It can apply pressure to my head as a manipulation tactic, but it can't make me do anything. I still have some amount of bodily autonomy.

"Careful with your thoughts there, child," the Light whispers.

"Ah, screw you," I say out loud, both middle fingers in the air. Light, it is so nice to have that finger back.

I stumble lethargically to a building and push through the front doors. Searching through a couple of the rooms, I find one with a tapestry on the wall. Ripping down the cloth, I lay down on the hard carpet, tossing the art over me as a makeshift blanket. My mind drifts into a safe reality separate from this one.

38

The University of Solace

Could the BlightStone be linked to the Freezing?
From the Journal of Azura Seren. Mino section, 29th
orbit

As I draw closer to the college, I feel it more strongly. The same strange magnetic feeling. I feel terrible for what I've done to the people in the burning building. But there's nothing I can do about it now. They're not human. They're not human. They're not human. I repeat it over and over in my mind until I believe it.

In the distance, I see something familiar. The top of it barely breaks above a building: a willow tree, like the one in Hollyard. My legs burn, but at least now there's some kind of end in sight. I push further. How long have I been walking? A day? Maybe two? I wish there were an easier way to track the passing of time. We'd be much further behind if Jaime and Elara had come along.

I walk another half mile drawing closer. The willow stands in front of the college like a beacon. A plot of grass surrounds it, edged with concrete sidewalks. The massive trunk still leaves me in awe. Its leaves droop sadly, brushing against the grass underneath.

The college isn't a singular building, but rather a group of seven. The tree stands in front of one that looks like some kind of research center. The building is almost made entirely of glass, standing thirty feet tall, meeting at a dense concrete roof. The faded support columns are cracked, showing hundreds of passings of wear. The design of the building is alien compared to any other building I've seen before.

Something is off. Where are all the Crits? There are none outside, yet signs of their presence are shown with trash, blood, and bones littering the once-pristine sidewalk.

I hear something in the distance. A faint, low groaning coming from multiple bodies. Are those … cattle?

I walk and feel the pull change directions. The impression I'm feeling is coming from the willow tree. Not the college. Maybe my strange abilities connected me to all the willows. Perhaps they aren't even willow trees, but something else entirely.

"I didn't bring you here for the college," the Light whispers. "You're here for that. Touch it," it urges.

I hesitate, remembering all the other times the Light directed me to touch something with my hands. Everything I touched, died, either by ice or fire. I extend my left hand anyway, seeing my regrown fingers, and touch the tree. I expected it to burst into flames. Instead, its energy surges through me as if I'd stolen the heat from a victim. But, unlike a human, the tree doesn't freeze. It glows brightly enough to be seen in the broad sunlight.

The bark under my palm moves and undulates. I lift my hand to see what's underneath. The bark splits, spreading to the sides, opening up like a curtain. It leaves a slit-shaped hole, revealing something inside. It's a green, porous stone, identical to the one Pladd had given me.

"Take it," the Light says. "Plant it and receive even more power as your soul becomes more aligned with my own." I pinch the rock and gently remove it from the tree. The bark closes back up, folding in on itself.

The object, a BlightStone, leaves a residue of dust in my hand. I feel a desire to crush it in my palm. It's what connected me to the Light. It's what caused me to kill others against my will. I want to destroy it. "Hey now, child …"

I can't bring myself to do it. I'm capable of so much already and the Light is offering more. I'm already bound to the Light, so why shouldn't I accept it? I pocket the small stone, being careful not to crush the fragile seed. I can't consume the BlightStone. Not yet anyway. I'll need an isolated planter box. Could I eat it? There's an impression from the Light as well—curiosity? It doesn't know either.

"We've been trying to extract that for weeks," a voice says, interrupting my train of thought. I turn around to see a Crit standing behind me. He's shorter than me by about a foot. One of his eyes rests higher than the other and he displays heavy acne scarring on both cheeks. I'm too startled to react. I should unsheathe my knife, but I don't. "I'd been told you'd show up to redeem us."

"Who told you that?" I demand harshly. I will not redeem these creatures. His face disgusts me. Could this … thing be a product of Crit inbreeding?

"Our queen, of course," the Crit says. "We've tried hundreds of different ways to open the tree up. Knives, axes, hammers, you name it. And then you show up and touch it. Just like he said you would."

"He?" The Light mirrors my thoughts. Who in the world would know such a thing? It seems like I'm the subject of some kind of prophecy. One that I am not privy to. Should I be surprised though, being connected to the burning Light itself?

Does he want me to give the stone to him? What if he attacks me for it? I could take him easily with my renewed power. I study him, standing defensively for any move he could pull.

He knew I'd be able to retrieve the BlightStone from the tree. Would that mean he knows about my abilities too? He wouldn't fight me; he has to know he's outmatched. One thing seems terribly off about the man, though. He seems strangely aware for being a Crit—speaking in perfect language, not like the other Crits I've met. Pladd isn't genetically a Crit, though he lived a Crit lifestyle. This abomination definitely is.

The man shrugs and waves his hand. "Come, let me introduce you to our queen," he says, turning to walk toward the college.

"You should kill him," the Light says hungrily. I could easily do it. He'd exposed his back to me, to a potential enemy. A rookie mistake I'd learned from Jaime. But I don't take the opportunity. Instead, I revel in the fact that I could. I figured the Light would punish me for refusing, but it doesn't.

The glass doors slide open automatically revealing a large open common area. Weeks ago, this would have fascinated me, but the magic of electricity had worn off. After learning about radios, rail guns, and cars, sliding glass doors aren't anything mind-blowing.

We walk by a group of four other Crits. Two men and two women. They sit in a circle chatting about potential lead contamination in Solace's water supply. Among them are stacks of papers. The sight of cannibalistic Crits having an intellectual conversation is as unsettling as Steeq's lack of concern for death.

"Why are you guys at the college? And not somewhere else?" I ask the man escorting me. We pass a few more Crits and no one shows any outward hostility.

"Our queen wanted to explore the deeper philosophical side of our species. He wanted to conduct research to see if we were as intelligent as your kind and how much it would take to teach us the human condition. There are tons of pristine psychology books in the library. Anything you want to learn, you can find here."

Elara would overflow with excitement if she came here. But an intelligent Crit? That seems impossible, wrong even. If I wasn't seeing it with my own eyes, I wouldn't believe him. Perhaps they are faking? But how? It doesn't make sense.

"But you guys still murder and eat other humans," I say. "Do any of you find anything wrong with that?"

"Do you find anything wrong with hunting deer, Caelius?" the man asks, somehow knowing my name. It sends a chill down my spine. "You don't classify us as humans. By your definition, we are different."

"How do you know my name?" I threaten.

He doesn't answer that question; instead, he continues his rant. "How can it be considered cannibalism if, in order to be called a cannibal, you have to eat meat of your own species? Many of us are human, and some do indulge in consumption of human flesh."

"Why do you do it? If you're so intelligent now, why do you guys consume human meat?"

"A lot of us do it for sport. It's in our DNA. Another reason for some may be tradition."

"What about you?" I ask. "Why are you a cannibal?"

"I don't eat meat, actually," he answers. "I'm vegan."

Many of the words he'd used prior went over my head, but I can infer what that means through context. My mouth drops. A cannibal who doesn't eat meat? Has the Darkness burned over? I actually laugh at the absurdity.

"Don't be so close-minded," the Crit jokes. "I'm a Crit genetically, but that doesn't mean I have to eat meat. We're omnivores, like you."

I don't know what an omnivore is, and I don't want to ask. "This is an abomination," the Light shouts in my head. It's just as bewildered as I am.

We approach a room at the end of a hallway. The door reads *QUEEN* in black marker. "We are here," the Crit says. "Don't forget to take off your shoes before entering."

I keep my shoes on. "Hey, I didn't catch your name?" I ask the vegan Crit.

"Petyr," he says with a smile.

Petyr. I've heard that name somewhere. Did Pladd mention it at some point? "Well, Petyr," I start, almost not finishing, "thank you for bringing me here. It was a pleasure to get to know you."

He nods and his smile widens. "Of course, sir. Any time."

He leaves and I push open the door in front of me. The room is dim, lit only by flames of a hearth. I'm reminded of the church basement. In the center of the room, facing the door, is a lavish leather chair. Seated, is a short man. A cloth hangs over his right shoulder, and he holds a glass of red liquid between his left fingers. The flickering flames briefly illuminate his face. I could recognize the pointy rat face from anywhere.

"Hello, Caelius," Mattias says, with a smirk. "Good to see you again."

39

The Queen

*I've heard reports of individuals who can freeze
the air around them.*
From the Journal of Azura Seren. Janio section, 29th orbit

An overwhelming guilt floods my body as my fight-or-flight reaction kicks in. I killed Mattias. Yet he sits here right in front of me. A walking corpse. My eyes adjust to the darkness, and he looks just like how I remember him. Except this time, he has an air about him. Some kind of unstated authority. So, this is who they chose as their queen.

"Mattias," I start before he cuts me off.

"Caelius, do you know how many times a day I replay that event in my head?" he says, standing up. The red liquid swishes around in his glass. "I've tried to convince myself that you did the right thing. That you did what you had to do. But I no longer think that's true."

"Mattias—"

"I'm not finished," he says. "When I say you can speak, speak. Until then, listen." I keep my mouth shut. "The look in your eyes before you let go of my hand. Before you killed me. I didn't know it, but I've seen the same look dozens of times now. You wanted me gone. You took the opportunity to kill me. Just as I now have the opportunity to kill you," he says, taking a sip of his drink. "Now you may speak."

"I'm sorry I let go, Mattias. I really did jump in to save you. I didn't want to die either! I've suffered, losing my fingers as a result of my actions," I cry out.

He observes me, looking at my hands and tilting his head curiously. "Why do you lie, old friend? Why did you and Oberon hate me so much?"

"We didn't hate you, Mattias. We—"

He cuts me off. "Lost your fingers." He scoffs, bitter. "What a sick joke." Mattias pulls out a knife and sets it on a table between us. He leans in close enough that I can smell the blood on his breath. "I lost more than you could ever understand."

With a sharp flick, the cape draped over his right arm flies behind his shoulder. Where his arm should be is nothing but a scarred stump.

Light burn me. I did that. I thought I had it hard, but my misfortune pales in comparison to his.

"Remind me again," Mattias says. "Do you like veal, Caelius?" He says my name with venom on his tongue. A Crit servant comes out and places two plates on the table next to us. "Please, sit."

I warily take a seat and Mattias does the same. The steak is adorned with broccoli, spinach, and butter, food I'd never had before joining the Horizon. Mattias continues when I don't say anything. "Can you believe there are wild cattle roaming around?" With one arm, he stuffs a napkin in his shirt. "I guess they don't like sticking around the Path, like the Brightest. When was the last time we shared a beef steak?"

He grabs the steak in one hand and tears at it with his straight teeth. He hadn't filed them down yet. I stare at the assortment of colors on my plate as he digs in. On the right of my plate is a fork. To the left is a serrated kitchen knife. I could kill him. Finish the job correctly.

"I butchered the calf myself. You don't have to worry," he says in between bites. I continue to stare at it. I don't trust him. How am I to know this isn't human meat? Would I know the difference between beef and human? The Light is awfully quiet.

What about after I kill him? The knife is sharp, but what if the consequences are sharper? Maybe I'd be elevated to his position as queen. The vision would become true.

"Eat. It," he demands after a few minutes. His plate is completely clean. My stomach does somersaults as I stare at the meal. I can't do this. "Eat it, or I'll shove the whole damn thing down your throat." Am I really going to fold under Mattias?

My hand lifts the steak knife from the table, trembling. He watches me intensely as I cut a piece off the mystery steak and hold it up with my fork. The pink center leaves blood on the plate. I feel like I'm going to vomit.

I gag when I stuff the tender meat into my mouth. The flavors are rich and the steak melts on my tongue, unlike the toughness of venison. The butter and spices enhance the flavor, too, creating a combination of flavors I've never experienced. It's delicious, but I can't bring myself to take another bite.

"Good boy," Mattias praises. Light burn him. Light burn him to hell.

"This isn't veal is it?" I ask, taking a breath.

"Why should it matter? Meat is meat," he dismisses. "It's also fun to watch you squirm." He leans in, taking a sip of his red drink. "That's the best part about being a butcher. All meat looks the same when cooked."

I resist the urge to gag again. "What do you want from me?" I push the unfinished plate away.

"What do I want?" he asks, incredulous. "You're the one who came here. I'm just trying to live peacefully, but you've come to screw it up a second time. How did you even find me? Come to finish the job you started?"

"I didn't. I—"

He cuts me off. "You took everything from me you know?" he says, digging up a previous conversation. He stands from his chair and paces toward me. "You took my arm. You took my job. You took Lyria. We were friends, Caelius. How come you wanted me gone?"

His eyes drill into me for a long moment. What do I say? He's not going to like any answer I provide. "We wanted you gone because you were annoying. But we didn't want you dead." He takes a step back looking offended. "No, actually you were downright mean and vile to us. You said that if there wasn't enough food, we wouldn't eat. You aided in the sabotage of Oberon's marriage."

Mattias lifts his chin up, trying to play off the grin his face holds. "You don't eat my food anyway? Why would I give food to someone as wasteful as you?" He gestures toward my uneaten meal. "Oberon's marriage was failing even before I stepped in. He told me himself."

I set my jaw, not saying a word. Mattias leans forward and sets his knife down on the tablecloth between us. He takes his finger and spins the knife lightly. When he lifts his forefinger, the knife continues spinning, the blade eventually pointing directly at me.

He shakes his head. "Tell me this, as I do not understand. Why are you here instead of with the rest of them?"

I don't want to tell him the truth, but I know I should. "I came looking for Oberon, who was exiled."

"Exiled?" Mattias asks, surprise covering his face.

"When I decided I was going to search for him, Hadrian exiled me as well. He told me to never come back," I explain, "but I found Oberon's crossbow at a nearby Crit camp." I leave the rest unsaid.

"That must be really hard for you. Oberon was the better of you two. He didn't deserve to die."

"No, he didn't," I say, taking a deep breath. "Now are you going to tell me how you got here?"

"It's only fair, I guess," Mattias says, getting more comfortable. "After you killed me, I drifted down the river. I don't know how many miles or if I was conscious for any of it. I'd finally washed up on a bank and was met by friends, real friends, who took me in, warmed me up, kept me fed, and gave me a home.

"When I found myself acquainted with the group, I was the smartest one of them all." He continues, "This was a challenge to some and a shock for most. I bested all of them in intellect. They wanted to test strength as well, but with clever wordplay, I got them to drop it. It didn't take long before they all wanted me as their queen. I don't entirely know why, but I've seemed to have found my name in the mouths of everyone. Maybe they wanted change and saw it within me."

"Crits don't change," I spit.

"What makes you say that?" Mattias asks. "Can a person not accept his failures and become a better man for it? Is it that hard to believe that people can walk away from their old lifestyles to embrace a new one?" I don't have a response, but he continues. "Remember in the forest when I promised to change? You tried killing me soon after."

I notice a face peek from a door. It's a child's face. He has to be less than four feet tall. Mattias sees my lack of attention and turns around. The boy hides behind the doorframe. "Tommy," Mattias calls. "It's okay, little one. You can come out. Say hi to uncle Caelius."

Tommy? Could it be? The boy comes out, his thumb hanging loosely from his mouth. The boy sits on Mattias's lap and waves his hand sluggishly toward me, making intense eye contact. Children have always creeped me out. His analytical eyes watch my every move.

"I hope Lyria will be happy when she learns that I'm taking good care of her child," Mattias says.

The world around me spins, when my suspicions are confirmed. She'd spent months searching for him. She hung herself when she believed he was dead. If only she knew.

I want to grab him and bring him back to his mother. But I know that won't end well for me. There's no way he'd let me just take him. He's likely already grown attached to this place. Attached to Mattias.

"You believe Oberon is dead, so why are you here, Caelius? Surely you didn't think you'd find him."

"I'm here to learn more about what happened thirty orbits ago."

"No, no!" Mattias shouts. "You promised you'd tell the truth! Why are you here?"

I look at him with disdain. "I'm here to destroy the college."

"Destroy the college?" Mattias's eyebrows flatten. "Why ever would you want to do that?"

I come up with a lie, but I don't use it. I sigh, not even wanting to bring them into this. "There are people who want to fix the world. They want to … make the Darkness habitable again." I bite the inside of my cheek. "Doing so would kill all plant life on Nivalis. So, I came here to destroy any bit of knowledge related to the Freezing." The idea sounds stupid in my ears as I say it aloud. Maybe the Light planted that idea into my head so I'd collect that BlightStone.

"We forge the chains we wear in life," he says. "You can't imagine living in a world where you don't have to travel constantly." I nod in response. "You're right, though. The college does contain the answer."

I meet his eyes and he presses a hand on the child's head, messing up his blond hair. Mattias continues. "My team found a publication. You would call it a history book now. It stated that the world had been overcome by a blight of some kind. A manufactured blight. You see, many passings ago, a group of scientists realized that crops don't grow well in the Darkness. Which is fine if there are just a couple hundred thousand people alive, but the world kept growing. Expanding into the millions, maybe billions." Mattias paces in his lavish room. The hearth pops, shifting the wood.

He continues his monologue: "Too many mouths to feed, not enough food. A tale older than time itself. Children died clutching their hungry stomachs. Men found food elsewhere, forming the first-ever cannibal group, predating the Freezing of the World." He takes another sip of his drink. "Ironic, right? You'd think they'd have resorted to cannibalism after the Freezing, but it found its roots long before."

"What does this have to do with the plants?"

"Remember what I said about interrupting?" A blood vessel makes itself visible on his head. "Also, what a stupid question. This has everything to do with the plants. These six scientists devised a way to allow the plants to grow in the dark, taking heat from the air instead of light from the sun. One genetically modified seed could change the chemistry of an entire acre of farmland to follow the same rules.

"The scientists injected themselves with a failsafe vaccine in case things went wrong. Their idea worked for many orbits, but the six passed before it got out of hand. Only their blood can reverse this blight." He shakes his head. "Them and their offspring." He looks at Tommy. "That boy is the key to fixing this all."

It clicks in my head. He's a direct descendant of one of the scientists. He's a Merida, right? His father is the infamous Jack Merida. A "who knows how many greats" grandson of one of the lab partners.

"Well, now you know the secret. I guess you could destroy this place now if you're so inclined." He sticks his arm out. "But you know as well as I that knowledge is a weapon." He's right. How would Elara react if she found out I knew the secret but kept it from her? Damn him for playing these games with me.

"Oh Light, what kind of host am I?" Mattias says. "I haven't even shown you my little pet." Mattias walks over to a box four feet high, covered by a blanket.

The blanket flies off the cage like a cape in the wind. Inside the cage is a man with scars all over his body. He's extremely malnourished and barely lucid. Hair on his once-bald head pokes through his scalp.

I gasp, standing up. I cross the room to get a closer look. Oberon lays curled up on the floor of the cage, trembling. "Oberon," I urge, grabbing the bars of the cage, shaking. He doesn't speak a word. "Get him out!" I yell. Light, what did they do to you?

"Of course, I'll let him out—under one condition," Mattias says. His smile shows that he's going to be extra difficult. "Bring me Lyria, and I'll let your friend go."

Lyria? Bring Lyria to him? I could do that. Easily. She was with the Brightest. How hard could it be? I could convince her if she knew her son was here.

But what kind of person would I be if I did that? If I brought her to this hellhole where she'd surely die. What if the Brightest already left Hollyard? They could be miles away by now.

"I can't do that. I don't know where she is!"

"She's with the Brightest, no? Find her, bring her, and Oberon is yours."

Sweat beads down my forehead. Would I even have time? Is it safe? I panic as I stare at the barely recognizable man in the cage. He curls into a ball, tears leaking down his face. It makes me sick seeing my best friend like this.

"Is there anything else I could do? I can't get Lyria. I'm sorry," I say.

"I know," he says, like he expected that answer. "There is one other thing I'll trade," Mattias says. "You carry it with you in your pocket."

My hands dig into my pant pocket, and I pull out the seed I extracted from the tree in front of the college. It's another BlightStone. Like the one from Hollyard.

I knew it was the item Hadrian desperately wanted; now I understand why. There was a reason he halted our progress to search for it. Now this man in front of me, a man I no longer recognize, wants it for himself. He wants power. The same power I carry in my hands—in my head. "Don't you dare," the Light whispers in my head. I barely hear it.

This Mattias is not the same Mattias I knew. He is colder, darker, more sinister. He watches me with his calculating eyes, reading my thoughts like an open book. Before he'd drifted away with that freezing river, he'd told Oberon and me that he wanted to become a better person.

He was self-aware in that moment and wanted to do right by us. And I took that from him.

The consequence of my action led to the Brightest not having a competent butcher. I'd lost my fingers and had to deal with the pain of knowing I'd killed someone. Not someone who was trying to hurt me or someone else. I'd killed a man who wasn't much different from myself. One of my own.

Now that man stands in front of me, arm outstretched. Behind him in the large cage is my friend. The one I'd thought was dead. The one I risked everything to find. And now Lyria's child, who was also presumed to be dead, clutches to Mattias's pant leg.

Dead men walking—apparitions only I can see.

"I'm waiting," Mattias says impatiently. Maybe I should just kill him. Could I bring myself to do that again? Could I really take the life of another man? Of a member of the Brightest? My hand trembles and I almost drop the stone.

"Tell me what this is," I demand, holding the stone above my head.

"Caelius, be rational." He drops his head sluggishly, impatient. His arm is still outstretched.

"Tell me what it is or I crush it under my boot." I'm not bluffing. The Light cries out but I ignore it. It wouldn't dare try to manipulate me, not when I finally have the position of power. I don't entirely know what it is or how important it's supposed to be. Mattias, Hadrian, and the Light itself seem to want it badly, which makes me skeptical.

Mattias sighs, dropping his hand. "It's a BlightStone."

"I know that, dingus."

"It's a concentrated by-product from the scientists' experiments. I don't know how they are formed."

"What happens if I cleanse the blight? With Tommy's blood?"

"You die. You seem to have touched the power. Your soul is intertwined with it. And who knows … you might kill everyone on Nivalis while you're at it. The flora would have to relearn how to survive and who knows if they'll be able to generate oxygen."

I really should crush it. My arm comes up, poised to throw it against the ground, but something makes me hesitate. "Please don't," the Light says in my head; is it … crying?

"If you crush that," Mattias says, "that BlightStone will just regenerate somewhere else. We'll find it again."

"Who's gonna unlock the next tree then, huh?" I ask.

"If you destroy that, I'll kill him in front of you." Mattias holds a knife up to Tommy's throat. "Oberon will be next. I'll chop him up and force you to eat him." I bite my lip. He's lost his mind.

I can't negotiate with the insane. No matter what I do, the outcome would be devastating. Would he seriously kill the child of the woman he wants? Would he bluff over something like that?

I lower my arm, holding the BlightStone in my palm. Mattias sheathes his knife and quickly plucks the tiny rock from my hand. "Thank you," he says, satisfied, admiring the stone. Tommy darts away into the other room. "As promised." The little man gently puts the rock into his pocket and unlatches Oberon's cage. Oberon twitches slightly.

Hate burns within me. I can feel the power of the willow rush through my muscles. I wish he would have died in that river. I should have held him down under. I should have choked him out with my bare hands.

Mattias opens a door and steps through. "Oh, and when you bring Lyria to me, there will be a more handsome reward waiting for you. I'm sure she wants to see her son again." With that, the door closes behind him and there's a click of a deadbolt lock.

I push out, intent on burning the entire place down. I feel the inferno building inside of me, but when I release, nothing happens. "I'm empty, Chosen. I need warmth. Your reserves are gone. I .... I can't. I'm sorry." I shake my head. I don't have time for this.

I drag Oberon out of the kennel and sling him over my shoulder. He's much lighter than I remember. I exit the room, wary of being attacked and killed by the surrounding Crits. Where did Mattias and Tommy go? Maybe I should have killed him when I had the chance. I couldn't bring myself to do it. But what about Oberon? He needs medical attention immediately. I need to get him to Dan first. I'll deal with Mattias another day.

I walk down the long hallway. The Crits stare at me, but they don't say or do anything. Oberon carried my body for miles after I jumped in the river to kill Mattias. Now it's time for me to do the same.

"Leaving so soon?" a voice says behind me. I struggle to turn around to see Petyr standing there. There is no malice or ill intent in the man's face. Just concern. "Be careful out there, friend," he says.

"Until next time," I say, not sure if there will be a next time. I liked the funny little man. He's different from the other Crits I'd run into. Oberon mumbles something, but it's unintelligible. "I know, buddy. I'm gonna get you some help, okay?"

40

The Chosen

*It terrifies me that these powerful individuals live
so close. The entire world lives in a twelve-
hundred-mile-long zone.*
From the Journal of Azura Seren. Janio section, 29th orbit

I don't know how long I walked. The sun provided enough energy for me to carry Oberon for Light knows how many miles back to the hotel. The Light grumbled in my ear for letting Mattias take the BlightStone from me. Unfortunately for the Light, Oberon is my priority. Not some rock. I'm relieved it hadn't tried attacking me for my failure.

Oberon is terribly malnourished; the previously 250-pound man weighed nearly half that. It is concerning, but it made the return trip much easier. Maybe Mattias tried feeding him but Oberon refused to eat.

Not a single Crit attacks me on the way back. Which is concerning. Maybe the Light had cleared the way for me, allowing me to return safely.

My foot pushes open the hotel doors and they swing open. Dan is preparing the dinner table by himself, placing silverware at the position I usually sit. He reacts quickly when he sees me, shouting, "Get him on the table." He sweeps everything off the table with his arm. Silverware and glasses of water fly off the surface. I set Oberon on his back, pushing the rest of the tablecloth off. Oberon's breath rattles through cracked lips. Dan's already in the kitchen, searching for something.

"Is everything okay?" Elara appears from around the corner. "What happened?" Jaime arrives behind her, holding a shortsword in his hand. Sweat beads down his face. He must have been training.

They both freeze when they see me. Elara keeps her hand close to her chest. Jaime does not lower his weapon.

"Where the hell have you been?" Jaime shouts. "We thought you died."

Dan returns from the kitchen holding a glass of water in one hand, a med kit in the other. I take a step back and let Dan do his work and address the two. Seeing their faces fills me with guilt. I'd just abandoned them to destroy some college. I didn't even get to do that.

"I'm sorry," I say, cringing. "I shouldn't have left without telling you. It all just happened so fast."

Jaime's shoulders relax and he lowers his sword. The siblings look at the sickly man on the dining table. "Is this him?" Jaime asks, pointing his blade at Oberon. I just nod. "Light," he swears. "Where was he?"

Dan removes a small knife from the bag and cuts open Oberon's shirt to get a better look at his wounds. I knew he was malnourished, but his thin body makes me concerned.

There are about ten or twelve cuts on both sides of his ribs, each a precise inch from the last. His torso looks like he has gills.

My teeth clench, not wanting to tell them, but I was gone for two days with no word. The least I could offer is the truth. I take a deep breath before speaking. "I went to the college." Elara's face twists in betrayal.

She doesn't say anything. She's not mad; instead her eyes well up with tears. My heart aches seeing her like this. I missed her so much.

"You were right, Jaime," I continue. "The college was filled with Crits. Except these ones … these ones were different. Unnatural." He raises his chin. I take that as a sign to continue. "They were smart—intelligent."

"How?" he asks.

"I met their queen," I tell them. "He was an old friend. One that should be dead."

Dan pulls out a bottle of alcohol and a few balls of cotton. He soaks one in the clear liquid and gently dabs one of Oberon's cuts. He grunts, his back arching in pain.

"Who?" Jaime demands, harsher this time.

"Mattias," I reply. "He was a butcher for the Brightest. He fell into a river, and I let him die. Unfortunately, like the cockroach he is, he survived and became the queen of the most dangerous group of Crits I've seen. Somehow, he civilized them, changed their culture." It had only been a couple of weeks since he was taken by the river. How did he manage to civilize so many Crits in such a short period of time? I continue explaining, "There was a vegan Crit who I met."

Jaime laughs. Under different circumstances, the sound would be welcome. "That's absurd," Jaime says. "Crits can't be vegan." He shakes his head, sheathing his sword in his scabbard. "Why did you even go in the first place?"

Elara's moist eyes meet mine. I betrayed her by going without her. I'm not sure what would hurt her more—a lie or the truth. "I wanted to find answers. I went alone because I didn't want you guys to get hurt."

"And did you find them?" Elara chokes.

The words hang in the air for what feels like hours. I see her pain. Maybe she understands? I take a breath and force the word out. "No."

Jaime crosses his arms and Elara rushes back to her room without saying another word. I'm startled by the Light speaking in my mind. "You're wasting your time with them. Go back and retrieve that BlightStone." I'm not sure if Jaime noticed me flinching.

"I know you're lying," Jaime says once Elara is out of earshot. He steps forward. "You found something. But you won't share it." I nod, meeting his eyes. "Whatever it might be, I trust that you have a good reason for not bringing it up."

I smile weakly. "You wouldn't believe me if I told you."

"Depends on if you tell me the truth."

Dan pulls out a spool of thread and a hooked needle. He tries to delicately weave the string through the eye, but his massive hands stop him. "Elara, I need your ..." He turns to see that Elara had left. Jaime takes the items from Dan and threads the needle with ease.

Dan nods in thanks, examining the first of many cuts on his ribs. He pinches the two sides of flesh together and inserts the needle through one side and out the other. The skin resists and Oberon winces in pain.

"Here, Dan." I fish out the purple petal from my pocket with my left hand. SpringStep's abilities to block pain are unmatched. Too bad it came with a price. The Light recoils in my mind upon seeing the petal.

Dan smiles, pinching it between his large fingers. Oberon visibly relaxes when the petal touches his tongue. I know the feeling of bliss. It's amazing, intoxicating. I wish I had some more for myself. "I figured you'd have taken all three by now," Dan says. "How's your chest?"

Before I can speak, Jaime shoves me to the ground. I land hard on my back, all the air expelled from my chest. He pins me down, tightly gripping my left wrist. "What the hell is this?" Jaime demands.

I can't speak before he rips open my shirt. He cuts open the bandages wrapped around my chest. He freezes, dropping his knife. Mouth agape, he tries speaking, but no words escape his lips.

"Huh." Dan shrugs. "That healed up really well."

"How is that possible?" Jaime finally says. "What the hell did you do?"

The Light squeals in glee, "Oh I like this one. There's something odd about him. Might he know Ms. Rivers?"

I struggle, trying to push Jaime off of me. "I don't know," I lie again. "It could be the SpringStep maybe."

Jaime squeezes my wrist even harder, fingernails digging into my skin. "Who are you really, Caelius?"

"He's mine, little Grafter," the Light says in my head. Jaime leaps backward, releasing me as if he heard it too. Perhaps he did. Fear masks his face as he steps away quickly, not breaking eye contact.

"You're"—his breath catches—"you're the Chosen."

41

The Prophet

*My age has begun to limit my abilities. But I've
been told I needn't worry about it for much longer.*
From the Journal of Azura Seren. Sebero section, 29th
orbit

Bang, bang, bang. My knuckles rap against Elara's
door. There's no response. "Elara," I yell, wiggling
the locked doorknob. "Elara, I'm sorry." Nothing.
Is she even in there?

"Please just leave," she shouts.

"Please, I just need answers. Your brother started
worshipping me. He called me the Chosen." The door
opens slightly, caught by the chain lock and she peeks out.

"What makes you think you deserve answers?" She's
right. I lied to her and denied her information. She has
every right to do the same.

"I don't. But something weird is happening to me, and you're the only person who can help."

"Jaime called you the Chosen, huh?" She sighs and curses under her breath. "Fine." The door closes so she can slide the chain lock, and the door swings open. I step into her room. "What happened?" she asks, annoyed. "Try not to lie or hide anything from me, because I'll know."

I nod my head and try to ease into it. "So. Um. How've you been?" She kicks me in the shin. I grunt, grabbing my leg in response.

"What is wrong with you?" she demands.

I need to rewind and fill her in. "Do you have a glass of water?" I say through clenched teeth. She sighs and grabs the glass from her nightstand, filling it with water from the bathroom. When she hands it to me I dip a finger into the lukewarm liquid.

"Woah what the hell?" she yells. I haven't even done anything. "Your hand?" She takes a step back, fear in her eyes.

I wave to her with all five of my restored fingers. I dip one in the water again and drain the heat from the glass. In moments, the water turns to ice. I leave behind an impression of my finger when I remove it. Her face is even more worried. Her mouth moves, but no words escape.

I hand her the glass, and she softly grazes the ice, likely not believing it's real. I press my finger into the cavity again and push heat outward. The ice melts into water, boiling seconds after.

The cup cracks and she drops it. "Ow!" she exclaims in pain. The glass shatters, spilling hot water all over the floor. She meets my eyes and instead of fear, there's realization. "Jaime's right," she whispers.

"What? Right about what?"

"Jaime follows the Chosen, a denomination of the Path. Meeting you is like meeting a ..." She snaps her fingers thinking of the word. "A prophet. Or like a humanized version of the Light, maybe."

I've never heard of the Chosen denomination. Hadrian never mentioned it in any of his teachings. Though the Light itself had called me its Chosen many times. "But I'm not the Light. I'm just a man."

"Not to him."

My stomach drops as I understand the scale of it all. Am I really some prophet, slated to arrive? Did his religion predict my coming? How? But what about Hadrian? Why isn't he this "Chosen?"

"Why the hell didn't you tell me sooner?"

"I didn't want you to freak out," I say, dropping my head. "I'm still trying to understand it myself."

"I was more freaked out thinking you died," she shouts. "When did this start happening?"

"When I touched that tiny willow tree. After my seizure," I say, fiddling with the eraser on her desk. "I left right after."

"It died, you know." She opens the black curtains to let light into the room. Lifeless buildings across the street obstruct the view. "The willow died the next day. After you left us."

"What about the other plants?"

"All the same." She leans on the windowsill, letting the natural light illuminate her figure. She turns to meet my eyes. "Except the SpringStep."

Curious. So, the SpringStep has different properties than the other four? We knew it couldn't be planted and grown artificially, but why?

"What did you really find at the university?" she says abruptly.

"Elara. I can't—"

She turns around to face me. "I told you the truth about Jaime. Don't you owe me that?" Her eyes stare at my forehead, rather than meeting my own.

I bite the inside of my cheek, knowing the truth will crush her. But isn't that what she wants?

"As we know, Nivalis is frozen over because the plants use thermosynthesis when in the dark. It's not some evolutionary breakthrough, but rather a manufactured blight." Elara listens intently, darkness over her eyes. "The six scientists in that headline, injected themselves with a cure—a reversal. Something that could reverse the blight." I take a breath before continuing, "The catch is, the plants would likely stop producing oxygen in response. It might kill all life on Nivalis."

She nods her head as if expecting my answer. "So that's it then?" she says, throwing her arms to the side. "All this work for nothing?" Her voice cracks. "I just want to do the right thing here. Please say you're telling the truth."

I nod.

"Oh, Light." She covers her mouth and a tear falls from her cheek. "So those six have been dead for over six hundred passings, and their magical cure died with them? So what now?"

"We just keep moving."

She scoffs, "You would say that, wouldn't you? So ready to just give up?" Her words cut deep. She's upset, but she's right. Giving up is what I do best. I gave up saving Mattias's life. I gave up looking for Oberon and when I did, they were both handed to me on a silver platter.

I shudder once again, thinking about the implications of giving Mattias the BlightStone. Was it a trade I should have made? Did I even have a choice?

Mattias said it "might" kill everything on Nivalis. Not that it "will." Do I tell her that? Will that make her feel better? Is it worth the risk? Should I mention that the cure is found in offspring. That there is at least one person alive who can reverse the Blight?

"I'm sorry," I whisper. She wipes her tears away and wraps her arms around my torso. She buries her head into my shoulder.

I hold her gently as she cries. I feel that familiar connection between us, asking me to draw the heat from her body. It's right there, tempting me stronger than SpringStep ever could.

I ignore it and hold her tighter.

"Guys," Oberon says lethargically. "I just had a terrible dream where Caelius came to save my life and carried me …" He looks at me in disbelief. "Oh no. It came true."

Dan put him in an empty room next to mine on the first floor to recover. A couple of blankets pin him to the mattress. With a bit of SpringStep, he seems much more coherent.

"Dick." I smile. "It's good to see you're okay."

"Well, duh." He shakes his head. "I've always been the better hunter." He tries moving but winces in pain. The SpringStep must be wearing off.

"What did Mattias do to you?"

"Mattias?" He looks shocked. "What do you mean? He died in the river." He seems to not remember. Could it be a trauma response or something deeper?

"It doesn't matter." I run my fingers through my hair.

"Must have been a stressful time then, huh? Your hair is already graying." He looks at the top of my head. Graying? I couldn't be.

I stand up from the chair and look at myself in the mirror. I brush my fingers through my thick head of hair and sure enough, the roots of my scalp are white. Stark white. Why?

"Hey, don't feel too bad about it though," Oberon says lethargically. "I went bald long ago." A moment passes before he connects the dots. "Wait, didn't you lose those fingers or am I just like really high right now?" His words drag, each one requiring a lot of energy to form.

"I'll tell you about it later." I rub my aching regrown fingers. There's still phantom pain, though there shouldn't be. "Oh, I found this." I open my shirt pocket and pull out one of Brena's painted stones. "*I love Daddy!*" it says. A faded heart is painted underneath the words.

Oberon's mouth drops and he takes the stone like he is receiving a kitten. "Brena," he whispers, lip trembling. "Where ...," he starts.

"It was in Hollyard. I picked it up from the rubble of your home before I came to look for you."

"My home?" He sadly looks into the distance. He must still be missing pieces of his memory.

Elara knocks and enters. She's looking to be in a much better mood. Oberon returns to his normal self and waves, showing a goofy grin.

"I've finished with my research," Elara says to me. "There's no reason to stay here anymore. I talked to Dan, and he agrees it's time to get back on the road."

"Yeah, I'd like to see my daughter again," Oberon says.

"I've already started packing things up. Same with Jaime. Just thought I'd let you know."

"Thanks, Elara, I'll get my things ready too."

"What about him? Is he able to walk?" she asks, pointing at Oberon.

"He's been through much worse. He'll be fine."

"I'll be fine," Oberon repeats.

She gives me a smile and leaves into the hallway, closing the door behind her. "Caelius, she's a cutie! Who is she?" Oberon drawls.

I realize I haven't even introduced everyone to Oberon. "That's Elara. She's the smart one of the group," I say. "Jaime is her brother, who you may remember. Dan, the big guy, patched you up, and Steeq is … Steeq. You'll meet him."

"Are you and Elara a thing?" Oberon asks, grinning wide-eyed.

I blush, chuckling. "No." I desperately try to hide my face. "She's too smart for me. We aren't a good match." Oberon laughs softly.

His laughter tapers off and he looks at me seriously. "How is she, Caelius?" he asks. "Brena? Is she okay?"

I hesitate, letting a couple of seconds pass. "I don't know," I say. "I left right after you did." Oberon nods in understanding. "Hadrian exiled you, right? Do you know why?"

"I don't know. I guess he didn't want me around anymore or something. Said I was a 'threat' to his regime? I'm not sure what that means. I mean, wasn't he prepping you to take over for him?"

"He was," I say. "I'm not taking his place. I'm better as a follower, not a leader."

"Better you than him." He shrugs, lips coming to a line.

"It's not gonna happen. After I left, he exiled me as well, making me an enemy of the Brightest. He said if I return, I'll be met with hostility."

Oberon's eyes go wide. "Really? He said that? So how am I supposed to see Brena again? He didn't even give me a chance to say goodbye."

Hearing that angers me. I know Hadrian is cruel. But at the very least, he should have allowed him to say his farewells. Did he lie to Dolora and Brena, telling them that Oberon left to go somewhere really quick?

He said that to me when I was a child. That bastard. I should have known this entire time he was responsible for my parents' deaths.

That lie put me through so much distress throughout my developmental passings. I can't imagine what Brena is going through right now. She probably believes she'll never see her dad again.

I know how that feels—growing up, always hoping they'd be there just over the next hill, waiting. And when they weren't, the weight of disappointment settling in, followed by the shame of ever believing they would be.

My face becomes red hot.

"Let's go then," I say. "Let's go see Brena."

42

The Gravestones

I see it. I understand it all. The world sings to me
in tones and vibrations. The BlightStone—a well
of infinite untapped power.
From the Journal of Azura Seren. Nevoro section, 29th
orbit

The road in front of us is long and treacherous. If my days are correct, the sun should be illuminating the Octoro Bridge very soon. We can intercept the Brightest there. I didn't have much to pack. Just myself, my rapier, and my clothes. The others have quite a bit. Dan has a portable greenhouse wagon and the rest of the Horizon has one other wagon for all their general belongings.

We don't have animals to do the heavy work for us, but Steeq modified the general wagon with a solar-powered engine and a battery. It moves slow—no faster than our walking speed—but at least we don't have to pull it behind us. Dan has to pull the greenhouse wagon behind him, though. The general wagon holds most of Jaime's weapons, Elara's equipment, and Steeq's … other stuff. Most of it looks like random junk, but he insisted on bringing it.

Steeq looks a bit worse for wear. He disappears more often than anyone else to "defecate," but I know what he's really doing. So does Jaime. Do the others suspect his addiction? When's a good time to bring it up? It would be torture for him to quit cold turkey while walking twenty miles a day, but maybe that's what he needs. As long as it wouldn't end up killing him.

Oberon is looking better. He is dangerously lanky now—a look that does not suit him at all. He looks like he went to hell and returned. I recognize his crossbow clipped to his belt. Just like old times. Jaime must have given it to him at some point.

Jaime still looks at me with reverence. Each word that escapes his mouth is one of respect. It unnerves me, but at least he isn't bowing at my feet. He carries himself differently, as if expecting to learn something from me, rather than the other way around.

The Light is quieter when I am around my friends, murmuring something only once or twice a day. Why is that?

The city of Solace shrinks in size as we leave it behind. It was a sad moment saying goodbye, but as with everything on Nivalis, we have to keep moving. It wouldn't be long before the Darkness found its way to the city, and we'd be forced out, anyway.

The road we walk is the same road the Brightest would have taken. It's cracked and destroyed by the hundreds of passings of people traveling on it. What do I hope to accomplish by confronting the Brightest again? Maybe we could just grab Brena and leave? Or would I have to confront Hadrian? Could I kill him if needed?

On a normal day, the Brightest would walk about three miles to keep up with the Bright Spot. We push nearly seven times that before we need to stop and rest.

We come across a few grave markers off the side of the road on our third day of travel. I almost ignore them before Dan says something.

"Caelius," he says. I walk over to him as he stares at the headstones. "Oberon," he says next. "Mattias, Efram." He lists off a few more names from the Brightest. Those who died on the trip. The list is shorter than I figured, but seeing our names there infuriates me.

Each grave marker has a mound of dirt in front of it. It's weird seeing my name as deceased. I'm dead to them. How many actually believe that? How many know I left? I get down on my hands and start digging.

"Caelius. What …?" Oberon asks. I ignore him and keep digging, shoving the dirt out of the way to uncover what the crew left behind. It's tradition in the Brightest to bury the deceased's most prized belonging with them. Dirt shuffles underneath my fingernails and the soil becomes muddier the deeper I dig.

My hand brushes against something hard. I dig around it, revealing a wooden lump. There it is. I know what it is before I even grip the item. I pull it out of the dirt to reveal my old crossbow. "C" is etched on the side.

I thought it had been stolen or destroyed. I'd lost it in one of the raids, but here it is, in my hands. I admire the craftsmanship, rubbing the dirt away with my thumb. "A crossbow?" Jaime asks.

"*My* crossbow," I say. It's the same crossbow I used to feed everyone. It's saved my life and others countless times. It had always been more than just a weapon to me.

That is, until I'd abandoned it for my sword. I'd abandoned it for a weapon made specifically for killing. Not providing. The rapier isn't made to hunt, to kill squirrels or deer. It's made to kill other humans. To kill others who also bear a sword. Or ones who don't.

I'd abandoned this crossbow as well as the person who carried it. I'd left someone who cared for people. Someone who wanted to keep everyone safe. Someone who used to hesitate before killing.

I didn't abandon him. I killed him.

Now I'm cold. Death doesn't bother me as it once had. I've killed so many people, masking them under the name "Crits," pretending they aren't human to make myself feel better.

The Brightest buried Caelius because he truly is dead. This crossbow isn't mine. Not anymore. I place the crossbow back into the pit. I start covering it back up with dirt until it's no longer visible.

"What are you doing?" Jaime asks. "That could be useful. An extra weapon never hurts."

"I'm not just burying a crossbow," I say. "I'm burying someone who died long ago. Someone who shares my name."

Oberon looks at me with sadness in his eyes. He knows that I'm not the same man he once knew. And neither is he. He holds his crossbow in his hands and looks at it deeply. After a moment, he walks over to his own headstone and digs.

We watch in silence as he buries his crossbow in the grave next to mine.

A couple of days pass and we come across a sign for a small village half a mile away. This one is smaller than Hollyard. A sign identifies it as "Overlook." Its population before the Freezing was nine hundred people.

Nine hundred seems like a lot. I can't even imagine trying to keep a town of nine hundred people fed and maintained. Even fifty is difficult. Although I'm sure back then, things were a lot easier.

"You guys stay here," I command the group. "Jaime and I are going to scout the area for anything that might be of use. It could also be dangerous." No one objects and they use this opportunity to relax a bit. Jaime follows me into the little town, eager to move quickly again.

The two of us walk through the small village when he speaks up. "Do you think it's called Overlook because people overlook this town in favor of the bridge?" I wasn't expecting him to crack a joke, and I chuckle a bit. He's always so serious, but this reminds me he is still human.

The little town is dingy and run down. Somehow it looks less maintained than Hollyard. Very few buildings still stand. Each house is held together by decaying, unpainted wood. Some houses slant completely to the side, daring to collapse. The town looks primitive even for pre-Freezing standards, like it was stuck a couple of hundred passings behind the rest of the world. It's not uncommon for villages to look like this one, but when compared to Solace, one would wonder why someone would choose to live here instead of the city, or Hollyard for that matter.

It is possible this place was abandoned before the Freezing. Though, surprisingly, cars line the road even here. How nice would it be to have one of those instead of walking? If only Steeq spent the time to make all of us motorized wagons.

"There's warmth nearby," the Light whispers. Did Jaime hear the Light too?

Movement. I notice it in the corner of my eye. Jaime sees my reaction and is on guard as well. We both ready our weapons. Someone—or something—is watching us. He and I study the surrounding area with our backs together, ready for what might come.

I hear whistling through the air. I don't have time to react before a crossbow bolt plants itself into the center of my chest. Pain sprouts from the area. I feel my reserves of heat drain from me as my wound stitches back together, spitting the arrow out onto the ground.

"What the hell was that?" Jaime asks, as two Crits appear behind a house. One wears a ghillie suit and holds a sickle, and the other holds a short sword. Where is the archer?

The first one runs at me. The female crit swings her sickle at my throat. My first instinct is to leap backward, but Jaime is at my back so I duck instead. The female Crit anticipates this and swings upward. I leap to the side, breaking my contact with Jaime. Metal sings from him and his opponent. A third attacker with a steel knife comes at us from the side. Where did they get weapons like these?

The first Crit is too close for my rapier so I use my other hand to sink my knife into her stomach. She gasps and swipes her sickle at my face. The blade misses, but I feel a slight cut on the bridge of my nose. I tug on my knife to unbury it from her guts. It resists and comes free with a second tug.

The third attacker lunges at me with his own knife. Jaime spins around and slashes him across the face. This doesn't stop him though. The Crit's knife sinks into my left shoulder and we fall to the ground. My hands grip his hairy arms. I could freeze him now, steal his warmth.

But I don't want to reveal my hand too early. In a moment, Jaime sticks his blade into the raider's kidneys. He screams and I shove him off with my feet.

Are we prepared to handle these Crits? They have more combat knowledge than most. The knife is still lodged between my shoulder blades, restricting movement. I could remove it but I don't have time to deal with the blood.

Would I bleed out with the Light's protection? I grunt as pain blossoms from my left pec. I'd been shot again, though it didn't dig deep enough to damage anything vital. The Crit stands on a roof, reloading her crossbow.

I rip the knife from my shoulder, blood soaking my shirt. I don't have any ranged weapons, but that isn't a problem.

"Jaime!" I yell, not sure what his situation is. I point to the raider on the rooftop and toss the knife to him. He catches it with one hand and throws it with precision. It spins through the air, whizzing as it flies and sticks into the ranger's skull. Her body falls backward and rolls off the roof.

Without time to think, I jam my index and middle fingers into the hole where the knife had once been and push outward, cauterizing the wound. It hurts like hell, and the rest of my body drops in temperature. It uses less heat than healing, but I'm still low on reserves. I won't be able to do that again until I draw in more.

Four Crits attack at once, thinking they could overwhelm us. Two run for me and the other two run for Jaime. I leap at the two coming at me, risking it all as I grab each of their legs with my hands. They can't react before I pull heat from the raider in my left hand and redirect it into the raider in my right hand. The left raider freezes, becoming a sculpture of ice. The right raider combusts into flames. He drops his weapon, trying to bat the fire away, but it's no use. He screams in pain as he bumps into the sculpture of his friend, which topples over, shattering across the ground.

In moments, the Crit on fire falls limply, the fire dying out, leaving a charred husk of a human being. I look at Jaime and he'd already made quick work of his two attackers. He stands in awe of what I have done. Even I'm shocked at what I just did.

Somehow, the two of us alone dispatched a whole group of Crits without breaking a sweat. Jaime and I, when paired together, are dangerous.

"Looks like your training is coming to good use," he jokes, breathing heavily. "Though you're gonna have to teach me how to do that fire stuff."

43

The Bridge

I do not know how many more like me there are.
From the Journal of Azura Seren. Nevoro section, 29th
orbit

The **Octoro Bridge expands in** front of us for a hundred miles. It's impossible to see the other end. The continent of Retuno.

The bridge is made of steel and has supports that stretch hundreds of feet into the sky. It's nearly as tall as some skyscrapers in Solace. Six hundred passings after the Freezing of the World and this bridge still stands. Without it, people couldn't cross continents, and the Darkness would eventually consume them.

"Oh Light," Oberon says. "That's them." He tries to push past me, but I stop him. A group of people with wagons walks on the bridge.

"Stay here," I command. "I don't know what he's capable of."

"Like hell," he says. "My daughter is over there."

I look intensely at him, daring him to try it. He takes the hint and backs off. Good. "Jaime, you stay here too. I need to do this alone."

"You got it."

I turn to face the Brightest. A few of them recognize me and start pointing; their faces are too far to make out. I pick out Hadrian in his white and gold-trimmed robes. He stands taller than the others, despite his actual height. Even far away, his air of authority imposes.

"Father Hadrian," I yell mockingly. My voice rings in my ears. It echoes back to me through the vast open space.

"Caelius?" he says. Even though he's a couple of hundred feet away, I hear him clearly, as if he is standing next to me. "Son? You're alive?"

Hearing him call me his son disgusts me. He said I wouldn't be his son if I returned. Clearly, he's doing it because others are around. He wouldn't dare ruin his image.

"Do not call me your son, for you are not my father. You killed him twenty passings ago and lied about it," I yell back. The dust of their bodies might still be in the water underneath me.

"I'm a leader, not your friend," he says. "I make decisions that are best for the group. You are better off not knowing the truth."

It stings to hear him admit it. I wanted to believe he didn't, that I was making it all up in my head. "You can freeze things and spit fire from your hands," I say. "You're not a priest sent by the Light. You're a fake and a fraud."

"I don't know what you're talking about," he says. "Come closer so we can chat. I'll welcome you and your new friends into the Brightest with open arms."

The idea of stepping on the bridge causes me to tremble. I tell myself it's just in my mind. The bridge isn't evil. The bridge didn't kill my parents. "You know exactly what I'm talking about. Because I can do it too. You wear gloves to not accidentally freeze someone. You don't eat because you get your energy from the sun. That's why we stay at the head of the Bright Spot."

"You're wrong, Caelius. I can't spit fire from my hands," he says. "If you claim that you can, then that implies that you stole something from me. Something that was rightfully mine. Something you're going to give back."

In a display of power, I grab the metal girder on the right side of the bridge and pull the heat from it. It takes everything I have to do so and frost webs out from the contact, creeping its way down the metal. The familiar frost pattern isn't just any pattern. It's my own, unique, like my own fingerprints. I've seen the same pattern creeping up the faces of Crits. The group of people steps away from the frozen bar. They see it with their own eyes.

"Caelius?" Oberon asks, shakily. "What did you do?"

"I am Chosen by the Light," I yell. "You are to be punished for your crimes and murders against your own followers, which include my mother and father."

"Who are you to decide punishment?" Hadrian says. "You admitted it yourself. You'd killed Mattias in cold blood." I see a few members shift uncomfortably at that news. This is the first time they've heard that side of the story. What they don't know is that Mattias still lives and breathes today. "Maybe that's why the Light chose you. It's the same reason it chose me all those passings ago. Because we do what needs to be done. Maybe we should both be held accountable for our crimes. I propose a sword fight to the death. No powers from the Light."

Hadrian dramatically whips his robe to the side, revealing his rapier. My stomach sinks. He is a better fencer than I could ever be. Unless I had an edge, I'd lose every fight against him.

"I got this. I can take an old man." Jaime steps forward, revealing the arsenal of weapons on his belt.

I stop him with the back of my hand. "No, Jaime. This is my fight. My punishment," I say. "I am the one who needs to do this. If this goes poorly for me, take care of the Horizon. Take care of Oberon and Brena if they decide to stay."

I look forward, seeing the golden man a hundred feet in front of me. It's time to cross my own bridges. I take a step forward, pressing my boot against the metal underneath. I feel the tension between us. The anticipation of the Brightest, Hadrian, and the Horizon.

Flashes of my parents assault my mind when my next foot lands. I see my mother's beautiful face. I feel her intense heart and love for me. She reminds me of Elara. Or perhaps Elara reminds me of her.

Step.

My father's spectacled eyes meet mine. Plastered on his face is a goofy smile. He was someone who always sought the best in people. He could laugh and joke even in the darkest of times. I see my father in Oberon and in Daniel. I seek comfort in them because they are the missing piece of my father.

Step.

I see the Light. Its physical form. It's impossible to comprehend. I could never describe it to anyone who hasn't seen it themselves. Light reflects from it, and new colors refract. Colors I've never seen before. This being assigned me to be its Chosen.

Step.

Lyria. A woman with passion. A woman dedicated to one thing. Finding her son. After this is over, I need to help her.

Step.

A hard-faced man. His name is Grafter. He doesn't carry the same young face. He's old with a beard. But those eyes. Those are Jaime's eyes.

Step.

Hadrian. He isn't part of a vision. Instead, he stands right in front of me with the Brightest behind him. "Caelius," he says formally. His clean, gold-trimmed white silk robe makes him look more regal and powerful than ever. His sun insignia on his chest reflects the light in the way only pure gold can. His beard is trimmed neatly to a point. He stands shorter than me, but at this very moment, he seems as tall as a skyscraper.

"Hadrian," I respond. This is the man who's taken advantage of me and my abilities my entire life. This is the man who took everything I've cared for: my mom, my dad, Oberon. This is the same man who's been grooming me to take his place. Twenty passings ago exactly, on this very bridge, he assumed parental rights over me after a little "accident."

It worked. I hate him for it. But I realize here and now as I look at him, I see only myself. Everything I never wanted.

"Your hair is turning white. I'm sorry it has to end like this," Hadrian says. I see sorrow and despair in his eyes. He really is regretful.

"I'm not." I draw my sword, and he does the same. I hold it up and study him.

Before calling, I start the attack. I strike not to hurt, but to test the waters. He is prepared, as I expected. He counters my move, feeling out the landscape for himself. The change in his posture shows me that he's impressed by my improvement. He takes this incursion a bit more seriously now. I guess all that training with Jaime might pay off.

I test the waters again, and he takes advantage when I extend a bit too far. He makes a warning slash against my thigh. My trousers split and pain screams throughout my leg. He could have killed me. He should have killed me. I need to be more careful.

No amount of SpringStep could prepare me for this fight. My body still moves as if made from lead. I make another mistake and know it immediately. I'm unable to correct myself as I'm punished with his blade sweeping across my side. The area feels warm as it bleeds.

I feel Jaime's judgment. He is reading every mistake I've made, knowing he wouldn't have made them.

"Caelius," Hadrian mocks, making a pouty face. Seeing it makes me angry and I attack once again. A lesson I had to learn while practicing with Jaime is to not let anger control your attacks. I wish we had spent more time on emotion management. I'm punished for a third time with a quick swipe across my cheek. I step back, left hand coming up to feel my face. Knowing Hadrian, that was the final warning slash. The next one, he'll use to kill me.

I know right there that he's bested me. I knew I couldn't defeat him, but I wanted to try anyway. He holds his sword up to my chest. My next error will lead to the end of this fight. I try to look for an advantage in my favor.

My distraction costs me greatly as my sword is lifted from my hand and launched through the air. Hadrian's signature move is to disarm, then attack.

"This is the end, then?" Hadrian says. All emotion is gone from him. He'd made his decision long ago and already come to terms with it. My sword clatters on the metal bridge when it lands.

Facing the end isn't as terrible as I thought it would be. I thought I'd die of old age or some kind of sickness. I thought maybe I would die like a hero against a Crit, losing to a knife made of bone and prepared for dinner.

I didn't think I'd die at the hands of the person who raised me. I'm not upset; I'm ready. I just hope he doesn't hurt Oberon, Jaime, or even Elara after this.

I come up with an idea. "You want my powers, right? You want to create fire with your hands?"

He doesn't say anything; instead he stares at me with those old eyes.

"Don't lose yourself to him," the Light says.

"How do you know that you'll get them if you kill me?" I continue. I'm not sure exactly how it works, but I'm betting he doesn't know either. He hesitates for just a moment.

He drops his sword just slightly. Just enough for me to gamble everything. I lunge forward toward Hadrian. His rapier sinks into my stomach, and I feel it break through the back. It's an odd feeling.

The knife in my right hand sinks into Hadrian's chest. I equipped it when he struck my cheek—a perfect misdirection. Hadrian's expression drops. There's true fear in his eyes for the first time. He spits blood and it runs down his chin.

"What were their names?" I demand.

He spits blood again, trying to speak. I twist my knife slightly and he tenses up. "Jer-Jerrin and M—M—Mayra."

My father and mother. He took them from me. My knife shoves upward and hits something hard. What? I can hardly think over his deafening screams.

"I know I said no powers," Hadrian grunts through gritted teeth. He grabs my face and I can feel the warmth draining from me. He's going to kill me and I can't move.

"That's it," the Light says. "Grab that."

I feel my eyes freezing over first. They slow, unable to move. They frost over, becoming blurry. My arms are still mobile. I position the edge of my knife underneath the hard lump in his chest and pitch it toward me. A small bloody stone falls out of the slit. It bounces off the rapier and onto the metal ground with a soft knock.

My heat doesn't return to me, but the pulling ceases. Hadrian stops, unable to move. His eyes are wide, shocked, as if I'd just severed a limb. With a strength I didn't know I had, I lift his body, carrying it over my head, and hurl him over the side of the bridge.

A drop from this height would feel like landing on concrete. It would be impossible for him to survive a fall like that. He falls, screaming before making a splash in the water.

I turn around to look at everyone watching, but something stops me. I can't turn as far as I want. I look down at Hadrian's sword sticking from my stomach. That's not supposed to be there.

Jaime, Oberon, and Dan rush to my aid. My arm isn't long enough to pull it out myself. "Jaime," I request. He knows immediately what he needs to do, carefully pulling the rapier from my stomach.

"Caelius, you need to lie down. Dan will help."

"I'm fine," I say, planning on cauterizing the wound. Hopefully, the Light will heal any internal damage.

Oberon pushes past me into the crowd. "Brena?" he yells. "Sweetie, where are you?" The crowd moves, revealing Dolora. She's distraught. "Where's Brena?" Oberon asks softly.

Dolora stands with her hands at her sides. Tears flow down her cheeks as she cries.

"Where is our daughter?!" Oberon yells at his wife. I look around the crowd, scanning faces. Pladd is still here, alive, except his hair is stark white. Maybe he converted to the Path. I make another pass, scanning faces. Someone's missing. The woman Oberon and I saved from hanging. Lyria is gone—and so is Brena. I feel sick to my stomach.

"I don't know," Dolora chokes out. "I thought you died." She moans in agony.

Oberon shouts. "You were supposed to keep her safe! You were supposed to keep an eye on her!" He grabs her by the shoulders and shakes her. "Now my baby girl is gone. You might as well have just killed her!"

Oberon huddles on the ground, hyperventilating. He brings his knees up to his chest and cries. Beef Iron Mutilator walks up and rubs his head against the pained man.

44

The Promise

Be warned: The power corrupts and anyone who draws upon it is dangerous to themselves and everyone around them.
From the Journal of Azura Seren. Nevoro section, 29th orbit

We take our final steps off the bridge, setting our feet on the continent of Retuno. It took us almost thirty days to cross. Luckily Reyus knew how to fish, providing everyone with enough food to last. Oberon hasn't said a single word. Meanwhile, Dan, Elara, Steeq, and Jaime integrate themselves into the Brightest. Dan provides homegrown food for everyone. Eventually, he's going to need a bigger greenhouse wagon. Or maybe a couple.

I caught Steeq a couple of times sniff SpringStep from his finger. That's going to be addressed. He doesn't seem as energetic and wiry as he usually does. Maybe his body balanced out, requiring the drug for stability. Elara collected the lump I harvested from Hadrian's chest and found it was another BlightStone. No one really knows what it is, other than me and her. We decided it would be best if we waited to plant it. The Light wanted me to take its power but hasn't yet attacked me for deciding to wait. We've come to a mutual agreement, accepting each other's roles.

It's odd knowing that the Light isn't some benevolent, omnipotent being. It's crass, reckless, and sporadic, like us mortals. What is this Light, truly?

What now? The Brightest look up to me for answers, but I don't have any for them. I wasn't supposed to take over Hadrian's place, but who else could? Jaime is the only one with enough grit to make tough decisions, but he's just a kid. I couldn't dare put a responsibility like this on him.

People wouldn't look to him for advice anyway. They'd look to me, regardless of my title. Unfortunately, Hadrian was right. I'm the only person suited to take his place. I hate it, but it needs to be done.

I look at Oberon, who walks next to me. He is hollowed out, a husk of his former self. He may have tried hiding it, but being held captive under Mattias really changed him.

That bastard. I should have killed him. Instead of letting him float down the river. I should have taken my hands and suffocated him in the dirt. If I see him again, I'm going to kill him.

My mind fuzzes at what needs to be done. We need to find Lyria and Brena, and then somehow convince Lyria to see Mattias so she can reunite with her own son. What lengths would she go to see him again?

Where would Lyria even have gone? She wouldn't have gone back to her previous camp, the one where she was tortured and abused. If so, she better not have taken Brena there.

My stomach turns. Oh Light. I hold my hands up in front of me, all ten fingers. Three restored by the Light. I shouldn't have this power. I rejected it and it was forced upon me.

I drop to the ground and pull out my knife. It's not delusion in my mind, but clarity. Clarity for the first time in weeks. I place my left hand on the dirt and roll the blade over my index and middle fingers on my left hand. It hurts like nothing else. I scream as the middle finger is removed. My forefinger is still connected, a large gash exposing the white bone underneath.

"Caelius? What the hell are you doing?" Oberon asks, shocked. I can't do this. I take a deep shaky breath, almost passing out. The forefinger is removed with force, detaching next to the other.

Tears roll down my face, turning the dirt into mud. "Caelius," the Light says in my head, confused. "What are you doing? Why are you rejecting my gift?"

I almost gave up until I heard its voice. That's why I'm doing this. This thing invaded me. I won't accept its help.

Screaming, I put my entire weight on the knife resting on my thumb. Blood spews out of each stump, darkening the ground.

My fingers lay in the dirt, separated from the rest of me. My hand is covered in blood.

I draw heat from the ground around me and it cools down significantly. I press my other hand to the wound and cauterize it, closing off the blood vessels. I wipe the blood off on my shirt, and Oberon stares at me with a wordless expression.

Many others around me witnessed it as well. The other BlightStone is nearby. I can feel its power, requesting I take it. "Let this moment be remembered from this day forward," I shout to the crowd. Every face turns to me. "I, Caelius, leader of the Brightest, am not Hadrian. Let my actions here reflect that when you doubt it."

It feels good to finally be respected. If I can make the crowd believe I'll never become Hadrian, hopefully I can convince myself as well.

I do not know what is in store for me in the future, but the Light places a single command in my head. "Grow."

Epilogue I

Lyria

Tell my son and daughter that I'm sorry.
From the Journal of Azura Seren. Dektoro section, 29th
orbit

Lyria couldn't explain how she knew where she was to go. It'd been days, maybe weeks since she left the Brightest. She'd followed the Path backward, walking by Solace, through Hollyard. The tree where she'd hung herself stood taller than ever.

She could feel it watching her, observing her. It disapproved of what she did. The rope remnant mocked her for her failure. She felt small—unwanted—unnoticed within the Brightest. She'd been labeled as "the one who tried killing herself." She feels at the rope scar on her neck with her right hand. It's not the kind of smooth one might feel against a baby's cheek, but smooth like rubber.

There were people who cared for her in the Brightest, but they'd all left her. Mattias drowned in the river. Caelius was missing, likely dead. Same with Oberon. Hadrian healed her but never spoke with her afterward.

"I'm tired," Brena whines. "My legs hurt. Miss Lyria, are we almost there?" Dragging her feels like dead weight. Lyria's left hand grips the child's arm harder.

"Yes, sweetie," she responds. "Don't let go of my hand, okay?" They were close. She could feel it.

Tommy said the same thing once, before he disappeared. Guilt wells up in her throat. She'd taken a child from her mother. She'd cemented in her mind that those who take children from their parents are evil people. She wasn't evil, was she?

Lyria had been taken forcefully from her parents. She'd been sold into the Meridas. The world had taken Tommy from her. Maybe this is revenge.

Maybe Tommy was right where he'd left her. She breaks from the road of the Path, taking an exit that would branch away for miles. Brena continued to complain. "I miss Mommy."

Lyria feels the air cooling around her. Are they getting closer to the back edge of the Bright Spot?

She and the child walk for days. She hardly could close her eyes to sleep. She could feel the effects of exhaustion on her body, but she would not dare make the same mistake with Brena as she did with Tommy. She'd closed her eyes for just a moment, and he was gone.

The landscape around her feels familiar. Pine trees along the road take shape and road signs read how far they are from Solace. She meant to look for Tommy in Solace, but when she arrived in Hollyard, the city in the distance was larger than she'd ever imagined. It would have taken her weeks to search Hollyard alone—dozens of passings if she dared explore the city. There just wasn't enough time. Nivalis doesn't wait for anyone. If you fall behind, you die.

They are close. Very close. Tommy had to be here. They'd cross the hill, and he'd be right there.

Smoke billows over the trees. Not bad for a six-passing-old child. She'd taught him well.

"Miss Lyria," Brena says, tugging on her blouse.

"Not now, honey," she replies, as they crest the hill. A group of colorful people sits by a campfire. Blobs of pink and blue hang a colored assortment of silk lace on a clothesline. Browns prepare food, cutting meat and tossing vegetables into a pot hung over the fire. A few children wearing red, pink, and purple run around, playing a game like tag.

She doesn't see Tommy among the purples or reds, but if he'd be anywhere, he'd be here. Men in purple lace march toward them when they notice their arrival. Their purple cloth hangs over their faces and shoulders. Layers on top of layers of lace fabric hide their pecs and genitals.

The man on the left is Okanakan. His accent confirms it. "Women. You two join us." His voice is deep, deeper than anyone's in the Brightest. Lyria feels a spike of fear. She knows what's next. It's time for her to stop running from it.

"Miss Lyria?" Brena cries, tugging again at her blouse.

"It's okay," she consoles. "Just stay close to me, alright?" Brena nods her head, sticking her thumb in her mouth. They follow the two men into the camp. They don't wear any weapons, but that didn't stop them from being dangerous. They are purples.

The men lead them to a tent erected at the edge of the camp. Its burlap cloth reminds Lyria of the same material the Brightest use for their maternity wagons. Giggling women pour out of the open slit of the tent. He's in there.

Lyria stops, letting go of Brena's hand. Lyria places both her own hands on the child's shoulders, dropping to her eye level. "Okay. Sweet Brena, you should stay out here, okay? Miss Lyria has some things she needs to do."

Her face is scared, stained with tears. One tear drops from the palm of the hand she's sucking on. "Please don't go."

The Okanakan man speaks in his low voice before Lyria can. "Both of you must go in."

Lyria turns on the man. "She's just a child." She didn't expect to hear pain in her own voice.

"Isn't that why you brought her here?"

Her stomach twists as if she's been punched in the gut. Is he right? Why did she bring her here? She knew exactly where she was going. She whimpers, grabbing Brena by the hand. "Come on, pumpkin."

Behind the veil of the tent, a solitary man dressed in red sits on a throne of wood. A dozen women in pink surround him, rubbing their bodies against his chair, arms, legs, and chest. Their fingers weave through his stark white hair and others caress his hard face with the back of their wrists. His bone-white irises are a fire of passion, accented by pitch-black eyeliner.

The women's thin pink lace shawls expose their natural beauty. A cleanly shaven front accentuates the crease where their legs meet their waists. The pink lace hides the color of their nipples, but not the shadows of their breasts. She was in that position once.

She moves to cover Brena's eyes, but the man in red speaks, stopping her in her tracks.

"Lyria Merida." His voice is cold like ice. His accent is Westcan. "I didn't think I'd see you again. I wondered if you'd ever answer my call." He smirks, exposing uncannily white teeth. His teeth didn't seem real. As if they were layered over his mouth, rather than inside. "I see you brought a new prize for me, yes?"

The Westcan man leans forward. Golden beads around his neck and waist clatter and chime. He is the only red who wears gold beads. The other reds wear only the full-body shawl. "What is your name, little one?" he asks devilishly. The grin on his face turns Lyria's stomach.

She speaks before the child can. "Jack, this is Brena," she says. "She's our daughter." His eyebrows raise and he sits back. A pink twirls a curl in his stark white hair. "So don't even think about laying a finger on her," Lyria warns. She knows Jack would never touch one of his own children. He may be a monster, but he's nowhere near as bad as one of those cannibals.

Pladd was able to change. Not everyone is irredeemable.

Jack exposes a toothy grin. His teeth unnerving Lyria once again. "Very well. Slade, retrieve me two shawls. One pink and one small red."

The Okanakan man nods and leaves the room. Pink and red? She couldn't be pink again. That's why she left in the first place. Did she have a choice? Could she be something else?

"I'm unfit to be a pink," she blurts. "After I had T— Brena, I am no longer fertile."

Jack leans forward, studying her. Did he catch her slipup? She'd be a blue or a green. Anything but a pink. "Perhaps you didn't know, Lyria Merida." He accentuated each syllable in her name. "The Meridas have changed their structure. Pinks don't need to be fertile in order to serve me."

Lyria's stomach turns again. When the purple man, named Slade, arrives with her pink shawl, she hurls the contents of her stomach into the dirt. The pink cloth didn't even have an accenting color. Her job would be to pleasure only. To pleasure Jack.

"You are going to be mine for the rest of your life, Lyria Merida."

Epilogue II

Mattias

*They're called BlightEaters. I know because I am
one myself. Trapped in this forest.*
From the Journal of Azura Seren. Unknown section,
unknown orbit

Mattias, **leader, and queen of** his new group, is respected. He has real friends now, those who care for him and want to see him succeed. Things have changed since the Brightest and he could never go back. After seeing him now and knowing what he's done, they would never welcome him back.

He remembers a time in the new group when he had nothing to eat but human meat. He'd hated the idea of eating another human back then, but after a while, it seemed to grow on him. It doesn't taste as bad as he thought it would. He makes a conscious effort to avoid eating the brain. Another member ate a brain in hopes of gaining the knowledge of that individual and went insane.

That was the driving catalyst for Mattias to start formal education.

Mattias didn't think he'd enjoy being the queen in a group of savages, but he's happier now than he ever has been. Because of the major reform, very few of them remain savages. Most learned that by putting their minds together, they can survive this.

He wonders how the Brightest are doing without him. How Caelius and Oberon could be doing. They should have just crossed the Octoro Bridge if he counted his days right. He and his party still remain at the college. They'll be shoved out eventually, but they enjoy their moment while they can.

Mattias steps out of his briefing room and onto a stage outdoors. The sun shines brightly and the crowd in front of him goes wild. It's crazy how many people devoted themselves to following him. He isn't anything special. He's just a guy with ideas. He's just a guy with passion.

Thomas, Lyria's son, sits on a rock, watching intently. The group had called him "Metal" before learning his true name. They even called Mattias "Chopper" before they started to just call him "Queen."

"Are you ready?" a woman asks. Her blond hair is stained by dirt and grime. Her teeth had been filed down to sharp points to tear meat apart easier. Mattias would never undergo the same procedure. He can't imagine the pain.

"I don't think I'll ever be ready," he responds.

Behind a curtain, two people carry a potted plant on a cart, careful not to touch it. It's a small willow tree, like the one in Hollyard. They grew it with the seed that Caelius extracted from the tree in the front.

The volume of the crowd increases. People yell and chant. Mattias takes it all in, letting it give him the confidence to do what needs to be done next.

"Touch it! Touch it! Touch it!" the crowd screams in unison. It's time to give them what they want.

Mattias sticks a finger out and touches the tree ever so slightly. A shock flows through him and he freezes, seizing violently on the stage. The crowd cheers in delight as he shakes. The pain is agony. His life flashes before his eyes, each decision playing out in mockery. Every one of those decisions led him right here. Maybe he should kill himself. To stop the infection before it grows.

"Hello, Chosen," a voice says in his mind.

After a few moments, Mattias stands up weakly. Two of the onstage helpers assist him up. A connection forms between them. Something new. Mattias grabs on to that connection. The onstage helpers freeze, their eyes frosting over first. A frost pattern forms from where Mattias grabs them. Their warmth fills Mattias with energy. The crowd cheers even louder.

There's a strange feeling in his right shoulder. What the heck? He looks down, watching the stump quickly extending in size. Is it … regrowing? The arm grows, turning at the elbow, forming the forearm. It is a painful process, but it feels so good. The end melds like clay, becoming his palm. Five fingers follow.

He feels the strength inside of him, longing to escape. He lets it take control. The energy expels from his body and bolts of yellow lightning shoot from his fingertips connecting to the bodies in the front row. The electricity bounces from body to body before dying out after a few jumps. The first three people are completely fried, and the last two shake uncontrollably. Hair sticks straight up on the heads of members next to the victims.

The crowd roars. People start moving around trying to get closer, as if wanting to be the next victims. They've been wanting this. Might as well give them what they ask for.

The End of The Bright Spot

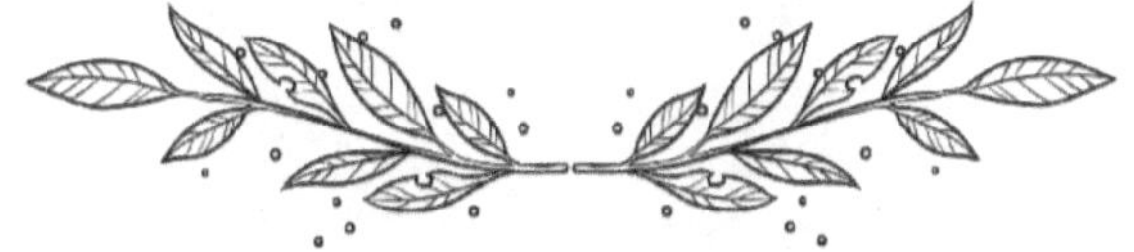

Glossary found in the Journal of Azura Seren

- **Nivalis**: A planet with a slow rotation around its sun. It takes twenty passings to complete a full orbit around the star. It's almost fully tidally locked, its own rotation drifting ever slowly.

- **Passing** (When used for time): 340 days, the length of time an area of land is illuminated by the sun.

- **Passing Section** (When used for location): A longitude section on Nivalis. The diameter of the Bright Spot spans the distance. There are twenty of these, each one labeled. It takes one passing (340 days) for the Bright Spot to move across a single section.

- **Orbit**: When Nivalis makes a full orbit around the sun. The Bright Spot would have circled the planet, taking twenty passings.

- **The Bright Spot**: A section of light and warmth illuminated by the sun about 1,200 miles in diameter. The only habitable land on Nivalis is within the Bright Spot.

- **SpringStep**: A purple flower. Its petals, when consumed, have a psychoactive effect, increasing cognitive function and pain relief. Its addictive nature makes the habit difficult to break.

- **BlightStone**: A concentrated well of power, linked to the light somehow. Can be used to create a BlightTree or a BlightEater.

- **BlightTree**: A tree that carries a BlightStone. Typically takes the form of a weeping willow tree.

- **BlightEater**: A person connected to the Light, granted with the ability to draw heat from nearby sources and convert that energy into something else.

- **Crit**: Genetically evolved to hunt and eat human flesh. They are typically shorter than humans, their pelvis lower, and their arms longer. This helps them run on all fours. Each hand has claws that extend almost double the length of each finger. Some have their teeth filed down to tear meat more easily. It is debated whether Crits are truly human.

Crit Clans

Most Crits separate into groups. The three main groups are the *Claw*, *Kreeturs*, and *Shearing*. These groups will camp out in sections of a city away from each other. Despite being the same species, Crit Clans often fight each other for various reasons. Each clan member emits pheromones of their respective group. It is unknown how the pheromones are produced.

Crit Clans typically elevate a single queen. This person is not gender-specific, typically delegating its role to a man. Like a beehive, when the queen is eliminated, the group typically tries to elevate a new queen or slowly dies off without any direction.

- **The Claw**: Its logo is depicted by a clawed hand. They typically scare their prey by disguising themselves with ghillie suits. One of three Crit groups in Solace.
- **Kreeturs**: Its logo is depicted by a wolf head, though most Crits can't draw to save their lives. Dumber than the other two groups, but more ferocious.
- **Shearing**: Its logo is depicted by a scythe. The third Crit group in Solace.

Passing Sections

1. Janero
2. Febro
3. Marto
4. Abro
5. Mino
6. Janao
7. Janio
8. Agero
9. Sebero
10. Octoro
11. Nevoro
12. Dektoro
13. Plino
14. Vereno

15. Turseno
16. Corono
17. Cayano
18. Hylano
19. Retuno
20. Fonalo

Notable Locations

- **Octoro Bridge:** connects continent of Octoro to the continent of Retuno, Octoro section

- **Retuno Bridge:** connects continent of Retuno to the continent of Octoro, Retuno section

- **The Luminous Forest:** forest in Illuxxia, Nevoro, Dektoro, Plino section

- **Misura's Point:** capital of Misura, Marto section

- **Westco:** capital of Barrenel, Mino section

- **Solace:** capital of Aurelia, Sebero section

- **Lunace:** capital of Illuxxia, Nevoro section

- **Velas:** capital of Okanako, Nevoro section

- **Elynsura:** capital of Elyndra, Turseno section

- **Hollyard:** suburb neighboring Solace

- **Overlook:** small town near Octoro Bridge, Sebero section

- **Myrren Tower:** city built around mysterious obelisk, near The Moon's Mountains, Corono section

Energy Transferences

- Thermal transference
- Acoustic transference
- Electrical transference
- Intuition transference
- Unknown

My research says there are more. But there is no more information available.

About the Author

Shawn Raben was born and raised in Chadron, Nebraska before moving to Wisconsin to pursue new opportunities. From a young age, he had a deep love for storytelling and a vivid imagination, often losing himself in tales of mystery, tragedy, and wonder. That lifelong passion for narrative grew into something more—a drive to explore the unknown and challenge how we see the world. The Bright Spot is his debut novel, the culmination of a dream years in the making.

www.ingramcontent.com/pod-product-compliance
Lightning Source LLC
Chambersburg PA
CBHW031202310726

48969CB00001B/188